I0676524

THE PRIME MINISTER'S WIFE

Doris Leslie

SAPERE
BOOKS

THE PRIME MINISTER'S WIFE

Published by Sapere Books.

24 Trafalgar Road, Ilkley, LS29 8HH

saperebooks.com

Copyright © Doris Leslie, 1961

Doris Leslie has asserted her right to be identified as the author of this work.
All rights reserved.

No part of this publication may be reproduced, stored in any retrieval system, or transmitted, in any form, or by any means, electronic, mechanical, photocopying, recording, or otherwise, without the prior written permission of the publishers.
This book is a work of fiction. Names, characters, businesses, organisations, places and events, other than those clearly in the public domain, are either the product of the author's imagination, or are used fictitiously.
Any resemblances to actual persons, living or dead, events or locales are purely coincidental.

ISBN: 978-0-85495-537-4

ACKNOWLEDGEMENTS

I am deeply indebted to the Staff and Reference Librarian of the Public Library at Bristol for much valuable assistance in my research; to the Staff of the Public Library at Cardiff for information concerning Greenmeadow (Pantgwynlais) and the Lewis family; to Messrs. John Murray for permission to quote excerpts from the letters of Disraeli and of Mary Anne Disraeli in the Official Biography by Moneypenny and Buckle; and to the National Trust for their courtesy in allowing me access to the letters and diaries of Mary Anne in possession of the Trust at Hughenden.

DORIS LESLIE

PART ONE: GREENMEADOW

ONE

On a summer's evening in the year 1815 a singular activity might have been observed in and about the ground floor front of a small and narrow house in a small and narrow way leading from the steep ascent of Bristol up to Clifton.

Had anyone been passing by on that evening in July, which was unlikely at an hour when village folk were at their suppers and the *ton* at its diversions, he or she would have seen a young lady with a kerchief on her head, determination in her face and a duster in her hand, busily engaged in polishing the panes of the ground floor front's bow window. Above the door hung a signboard, glossy in its recent coat of paint, and bearing the gilt-lettered legend:

MISS EVANS
Milliner
MANTUA MAKER
Robes

The diminution was deliberate; for, although Miss Evans could rightly claim distinction as a milliner, having served her apprenticeship with a Madame 'Thing' of Exeter and could make a cap or bonnet with the best of them, she was somewhat less proficient in the making of a mantua or robe. Indeed, her knowledge of such extended no farther than the altering of her mama's cast-offs to fit herself. Yet, if put to it, Miss Evans had no doubt that she could do as well or better with her robes and modes and whatnot than any Mesdames

Thing-me-Bobs of Exeter or Bristol, or even of London come to that. For the present, however, let this, her latest, or to be exact, her first and only model, suffice to tempt the Quality with the opening, upon the morrow, of the season and her salon. *(Never call it a shop.)*

And now, having polished her panes until they shone in the last of the sun to reflect a rose-star in each, Miss Evans — justifiably complacent — surveyed her sole exhibit.

Elegantly topical in red, white and blue — red for its ribbons, white for its lace frill, blue for its nosegay of forget-me-nots — it was poised on a hatstand converted from a candlestick and labelled *The Waterloo Cap*.

Islanded in solitude, it flaunted enticement — too solitary, perhaps? For, despite that Madame 'Thing' had always laid importance on under-dressing — window under-dressing, be it understood — 'The same,' so Madame had instructed her apprentices, 'applies to caps and every kind of headgear, *modes et robes*. Simplicity, young ladies, is the hallmark of the tonnish, the goal and aim and purpose of the *chic*.' Yet, Miss Evans reflected, one might overdo 'simplicity' in under-dress of windows. Some additional support: a pair of gloves, pantoufles, a length of gauze, a shoulder scarf, would surely not detract from but enrich temptation. And nothing, certainly, more tempting than this, *her* Waterloo, had been seen in Clifton where Fashion, in the season, flocked to the Hotwells in running for the rivalry of Bath.

With Miss Evans to think was to act, and dallying no longer, she darted through the door that opened directly on the street giving access to and egress from the salon. These premises, of which she had been tenant for barely two weeks, were let unfurnished, and the decorations undertaken by herself. Three days' hard work and several pails of soapsuds had eventually removed from the walls the layers of dirt that hid their original colour: a peculiarly gentle shade of pink, known in millinery circles as 'Maiden's Blush'. She had polished the floorboards with beeswax to render them slippery as glass. She had draped the bow window with curtains of sprigged muslin, and from two tea chests bought of the local grocer for fourpence a piece, she had contrived, and covered with black velvet, a raised platform or dais for the display in the window of her wares.

In all these manoeuvres her landlady, Miss Graham, took the keenest interest, gave much gratuitous advice and the loan of a pair of brown spotted china dogs, one of which lacked a paw, the other an ear. These, received with rapture by Miss Evans who privately thought them too hideous for words, she placed on the mantelshelf having nothing else to put there.

The furnishings of her salon, which admittedly were wanting, consisted of an oval mirror in a very tarnished frame, re-gilded by Miss Evans and purchased at an auction in Bristol along with three chairs, a tallboy and a rug, a trifle threadbare, knocked down for a guinea the lot. These preliminary outlays had sadly diminished her capital, hoarded in a stocking and saved from the pin money of sixpence a week doled by her mama, with a bonus of ten shillings at Christmas from her Uncle James Viney in Gloucester. By dint of strictest economy she had saved enough in eighteen months to assert her independence, though not without some opposition from her mother.

'That a daughter of mine should sink herself so low. Millinery! I'll die of shame.'

'But,' was the gentle reminder, 'you didn't think it low, nor did you die of shame when you apprenticed me to millinery, so why die of it now?'

'That was different,' her mother had tearfully retorted. 'I paid ten guineas to Madame for your apprenticeship which I could ill afford, having bought your brother a commission in the army and in case you should never find a husband,' her tone had suggested little hope of that, 'so you may earn a living against a rainy day.'

'Which came,' rejoined Miss Evans, 'raining cats and dogs, when you went off and married Mr Yate.'

'Dear heaven,' Mrs Yate appealed, 'was ever woman so abused by her own daughter? To disgrace my name — the revered name of Viney — with a *shop*!'

'A salon,' Miss Evans inflexibly corrected, 'and your name has not been Viney, Ma, for five and twenty years. So how can I disgrace it now?'

Avoiding direct answer to that question, 'And there's no rhyme nor reason in it,' wailed Mrs Yate, 'while I can afford to keep you.'

'There may be no rhyme in it,' Miss Evans had agreed, 'but plenty reason. For granted that you *can* afford to keep me, you can't afford to keep your Mr Yate as well.'

So that had been the gist of it, and several such arguments, to result in Mrs Yate's capitulation.

On her knees before the tallboy on this, the eve of her great day, Miss Evans rummaged in a bottom drawer to bring forth a long Angola shawl of bright amber with a garish floral border, a gift from her Uncle Viney for her twenty-first birthday, worn only once at a ball in the Bristol Assembly Rooms, and now put into stock.

'Yet I somehow fancy,' said Miss Evans, who for want of better audience would often talk to herself, 'that it would look frightful with red, white and blue.'

She pulled out another drawer, turned all in it topsy-turvy to find what she sought: a pair of lilac kid gloves elbow length, pearl-buttoned, and the slippers — or pantoufles — of striped satin, blue and white. From these, and a miscellany of oddments purchased in Bristol at last January's sales, she made her selection, choosing the pantoufles, the gloves, and a parasol of fluted blue silk arranged with careful negligence on the dais in the window where presided the Waterloo cap.

Dusk was falling, colours fading, a near church clock chiming eight sonorous strokes. 'Dear me,' said Miss Evans, 'and I must be going, else Ma will be throwing a fit.'

She was loath to disturb the effect of her display, yet to leave it exposed to the danger of thieves would be courting disaster. She must lock all away in the tallboy for safety. This done, and removing from her head the kerchief replaced by a modest chip bonnet, she prepared to depart and was stayed by the voice of Miss Graham in the doorway leading to that lady's private quarters.

'Still here? I thought,' exclaimed Miss Graham in tones of liveliest amaze, 'that you had gone hours ago.'

This was a slight fabrication. Miss Graham, having listened from her parlour above to her tenant's every movement below, was perfectly aware that Miss Evans had not gone; and, imbued with curiosity, had come down to see why she lingered. Could she be expecting — oh, surely not! — a follower? Since Miss Graham, through force of circumstances, much reduced, had advertised in the *Bristol Mirror* her ground floor front to let *(Modes, Robes, or Millinery only)*, she had suffered many anxious qualms regarding the propriety of ways such as these to meet her impoverished means. True, she had chosen Miss Evans from six other likely applicants for the proffered tenancy, since, not only did Miss Evans reside in Clifton with her mother, Mrs Yate, she was, as careful enquiry had elicited, the daughter of a naval officer deceased. Moreover, the high cost of living due to heavy war taxation had been a prodigious drain on Miss Graham's slender resources. The additional seven and sixpence a week from the rent of her ground floor front, millinery or nothing, would supply her with some little extra comforts sorely needed.

Small and narrow as her house, a sprightly virgin of fifty was Miss Graham. Her hair, whose golden tint discreetly applied from the contents of a bottle and arranged in juvenile curls around her forehead, framed a withered little face of insignificant features save for a nose disproportionately large for the rest of her. A clinging mull muslin, puff-sleeved and high-sashed, her habitual style of dress, was more suited to fifteen than fifty; and she affected a penchant for childish bonnets that might possibly be offered, decided Miss Evans, at terms reduced with the proviso of recommendation.

'Pray, Miss Evans,' was the winning invitation, 'won't you step up to the parlour for a dish of tea? The kettle's on the boil and my ratafees are new baked. I'll be bound, so busy as you are getting ready for tomorrow, that you have had nor bite nor sup all day.'

'I thank you kindly, ma'am, but,' Miss Evans bobbed, unconscious of Miss Graham's pout at that respectful 'ma'am' which placed her high in years of seniority to 'miss', 'I have had a sandwich.'

'A sandwich!' cried Miss Graham. 'Is that *all*? You must be starving. Do let me persuade you, dear Miss Evans.'

Dear Miss Evans was persuaded, for if not starving she was thirsting for a dish of tea; and willingly she stepped, in the wake of her hostess, up the spiral staircase to the parlour.

This apartment, even smaller and more limited for space than the ground floor front in that it could boast no bow window, was over-filled with furniture inherited, Miss Graham sighingly revealed, from her Poor Papa's ancestral seat in Staffordshire; and which led her visitor to think must have been a castle, second only in magnificence to Blenheim. Further revelation disclosed a baronetcy in abeyance, the Rightful Heir, Miss Graham's paternal great grandfather, having disappeared mysteriously under Anne. And since there was none but daughters to inherit, the title still awaited a male heir to claim it.

Miss Evans, while duly impressed, forbore to ask why Miss Graham's Poor Papa who, from all account, should surely have been Rich Papa, had not himself if a direct descendant, claimed it. Miss Graham, however, leaving the baronetcy still in abeyance, proceeded to tell of her niece, 'My poor brother's daughter. *She* married into the Dragoons — a Major Vernon — wounded but not mortally, thank God, at Waterloo. My brother, years and *years* older than I, is, alas, gone before —' which, cruelly reflected Miss Evans, must have made him about ninety when he went — 'so that I and my niece,' Miss Graham was in haste to add, 'are almost of one age. Her husband, the major, recently took the name of Vernon-Graham, hyphenated, we being of more ancient lineage. My niece, Dottie, short for Dorothea, with the major and the three darling children, will soon be coming to the Hotwells for the cure.'

Miss Evans brightened. The niece, Dottie, if not the darling children, might augur well for custom.

'And I,' Miss Graham indicated coyly, 'am — hee, hee — a *great-aunt!* Isn't it ridiculous?'

Miss Evans, with an upward look from eyes that were neither blue nor grey but of that colour mistakenly called violet, agreed that it was indeed — ridiculous.

The kettle, hissing merrily above a spirit lamp on a near side table, brought Miss Graham to her feet with a little scream. 'Stupid me! I've let it boil over!' Tea was poured; ratafia cakes, in a silver (plated) basket, were offered. 'Pray, Miss Evans, try one of these. I made them myself. I hope you will find them to your liking. Now tell me —'

So across the teacups confidences were exchanged, or, by Miss Graham, extracted.

'Your papa, was he,' she asked in a suitably hushed voice, 'killed in naval action?'

'Yes, ma'am. I was an infant in arms when he died a hero's death at the Battle of Traf —' Miss Evans stopped herself in time. She had almost said Trafalgar, which would give her barely ten years now; and with another uplift of her eyes ceilingwards, she deftly substituted, 'in sea-battle.'

Miss Graham shook her curls and sighed. 'These wicked, wicked wars —' And Miss Evans sighed in unison, much relieved to find she was not pressed to furnish more particulars concerning the heroic death of her papa; for although a naval officer, having been promoted from the rank of captain's servant to that of a lieutenant a year or two before his marriage, he did not die in naval battle nor did he die at sea, but ashore in the West Indies of a fever.

'And before you came to Clifton,' Miss Graham carefully avoided the millinery apprenticeship, 'you lived, with your mama, at — you did tell me, but my memory — hee, hee! — is like a sieve.'

Miss Evans, who certainly had not told Miss Graham where she lived with her mama before she came to Clifton, nor indeed any more concerning herself than she deemed proper for her landlady to know, answered with becoming modesty, 'In Devon, ma'am, near Exeter where I was born. And when my father went to sea again, my mother, my brother and I — we lived with my grandfather Evans, the squire of Brampford Park.'

'Brampford *Park*?' Miss Graham's negligible eyebrows shot up to her gold fringe of curls. 'It must have been a considerable property.'

'It was,' Miss Evans softly stressed, 'a considerable property, until — the fire.'

'The fire?' echoed Miss Graham, parrot-wise.

'Destroyed.' Miss Evans lowered her remarkably long lashes. 'Burnt. To the ground. No stick nor stone left standing.' And this was true enough in that no stick nor stone of Brampford Park had ever stood, save in the imagination of Miss Evans. Nor was her grandfather the squire of a property, considerable or otherwise, having been a farmer, and a tenant farmer at that, of a small holding in the village of Brampford Speke, glorified by Miss Evans to 'Park'.

There, in early childhood, she had lived and laboured in the farmyard, the cowsheds and the dairy. Then, on her grandfather's death and on her mother's remarriage, she had been sent to her Uncle Viney at Gloucester. An officer in the Royal Artillery, the pride of and most distinguished member of the family, he had seen much service abroad and in later life was to receive a knighthood and the Companionship of the Bath. And *a miserly, crotchety, crusty old bear was he,* so ungratefully we have it from Miss Evans; for, crotchety, crusty, or bearish notwithstanding, he had paid for her schooling that she be taught to read and write and lose her country accent; but she still must keep a guard upon her tongue which, in moments of forgetfulness, would revert to its Devonshire burr.

She had often been puzzled as to the reason for the long estrangement between her mother and her nearest relatives. That Mrs Yate had married not once but twice beneath her, she had learned from Uncle Viney. Her mother's marriage to Lieutenant Evans, RN, had been a love match, a romantic elopement and, in fact, a double wedding in that her mother's twin sister, Bridget, had been married at the same time and in the same church at Plymouth to a friend of John Evans, a Lieutenant Munn. A brief account of this event in the *Exeter Flying Post* reports the brides, Bridget and Eleanor Viney, as *agreeable young ladies with handsome fortunes*. Their fortunes, unless much exaggerated, must indeed for those days have been handsome, amounting, so rumour gave it, to something in the region of five thousand pounds each, bequeathed to the orphaned twins by their mother. How or when Eleanor's portion was dissipated is not known, but if Mrs Evans, when widowed, had been the 'Guest of Charity', as she often deplored, it would seem that her two marriages had consumed the better part of it. She may, however, have still retained an adequate competence when, as a widow, she was wooed again and won by Mr Yate.

This second misalliance so deeply offended the Family, emphasised by Uncle Viney, as the Head of it, in Capitals, that Eleanor would seem to have been shunned. 'Yate, a ne'er do well, a nobody who scraped a living — how? At the best a toastmaster, at the worst — a traveller.'

When Miss Evans wished to know why a traveller — one who travelled and therefore must have means — should be scorned by Uncle Viney, she was curtly told, 'Commercial', which left her none the wiser. But that Mr Yate had ceased to travel when he married her mama was the primary cause of her venture as the tenant of Miss Graham's ground-floor front.

Her credentials thus presented with a social status and background comparable at least to that of Miss Graham, she sat remotely gazing at the middle distance as if she saw in it the vanished splendours of her past.

'Your brother,' persisted Miss Graham, who had lapped up this intelligence as a kitten laps up cream, 'your brother — he is also in the Navy?'

Roused from her reverie and with a pretty show of blinking, Miss Evans replied, 'My —? Oh, my brother. No. He is in the army, but was not at Waterloo, being stationed with his regiment, the Twenty-ninth Foot, in Mauritius.'

And, having spiced her potpourri of fiction with this one indubitable fact, *That's quite enough, old Poke-Nose,* Miss Evans said, *from you!* But this she did not say aloud. What she did say, setting down her cup, rising from her chair, was effusively, 'Obliged, ma'am, I'm sure, for your kindness and the delicious tea. I have never been more sweetly entertained. Your ratafees, I declare, are perfection. If I may, I'll beg from you the recipe. Of all things I would love to stay longer, but I daresn't. My ma — er — my mama will be in a rare taking.'

'I, too,' Miss Graham graciously conceded, 'have much enjoyed our little chat, and I hope this is the first of many other pleasant meetings. Most of the lady residents in Clifton are elderly, not to say *old*; I have often longed for a friend nearer to my age, and I trust I have found one, Miss Evans dear, in you. Wait —' from the mantelshelf she took a tinderbox and lit a taper — 'Allow me to light you down the stairs. 'Tis growing dark.'

So with mutual curtsies and affectionate farewells they parted at Miss Graham's narrow door.

It was some ten minutes' walk to the house where Miss Evans's mother lodged at the upper end of Park Street, on the heights of Clifton village; but the church clock chiming nine set Miss Evans to a run up that steep ascent. Pausing on the hilltop to recover breath she stood savouring the mingled cool sweet smell of new-mown grass and unseen dew-drenched flowers from near gardens. In the bowl of the city below she could see the lamps of Bristol circling the pewter-coloured dusk like a necklace of gold on grey velvet. Through the gathering twilight she glimpsed the tree-embowered deep ravine dividing two counties, with the river Avon, out of sight at the foot of those rocky cliffs, rushing ever onwards to the sea. And dark against the dying afterglow of sunset she discerned the high plateau of the Downs that seemed to nudge the low-swung crescent moon and one great ice-green star, so close to earth it was as if a far-flung stone could reach it. Then, as night swept softly down upon that dimmed enchantment, and as she turned to pull the bell of the front door, she heard approaching footsteps on the cobbled stones behind her.

Even in the frail light she recognised the face of him who, with a long stare and a momentary halt, passed on; nor did he look back.

Well, now, decidedly this, said Miss Evans to herself, *can't be chance — or is it? Four times in three days. He all but stopped to speak. Am I watched? Am I followed? Who is he — what is he? And why does he prowl about the village at these unconscionable hours and always when the* Pump Room *it be closed, so he can't have come from there if he be here to take the waters...* And looking round to see if he were looking round at her, which he, disappointingly, was not, she pulled the bell.

A chubby, round-faced, rosy-cheeked child answered it and told her in broad Somerset without comma or full stop, 'Your ma miss is skeered as you was strangled on the Downs like that poor girl last Sunday with 'er stockin' an' on the Sabbath too bein' found under a bush an' 'er legs stickin' out an' nothin' on 'er but 'er shift an' there be col' mutton miss for you shall I bring it up?'

'Yes, Nina, if you please.'

From a tray on the hall table Miss Evans took a lighted candle and climbed the three flights of stairs to the third-floor back, consisting of a parlour and bedroom rented by Mrs Yate for herself and her husband, with use of the kitchen in the basement. Two attic rooms under the eaves were respectively allotted to Mrs Yate's daughter and her thirteen-year-old maid, Nina Rook.

'Mary Anne?' The voice of Mrs Yate, querulous and high-pitched, shrilled through the half-open door. 'Is that you? At last! I thought —'

'Yes, Ma, and what did you think?'

Miss Evans, or Mary Anne, as henceforth we shall know her and as throughout her life she was known — although the record of her birth in the parish register of St Sidwell's, Exeter, gives her baptismal name as Marianne — went in. Thriftily snuffing the candle, she placed it on the sideboard, and added, with a smile showing dimples, 'Did you think I'd been murdered or raped?'

'Goodness gracious, girl!' Mrs Yate raised eyes and hands to heaven, 'the things you say. You're wanton. Lost to all maidenly reserve. And how many times must I tell you not to call me "Ma"? "Mama" is the proper mode of address from a young lady to her mother, but despite all my efforts to make you one you will *never* be a lady. And now to bring me to shame with a shop!'

Mary Anne took off her bonnet and gloves and, seating herself at the table, said, 'Ma — beg pardon — Mama, you're old-fashioned. Values, and by values I mean not only money values but social values too, have changed. We've been at war for fifteen years, remember, and now that Boney's finished we likely may be faced with another war. At home.'

'You're romancing,' said Mrs Yate, 'as usual. I don't know from where you get all your fancy ideas.'

'They're not fancy ideas.' Mary Anne lost her smile. 'And I'm not romancing. I only wish I were. There'll be war among ourselves here in England, you'll see. It mayn't be a war of bloodshed, though there be signs of combustion all over the country. You don't read the news-sheets, Ma, but I do. I can read them for nothing in the circulating library, and I saw in the *London Times* how processions of starving men, 'human scarecrows' as was quoted from one of the speeches in Parliament, go marching through towns and villages flying banners and yelling "Bread or Blood!" like they did in the French Revolution.'

'Lord help us!' gasped her mother.

'The Lord helps those,' said Mary Anne, 'who helps theirselves.' She helped herself to a slice of bread cut from the loaf before her. Spreading butter thick upon it, she conveyed the slice to her mouth. 'And them — those human scarecrows,' she continued while she munched, 'they be helping theirselves by breaking the machines in the engine-controlled factories all on account of the Regent's high living. Much he cares if the needy go grubbing pigs' swill for their food and eating snails — they who fought to win his wars. And with the price of bread soaring — why, look at this loaf —' she stuck her knife in it — 'a shilling! That be the cost of it today. If *we* can't afford to pay a shilling for a loaf, how can

21

them poor wretches buy so much as a crust who haven't a shilling piece between them? So you see, Ma, women'll have to work to earn their bread, same as me. I wouldn't want to be a burden on you. Besides, you've always said you apprenticed me to millinery that I might have a living in my hands.' She held them out, small and slender-fingered. 'It would be a sin to waste that ten guineas you did spend on my apprenticeship if I do nothing with it.'

'I can't — I can't —' moaned Mrs Yate, to whom only the last few words of this monologue had conveyed any sense at all, 'stand much more of you or your talk — so low and common. One would think you'd been brought up in the gutter, though goodness knows I've tried my best, *and* your Uncle Viney with your schooling. But you can't make a silk purse from a sow's ear, that's plain. What have I done to deserve it?'

The entrance of the little maid with the remains of a cold leg of mutton circumvented an answer to that. Setting the dish, a jar of pickles, and a crust of bread on the table, Nina, adenoidally breathing down the neck of Mary Anne, whispered, 'Which be all there is for you miss the Maister's supper keepin' hot a boilin' fowl not to be carved Missus says, till 'e come 'ome but I'll bring 'ee a pint o' porter if you like, miss.'

Miss indicating that she would like, the pint was brought in a Toby jug.

'Porter!' cried Mrs Yate. 'That's your papa's porter. You can't drink that.'

'Can't I?' smiled Mary Anne; and lifting the jug in both hands she lowered her lips to it and drank a full draught.

'I might,' declared her mother, 'be a fly on the wall, so much you heed me. You will be my death, you wicked girl!' She clutched her bodice in the region of her heart. 'My palpitations—'

'Porter,' said Mary Anne, 'is good for palpitations.' She left her seat to offer the Toby jug. 'Come, Ma, take a sip. 'Twill do you a power of good.'

'No.' Shuddering, her mother turned her head away. 'Brandy. A drop of brandy. You will find the bottle in the sideboard. Your papa bought it specially for me to take when I come over poorly.'

Mary Anne went to the sideboard, pulled open the drawer of its zinc-lined cellarette, and found the brandy bottle. It was empty.

'Well, I never!' ejaculated Mrs Yate. 'And it was full last night.'

'Perhaps Mr Yate,' said Mary Anne, the dimples much in evidence, 'came over poorly, too.'

'Oh!' Her mother recoiled. 'I hope and trust not. But if he had —' she shot a stabbing look at her demurely smiling daughter — 'he would never tell me. Always considerate, *he* is, of my feelings, which is more,' she added pointedly, 'than I can say of some.'

We must allow her cause for grievance. A faded little blonde, whose not too well-worn prettiness went veiled in a constant martyrdom, long-sufferingly endured, she had it fixed she was the victim of an unjust, ill-starred fate. Widowed in her twenties, left with two small children, 'cut adrift' from her nearest and dearest and 'dragged to the depths of low living,' as she termed it, on a farm, her dear John's parentage being 'not — not *quite*,' she must now be confronted with 'a Viper nurtured at the Breast.' Was ever a mother so humiliated and misused? Or was ever a daughter so shameless and self-willed? To answer an advertisement for a room to let so she might open a shop, in Mrs Yate's estimation only second to a stew, and without a word, mark you, to her! That clatterpate Miss Graham would never have done talking. Was this monstrous, base ingratitude a mother's just reward for a life of sacrifice and toil? Sharper than a Serpent's Tooth…

Some such complaints as these were the running commentary to Mary Anne's cold supper. To be sure, they were no new complaints, although to what extent had been her mother's life of sacrifice and toil she was at some loss to know. For if anyone had toiled it had not been Mrs Yate, but Mary Anne.

Yet her childhood, nostalgically reviewed, had been happy enough down on that Devonshire farm. She had only to close her eyes to see the shadowed cow-stalls… Sun-shafts, dagger-bright, thrust through the open doorway cleaving dark umber recesses where Molly and Sally and Clover and Sue stood patiently waiting the ease of their burdensome milk bags. Light falling on those satin flanks turned them to honey gold; and with that recurrent memory would come a haunting whiff of damp straw, hay, ammonia and dung. She saw the gentle enquiring turn of a head, the greenish dribble from soft grey chewing lips, the swish of a welcoming tail, and herself, very small, on a stool, her cheek pressed to a warm, sleek side while her coaxing fingers drew from full udders their rich grateful yield. She could hear again the foaming plash of milk in the pail and her grandfather standing over her saying, "Ands like a boy's 'ands you 'ave. There be no better 'ands for milkin' than a boy's unless they be your'n, Mary Anne.'

But he would lend no quarter to a laggard. Up she must be with the sun and the cows, her milking stool and 'Gran'fer' Evans too.

Her brother John, however, for all he had boy's hands, would have naught to do with milking. Destined for the army, he was sent to school at Taunton. Their mother spared no expense on educating him; and save for occasional visits to Brampford Speke, his holidays were spent with Uncle Viney in Gloucester. Sowdons, the Evans's farm, was not considered by his mother and his uncle to be a suitable environment for a budding officer and gentleman.

John, seen through the haze of distance, was a long-legged, lordly being with a face like a girl's, hair smooth and shining, and eyes of a startling blue. He would talk very big of himself and of a game called cricket in which, it appeared, he excelled, and that his sister believed had to do with an insect. The exposure of her ignorance in a leading question: 'Where do you foind them crickets to play with? We h'ant none 'ere, but grass'oppers a-plenty —' brought hoots of derisive laughter and scorn unmitigated on her for 'a dizzard, dolt, a bumpkin', and never let him be seen walking out with her in Exeter when their grandfather drove them over in his gig on market day, lest he should meet with some of his 'fellows' who lived there. He had a pet name for her, 'Whizz', derived from her country accent and would mimic it teasingly. 'Where do you foind —' till she let fly at him tooth and claw, to leave a bleeding scratch on 'them lily-whoite 'ands o' your'n. Foine 'ands for milkin' they be, I'll say!' And they were at it together, rough and tumble, he the victor, to fling her face downwards on the dung-heap to split his sides at sight of her covered with the muck, that she must up at him again kicking his shins till he, still laughing, held her wrist and called, 'A pax!' and told her he would show her how to deal a straight right-hander and not to hit below the belt.

Then he took his handkerchief, spat on it, cleaned the dirt from her face and gave her as peace offering a bull's-eye with bits of fluff from his pocket sticking to it. And even now the taste of peppermint always gave her thought of John, whom she seldom saw since he had been gazetted to the army… Darling John, who was always in debt and always helped out by Mama.

There was yet another memory, more vivid than any of these.

Autumn time, it must have been, for the drift of woodsmoke blown in at the cowshed door with a flurry of brittle leaves and a footfall in the stable yard beyond, where the white fantails winged down from their cote to peck at the grain she had scattered to the hens; a footfall lighter, yet firmer than that of a shuffling, thick, booted farm lad; and the voice of a stranger who hailed her where she sat at her milking.

'Will you sell me a draught fresh from the cow, little maid?'

A gentleman, a 'foreigner', as strangers were called in those parts, stood there in the doorway. She knew he was a gentleman for his clipped speech, his fine suit of broadcloth, and the way he raised his beaver to her bob.

'Sure, sir, I'll gie you a drink an' welcome, so be's you wait till I be done with this 'un 'ere. I daresn't leave 'er 'arf full.'

So he waited, idly tapping his cane to the toe of his silver buckled shoe. Then, when she was done, she led him across the yard to the dairy, dipped a cup in the new milk set aside for skimming, and offered it; but when he would have slid a crown piece in her palm she put her hands behind her back and told him: 'No, sir, I thank 'ee. We've more 'n enough an' to spare.'

At which he touched a finger to her eyelashes and asked, 'Who gave you these, an inch long? You could hang rings on them. And eyes like those flowers called Love-in-a-Mist?'

She shook her head. 'I dunno, sir. I be seemin' allus to have 'ad 'em, and my eyes, since I be born.'

Then he laughed and called her, 'True daughter of Devon — sweet as a Devonshire rose.' But for all she refused it, he insisted she accept the crown piece — 'to buy yourself a riband or some lollipops or such, when you go fairing.' And with a courtly bow he went upon his way.

She often wondered who he was and whence he came, and often, too, would look for him around the farm, along the lanes, but not for many years to come was she destined to meet with that 'foreigner' again.

While thinking back upon this chance encounter, and lost to her mother's lamentations, a stumble on the landing and a loud 'Goddamme! Where's the light? I've barked me shins!' announced the approach of Mr Yate.

His wife, in a flutter, went to meet him; Mary Anne drank the last of the porter and stayed seated, when Mr Yate, flinging wide the door, proclaimed his presence.

'Here we are!'

An imposing presence was that of Mr Yate, broad of chest and shoulder, inclined to a paunch accentuated by a large expanse of white marcella waistcoat. The gilt buttons of his well-tailored raven-blue suit shone like little harvest moons. A high, starched cravat concealed all but one of his three chins; and his face, expansive as the rest of him, was crowned by a crop of suspiciously auburn Neronian curls.

'Hah, my chick!' On his 'chick's' eagerly expectant lips he planted a resounding kiss. 'I bring you news. Good news. Brave news!'

Mary Anne swung round in her chair. 'Is Boney dead?'

'Buonaparrte?' He gave to the name its Corsican pronunciation with an emphatic rolling of the r and a simultaneous up-rolling of his eyes. 'What have we to do with Buonaparrte? Wellington, thank Gard, has done for him. No. My news is of a more — hic — pardon me,' politely he belched, 'of a more personal nature, which calls —' his glance swerved to the Toby jug, thence to the sideboard and back again to Mary Anne — 'which calls for cel-hic-bration.'

'Angel!' ecstatically cried Mrs Yate. 'Is it — have you — *are* you —?'

'It is, and I have, and I am,' declared Mr Yate taking her into his arms. 'Let us drink to this most auspish-hic-shus —' over the nestling head of his wife he addressed his wife's daughter — 'Child, bring forth a bottle.'

'A bottle of what?' Mary Anne asked, still seated. 'And from where am I to bring it?'

Mr Yate waved a hand, and settling his third chin in his cravat, said airily, 'From Mount Olympus — hah? Or if Bacchus be not disposed to oblige, then descend you to the Pluton-hic-depths of the cellar where, with permission of our good landlady, I have laid me down a dozen of the best in anticip-hic-ation of this joyous event.'

'I am going to bed,' said Mary Anne, rising. 'I'm tired.'

'Tired?' Mr Yate fumbled for his quizzing-glass, suspended by a black watered ribbon to rest on his bulging waistcoat. 'You, a nymph,' leeringly he side-glassed her, 'tired? Look at *me*—'

Mary Anne wrinkled a tip-tilted nose. 'Yes, I'm looking.'

'I — hah — am twice your age, and am I tired? No. Am I buoyant? Yes.' Detaching himself from his wife, he strode to the sideboard, pulled open the cellarette and took from it the brandy flask. Holding it neck downwards to the candlelight he solemnly pronounced it 'Dead,' and, unsteadily revolving, screwed an eye at the table, 'as mutton. I come prepared for the fatted calf and what am I offered? A bone.'

'There's a fowl,' said his wife, 'if it is not overdone by this time. Mary Anne, ring the bell for Rook.'

Mary Anne got up. 'Nina has enough to do fetching and carrying all day and half the night. I'll see to it.'

She made for the door and was caught back by Mr Yate, boisterously declaring, 'Here's a thing, and a very pretty thing. What shall we do with this very pretty — hic?'

'You seem,' said Mary Anne, 'to have the hiccups.'

'In'jeshion, me darling. Never mind the fowl. I have already supped.'

'Which,' said Mary Anne, dodging an effluvium of brandy, rum and other sorts, 'is evident.'

'Shall we then descend into the cellar together?' suggested Mr Yate, his arm enveloping her waist, while with the fingertips of his unemployed hand he wafted a kiss to his wife's elevated eyebrows; then of a sudden he burst into song: *How happy could I be with either, Were t'other dear charmer away — ay — ay-hic!'* and, as suddenly ceasing, released Mary Anne to make her and her mother a leg. 'Mesdames, behold me here and at all time hereafter your devoted husband, father and Master of the Ceremonies at the Clif-*hic*-ton Assembly Rooms. Mesdames, at your service — Thomas Yate.'

TWO

That Victory July and August brought visitors in unprecedented numbers to the Hotwells. The apartment houses on the Polygon and the Parades, patronised by the élite, were besieged with requests for accommodation. Such an influx of oldcomers, newcomers, and persons, who, in the opinion of Miss Graham, had no right to be there, were never before seen in Clifton.

'Dreadful businessmen from Cardiff, and their wives, dressed to kill. Simply smothered in jewels — how *do* they get their money? Tradespeople and all sorts, and no offence intended, Miss Evans dear, to you. Millinery can scarcely be called trade.'

Miss Evans may have hoped it could. She welcomed the flamboyant ladies of rich city merchants and nabobs, who, passing to and from the Hotwells, would pause to look in at her bottle-panes. And they did more than look; they bought. Within a week of its appearance the Waterloo cap had been sold and copied in various colours and under various names: The 'Wellington', the 'Victory', the 'Princess Charlotte', in compliment to the young daughter of the Regent.

Miss Graham's qualms assuaged, she spent much of her time in the upper window of the little house in Culver Street, watching the elegant and not so elegant deposited in carriages, hackneys or sedans at her door. For, signboard or not, tenanted or nothing, it was still her door, and her interest in what Miss Evans called her 'cleeontell' not entirely impersonal. It may be that Miss Graham regretted she had let her ground floor front in this so select a neighbourhood at so low a rent, when it would seem Miss Evans was making money hand over fist, selling caps, hats, bonnets, scarves, and buying, if you please, materials at sale price, as Miss Graham could vouch for, she herself having bought a remnant of that same lilac sarsenet for half a crown, and sold by Miss Evans at twelve shillings. Did you ever!

Thus to her cronies in the Pump Room, where twice weekly she and they foregathered to drink the waters, so good for the — ahem. And only think! A guinea for a mob composed of net and lace, not even *real*, and no trimming but one teeny-weeny rose. Downright robbery, Miss Graham called it.

None the less she coveted the mob, and, with gentlest hints, conveyed that it was just the thing for her but *far* beyond her means, Miss Evans dear.

Miss Evans made rapid calculation to assure her, 'You shall have it at cost price of — sixteen shillings.'

'Six-*teen*?' Miss Graham's button mouth fell open. 'That's more than two weeks' rent. I cannot possibly afford —'

'Fifteen then — or, if you prefer it, two weeks' rent free and not one penny more than sixpence do I make on it. Do you know what such a cap as this would cost in Bath?'

Miss Graham did not know.

'Two guineas,' stated the unblushing Mary Anne. 'I saw this self-same model cribbed from *my* creation in Gould's of Milsom Street when I was there last Monday.'

That Miss Evans had been in Bath last Monday was news to Miss Graham, and indeed to Mary Anne, who if truth, which she regrettably was not particular to tell, were told, had not been in Bath for a year of Mondays. But what of that? A girl who had a living in her hands must, in all fairness to the money spent on it, make that living good. And so, 'Fifteen shillings,' she hard-heartedly repeated. 'Or my rent for two weeks free and call it quits.'

Miss Graham was beguiled; and the transaction completed, satisfactorily at least for Mary Anne, with the addition of a chequered ribbon, blue and white, thrown in 'so you can wear it tied under the chin by day, or, without the ribbon, as a turban for evenings.'

'I'll wear it,' Miss Graham delightedly declared, 'when I go to the Victory Ball.'

She had just heard from her niece, Mrs Vernon-Graham, that she, the major and the three darling children would be at the Hotwells in time for the ball — 'which you, Miss Evans, will of course attend, now that Mr Yate, your step-papa, is *persona grata* at the Rooms.'

Mary Anne withheld her doubt of that, for if Mr Yate, as Master of the Ceremonies, were *persona grata* at the Rooms, she most certainly was not.

Following the rules and example observed by Nash, immortal Beau of Bath, Mr Yate had debarred from that circle, exclusive to the nobility or gentlefolk, any plebeian intrusion; and by plebeian, he had made it clear to Mary Anne, 'any person of either sex involved in trade'. Therefore, unless he perjure himself by presenting her masked and in a false name as the Lady Mary X, or the Honourable Miss Y, she could not, his beloved daughter though she were, be received in the Rooms by him.

'There, you see,' bemoaned her mother, 'how you have ruined your chances, you bad girl! Your papa, in honour bound to his great calling, cannot break rules in your favour. You keep a shop to your disgrace — and mine — and so are banned henceforth from high society.'

'Alas, too true,' murmured Mr Yate, pouring liberal sherry into a liberal glass to taste with a relishing smack of his lips. 'A sample,' said he, 'submitted for my approval by Harvey of Bristol, at half the price paid by my predecessah for an inferior quality in Bath. This,' he refilled his glass and drank again, 'is excellent.'

'It don't matter a row of pins to me,' surlily said Mary Anne, 'if I do or don't go to the ball. What time have I for prancing and dancing, kept busy from morning till late in the night to deck out those ladies who do?'

Among those ladies who did were Mrs Vernon-Graham and the darling children. Their descent on the salon, a few days after their arrival at the spa, had been urged by Miss Graham on a tacit understanding between her tenant and herself concerning a 'tweeny-weeny what d'you call it? — commission. I am a positive babe in the wood — hee, hee! — at money matters. Or would it be a something small per cent on any purchase they — you know?'

Mary Anne, it seemed, knew very well. 'Shall we say, then, two per cent?'

'Oh, my dear *soul*,' screamed Miss Graham, 'what a little skinflint — hee, hee! Make it four — but,' she artlessly apologised, 'I never could do sums, so you must tell me exactly how much that would be on a guinea. Something near to *nothing* I am sure. Or, if you would rather — say an increase of two shillings a week in the rent to make up for — you know — those two weeks' rent free.'

'Certainly not,' was the decisive rejoinder. 'Those two weeks' rent free were a more than fair exchange for a cap at less than cost price. Besides, an agreement,' said Mary Anne, 'is an agreement. I took the premises in writing which each of us signed, at a weekly rental of seven and six, and that is sixpence too much. For look you, ma'am, the season will not last for ever, in which case I would have to give you a week's notice, so you'd be out o' pocket and I'd be out o' work.' Then, seeing Miss Graham lip-fallen, 'suppose we split the difference,' she magnanimously offered, 'and make it three per cent on any custom you may bring?'

So three per cent it was; and the deal barely concluded when Mrs and the Misses Vernon-Graham paid their first visit to the salon, in bulk.

In bulk, very truly; since, not only did the darling children prove to be a well-grown buxom trio whose joint ages could scarcely have been less than sixty-five, but their mother, Dottie — 'short for Dorothea' — was florid, stout, and hearty as her offspring. The four of them took up what little space the salon could afford, and when Mrs Vernon-Graham deposited herself on the smallest of Mary Anne's small chairs, it ominously creaked beneath her weight. Perspiring freely, for the day was warm and she unseasonably clad in ruby cloth with epaulettes gold-braided in military fashion, she sat, beaming indulgence on her daughters. They, in India muslin — damped, as worn by the tonnish, to cling, and which transparently revealed an unshapely show of leg in flesh-pink stockings — were rhapsodic. They bounced from cap to bonnet, snatching each a sample to ram upon her head, while Mary Anne, agonised for the fate of her cherished creations, was hard put not to snatch them off again. Having tried on and discarded her entire stock, not excluding pantoufles and gloves, pronounced too tight a fit and, 'Oh, look, Miss Er-um, I'm bitterly sorry but I think I've burst open a seam.'

''Tis of no consequence,' Mary Anne returned brightly, *'mamoyzelle.'* For thus, in her apprenticeship, had she been schooled to address the maidenly; and retrieving the glove with

34

a smile on her face and murder in her heart, 'what now of this Leghorn for *mamoyzelle*? Or this cap, as favoured by and named for 'Er Royal Highness Princess Charlotte?'

It was declared by the three to be 'heaven'. 'Mama, we must, we positively *must* have this angel of a cap named for —'

'— and worn by,' squeaked Miss Graham from the background.

'— the Princess Charlotte. Do, Mama,' pleaded Pippie, short for Phillipa, 'let us have it copied. Could you copy it, Miss, in different shades? I would adore it in yellow.'

'And I in rose pink —'

'And pea green for me —' chorused her sisters.

'Providing, my loves, that the price,' their mama cautioned them, 'be not too — How much for the three, Miss Ah-um?'

'The price of this model, madame, is two guineas — but,' amended Mary Anne with a lift of her brows at Miss Graham who was excitedly counting on her fingers, 'for your *obleegement*, ma'am, shall we say five guineas for the three?'

'Well, that's fair enough,' boomed Mrs Vernon-Graham. 'And how soon can my daughters have the caps?'

'If I may take the measurements of the young ladies' heads I can promise them to you, madame, next week.'

'Next *week*?' came concerted protest from the sisters. 'We can't wait until next week. We want them to wear at church this Sunday.'

'It is already Friday, *maymoyzelles*,' hedged Mary Anne, 'and I am bound to deliver by tomorrow two turbans and a bonnet to the Countess of — now, let me see,' giving time for this improviso to sink in, and ignoring a stifled scream from Miss Graham, 'if I and my — my apprentices,' she murmured, 'work at them day and night, I think I can promise you shall have the caps, *maymoyzelles*, by tomorrow evening. Now, if you will allow me —'

From the reticule suspended on a cord at her waist she took a tape and the necessary measurements, and was declared by Dillie, short for Delia, to be 'a little duck, and what long eyelashes!' And, 'Look, Mama, here's a dream of a scarf. I'd die to wear such a scarf at the Victory Ball.'

'So,' shrieked Pippie, 'would I. Dillie, Lissie —' short for Alicia — 'do you see those cunning little tassels? Mama, you can't refuse.'

'And if I can't,' Mama with mammoth playfulness returned, 'I shall be ruined. How much, Miss — Um, for the three scarves?'

'Three guineas, madame.'

'Each,' hopefully prompted the fluttering Miss Graham.

'Never,' her massive niece sonorously queried, 'three guineas *each*, Miss Er —?'

'No, madame.' Turning a cold shoulder on Miss Graham, whose long nose was a-quiver in joyful anticipation of — more counting on the fingers — 'Three guineas for the three,' pronounced Miss Evans. 'That is, if I can procure more of the material. This 'ere — this *h*ere — scarf came from Bond Street in London. I shall have to try and match it.'

'You must let me know then, in good time,' bayed Mrs Vernon-Graham, 'if you *can* match it. Come, girls.' Ard, when at last the four of them were safely off the premises, Miss Graham hysterically flung herself at Mary Anne.

'You naughty — naughty — hee! I know 'tis wicked in me to encourage such outrageous — only she has *millions* compared to poor little me. The Vernons have the money and the Grahams have the breed — and I a party to it. Poor dear Papa must be positively *turning* — my own flesh and blood, too, though you'd never think it, she's so enormous, and the girls — what they'll be like at her age — and she so near to mine, but everybody says I look at least fifteen years younger. She takes after my poor brother, so very much my senior, a great *big* man, and I'm such a teeny-weeny — and when I think of the profit you will make on eight guineas, which gives me something shillings, doesn't it? I can't do it in my head, being just a babe unborn at sums. But take it how you will, dear, 'tis all due to me whatever either of us makes, seeing that I simply *dragged* them here by force. They didn't want to come having planned to shop in Bath but I told them they'd pay double there and you didn't really, did you — artful little puss! — sell those turbans to a countess? Do tell.'

Mary Anne showed dimples as Miss Graham paused for breath. 'I'll tell you this. One good turn deserves another, so for once — and once only, mind — we'll forget the commission and go halves.'

That same afternoon, having at last rid herself of Miss Graham, Mary Anne, who for five hours on end had sat diligently cutting, pinning, stitching, drank a cup of milk, ate some stale ratafias presented by her landlady, and put away her work at four o'clock. Although she did not usually close the salon until evening, today was an exception and with no time to be lost.

So we find her in a hackney, driving down to Bristol where, at a wholesale mercer's in King Street, whose representative, a smirking persuasive young man, had recently left his card at her salon, she made some necessary purchases including a length of material 'from Bond Street' with payment down, at discount, and the promise of repeated orders.

Having spent too much already on the hackney, she had not enough money in her purse to pay for another, or even a chair were there one to be seen. The sun was near its setting when she gained the heights of Clifton and, aware of a footstep behind her, turned, saw, and hurried on.

So he was here again. She had not seen him for three weeks and believed him gone for good; but no! Either he had ceased to track her, if he ever, by intention, did, or he may have been away or sick, or — her heart quickened — could he be a ghost? So solemnly, so slowly did he walk to put her in a fright, that she must break into a run, nor stopped until she came to Culver Street. But, when from the doorway of her salon she looked for him who dogged her, he had vanished.

'Mercy me!' said Mary Anne, 'I sure am 'aunted —' although, if a ghost, he was a most substantial one. These few glimpses he allowed her had revealed him to be personable, handsome-seeming, and well built. And could an apparition, or whatever, walk with so heavy and so firm a tread? However, once inside her precincts, she had no time for trepidation, speculation, silly fears, with three caps to be delivered on the morrow.

Accordingly, the next evening, having fulfilled her commitments, she presented herself with a bandbox on her arm at the house in the Polygon, where lodged the Vernon-Grahams.

A liveried manservant answered the doorbell and, with one look at her and another at the bandbox loftily to decide her state and mission, admitted her to an elegant apartment on the right of the entrance hall.

A babel of voices was hushed to the deprecatory announcement: 'A young person, ma'am, to see you.'

She had a confused impression of a room full of giantesses, one giant, and a pigmy, outstretched on a sofa, his leg in a bandage, his arm in a sling. Her startled vision, clearing, disclosed this assemblage to be the Misses Vernon-Graham, their mother, voluminous in amethyst, their father, the major, presumably returned from Waterloo; and, standing on the hearthrug, his back to the fireless grate, a tall gentleman in a corbeau-coloured coat.

A glance of recognition stole between them. Mary Anne lowered her lashes, curtsied, was surrounded, the bandbox ripped from her arm, its lid opened, its contents rifled, amid Ohs and Ahs of admiration and the insistent chorus: 'Come with us, Miss Um, that we may try them on at once!' And they surged with 'Miss Um' to the door.

'Now, now, girls,' their mother admonished, 'what will our visitor think? Pray, sir,' to the tall gentleman, 'excuse this intrusion. Our little milliner — you understand?'

'Bonnets?' He, upon the sofa, raised himself on an elbow and in a voice, strongly at variance with his bantam size, demanded; 'What d'ye want with bonnets and fingle-fangles, hey? Haven't you enough already? D'ye think I'm made of money?'

'No, Papa, you're made of *love*.' Pippie rushed to kiss him. 'And they're caps, not bonnets. You wouldn't — would you — grudge us a new cap for high days, as worn by the Princess Charlotte? Miss Thingummy here has the sweetest collection. Dear Papa, *don't* be a grump.'

'Hey?' The diminutive major withdrew from his daughter's emphatic embrace. 'Have a care. You'll bring me on a blooding if you come at me like a battalion. Caps! And who pays for them, hey? Damme, sir,' to his guest, 'if you, as a bachelor, are not to be envied. Thank your stars you have no daughters, or none,' with a sly chuckle, 'to speak of.'

Said the gentleman, pompously, 'Sir, had I three daughters, or, haply, three graces such as these,' he bowed to them severally, 'I would, indeed, thank my stars.' But his eyes were not for the three graces, as they hustled Mary Anne — caps, bandbox and all — from the room. Nor, when they returned, each with a cap on her head, did he watch them revolve for their papa's inspection. No, so Mary Anne, from beneath downcast lashes, was encouraged to see, he watched her. As did the major. And: 'Miss,' said his wife with frigidity, 'kindly send your account for the total with the scarves.'

'Scarves!' ejaculated the major.

'Yes, Papa, for the Victory Ball,' chimed his vociferous daughters. 'New scarves will furbish up our last year's gowns that are completely *démodé*, and Miss Thing-me-bob has all the latest —'

'Thank you, Miss Er. Good evening.'

Like a galleon in full sail, Mrs Vernon-Graham swept Mary Anne to the door; where, modestly, she curtsied to the ladies, to the gentlemen, and was halted in her exit by the major.

'Here, Miss — Who? What's your name, m'dear?'

His daughters in unison giggled; his wife shot him a lethal look; and Mary Anne with another curtsy, murmured:

'If you please, sir, Evans.'

'Evans?' The reclining major raised a quizzing glass. 'That's a Welsh name, surely? Charming — ah — charmed.' And disregardful of his lady's glare, he presented his guest whom Mary Anne was disappointed to perceive at closer quarters to be elderly: thirty-ish at least, with hair greying at the temples. 'Here we have a compatriot of yours. Mr Wyndham Lewis,' said the major.

THREE

The Victory Ball kept the gossips busy for weeks after it was over. Gleanings garnered by Miss Graham and offered in sheaves to Miss Evans lost nothing by embellishment.

'My dear! Some of the greatest families attended, among them Lord and Lady William Crichton-Stuart — he stands for Parliament in the Borough of Cardiff, brother of the marquis of Bute. The late marquis, their father, caused quite a scandal concerning the Princess Dowager, mother of our poor mad King, when he was prime minister. Not the King — hee, hee! — the marquis. He was only an earl then. *Ages* ago, in the sixties, long before you — and I — were born. And who else, now? Let me see. Oh, yes, Sir Somebody and Lady Northcote, come from Pynes in Devon. Did you visit Lady Northcote when you served as apprentice in — No, how stupid of me. I forgot. Of course,' purred the kittenish Miss Graham, 'you would not have visited at Pynes.'

'On the contrary,' was the apocryphal correction. 'I often visited the Northcotes at Pynes when I lived at Brampford Park with my grandfather, the squire.'

'Really?' Miss Graham took a moment's breath to swallow this before proceeding. 'Only think! Dottie's three girls were the belles of the ball — surrounded by partners, never once wallflowers, nor — hee, hee! — was I. 'Twas your turban that did it, my dear. So becoming.'

Mr Wyndham Lewis, with whom Miss Graham danced the cotillon, had paid her — 'the most *lavish* compliments. Perfidious wretch, I told him, "'Tis my turban, not I that attracts. My milliner, Miss Evans," I said, "made it for me," hoping he might recommend you to his mother, if he has a mother and were she coming to the Hotwells for the cure. "Miss Evans," I told him, "is my tenant — *quite* a cut above a milliner, daughter of a naval officer and so clever with her fingers. Like all of us since these dreadful wars, she has to turn them to earn an honest penny. So you can't say I don't do my best to bring you custom.'"

Mary Anne, with heightened colour, went on stitching.

'But Mr Lewis,' twittered Miss Graham, 'did not single little *me* for marked attention. 'Twas Pippie in particular he favoured, and would not *believe* she is my niece. And I didn't say *great*-niece, neither. "Impossible," he said, "you might be sisters..." My dear,' conspiratorially Miss Graham edged her chair nearer to the silent Mary Anne, 'if I tell you a secret you must not repeat it to a living *soul* until it is a *fait accompli*. He, Mr Lewis, is paying court to Pippie. 'Twould be a prodigious match, even for her who will have five thousand. He's a Justice of the Peace and Deputy Lieutenant of Glamorganshire, with vast estates, near Cardiff, and a castle — a quite unpronounceable name, all consonants. Pantingsomething, Welsh for Greenmeadow. His grandfather made a fortune from coal which, like beer, is accepted and *quite* correct, though wine is not, which I can never understand. And, my dear, he never took his eyes off Pippie, led her three times in the quadrille. Such a pity her feet are so big — outsize, my dear. She takes after Dottie. And just fancy! The next day when he visited the major — they are old acquaintances, you know — he brought bouquets for the girls and *red roses* for Pippie. Well, we all know what red roses mean.'

'I don't. What,' asked Mary Anne, still intent on her sewing, 'do they mean?'

'La, for gracious sake!' cried Miss Graham skittishly. 'Was there ever such a little innocent? Red roses for love, of course.'

'Oh?' said Mary Anne.

'So now we're all on tenterhooks waiting for him to declare his intentions. Will he, won't he ... and I am sure he *will*.'

And when Miss Graham had talked herself exhausted and retired to her parlour, Mary Anne laid aside her work and sat idle while she too might have wondered: *Will he, won't he?*

Her mind went searching back.

The very day after her meeting with Mr Wyndham Lewis at the Vernon-Grahams' she had again been followed, but now, with the privilege of introduction, he had gained her side to say, 'Miss Evans — is it? Yes, it *is*!' as if she had dropped from the sky. 'May I be permitted to escort you to your door? You live in Park Street, do you not?'

He knew that, and more besides. He knew the very time she left her salon. He must have read the signboard and had therefore known her name and all about her long before she knew of him. *But,* she sourly reflected, *if he thinks he can go on chasing me while he hunts bigger game, he is mightily mistaken.* Hunting. Yes. He came here every season — not for the cure, he told her, but for the hunting in the Mendips. He had permanent lodgings at Clifton. Cubbing would start in a week or two. Did Miss Evans ride to hounds?

No. Miss Evans rode, but not to hounds. She used to ride cross-saddle down on her grandfather's farm in Devon, and sometimes she would ride a steer, bare-backed... A smile played about her lips as she recalled how she had admitted that, with no mincing of her words. Let him see and judge her for what she was. A little milliner, country born and bred, who 'could never,' as her mother always told her, 'be a lady.'

She must allow that his approach, even if he so often waylaid her, was exemplary. What harm in a five-minute walk through the dusk to her door? But although he hung around obviously hinting to be invited in, she never did. She dared not invite him unexpected, lest her mother should be in her tantrums and Mr Yate in his cups. Besides, easy come, easy go. Did she want him to go? She couldn't honestly say. Her heart was not entangled — yet. Too old for her, seeming. Grave and stolid. Kindly. Ever so polite, which was more than could be said of the curate, Mr What's-his-name, who had come courting of her when she had lived with Uncle Viney. No, she couldn't have fancied the curate. He had pimples. But how Uncle Viney had raged at her for refusing such a match: related to the peerage, an Eton scholar and a graduate of Oxford. Who did Mary Anne think she was? A girl without a penny, brought up in a sty? She should be down on her knees thanking God that one so far above her had asked for her hand...

Would she refuse Mr Lewis if he asked for her hand? *Why should he? What have you to give him who has all to give you? What's he after? That's it — what's he after?* Her eyes narrowed. *If he thinks to play fast and loose with a girl who earns her livin', then what he plays for he'll not get. So let him stew.*

With which she put away her work. No hurry now to complete it. The season was in its decline, with a consequent depreciation of her 'cleeontell'. Few, of late, were the ladies who paused to look in at her window, fewer those who came to buy, while mounting bills from the mercer's must be met; and how to pay her rent in the winter months ahead with this steady fall in custom was a greater problem than Mr Lewis's intentions to her, or to Miss Pippie. *Neck and neck we run,* said Mary Anne to herself. *A race between the tortoise and — no, not the hare, the elephant!*

She tidied her salon, and, on hands and knees, picked up scattered threads and pins. And when everything was spick and span and ready for the morning — and, God send, a customer, if it were only one, but better two — she put on her bonnet, and in the mirror saw a shape reflected from behind the bottle-panes.

'I happened to be passing,' he greeted her as she came out. 'Do you go home, Miss Evans? If so, may I escort you?'

'Thank you, sir, I —'

'The evenings draw in. You should not walk alone at this hour.'

'It is no distance to my home, sir.'

'Still, unlawful persons may be loitering. There is a gipsy encampment on the Downs, I hear.'

'Yes, the gipsies often come around these parts, but they'd do no harm to me. I like the gipsies. I often used to play with the gipsy children when I was young.'

'When you were young.' A side-long glance revealed his eyes crinkling at the corners in a smile as he echoed her. 'And you are now — so old?'

'Yes, sir. Twenty-two, which, as my mother says —' She curbed her tongue. Best not repeat what her mother had said: *A girl who goes uncourted after one-and-twenty is like to go unwed. A nice thing to be saddled all my life with an old maid.*

'Your mother? I would be honoured,' said he, measuring his long stride to her short one, 'if you would present me to your mother.'

'Yes, sir. With pleasure, but,' floundered Mary Anne, 'she is … she's poorly.'

'I am grieved to hear that. Nothing serious, I hope?'

''Tis the palpitations, sir,' from which Mary Anne herself, at that moment, seemed to suffer.

They had now passed some way beyond the upper end of Park Street, and slowing his steps as they came to the hilltop, 'It is hard to believe,' Mr Lewis said, 'that the city lies so near.'

Together they surveyed the scene of the high level plains of Durdham and Kingsweston, cleft by equal height of rock on either side the river, 'which,' he reflected, 'suggests some convulsion of nature in ages past. It has been proposed to unite these two counties by means of a bridge across the Avon, though to my mind it would detract from the beauty of the view. What a beautiful sunset.' Then, from contemplation of the gold and saffron clouds girdled with a fringe of fading red, he brought his gaze earthwards, and peering down at the sheep-nibbled grass: 'Ah, *hippocrepis comosa*, I see. Indigenous to these parts. Are you interested in botany, Miss Evans?'

'I like all flowers, but I know naught of their names in Latin. It was Latin you were speaking, sir? Or Greek?'

He turned his head; in that half-light his eyes, deep-set under shelving brows, weighed on hers that met his warm look and fled from it.

'It is the name, a hybrid of Greek and Latin, that Linnaeus, the greatest of all botanists, gave to the tufted horseshoe vetch. *Hippo*, from the Greek, "a horse", *crepis*, the Latin for "plant", and *comosa* for —' he stopped and plucked a stalk with narrow leaves where the small bluish-purple petals clustered — 'for its hairy stem.'

She believed him very learned; but so he would be, as a Justice of the Peace.

Slowly the colours in the sky dissolved, or were hidden as if a grey mantle of smoke had been drawn about those fiery cloud-pennons; and a dreaming stillness fell upon the sombre green, dimly patterned with spectral grazing sheep. 'How late it grows,' she murmured. 'I must hurry. My mother'll be anxious.'

And not another word passed between them as they retraced their steps to her door, when, 'Am I not,' he asked her, and again that smile hovered, 'to be invited in?'

Ah, she had thought it was coming to that! So now what to do? She visualised the table spread for her supper: cold beef, last Sunday's joint left over, the tarnished cruet, stale mustard, wine stains on the cloth, not to be renewed until next Monday's wash. But she knew there was a steak-and-kidney pie for Mr Yate, having baked it herself that same morning early before she went to work. There'd be more than enough for two.

'My mother, sir,' she faltered, 'would be pleased, I'm sure, only that she's not entertainin' any visitors at present, if you will excuse —'

He bowed. 'I am at your service whenever it may be to your convenience and that of Mrs Evans, your mother, to receive me.'

'Mrs Yate, sir, is my mother's name.' She was glad of the diversion to tell him, 'My stepfather, Mr Yate, is Master of the Ceremonies at the Assembly Rooms.'

'Is that so? Then why do I never see you there? You were not at the Victory Ball. I looked for you.'

She was in greatest trouble now, and needs must blurt, ''Tis against the rules, sir — I am not — you see, I — I keep a shop and, please, sir — I must be goin'.' A flurried glance over her shoulder had perceived the looming shape of Mr Yate. 'I'll bid you good evening, sir.' She sketched a curtsy, but before her hand could reach the doorbell she was hailed, and her heart sank to her sandals.

'Wait, Mary Anne!'

No escape; he had covered the ground and was there in less time than it took him to tell, 'I've left me latchkey at home.'

Point device in mulberry cloth, grey kerseymeres and a yellow waistcoat decorated with blue monkeys upholding green umbrellas, Mr Yate was even more than usually imposing.

'Why! Unless my sight deceives me,' he cried, settling his chins in his cravat, 'Mr Wyndham Lewis, is it not? Did you pull the bell, me darling? Sir,' profusely bowing, he presented, 'my daughtah, with whom I see you are already acquainted.'

'I had the pleasure of meeting Miss Evans,' said Mr Wyndham Lewis stiffly, 'at the house of Major and Mrs Vernon-Graham.'

Mr Yate — who, Mary Anne was thankful to note, had neither dined nor, unduly, wined in Bristol, where from the chalk on his ungloved fingers she guessed he had been playing billiards — received and dismissed this information with the unsurprised announcement, 'Hah, yes. Mrs Vernon-Graham's aunt is under some slight — hum — obligation to my daughtah, and —'

Here the door was opened; and Mary Anne, with another hasty bob to Mr Lewis, went, or rather bolted, in.

'Goodness gracious, child! Pray,' her mother peevishly entreated, 'don't burst upon me like a whirlwind. Is anything amiss?'

'There's a gentleman — a visitor — below.' Mary Anne cast a look of dismay at the table laid ready for her supper: the cold beef, the pickle jar, a heel of cheese, a cottage loaf. 'Mr Yate will ask him up, for sure.'

'A gentleman?' Mrs Yate was on her feet and tiptoe at the looking-glass. 'My hair! I washed it this afternoon and have not put the tongs to it — it's scarcely dry — not fit to be seen. Go fetch me a cap, quick. I hear them on the stairs. You will find one new laundered in the tallboy drawer. Make haste.'

But for all the haste she made, the cap was not forthcoming. Mr Yate and his visitor were in the room to bar her exit, while her mother, full of smiles, dipped a bob, and, in a hissing whisper bade her daughter, 'Clear the table! Don't stand there gaping. Never mind the cap.'

'My love —' rising with professional aplomb to the occasion, Mr Yate presented Mr Wyndham Lewis to his wife. 'We are much indebted to Mr Lewis,' he said largely, 'for his — hah — courteseh in escorting our deah child in safeteh from the house of Miss Graham to this door, fearing she be set upon by footpads.'

'How very kind of Mr Lewis.' Again Mrs Yate curtsied. 'Pray, sir, be seated.'

'Will you join me in a glass of wine, sir?' invited Mr Yate.

Wine from the cellarette was instantly produced, and, while Mr Yate engaged his guest in talk, Mary Anne divested the table of its unsightly spread; then, unobserved by any save Mr Wyndham Lewis, she slipped away.

At her dormer window she sat gazing out at the star-sprinkled sky. He would not stay long down there, surely? Mr Yate must be dressed in full regalia to attend the Rooms at nine o'clock… Well, what to make of this? A prodigious match. Justice of the Peace. Deputy Lieutenant of his county. A castle in Wales.

Leaning her elbows on the windowsill she laid cold hands to her hot cheeks. If his intentions were not all they should be, would he have asked to meet her mother? Unless, more like, he was passing the time till the cubbing started — and that'd be next week. *So he'll have more to do than hang around the salon peeking in at the window to lie in wait for me while Miss Pippie* — a little laugh escaped her — *waits for him!*

The sound of voices below caused her stealthily to open the casement, craning her neck to look down at Mr Lewis's departure, boisterously sped by Mr Yate.

'Immenseleh gratified, I'm shaw. I will be seeing you anon, sir... A game of whist? With the greatest of pleasure. Lady Northcote, yourself and Major and Mrs Vernon-Graham? Very good, sir, I will arrange it. What a balmy evening!'

From her eyrie Mary Anne watched Mr Lewis out of sight. He had a fine pair of shoulders, handsome calves. A castle.

She waited a while and heard her mother pleading at the parlour door: 'Thomas, pray have something to eat before you go. There's steak-and-kidney pie. Rook can warm it in ten minutes. I had Mary Anne make it specially for you. It is not right you should go so long without food.'

'I have no time to eat. I will sup at the Rooms. Keep the pie for my dinner tomorrow.'

And her mother: 'What did he mean by telling you they met at the Vernon-Grahams? She doesn't visit *them*. She doesn't, to my knowledge, visit anyone who *is* anyone. But she's so secretive and sly you can never know what she may be up to. Look how she went behind our backs and opened that shop — to kill me! And now this Mr Lewis. I don't know, I'm sure, what to make of him, or what he thinks to make of *her*, dancing attendance and seeing her home … lays herself open to…'

Mary Anne strained her ears for more, but the voice of Mrs Yate was lowered, and facetiously capped by her husband's reply: 'What to make of it, my love, may be the making of her bed — hah — marriage bed or not. What's the odds so she may lie on it? Lewis has money to burn and to pay — for his fancy!'

And her mother's faint reproof: 'Thomas, *dear.*'

Well, by damn, said Mary Anne, disgracefully to herself, *and did I wear the breeks and not the petticoats I'd call you out for that, Mister Ceremon-yus Yate!* She listened for the slam of the front door; and when her mother was safe in her room and Nina Rook snoring in hers, she — who could not, if her stepfather could, go so long without food — went down to forage in the larder to soothe her empty stomach and her indignation by finishing the steak-and-kidney pie.

FOUR

It is likely that the interest in millinery evinced by Mr Lewis did not pass unnoticed by Miss Graham, and that the Pump Room, to whom she unburdened, may have been equally intrigued to hear how, 'That baggage, my dears, for so she is, comes tripping out to meet him at the door — *my* door — and off they go together in the *evening!*' That these delinquencies occurred in the evening was acknowledged by the Pump Room to hold a decidedly deplorable significance.

'For,' declared Miss Graham, 'I always had my doubts of her, the way she never looks you in the face with her talk of "my grandfather, the squire". And as for visiting the Northcotes at Pynes —'

Heads together, sipping the waters, round-eyed above the tumblers' brims, the Pump Room heard how Lady Northcote had vowed she had never set eyes on the creature. Such deceit, making of Miss Graham's name a byword in the neighbourhood; and, of course, after this she would have to give the hussy a week's notice. She could not possibly countenance such goings-on in or about *her* house.

The Pump Room was, with reservations, sympathetic. A shocking predicament truly, poor Miss Graham, in particular as this person's stepfather held a responsible position in Clifton; and, now they came to think of it, was it not rather *odd* that while Miss Evans's mama, Mrs Yate, often visited the Rooms for a game of whist, her daughter never once…

The heart of the Pump Room bled for Mrs Yate, poor lady — and a lady, mark you, every inch. How she must suffer —

and admitted she *had* suffered, and was not yet recovered from the shock of hearing that her daughter, unknown to her, should have rented a room from Miss Graham to open, of all things, a shop!

There could have been no spinster in the whole West Country in more sorry case than was Miss Graham. Not only must she run the gauntlet of the Pump Room's disapproval concerning her association with the odious Miss Evans, but she had also forfeited the good will and distant hope of a 'little something' from her niece, to relieve her of her 'difficulties'. Not that she could count on a penny piece from Dottie, yet in view of the major's near promotion to a colonel and a recent legacy from a wealthy uncle — 'a mere windfall', Dottie called it — of another five hundred a year, a teeny-*weeny* gift at Christmas would not have come amiss and might have been expected, but not now. No. Certainly not now.

That Mr Wyndham Lewis had ceased his attentions to Pippie was bad enough. That he should have transferred them to 'a nobody — a shop-girl — an adventuress,' sobbed Miss Graham to the chilly silence of the Pump Room, 'as if it were *my* fault,' had caused a rupture, unforgivable, between the Vernon-Grahams and herself. 'She, Dottie — I have never known her so enraged. She always shouts, but yesterday, my dears, she came *roaring* at me like a lion — lioness, I mean — to accuse me of encouraging clandestine meetings in my house between Mr Wyndham Lewis and that — a dreadful word which I simply can't repeat. And what use,' wept Miss Graham, 'to swear on the Bible, as I was ready to do, that I knew of no meetings more than that I've seen him marching up and down before my door, waiting for her to come out. And now Dottie and the girls,' declared Miss Graham in another burst of tears, 'refuse to speak to me.'

Meanwhile, Mary Anne in her deserted salon, still defiantly upheld her sign above Miss Graham's door. Soon, very soon, that sign must be taken down, and herself and her belongings taken out. Miss Graham had made that very clear in one climactic interview.

'A word with you, Miss Evans, if you please.' Her hair in bunches of curl-papers, which in her agitation she had forgotten to remove, Miss Graham descended on the salon just as Mary Anne was about to lock up at the end of the day.

'Certainly, Miss Graham. You look pale. Are you not well?'

'Yes. No. How,' bleated Miss Graham in staccato agony, 'can I be well? Confronted. Monstrous perfidy.'

'Perfidy?' echoed the innocent Miss Evans. 'What can you mean?'

'Mean,' was the reply distractedly, 'that I've been — robbed!'

'For gracious sake!' Mary Anne cast widening eyes at the quivering Miss Graham. 'Do you mean you've had thieves in the house?'

'Yes. No. Yes! One thief. Robbed. Good name. Reputation. You.' A bony finger stabbed the air. 'You snake!'

'What?' cried Mary Anne with the smallest of grins. 'Do I hear aright? You said —'

'— say,' gurgled Miss Graham, 'again. Snake. Never dreamed. Betrayed. Knew full well he fancied Pip-ip-ip — Oh!'

'Pray, ma'am, compose yourself,' begged Mary Anne. Her hands urged the tottering Miss Graham to a chair; and running to the bureau she took from a drawer a vinaigrette, saying, 'Dear, dear, I fear you 'ave the palpitations. My ma, she suffers chronic from the palpitations. Don't take on so, ma'am. Smell this.'

The vinaigrette was applied to the pinkened tip of Miss Graham's poor old nose. 'Never thought — never dreamed.

Always so trusting. Should have known. Give — a'tchew!' Frenziedly inhaling, Miss Graham sneezed. 'They're very strong. I give —' she wiped from her eyes a torrent of tears due to smelling salts as much as to emotion — 'one week's notice. From today.'

'Well, now,' said Mary Anne, the grin expanding into dimples, 'two minds think alike, do they not? I myself had intended to give you a week's notice from next Friday, when I pay my rent.'

'Oh, you did, did you? Merciful heav —' blubbered Miss Graham. 'Was ever such — *you* to give *me* — hee-hee!' And she fell into laughing hysterics.

'Well, it's all the same who gives it,' with provoking calm said Mary Anne. 'Come to yourself, ma'am, do. Another little sniff?'

'Fiend!' shrieked Miss Graham, dashing the vinaigrette to the floor and rising to her feet, every curl-paper a-bob. 'How have I bee-een mista-a-ken in — hee-hee!'

'That, then, is decided,' said Mary Anne, stooping to retrieve the vinaigrette. 'La, now, how vexing. You've cracked it. A family heirloom, too, presented by Queen Charlotte to my grandmother Evans when she was lady-in-waiting to 'Er Majesty. I'll 'ave to stick it up with glue.'

'Don't,' screamed Miss Graham, 'tell such tarry-diddles! Grandmother — lady-in — Liar! You've done me and mine such wicked wrong as never, never, *never* —' at each repetition, the word soared to a shrieking crescendo — 'can I forgive.'

'I am but 'uman,' Mary Anne said gently, 'and have but 'uman understanding, and for the life of me I cannot understand what *is* all this to-do. And pray, ma'am, I beg you not to speak so loud, your voice rings very shrill. Whatever will the neighbours think?'

At this reminder of neighbours, Miss Graham, opening her mouth to scream again, promptly closed it, suffered herself to be led away and comforted with camomile tea. Indeed, so anxious for and attentive to her plight was Mary Anne that the poor lady inclined to think she had been a trifle 'hasty'. For if Mr Wyndham Lewis were acquainted with the Yates, might it not have been with their knowledge and consent that he should escort their daughter to her home now that the days were drawing in and all those nasty gipsies on the Downs? And what did she mean by saying she would give in *her* notice? Nor, on quieter reflection, was Miss Graham disposed to quarrel with her bread and butter. Seven and sixpence a week was, after all, seven and sixpence a week, and in these hard times… Oh, dear!

Mary Anne, meanwhile, on her homeward way, and for once unpursued by Mr Lewis who had evidently not yet returned from the hunt, inclined likewise to think she had been 'hasty'. For if she closed the salon, even though almost all the profits of these last few months had been swallowed by outgoing and overhead expenses, what other means had she of livelihood? Must she always be dependent on her mother for her every need, and suffer the continuous reproach of her failure to 'settle herself', which in Mrs Yate's scheme of things was the sole aim and purpose of feminine existence? *It sure is a curse,* thought Mary Anne, *to be born a girl.* Had she been born a boy she'd have gone for a soldier, or better had she not been born at all… How to face the empty years ahead, nagged at, scolded, morning, noon and night, given less than second place to that drink-sodden, posturing ass, Mr Yate? No, she could not endure life in Clifton, growing older and older until… Would she turn into a giggling Miss Graham? Never that. Sooner have taken the curate, pimples and all. Or she might advertise herself as a lady's companion. *Adaptable, willing, good-tempered, highest references* — easy to fake. Or if the worst came to the worst she could offer her services to Madame in Exeter again. Madame always used to say she had a 'knack'. It wouldn't bring in much, Madame being mingy, but at least it would be something.

A pretty coil, Mary Anne thought savagely, *and all a'cause of him hanging round with naught to speak that can't be shouted on the rooftops. I'd like to tell him a thing or two, I would, for the trouble he has brought to me, losing of my salon, not that it's much loss with the winter comin' and the season closed, and those half dozen unbleached chips, two parasols, and twenty yards of rainbow gauze not paid for… What'll I do?*

But more to the point was, what would Mr Lewis do? A question of less concern to Mary Anne than to her mother.

In the shared privacy of the nuptial couch, Mrs Yate brooded on certain of her husband's jocular remarks regarding Mr Lewis's intentions. Dear Thomas, always so thoughtful for her ease of mind that he would turn gravest matters to a jest. 'Still,' said Mrs Yate to the hump beside her, dimly discernible in the low-burnt wick of a night-light, 'if, because of her lowly occupation, he thinks he can — Thomas!' She poked, none too gently, the hump. 'Do you hear?'

''M? Yip-a-ah.'

An unmistakable sound, not a snore, accompanied by a pungent aroma, assailed the shrinking nostrils and ears of Mrs Yate. 'Thomas! Really! What *have* you had to drink — or eat?'

'Roass' pork,' murmured Mr Yate, 'an' claret don' agree. D'injes'shun.'

'Yes,' the hand of Mrs Yate explored her husband's lower parts, 'you seem to be very distended. You shall have a blue pill in the morning. Thomas?'

'Yip?'

'Would it not be advisable for you to ask his intentions? Surely, as her father-in-law —'

'Loco — hic — paren'sis,' agreed Mr Yate. 'I'll ask 'm for th' pony loss' me at whisk. Tol'm no 'urry. Said wri' a bill — a-ah-ah,' yawned Mr Yate. 'Lem' go slee'.'

'Thomas.' Again the hand of Mrs Yate went voyaging to discover her husband's head that, bereft of its wig, was naked to the touch save for a sparse fringe of hair at the base of his skull; and on this his wife's fingers closed, with some violence, to pull. 'Thomas! *Will* you listen?'

From the dawn of a pleasant peculiar dream of nude maidens at play with a pig from whose jaws was ejected a flagon of wine, Mr Yate was painfully aroused to wakefulness.

'Hey! Yip — leg'go. Tha hurss. Whass a do?'

'Thomas, I insist if you have any love or thought for me or my daughter that you bring Mr Lewis to the point and so save her honour — if she has any honour left to save — Thomas, do you hear me?'

An affirmative grunt issued from the pillow.

'Faugh!' His wife pinched her nose. 'You smell like a tap room. Was ever woman put to suffer as am I? Where have you been, and with *whom* have you been, till all hours of the night — raddled to the hilt? You will explain yourself *and* your indigestion tomorrow, Mr Yate, or I'll know the reason why — and so will you!'

It is possible this oblique threat did persuade Mr Yate to approach Mr Lewis regarding his 'intentions', in view of news retailed by Miss Graham to the Pump Room.

She had seen, and with her own ears heard, Mr Lewis enter That Person's 'salon' as she called it, and — no, Miss Graham could not bring herself to tell what she had heard Mr Lewis say and had — gracious heaven! — seen him do.

Pressure brought to bear, under strictest confidence be it understood, induced Miss Graham to divulge.

'My dears! Can you conceive my horror when I heard *this* greeting from him to her. "My darling —" just imagine! — "Come down from that step-ladder at once. Do you want to break your lovely neck?"' Positively, yes. That was what Miss Graham from her spiral staircase heard; and later, from her window, saw Miss Evans emerge on the arm of Mr Lewis while the two of them stood staring up at that abominable signboard and then — oh, shocking — Mr Lewis stooped to *kiss* the creature under her poke bonnet, saying, 'This sign shall hang, a sweet memento of —' something or other which Miss Graham's burning ear, pressed to the pane, had unfortunately missed — 'above my study door at home.'

Soon to be the home of Mary Anne.

A miracle had happened, was happening; and she, formally betrothed to Mr Wyndham Lewis.

The cat was put among the pigeons in the Pump Room with a vengeance. Never in the annals of Clifton had any such surfeit of gossip been scattered, swooped upon, pecked over, spewed, and pecked again. Betrothed. She — he — to *her*, that scheming little artful jade. A cruel blow indeed was this to all aspiring mamas, with one exception. Did Miss Evans's mama now deplore her bitter fate in having borne a daughter so abandoned, lost, self-willed, deceitful, sly, etcetera? It may safely be conjectured she did not.

Mrs Yate, however grudgingly, must admit that Mary Anne, for all her slyness and deceit in her encouragement of Mr Lewis's advances *and* without her mother's knowledge, had managed to secure for herself, all unaided, a match of breathtaking brilliance beyond the dreams of Mrs Yate or any other matron, mother of a maid, in the two counties.

Major Viney, uncle of the bride-to-be, who had received the news in a letter post-haste from his sister, returned a prompt congratulatory reply expressing his delight at the prospective marriage of his dearly loved niece to a gentleman known by name to him as of greatest means and impeccable position in the county of Glamorganshire. Moreover, Major Viney would deem it his privilege to give away his beloved Mary Anne to Mr Lewis at the altar. And to this effusion he inscribed himself *Your ever affectionate and devoted brother James.*

By which startling change of front it would seem that the misalliances of Mrs Yate had been forgiven and forgotten, and she united with the head of the family to bask in his beatitude and Mary Anne's reflected glory. All was joy unbounded in the heart of Mrs Yate; but what of the heart of Mary Anne?

When, a day or two after her difference of opinion with Miss Graham had been amicably settled, more or less, she found Mr Lewis promenading up and down outside the salon door, was she taken by surprise? Not at all. Such perambulations on the part of Mr Lewis, as we already know, were not of uncommon occurrence. What did surprise her, however, was his apparent perturbation and disordered appearance, for which he offered no apology. He was in hunting pink, had a cut on his cheek, no hat on his head, and on each knee of his white buckskin breeches a muddy green stain betokening a toss.

'Miss Evans, pray, a word with you — I have but just left him, your fa — your father-in-law. Called at my lodgings — there when I returned.' Which information, delivered in a series of almost unintelligible jerks, had given Mary Anne to doubt of his sobriety.

'My — Mr Yate? What,' she had asked, as Mr Lewis ranged himself alongside to walk with her up Culver Street, 'did he want with you, sir?'

'He —' the face of Mr Lewis turned as scarlet as his coat — 'he, Mr Yate, suggested my intentions may have compromised… My dear Miss Evans, pray believe I would cut off my right hand sooner than have caused you one moment's embarrassment. How can I forgive myself?'

They had now gained the hilltop and there, in the evening dusk they stood, she collecting her wits to digest this astonishing announcement; he stammering, eyes feasting on her face with its tip-tilted impertinent nose, the dimpled chin, the ripe mouth a-quiver, red underlip drawn in, half fearful, wholly wondering, and all of her — delicious.

'I have this to say,' and he surprised himself to say it, 'I am in that degree of adoration I would gladly die for you if I am not to — live with you.'

'Sir!' cried Mary Anne, finding voice to blaze at him, 'but this is outrageous. 'Ow dare you so insult me!'

'Insult? Good God! Is my esteem — my — my unbounded love to be repulsed, discarded as an insult? Miss Evans,' he implored, 'if you will only hear me. From the moment I first saw you — yes, I saw you long before you ever knew of my existence, and I followed you —'

'You did indeed!' snapped Mary Anne, but with ever so little a smirk. 'I thought you was a ghost, the way you 'aunted me. 'Tisn't gentleman-like to take advantage of a poor girl what 'as — 'as to earn her living.'

'You should never — you shall never,' panted Mr Lewis, 'have to earn your living if you will give me the right to protect you.'

'Well, I'm —' Mary Anne lost her breath and her temper. 'What d'you mean, "protect"? So that's what you're after, is it? I might have guessed as much, the way you've been followin' me. I'll thank you, sir, to go your ways and leave me to go mine. I may be a milliner but I am not a —' Again she caught her underlip to stay the word upon it, learned from loose talk of her associates in Exeter. And to cover her confusion she stamped her foot on the turf to bring his arms about her in a frenzy.

'Child! Am I so — awkward in my speech or do you wilfully misunderstand? No, don't struggle.' He held her fast. 'Don't be afraid. I want you, yes, but with the right to have, to hold and to protect you as my — wife.'

'Your...? Lawks!' breathed Mary Anne, white now as he was red. And then, recovering, 'If you be makin' game of me, I'll — let me go!'

'I will never let you go. I want — I must —' He was blushful, incoherent as a schoolboy in these first belated throes of love. True, he had tasted to his fill of sordid promiscuous adventure. But this was different; and he, who till this moment had not contemplated marriage as a means to the much desired end of his pursuit, could not, with her eyes wonder-charged, upraised to his, envisage a happier conclusion to his self-chosen celibacy. So: 'All I have,' came the husky murmur, 'is yours if you will take me.'

That was the gist of it; there in the close shadowed dark, his face, an indistinct blur above her own, streaked with dirt and a trickle of blood where an overhanging bough in the hunting field had scraped it.

She put a finger to his cheek and said, 'Whatever 'ave you done to yourself, Mr Lewis? Come home with me. I'll bathe it in witch hazel.'

Then, his lips clumsily seeking, found hers with his words warm upon them. 'Dear. My love… Is this your answer?'

And she, in a tremble, 'Give me time. I'll have to think.'

All that sleepless night in her bed under the eaves she thought, and thought again of his astounding declaration while her mind strove to tabulate the incalculable possibilities he offered her, *if you will take me…* But what had she to offer him? A girl without a penny and nothing much in looks to recommend her, leastways not so far as her idea of looks should be. *Besides, he hardly knows me more'n "Ow d'ye do may I see you to your door and Hippocreepin' what's its name and you're so young and lovely…' Lovely, huh! No accounting for tastes — but young, yes, too young for him. More'n twelve years' difference. He'd be set now in his ways. A proper old bachelor. 'All I have is yours.' All he has. A castle. Hunting stables. Carriages. A coach and horses. Servants. Dozens of them, shouldn't wonder. I'd feel mortal strange among his highty-tighty servants. Who'd ever have believed? And him stuttering and bashful as a farm lad or the curate. 'Don't call me sir. Call me Wyndham.'* As if she'd dare, and him a Justice of the Peace! She'd have to mind her speech and manners. What could he see in her, for goodness' sake? A pretty face, or someone to look after him in his old age, a kind of housekeeper? — which, maybe, was all he *did* want. And she was not so sure of that, the way he…

She laid the back of her hand to her mouth that seemed still to hold the heat of his kiss. He had said, 'I love you,' but … did she love him? What was this love she'd read of in bits of poetry, by that Lord Byron everyone was talkin' of? Not that she knew aught to do with poetry, and less to do with love. She had never thought about it, not this way…

She wondered if her mother had been in love with Mr Yate. Bald as a coot without his wig, as Mary Anne had seen when once she walked into their bedroom by mistake when he was dressing. Did Mr Lewis wear a wig? She wouldn't know till she was married. There was much she wouldn't know till she was married. She burned, and buried her face in the pillow to cool it and thought, *If only he were younger, handsomer, not so staid and proper. Well, you can't have everything. A castle…*

Dawn was in the sky, piercing a cleft in the curtains, when, just before sleep came to her she chuckled, 'Whatever will Miss Graham say to this?'

What Miss Graham said to that, which shook the Pump Room to its delicate foundations, went unheeded or unheard by Mary Anne. All that she had hitherto accepted as an integral part of her daily life had now dissolved entirely away. Neither persons, personalities, nothing said, nothing done, had any bearing on or relation to reality. Her mother, Mr Yate, Miss Graham, even Mr Lewis, her acknowledged affianced, were but phantoms in one long unending dream. Yet despite these unconformable conditions, she strove outwardly, at all events, and for the short time left to her before her wedding day, to follow the pattern of her previous existence.

The salon still stayed open to chance custom; the signboard, creaking in the late October winds, still swung above the door; and through that door, Mr Wyndham Lewis would be admitted by Miss Graham genuflecting, wreathed in smiles, and invited to her parlour for a dish of tea.

Once recovered from the cataclysmic shock of the betrothal, Miss Graham and the Pump Room had come to accept, as one accepts a climate, the inevitable. This being so, Miss Graham looked ahead and past the pending loss of her weekly income, with an eye to some future advantage. Twice-yearly long, extended visits to Greenmeadow in capacity of helpmeet, friend, adviser to Mrs Wyndham Lewis *(Did you ever!)* might amply atone for the loss of seven and sixpence a week. Which hopeful hypothesis may have prompted her rapturous reception of and eulogy to Mr Wyndham Lewis.

'Such a charming gentleman, so courteous, distinguished, so well-bred, so handsome...' The string of adjectives was inexhaustible.

'Handsome?' doubtfully repeated Mary Anne.

'Certainly he's handsome,' gushed Miss Graham, 'and as fine a pair of calves as ever I did see.' And who would Miss Evans be having as her bridesmaids? If by any happy chance Miss Graham might be honoured to walk behind Miss Evans to the altar in palest blue muslin with a wreath of rosebuds... Oh, how disappointing. No bridesmaids? A quiet wedding. Really? But not *too* quiet, Miss Evans dear, Miss Graham begged. Her bosom friends would *surely* be invited.

Miss Evans said she had no bosom friends.

'You have one,' Miss Graham told her archly, 'one who loves you as a sister. You will, you *must*, dearest Miss Evans, allow me the joy of attending you as bridesmaid. Three times a bridesmaid, never a bride — hee, hee! And I've only been a bridesmaid once, so I have two more left, and still may hope. I can hardly bear to *wait* for the Great Day.'

Nor, it seemed, could Mr Lewis.

Mary Anne had intimated that she would like a springtime wedding, but her lover would have none of that. Six months was an eternity. If he waited so long he might lose her to someone younger than himself.

'You are not so old,' protested Mary Anne. 'What's twelve years' difference? Better this way than t'other. I couldn't abide to marry a man all that much younger than me.'

'Than I,' he automatically corrected.

'Than I. In which case you'd be only eleven. I wish —'

'What,' he took her hand to kiss, 'do you wish?'

She looked up at his face, down-bent to hers, marking the grey at his temples, the thin shaven lips, his deep-set eyes, surprisingly tear-misted. She had come to know him sentimental; and she, who was not, said sighingly, 'I wish I'd had more schooling. You'll have to take me as I am and teach me — everything. I know I don't always talk right. Are you sure you want me, Mr Lewis?'

For answer he gathered her into his arms and felt her breath in a sob on his lips.

FIVE

At Mary Anne's insistence none but closest relatives on either side were to be invited to the 'quiet' wedding. A reception in the Assembly Rooms, attended by the *ton* of Clifton, had been discussed and encouraged by the Master of the Ceremonies, since the bride of Mr Lewis could no longer be debarred from Clifton's high society. Yet, when the estimate per head for a possible one hundred guests had been offered by Mr Yate to his wife, she flung the sheet of paper in his face, demanding, 'And who, may I ask, is to pay for these refreshments to say nothing of nine dozen bottles of champagne?'

'Will not Mr Wyndham Lewis,' suggested Mr Yate, '— hah — hold himself responsible for —'

'So!' came the forceful interruption. 'I may be sunk to beggary, held responsible for *you*, but I will not sink to beg from my daughter's intended.'

'Beggareh!' ejaculated Mr Yate. 'What talk is this of beggareh?' It had occurred to him more than once, since Mary Anne's engagement, that his gentle Eleanor had 'turned on him', as he heart-brokenly accused her, 'as if my dove had — hah — taken to itself an eagle's claws to tear the very heart out of my bodeh!'

'Fiddle!' was his dove's reply to that. 'You can't tell me! I know what I know.'

'And what,' wheedled Mr Yate, 'does my pretty little angel know? That her ogre of a husband who worships the ground she walks on would lay down his life for her?'

'To lay down the money for your vintner's bill would be more to the point,' his wife retorted. 'And hearken here, Mr Yate. There will be no reception at *my* expense, nor at Mr Lewis's, in your Assembly Rooms. That's flat.' On which immense admission Mrs Yate closed her lips.

Mr Yate opened his to say, crestfallen, 'As you will, my deah.' And so it was.

Invitations were issued to Mrs Yate's widowed twin sister, Mrs Munn, who lived in the north near Newcastle and was certain not to undertake so long a journey; and to Major Viney, who accepted by return in the polite third person.

'Not that you may hope for much in the way of a gift from him,' Mrs Yate told Mary Anne. 'Your uncle's no fool. He and his money were never soon parted.'

Nor did he prove himself on this occasion foolish, his choice of a gift being a set of four salt cellars. 'And not even silver at that,' said Mrs Yate. 'He always was as mean as they make them. But God be thanked that you, my girl, won't want for silver, nor gold salt cellars now.'

Mrs Munn, whom Mary Anne had not seen since early childhood, sent a china tea service of which three cups were found to be broken and the teapot cracked.

'Bought second hand, I'll be bound,' said Mrs Yate; and peering closer, 'No, it isn't, then. This is one of her own wedding gifts — yes, as I live, it is. Well do I remember this chaney tea service as given to your Aunt Bridget by our Great-aunt Mary Anne, after whom you were named and from whom your aunt and I had expectations. So may we expect! And she dead and buried these twenty years or more.'

The Lewis family was represented by Wyndham's elder brother Henry, his second brother, the Reverend William Pryce Lewis, and their respective wives and daughters, who arrived the night before the wedding and sent lavish gifts in advance: a silver tea-and-coffee service from the Reverend William, and a handsome set of Bristol glass from Henry.

From the bridegroom to the bride a necklace of fabulous pearls, and from the bride to the bridegroom a pair of ebony-backed hairbrushes with his monogram in gold, bought with the last of her savings. The rest had been spent on her modest trousseau, most of which she made herself, with exception of her wedding gown; and this, to her design, was made by a little seamstress in Bristol.

The wedding date had been fixed for December 21, and the honeymoon was to be spent at Greenmeadow.

During these few weeks of preparation Mr Lewis was back and forth from Wales, putting his house in order to receive his bride. And, while those last days sped by, Mary Anne sewed into her bonnet of white satin straw with its cluster of orange blossom, heaven alone knew what of doubts and fears, forebodings and high hopes…

'With my body I thee worship, with all my worldly goods I thee endow.'

Firmly spoken were her bridegroom's words as she stood beside him at the altar on that raw December day. A stray sunbeam wandered through the stained glass of a window, lighting the blossom in her bonnet, turning to rosy pink the fall of her gauze veil.

'Happy be the b-b-bride,' wept Miss Graham in her handkerchief, 'on whom the s-sun shines.' Although gowned in sky blue she was not a bridesmaid, for Mary Anne determinedly had none. She had, however, given Miss Graham a cap for the occasion, received with gushful thanks and blessings. Mrs Yate, in magenta *gros de Naples* and a turban of silver lamé, made for her by Mary Anne, quite outshone the Lewis wives, disparaged in one glance as 'dowds'. She, too, was sobbing; the sisters-in-law, tearlessly, were sobbing; their daughters, hopefully, were sobbing, expectant of their turn to come. 'Shall we have to call her "Aunt"?' they whispered. 'She might have asked us to be bridesmaids…'

Mr Yate, in a buff-coloured coat and sage green kerseymeres with a set of sparkling paste buttons, was best man. And Uncle Viney in black, with a blue and white striped waistcoat and the very latest thing in Brummel trousers strapped under his boots, gave the bride away… And she was given. The organ pealed; boys' voices sang, and, leaning on her husband's arm, attended by her mother, Mr Yate and Uncle Viney, Mary Anne was led into the vestry to sign her maiden name for the last time. The witnesses were her uncle James Viney and her stepfather, who, since early morning, had been actively engaged in the Assembly Rooms superintending the setting of the table for the breakfast. As result of which, and some necessary sampling of the champagne, he affixed to his signature so tremulous a *T* and final *E* that the record in the register of the parish church at Clifton is inscribed for posterity: *A. Yates.*

Under a gigantic wedding bell of white flowers (artificial) contrived and presented by the stepfather of the bride, she stood to receive congratulations, her smile fixed, her bridegroom bowing, flushed, and looking, she thought, ten years younger in this, his hour. Was it hers? Her life known and lived as Mary Anne Evans was gone; and Mary Anne Lewis, as henceforth would she be, was merged in him, bound to him, now and for ever, 'till death us do part'.

SIX

Pantgwynlais, Greenmeadow: rightly named for its green apron, wide stretched to the valley of the Taff that winds its shining way between hills near and distant. A lovely way to follow in a phaeton, and explore the varied views it offered and the land that it embraced, of which she now was chatelaine. Yet Greenmeadow was nothing of a 'castle'. A sizable but not overpowering mansion, built on the site of a Cistercian monastery, it had grown in grandeur from report of the Pump Room, and Miss Graham, with another and major discrepancy: Wyndham Lewis was not the owner but the tenant of Greenmeadow, leased from his brother Henry who had inherited the estate from an uncle. But, for Mary Anne, Greenmeadow was a home; or she, a born home-maker, made it so in her first year of marriage.

And now, with a second year drawing to its close, she could look back and see herself moulded to her husband's pattern while strategically conforming to her own.

This entire reorientation of her life and being had presented no discolourment to detract from the bright overtones of her surroundings to which, with chameleon versatility, she soon became adapted. She had no regrets, nor, perhaps to his surprise, had he. For, while he may have doubted the effect of Mary Anne upon his family, he soon discovered she could hold her own against the chilliest reception. Moreover, as a woman — never mind that she were wife — he thoroughly and physically enjoyed her.

Although by no means ignorant of nuptial obligations, the furtive hints and giggles of apprentice-room confederates had not prepared her for the shock of her initiation.

Appeased and satiated he had slept, but she did not. Bruised and battered, achingly she watched the night fade into wintry dawn to find him there beside her, one hand, open-palmed, flung out across her breasts. She pushed it away, heard him grunt in his sleep — *And if this be how he worships me, I'd best go hang myself,* had been her stunned recoil from hymeneal experience.

Lifting her outraged body on an elbow she looked down at his face, turned to her and half-hidden in the pillow, his hair disordered, but at least his own. No wig... So this was marriage. She had nothing more to learn. She'd learned enough.

Then she told herself fiercely, *Lord sakes! And you raised on a farm to take on for what's natural as breath to the cows and the sows. But the least God can do to make up for* this *is to send me a baby...*

That was two years ago, all but a month, and God had not sent her a baby. 'Never mind,' Wyndham consoled her, 'there's plenty of time. You are still young.' And, once resigned and accustomed to 'this', she was happy. If his interests were divided between her and his hounds, his coalmine, and the ironworks in which he had lately acquired a share; and although the first heat of his ardour had cooled, he was none the less fond, and, after his fashion, was faithful.

To be sure there were obstructions to be overcome in her domestic role as mistress of his house, the full sovereignty of which, until her arrival, had been represented by one Mrs Jones. But Miss Evans had not been Mrs Lewis for a week before she decided to reorganise her household in her own time and in her own way.

For a month she left Mrs Jones to her housekeeping devices, during which interval, when the domestic staff had retired to their quarters for the night, Mary Anne surveyed the situation.

Her investigations found much to be deplored; in the larder a rime of greenish mould collected on the open-lidded jars of preserves and bottled fruits unsystematically ranged alongside pickled onions with a prevalent smell of mice. 'And,' said Mary Anne, 'no wonder, while the cat feasts on a capon. Shoo! Be off, you slinking thief. But who can eat it now? Best take it to the yard with you. Go on!' Followed by the capon hurled after it, the shocked cat went flying, tail up. In the kitchen crumbs unswept and beetles swarming, to be shudderingly scuttled with a broom; in the dairy, bowls of cream neglected, turning sour; and in the linen cupboard, the doors of which had not been locked, were sheets from the laundry still damp to the touch. Armed with half a dozen of these, much in need of repair, Mary Anne, next morning, busily set about to darn and patch and mend.

It required courage, though she had her share of that, to summon Mrs Jones for inquisition to her parlour.

Truculent, hatchet-faced and lean was Mrs Jones, in unrelieved black taffetas, hissing to her entrance as if she lodged beneath her petticoats a colony of snakes.

'You was wishful to speak with me, ma'am?'

'Yes, Mrs Jones.' Mary Anne induced a smile. 'I want to know how many servants indoors and out do we — do you,' she substituted tactfully, 'employ?'

Mrs Jones folded her arms. 'I have naught to do, ma'am, look you, with the men out of doors nor the gardeners whatever but as for the domestics in the house there is twelve to live in besides myself and Mr Jenkins, not to count Hew

Morgan the boot-boy from over the mountain, and Bronwen his sister the dairymaid, come daily.'

'And of these twelve,' daringly enquired Mary Anne, 'is there none to clean the kitchen and get rid of the black beetles? I had occasion to go down last night for — for a biscuit as I was feeling hungry, and I saw —' She closed her eyes and added faintly, 'I've a horror of black beetles.'

'As with all self-respecting ladies, ma'am, and never,' uttered Mrs Jones, 'have I been accused of favouring vermin with an abhorrence by me of black beetles second only to the devil, nor stinting of food that madam should go hungry, having but to ring the bell and order what is wanted — no matter how late is the hour, mind. Excuse me.'

'No one, Mrs Jones, would accuse, you of favouring vermin. It is only, if I may suggest, that crumbs or leavings from the table should be swept up by a kitchen-maid last thing at night and powdered borax sprinkled, which I'm told is death to beetles, and a trap laid for the mice. And, Mrs Jones, if the cream is set by in bowls packed round with ice, for even in this wintry weather it may turn if left standing too long —' Mary Anne politely paused, at which the tow-coloured hair of Mrs Jones, arranged in rolls and puffs above her forehead with one puff paramount, now appeared to rise as might the crest of an angry cockatoo.

'Indeed, ma'am, if there is in my duties for that you may find fault I would ask your pardon. Never a beetle nor mouse have I seen in the kitchen whatever, and should the cream be sour Dai Gower the cook it is, and not myself, should be called to account — for look you, ma'am, it is not usual for the lady of the house to walk by night and open of my cupboards and take my laundered sheets to turn them inside out and sides to middle — and if,' said Mrs Jones, the crest again uprisen, 'you would wish to make a change there is one month's notice I will give you.'

'As *you* wish, Mrs Jones,' mildly suggested Mary Anne.

A moment's listening quiet passed.

'From today, then, is it?' Buttoning her mouth as if she never meant to open it again, Mrs Jones made a move towards the door and turned. 'There is wishful I am to give satisfaction, which is it seeming I do not, but before that I begin to pack—'

'To pack, Mrs Jones? You surely aren't packing to go now?'

'Tomorrow,' Mrs Jones said firmly. 'I will go tomorrow, though I forfeit my month's wages, mind. It is not usual for a housekeeper should demean herself to wait her month where she is spied upon and called to task for this and that. Excuse me.'

'Mrs Jones, I think that you misunderstand —'

'There is no misunderstanding, ma'am, by me whatever. I know my duties and if I do not give you satisfaction there is better you replace me with a housekeeper who does, and since change one change all I doubt me not that Mr Jenkins the butler and Dai Gower the cook they will be leaving with me, Mr Jenkins he not caring for his silver to be counted and the cook his capon given to the cat.'

'I did not give the capon to the cat, Mrs Jones. The cat had it on the pantry floor when I —'

'It is not usual, ma'am, excuse me, for the lady of the house to go into the pantry, and the marchioness at Cardiff begging for a butler, she having dismissed her last, an Englishman from Bath, and him found by his lordship laid out in the dining room with a bottle in each hand, and her ladyship asking of me always to go back to her who served the castle before that I was wed, him — God rest his soul — having fallen down the mineshaft to leave me widowed and back to earn my living board and keep, which I have done and gladly at Pantgwynlais these ten years, and no interference of my duties, mind. Excuse me.' And Mrs Jones tossed herself out of the room.

In the reorganisation of her household, resultant on the exodus of Mrs Jones, with Mr Jenkins the butler and Dai Gower the cook, Mary Anne had her husband's full support. Having found that Jenkins had appropriated certain sundries of silver and wine, Wyndham advised what he called a 'full sweep' of all the upper servants.

'And no more housekeepers for me,' said Mary Anne. 'Henceforth *I'll* be the keeper of your house.'

By the defeat of Mrs Jones she had gained confidence to face and overcome hostility from another and more formidable front. Her sisters-in-law, Mrs (the Reverend) William and Mrs Henry of Park, were mutually agreed that Wyndham ought to have done better for himself. The Misses Price, the Misses Thomas the Rectory, to say nothing of Miss Vernon-Graham — who, it was reputed, had a dower of five thousand — any of these had been in the running until this 'Evans person' set her cap at him, and who knew better how to set it, since the making of caps was her — should they say — hobby?

They said 'hobby' — with tacit avoidance of the shop that led her to appear in a bonnet smothered in poppies — and scarlet ones, too — at the castle garden party to which, as Wyndham's wife, she would *have* to be invited. Yet it had been observed that the greeting of the marchioness was distinctly cool and that her ladyship presented her to none above the Dean and Mrs Dean. Not so the marquis who had walked her off, as Mrs Henry had witnessed, to an arbour behind the rhododendrons, 'with a dish of strawberries shared between them, and no plates —'

'How truly shocking!' gasped Mrs William.

'Yes, Mrs William, shocking indeed.' And with her own eyes Mrs Henry had seen Mrs Wyndham and the marquis picking at the fruit with the dish on his lordship's knees — 'and she whispering and giggling in his lordship's ear,' again Mrs Henry vouched for this. 'And later they were joined by our revered Member, Lord William Crichton-Stuart, all three talking *politics* together, mind! And she bold as brass to air her views, for all around and passing by to hear —' as Mrs Henry, passing by with Mrs Thomas the Rectory had heard Mrs Wyndham put in *her* word about — 'just think of it — the *Corn Laws.*'

'Imagine!'

'Yes, so unbecoming in a lady to discuss such subjects, and with Wyndham a staunch Tory to be saddled with a wife who brazenly declares herself a Whig and worse than that a Radical as near as makes no matter, and if I recall it rightly —' with some concentrative effort Mrs Henry did recall how Mrs Wyndham had condemned '"this prohibition of imported corn"…'

'However,' interrupted Mrs William, 'could she have known of that?'

'From the news-sheets, likely, which she is always reading.'

'Well, I'm sure!' breathed Mrs William. But there was more to come.

'"The cost of wheat at eighty shillings to the quarter," she said — and don't ask me how she knew of *that* — "is a terrible price to pay, and means that the poor labourer must starve or steal."'

'Gracious goodness!' Mrs William's eyes were popping. 'Is this to be believed?'

'Believe it or believe it not, that was what I heard her say. And, "We look to you, Lord William, to voice in Parliament the needs of these poor creatures. It was bread or the want of it that set the fuse in France," she said, "to start the revolution."'

'Mercy on us!'

'I assure you, Mrs William, I did not dare to look Mrs Price in the face. I hurried her away, but as we went I heard his lordship tell Lord William — you know how loud the marquis speaks — 'Take warning, Bill, you'd best stand down that Mrs Wyndham Lewis may stand up, as the first lady Member of Parliament' — to set them all three laughing as at the greatest joke, and she the noisiest. So shaming for the family.' And what the gentlemen could see in her, Mrs Henry, Mrs William, and their daughters could not understand. 'Yet better Wyndham should have married her than —'

Eyes went up and voices down. Wyndham, oh, too dreadfully, had strayed from the straight and narrow path of Pantgwynlais to follow a factory girl, whom he had seen in Bristol going *barefoot* to her work and he... No, never say it! It was, however, said, and said again, to be floated into legend, since Wyndham had disclosed his awful secret to his Reverend brother William; and, for his conscience's ease, to Mary Anne.

She received his confession three months after marriage, delivered with some humming and hah-ing while she heard him out in silence, until, 'All gentlemen,' she said, 'will have their fancies, but not all will tell their wives. It is good of you to tell me. I never need have known.'

'You would have known — were bound to know, if not from me, from others. Not that society looks askance at any such — hum — pre-marital adventures, but —'

'Where is she?'

'In Ireland. She is Irish. I sent her back there with her — h'm — her child.'

'Her —?' Mary Anne caught her breath. '*Your* child?'

'As so I was informed. I have no positive proof.'

'Is it a girl or a boy?'

'A girl. She is in a convent school. Both she and the — her mother are well provided for.'

'I'm glad of that. I shouldn't like to think you'd thrown her out for me.'

Astonishment at her undismayed acceptance of his 'fancy' was slightly impregnated with vexation. He had come prepared for a scene, vapours, tears, which would have been a womanly acknowledgement of his masculine prerogative. But not this unfeminine interest in and approval of it. 'Hem — the episode,' said Wyndham stiffly, 'occurred before I met you.'

'That don't make no difference. Did you love her?'

This really was going too far.

'Love,' he frowned a little, 'is not a term one associates with a passing liaison. That I have told you this is surely token enough of my esteem and affection for my wife.'

'Thank you very much,' said Mary Anne.

She was looking back upon that incident one morning in November, 1817, when a mild sun and soft west wind had tempted her out on the terrace. Yes, his half-abashed, half-defiant revelation — a smile played about her lips as she recalled it — had marked a subtle change in their relationship. He, who may have questioned his wisdom in having too readily succumbed to an infatuation, ceased to doubt; and this the more surprising in that he, a man of few complexities, had entered into marriage with the possessive instinct uppermost, unready to reject those compulsions implicit to the squirearchy of ownership.

According to his tenets a wife must be as much her husband's sole monopoly as were the lands he overlorded: a chattel of his house, a hostess for his table, her body for his use, leashed within the bounds of legalised concubinage. So Wyndham, in common with others of his kind and time, had recognised the wedded state; and now his home and heart were hers to do with as she would.

This utter abnegation of all he hitherto had lived by and which owed nothing to physical desire was, for her, although she did not know it, a greater conquest than the mere material advantage his name and wealth could give. And in those early years of marriage she enjoyed to the full all and more than he could give, soon to establish herself as a leader of local society. John, stationed with his regiment in Ireland, heard of dinner parties at Greenmeadow and a hunt ball — *a fine blow-out with drinkables and some devilish good fun... The whole house turned topsy-turvy.*

But 'good fun', however 'devilish', with or without Wyndham's approval, was not enough to fill her life. Her boundless energy sought a wider field of active interest than Cardiff or Greenmeadow could afford.

Seated there on the terrace, her sewing in her lap and her hands idle, her eyes searched the distant view beyond the slope of meadow to the river that, like a gleaming serpent, went twisting through the droop of golden willows on its banks. Autumn, as if to atone for a wet and dreary summer, had stayed, marking time on the advent of winter, with a gracious spread of bronze and copper not yet yellowed to the slow death-fall of leaves. From far off she could hear the brittle yelp of hounds hot on the scent, but no sight of them nor of the field. One of the gardeners, digging a bed below the terrace, straightened his back, his sharp nose pointing westwards.

'There is seeming they have found over the mountain, and here is Gwilym Owen the Papers coming up the drive. Will I fetch them to you, ma'am, to save him the walk?'

'Yes, Davies, if you please.'

Gwilym Owen the Papers waylaid, and the news-sheets delivered, she unfolded the first and saw the page black-bordered... 'Oh, no!' Her breath caught in her throat as she read the staring headlines.

DEATH OF THE PRINCESS CHARLOTTE

The heiress of England dead — of a stillborn son!

The paper dropped from her hand. Davies, inquisitively hovering, stooped to recover it. He could read Welsh but no English. Her whitened face gave him to ask, 'There is bad news, ma'am, is it?'

'Bad and sad, Davies,' she answered, and told him.

'God's will be done.' He bared his head, revealing a thatch of black wiry hair. 'The Lord giveth and the Lord taketh away. Dear to goodness, there is grief for us, our future Queen and Prince of Wales born to be King, gone together. There is like a judgement has fallen on the Regent for his ungodliness and fornication and the poor old King his father, crazy mad out of his mind. There is no good has come to Wales since the first German George did sit in the place of the King over the water, and say it I will.'

'And say it you won't!' She turned on him sharp. 'There is but one King for Britain, sick in mind though he may be, and no Prince of Wales but the Regent while his father lives. This is treasonable talk, and if you give voice to it, as I've no doubt you do with your fellows in the Cow and Snuffers, you'll find yourself on the gallows. Back now to your work. I want that bed a blaze of tulips come the spring.'

And as, sheepishly, he went from her, *Well, well, to think of him,* she said to herself, *a Jacobite, hot for that miserable drunkard Charles Stuart, dead near on thirty years. But it's a pointer to show the way the wind blows in these parts, warm or warmer for the Tories than any one of us. I wonder...*

And still wondering, she took up her sewing, while her thoughts were busy to buzz around the 'pointer'. *Now suppose,* she mused, *Lord William should stand down at the next election? He may be thinking of it. Remember how he and the marquis quizzed me last year at the castle garden party — who in his place will stand up? There's one I could name and none so likely with half the county in his pocket — and none so able nor so steady. True as steel he'd be. Not like some of them, who seek the honour for theirselves and not their country. He'd have no need to give up his hunting, neither, and him Master of the Hounds. He'd not do that to be prime minister. But he'd have to take a house in London. I'd like a house in London — not to live in all the year, but to visit time to time and see the sights. There'd be sights enough in London, I'll be bound — the Regent not the least of 'em, to say naught of his fine ladies and that poor princess, his wife, though she be leading him a dance from all accounts...* Talk of which had flown from Carlton House so far afield as Cardiff.

Late that afternoon when Wyndham, returned from the hunt, sat relaxed before the fire in the hall, his riding boots off, his slippers on, his legs in their mud-splashed buckskins stretched to the blaze while he drank tea and ate hot buttered scones, she brought him the *Cardiff Times*. He was staggered.

'We had great hopes of her,' he said, 'with that fine young Prince Leopold as Consort. He is sound, mark you, and might well have been a power behind the throne to bring about a democratic monarchy which is what this country needs and which the old King — "Farmer George" they used to call him when I was a lad — might himself have done had he been spared his wits. He was popular among the lower orders, as the Regent never was and never will be. The tragic loss of that young life may be the turning point. There's trouble enough already on the brew with agrarian unrest and burning of the hayricks, and this is likely to bring matters to a head. A national disaster. I'll have another cup, my dear.'

'But why,' asked Mary Anne as she refilled his cup, 'should the death of Princess Charlotte, sad though it is, be a national disaster?'

'Why? Because,' Wyndham indulgently explained, 'the Regent can go right ahead with his persecution of his wife. He's having her watched on her travels abroad to divide the country for and against him. He'll not scruple — now there's no daughter between them — to snatch at every straw to gain his ends. This double tragedy has lost him two potential heirs. He will stop at nothing to secure a direct succession.'

'But there's all his brothers,' put in Mary Anne, offering him scones.

'Yes, his brothers — and what of them?' He took a scone, and said, 'These are very greasy. Give me a napkin.'

'Here.' She gave him her handkerchief. 'You were saying about the Regent's brothers. There's the Duke of York.'

'Whose barren duchess is dying, and after York comes Clarence with his Jordan and a horde of little Fitzes. Prinny married Princess Caroline to get him an heir, and now it seems he'll have to try again, by fair means or — by foul.'

Which prophesy was soon to be fulfilled.

In January of the new year the 'unshackling' process, as the Regent called his first attempt to free himself from his unhappy wife, was launched on an astonished public. But that sensational enquiry known as the 'Milan Commission' did not proceed quite according to plan. The Princess of Wales, whose rollicking adventures from Genoa to Jericho by way of Carlsruhe, clad in a scarlet riding habit with half a scooped-out pumpkin on her head — 'to keep it cool' was the reason she gave to her horrified hosts — had caused the gravest consternation to the Whigs and much Homeric mirth to the Tories.

'Parliament,' was Wyndham's report of it to Mary Anne, 'stands, a house divided. Here's Brougham, loud in her defence and backed by all his Whigs with the mob at their heels to exploit her.'

'And drag her name in the gutter,' Mary Anne hotly rejoined. 'There's not a pin to choose between the parties, both hollering one against the other for their own gain and never mind whose cost — the Tories to make that poor lady their scapegoat, who I'm certain is mad as a puss — or the King. After all, he's her uncle and she may have got it from him. And the Whigs on her side to defend her, not from chivalry — oh, no, don't you believe it — but because they see a loophole to slip in and put the Tories out with the exposement of —'

'Exposure,' corrected her husband.

'Exposure, then, of her goings-on. I can't pick and choose my words. I'm no politician.'

Wyndham quirked an eyebrow. 'I'm not so sure of that.'

''Tis a nasty business,' reflected Mary Anne as she watched him pouring port from the decanter at his elbow. 'Who knows what'll be the end of it?'

'A general election,' said he, and drained his glass, 'will be the end of it.'

'Which, being so,' she was on her feet to tell him, 'that's the last you'll have tonight. There's all but a bottle of port since your supper a-top of claret, Madeira and brandy. You'll be full o' gout afore you're fifty, and on crutches, God forbid, and then what of your hunting?'

He pulled her down on to his knee. 'What's one bottle of port to a three-bottle man?'

'A bottle too much.' She stroked back from his forehead a lock of his hair. 'I want you well and strong, in body as in mind, but if you souse yourself in wine you'll blunt your senses. And if there is to be a general election I want to see you *in* it, not as a looker-on, but as the chosen candidate for Cardiff!'

SEVEN

So from merest trifles are destinies decided; a chance word spoken, a small seed dropped to bring forth, with the ripening years, its rich harvest. But since she had been given no gift of second sight, Mary Anne could not foretell how that she, so inconsiderable a pawn on the chequer-board of fate, had in one opening gambit determined the future, not only of her husband and herself but of another, who, as yet unknown to her and to the world, was to inscribe his name on the scroll of immortality.

That for the years ahead; while in the years between, kings, queens and men alike were moved by one inexorable hand to play out the game to its end.

In his castle at Windsor, a shadow among shadows, dwelled an old man, blind and deaf, lost of his senses, lost to his people, forgotten by Death who, remorselessly, had passed him by. But beyond his padded walls the stream of life flowed on, gathering impetus to turn the tide of change in the dawn of a new age: an age of transition, of social and political revolt; of new forces rising, old shibboleths dying, of new voices speaking for those who had never dared speak of their 'rights'.

Up in Manchester, a monster meeting was held, led by the fiery Radical Hunt, demanding universal suffrage, a new word. The magistrates, alarmed at sight of that vast multitude assembled in St Peter's Fields, ordered a charge of cavalry to arrest the speaker and disperse with lance and sabre some unarmed sixty thousand men and their wives, many of whom were injured if not killed.

It was a holocaust of wounded, dead and dying; a storm to fan indignant outcries in a blaze that threatened to demolish a generation of Toryism. In London, lampoons depicting a mounted horseman brandishing a blood-stained sword and trampling down a heap of shrieking women, were dangled in the faces of the clubmen of St James's. Younger members, scarred and limping from their wounds at Waterloo, asked, 'Is this for what we fought? Is this for what our fellows died?' And on every lip arose the question: 'Why?'

'Yes, why?' echoed Mary Anne, her eyes glued to the news-sheets. 'What's wrong with our rulers and the ruled that such an outrage as this Peterloo can follow hard on Waterloo? It says here there's more'n a hundred women wounded and two of them killed, besides eleven men. It's downright murder to have called out those Hussars to savage helpless women.'

'Who should remain helpless,' Wyndham inimically replied. 'If women choose to support their menfolk in blatant mutiny, then they must risk the consequences even to their lives.'

'As I'd risk my life,' she retorted, 'to support you. And some day when you stand on the hustings to face a volley of rotten apples and potatoes hurled by Whiggish Radicals, or whatever these hatemongers may call themselves, I'll be there beside you to take my share and part in it. So now!'

'Is that a threat,' he enquired with a twinkle, 'or a promise?'

To which she answered cryptically, 'You'll see.'

The long clouded life of George III had come to its merciful end, almost simultaneously with that of his fourth son, the Duke of Kent.

None could guess, least of all Mary Anne and one other, a schoolboy still in his teens and deep in his studies at Dr Cogan's Academy near Epping, how the death of this royal prince would affect their whole futures to be centred in the life of his daughter, the infant Princess Alexandrina Victoria.

Unmoved by her widowed mother's noisy lamentations, the little 'Drina', an exceedingly fat and plain child just finding her feet, waddled clumsily to and from the outstretched arms of her doting ladies; or, contentedly playing with her fingers, in her cot she would lie while her father and grandfather lay in their coffins.

The accession of her uncle, George IV, brought to her small life no change of circumstance, and none to him or his subjects more than that of title. The curtain fallen on a pitiable figure, sightless, senseless, talking with the dead, singing hymns and praying in its hoarse cracked voice, rose again on the long awaited entrance of the First Gentleman. He, who, for ten years, had been standing by as understudy to the leading part, now, at last, was called upon to play it. And play it he did, in the opening scene, with truly dramatic effect. Pending his coronation that in all decency could not take place in less than a year of happy mourning, the King set in motion his final abortive attempt to release himself from his marriage and his detested wife.

In taverns old men, heads together over tankards, hushed voices to speak of 'this new King George', who was anything but new, having reigned for a decade as virtual monarch. And a fine job he'd made of his regency, spending the nation's money right and left, on his women, on his drink, on his houses and his orgies, and that Pavilion of his down at Brighton with its onion-shaped cupolas and towers 'full of Chinamen', or so rumour gave it. And now to drag the Queen's name in the gutter. A divorce! It shook the country. It took precedence above all other topics of the day, even more than had the general election, which in the surprising sequence of that year's events held second place in national affairs. But not in the affairs of Mary Anne.

For her the general election had been the breath of life, an ambition realised in which she, too, if on a smaller stage, had played her part.

When it became known that Lord William Crichton-Stuart did not intend to stand at this election, she gave Wyndham no peace until she had wrenched from him the promise to offer himself, and was readily accepted, as Cardiff's prospective Tory candidate.

EIGHT

During the weeks before polling day, Mary Anne, heedless of Wyndham's objections, enthusiastically undertook her canvassing campaign.

'Lord William,' she reported, 'tells me they're a tougher lot than last time.'

'When,' enquired Wyndham coldly, 'did you see Lord William?'

'This morning in Cardiff. I drove into town to buy you a barrel of oysters, the last you'll get this season. There'll be no more months with an R in them till September, and you know how you're partial to oysters. Very dear they were, too. Six shillings. He — Lord William — was standing on the pavement outside the Angel and he waved his stick at the carriage to stop.'

'The deuce he did!'

'The deuce,' she mimicked, 'he did! And you don't have to glare at me as if I was a Gorman —'

'Gorgon,' murmured Wyndham.

'And then,' she continued, undaunted by the glare, 'I asked him to step in and told Thomas to drive on, and then we talked.'

'You mean *you* talked.'

'Well, someone's got to talk to bring you in your votes, and if you don't do the talking, who will?' Allowing a moment's pause for that to sink in, 'So,' said Mary Anne with a private little grin, 'I pumped him.'

'You —?'

'Pumped him. As to my means of approach when I start canvassing, since it's evident you'll not speak up so strong for yourself as you should, or as I can.'

'God help me,' muttered Wyndham.

'Yes, you'll need His help and mine too when you go to the polls. Lord William says that Ludlow, the Whig, is plugging —'

'Plugging?' queried Wyndham, eyebrows up.

'Oh, for goodness' sake! It's what Lord William called it — "plugging the Regent's" — beg his pardon, the King's — "tyrannical outrageous persecution of the Queen." He said I must show myself sympathetic to her for in the end she may be induced to stay out of the country, but not if the Tories go slinging filth in her face. It'll only bring her back to save it, so they say.'

'Or so Lord William says?' her husband offered drily. 'I can't think why he doesn't stand again, since he seems to have primed you so thoroughly — for me.'

'No.' She planted a kiss on his forehead. 'For me! Just you wait till I get going.'

She got going the next day.

Flaunting Wyndham's colours she drove herself through Cardiff in a curricle, with rosettes on the horses' heads, on her whip, on her bonnet and the hat of her footman up behind. She combed the lowest quarters of the city, winning hearts of mothers with admiration of and kisses for their babies; and, in the case of the 'tougher', a kiss for the fathers too; a blacksmith, a butcher, a baker, all three of them vigorous Whigs, were won by the same irresistible bribe, and maybe the promise of more.

Undeterred by gaping crowds who followed at her heels to jeer or cheer or heckle, and to whom she gave as good as she was given, she came home with a flea and a list of the names she had secured.

'Not a Whig,' she triumphantly told Wyndham, 'but hasn't had it from me pat. I had an answer for them all. Every time they called my bluff to shout me down, I shouted up!'

'I'll lay my shirt you did,' said Wyndham uneasily.

'Yes, I'm hoarse as a crow and itchin' all over, but I've got 'em. Or,' she amended, 'at least I've not lost you a vote and may have won you a score from the Whig, whose promises, I told them, aren't worth a tinker's curse.'

Wyndham blinked.

"He'll over-ride you and your liberties,' I said. 'He's politically unfaithful. He only wants your vote and then he'll use the lash. You'll be in worser case than you are now."

'Which is precisely,' was Wyndham's succinct rejoinder, 'what Ludlow, my opponent, says of me.'

'Exactly so!' cried Mary Anne. 'I spiked his guns. And I don't mind telling you that yesterday I went down to the hustings — no, you're not to fuss — they all know and look for me now, and I stood among the crowd and took notes of what Ludlow had given 'em the day before, and dished it up to them with frills like lamb cutlets. Laugh! I thought I should ha' died the way they swallered Ludlow's stuff fed to them by me. "The whole responsibility of the British Constitution rests with you," I told 'em. *"You!"* She jumped from her chair to point a finger at the startled Wyndham. "'You, who hold the future of your country in your hands. Vote for Lewis, for your lives and for your liberties —" and I didn't half have to yell to be heard above the cheering — "vote for Ludlow and be crushed beneath the iron heel of sham democracy. Why, the very word —" which you tipped me, Wyn, or rather that I cribbed from a speech of yours I found lyin' on your desk — "the very word derives," I told them, "from the Greek *demos*, the mob," and that impressed them proper. They took me for a Blue. "Do you want to be crushed by the mob and see your house and your hayricks burning?" — for I've been at the farmers too — "as did Rome while Nero fiddled? Don't let them Whigs fiddle you," I said. And believe me, Wyn, it worked!'

It did, to gain for Lewis an all but double majority vote.

'We're off!' cried Mary Anne, when the poll returned the figures. 'On to London. For you'll have to live in London most time of the year, now you're a Member of Parliament!'

PART TWO: PASTURES NEW

NINE

London in the 1820s: City of action, of revolt, where the loyal mob disturbances caused by the sensational trial of Queen Caroline passed as a storm cloud in the sunburst of Coronation Year. A city of contrasts where the foetid dens and brothels of Old Drury sprawled within walking distance of that gracious crescent built by Nash for the Regent's drive from Carlton House to his park beyond Mary-le-bone marshes. A city of enchantment where the dandies of St James's sought to outrival in dress, if not in wit, the greatest dandy of them all, their corpulent, ageing King: he, whose unerring connoisseurship never wavered in pursuit of Old Masters and new mistresses; whose Pavilion down at Brighton grew ever more crowded and more curious, more Bacchanalian his revels, more extravagant his tastes.

A far cry from the tender hills and valleys of Pantgwynlais was the mansion at Grosvenor Gate, Park Lane, bought by Wyndham Lewis for his wife. She, heretofore so easily adaptable to her surroundings, now found herself a stranger in this strange, exciting world. Not for her that carnival parade of self-indulgence, where a mushroom growth of middle-class society enriched by post-war redistribution of wealth, aped the follies and the foibles of an over-taxed and moribund aristocracy. Not to her door were cards of invitation delivered daily by cockaded footmen; nor for her the brilliant soirées of the *ton* who flocked to Holland House; nor even to the less impeccable but more entertaining salon of the lovely Lady

Blessington, whose marriage to her complaisant earl could never quite obliterate an equivocal past.

By such hostesses as these, and others, each a queen in her own right, the wife of a Welsh country squire and inconspicuous Member of Parliament was not, let us face it, 'received'. While her husband, at his sessions in the House, vainly strove to catch the Speaker's eye, Mary Anne, at her window in Grosvenor Gate, looked enviously down at the stream of carriages driving into and out of the park.

Imagination rioted in letters to John of a wonderful Cinderella ball. *Fancy your little Whizz partnered by our noble Hero, the great Duke of Wellington, and in her own house… It was a Fairyland!* John heard of walls hung with blue damask, white muslin and rose silk wreathed with flowers. There were thousands of wax candles, more flowers lining the staircase, draping the balustrade, *and a windmill with* real sails *and a stream filled with gold and silver fish.* (A 'Fairyland' doubtless borrowed from descriptions of Carlton House banquets in Regency days.) *If only darling John could see all my distinguished visitors…*

No wonder then, that 'darling John', whether or not he was likely to see them, applied to 'little Whizz' to pull him out of debt, only to fall more deeply in again, until Wyndham very firmly put his foot down.

'I'll not give another groat to your good-for-nothing brother, keeping horses, gigs and women at *my* expense.' *Or our expense,* thought Mary Anne, who may have had in mind some better use for Wyndham's money when, in 1826, Lord William decided to stand again for Cardiff at the forthcoming election, and she urged her husband's attention to the candidature of Aldeburgh in Suffolk. He must not, she insisted, retire from Parliament while here was a seat going begging for the right man. Yet was Wyndham, she wondered, the right man for any seat?

Only once, in these five years, had he caught the Speaker's eye, diffidently to address the House in support of the Anti-Reform Party who heard him in deadly silence split by derisive Opposition jeers. But a full report of this reception to his maiden speech was not told to Mary Anne. She, shifting doubt and ever staunch in her belief that Wyndham would ultimately take his place on the front bench, was unflagging in her efforts during the next electoral campaign to bring him in once more a good majority for Aldeburgh.

It was shortly after this that she became acquainted with Rosina, wife of Edward Bulwer. A young writer, launched by and madly infatuated with the notorious Lady Caroline Lamb, he had emerged from country life obscurity to a house in Hertford Street.

Between Mrs Wyndham Lewis and Mrs Edward Bulwer, acquaintance blossomed into questionable friendship; and if Mrs Lewis were aware that Mrs Bulwer confided to her dearer friends how 'that *outré* little creature sticks to me like a limpet and will not be shaken off,' Mrs Lewis may have had good reason so to stick.

Rosina, whose beauty had devastated the young Edward to lose him his fond mama's affection and her financial support, entertained with lavish indiscrimination. The high world, the low world, the half world, all and any were welcome to the Bulwers' open house. More decorative than domesticated was Rosina when she and Edward, still mutually adoring despite their frequent rows, gleefully descended upon London. But Edward's volatile gifts and caustic pen did not, at that time, make him independent of his mother.

Mrs Bulwer-Lytton — she had tacked her maiden name to that of her dead husband when she had inherited her father's wealth — strongly opposed her Edward's choice. The fair Rosina Wheeler had no fortune but her face. Born of an Irish father who drank himself to death, and of a mother who professed to be an atheist and led a sect of cranks at Caen, Rosina had migrated back and forth from France to Ireland, and to London via Guernsey, of which her mother's uncle was the Governor. Too sophisticated for her years, and until she and Edward met, Rosina still surprisingly *virgo intacta*, was discovered — even as Edward had been — by the youth-greedy Caroline Lamb. That association was the lovely Rosina's undoing. Lady Caroline, to whom boys and girls alike were equal quarry to be chased, devoured, cast aside, had found in this, her latest protégée, another delightful diversion.

With Caroline, Rosina skimmed the cream of social London's superfluities and, delving deeper, tasted of new undreamed experience, to learn from her captivating mentor much that was not good for her to know.

It must have greatly intrigued Lady Caroline to throw together two young people both entangled in her coils, and to watch their growing passion, re-fuelled from the burnt-out fires of her mischievous experiments with each. It was a marriage doomed to fatal consequence, brushed by Caroline's distorted magic, to lose themselves in tainted love.

And this radiant beauty, the irresponsible raffish Rosina, was the doubtful friend of Mary Anne.

Rosina may have realised how 'that *outré* little creature', holding her husband and his purse strings in her hand, might prove to be a useful source to tap; while Mary Anne, for her part, was well aware that Edward's certain income of two hundred a year and an uncertain supplement from penmanship could scarcely suffice to maintain a house in Mayfair, to say nothing of one baby — and a second, as confided by Rosina, on the way.

'If, my dear,' said Mary Anne, 'you would allow me to offer the smallest little loan to cover the expenses of your lying-in, I'd regard it as my pleasure. Here am I, a wife since the year of Waterloo, and have never been blessed with a child. None will ever know,' she sighed, 'how I've longed for a child.'

Which may or may not have been so great a longing as that deep-drawn sigh conveyed. True, in her early wedded life she had hoped for that which might have been and, as the years went on, had resignedly accepted what she knew could never be.

But: 'My sweetest girl!' was the somewhat too elaborate protest to Mary Anne's suggestion. 'I could not possibly… Such an angel as you are! I would not dream of taking advantage of your great-hearted generosity; of course we are living far beyond our means, but who does not? Your dear self excepted, married to the Mint! No, no, you can't deny it. That magnificent house, furnished in such exquisite taste.' ('Shrieking yellow curtains, my dears, for her drawing room, and in the middle of the floor an ottoman upholstered in sapphire blue.' Thus Rosina's version, to her circle of admirers, of her 'sweetest girl's' 'exquisite taste'.) And, 'No, my love, I simply couldn't think of it!' she, a trifle less elaborately, pursued, 'even though I've lent my diamond tiara to *mon oncle*.'

'To your uncle?' innocently queried Mary Anne.

'Oh, dear me!' Rosina pealed with laughter. 'Yes. My uncle Moses in St Mary Axe, only for goodness' sake treat this as confidential. Pups —' her name for Edward; his for her was 'Poodle' — 'would never have done raging if he knew.'

'Ah,' Mary Anne nodded, understandingly, 'I see.'

'I'm sure you don't.' The laughter left Rosina's eyes; her voice held an edge, razor-sharp, to it. 'You? The pampered pet of a rich old man? How could —'

'He's not old!' hotly interrupted Mary Anne.

'Old for me,' shrugged Rosina, 'if not so old for *you*. But as I was saying, how can you know what it is to jump at each knock at your door, nor to dread the grin on your footman's face when he announces: "A person in the 'all to see you, ma'am, most urgent."'

She snapped her jaws together as she flung this out and sat, sulky-mouthed, while Mary Anne, still nodding, said, 'I do know, see? I've not always had it easy. Till Mr Lewis came along I had to earn my living, and a poor enough living at that. I kept a shop.'

'A shop?' Rosina flicked her a look of disdainful incredulity.

'S-H-O-P, shop,' defiantly repeated Mary Anne. 'Millinery. Caps and bonnets. *Modes et Robes* and what-not.'

'Really?'

'Yes, *ray-ah-lly*!' was the impish mimicry of Rosina's tonnish drawl. 'Everyone has their ups and downs. Mr Lewis and I happen to be up, but if those Whigs come in again to bring about reform, then we'll *all* of us be down.'

'Well, to be sure!' ejaculated Rosina, 'you might be an echo of Edward. He's a red-hot Radical, too.'

'A Rad —' Mary Anne turned on her sharply — 'What d'you mean by "too"? I'm no Radical, God forbid, though I have an open mind on this question of reform. It's coming and it's needed and that's what I keep on telling Wyndham. One has to move with the times, and the times are changing. The whole world is changing as it has since the beginning when those old Ancient Britons went about mother-naked, painted blue before the Greeks — or was it the Romans? — came to teach them manners. And some day someone among those parliamentary bigwigs who say all and do nothing, will up to teach *us* manners and how we should be governed. But not by Radicals, no, and not by Whigs.'

'Perhaps,' Rosina bantered prettily, 'by Mr Wyndham Lewis.'

'And better him,' flashed Mary Anne, 'than some others I could name. And if Mr Bulwer has such leanings as you say, then I say I'll withdraw my offer. I'll have naught to do with the coming into this unsettled world of another little red-hot Radical.'

'But *I* am not a Radical,' Rosina hastily assured her. 'Nor have I Edward's confidence in his political affairs. I leave all that to his odious mama. She's a professed Tory, but is so besottedly enamoured of her beloved son that she'll agree to disagree with him, except where I'm concerned — the old bitch! Just imagine, not once did she come to visit me or her grandchild, my precious little Emily, during my confinement, although she all but killed me — Emily, I mean — and she has never seen her yet. Much help can I hope from dear Mama-in-law when my time comes again. And this time,' with a look, more disgustful than tender, Rosina laid a hand against her body, 'maybe it *will* kill me, for God alone knows how we can afford to pay the midwife, let alone the doctor.'

Mary Anne got up to go. 'When do you expect?'

'Well,' Rosina allowed her eyes to wander, 'as far as one can judge, in the … the new year.'

'So soon?' A direct cool gaze raked Rosina's slender figure top to toe. 'You don't show a sign.'

'It is deceptively easy for a clever modiste, as you, my dear, should know,' was the saccharine reply, 'to disguise these little delicacies. Yes?'

Mary Anne sat down again. '*One good turn deserves another* has always been my motto, and I find it pays.'

'I fear,' Rosina smoothly said, 'that if any point of payment, or repayment, should arise from your overwhelmingly generous offer, I must be frank with you, my dearest girl, and tell you here and now that I may never, never,' she clasped her hands in prayerful gesture, 'be able to repay you, either in gratitude or —'

'I don't want repayment,' broke in Mary Anne. 'We can both be in each other's debt, come to that. Look, if I 'elp you —' in her eagerness she let fall an aitch and forgot to pick it up — 'you can 'elp me. I tell you I'm sick of lookin' through my window panes at London life. I want to be *of* it and *in* it, and I'm not. I don't mean in society. I don't give a fig for society as such, and what little I've seen of the *O Mond* don't make me anxious to see more. No. What I want is to meet people, writers, politicians, that kind of people, men — and women, too — who don't just live for playing high and drinking deep at Crockford's, nor waltzing at Almack's nor driving in the park. I can drive in the park any day in the week, *and* in my own carriage and pair. But let us, as they say in French, *retournons ah noo mootons.*' Up went Rosina's eyebrows. 'And you needn't stare. You're not the only one who can speak French, though you who've lived in France have the advantage over me of a good accent. My *mam'zelle* who gives me French lessons says my accent is *ex-ec-rable*. But you don't need a good accent to read French to yourself. I've learned a lot from La Rochefoucoo. Wasn't it Rochefoucoo who said, *C'est une grande habilitay que de savvah cachay son habilitay* — "It's a very clever thing to know how to hide one's cleverness"?'

'In which,' Rosina commented with smiles, 'you excel.'

Mary Anne lowered her lashes. 'You flatter me.'

'No one,' purred Rosina, 'could flatter *you*, my love.'

'Why, now!' Mary Anne eyed her in simple wonder. 'How well you know me. Better even than you know yourself.' An ormolu clock on the mantelshelf chimed four silvery strokes. 'For gracious' sake!' She started up. 'Is that the time? And here am I chattering away, and Wyndham's dinner, his favourite — roast loin of lamb and onion sauce — done to cinders. We never dine late unless there's company. I'll have to hurry. And remember, *One good turn*... And if it's a girl I'll be godmama, if it's a boy I won't. He might follow in his pa's footsteps as a Radical, but in any case, my dear, I'll foot the bill so you can let the bums go hang. Think it over.

Rosina thought it over to the satisfaction of them both. For, if Mrs Edward Bulwer were mistaken in her calculations or in her condition, she would not have been the first young disappointed wife. And if when she received from Mrs Wyndham Lewis a letter marked *Strictly Confidential*, containing a bank note for two hundred guineas *to await the Happy Event*, who could blame Rosina if that event were not, unhappily, forthcoming?

'I guessed as much,' said Mary Anne when Rosina tearfully confessed to this calamity. 'I knew you was marked for a miss if you ever was likely. Best put it in your stocking. You don't have to send it back. It may yet come in useful when my god-daughter arrives.'

Whether or no Rosina did put it in her stocking is debatable, but when the Bulwer's second child did eventually arrive, the girl that Mary Anne had hoped to sponsor was a boy.

TEN

The splendours of the Regency that, like some colourful lingering ghost, still haunted the corridors of memory, had vanished. King George IV was dead, and with him died the tattered remnants of that spectacular era which he had made essentially his own. As King he was scarcely known to his people; nor, during the last three years of his reign, was he seen again at Brighton, and that exuberant folly of his, the Pavilion, knew him no more.

The new King, his brother, William, who since the death of the Duke of York had become of some importance to the nation as heir presumptive to the throne, now, in his sixties, ascended it. He, too, was scarcely known to his people, having lived these last few years in almost complete seclusion at Bushey with his young duchess Adelaide.

The scandal of his long association with 'that play actress, the Jordan', in which those of a former decade had delighted, was forgotten; yet while few of his subjects had ever seen him, all knew what to expect. An amiable, somewhat eccentric old gentleman whose early youth and young manhood had been spent at sea; who had fought, but without distinction, in his father's wars and who, as Lord High Admiral, had been thrown out of office for unorthodox behaviour.

Yet there were some who saw, or hoped to see, in this fourth William, the first monarch for over a century who did not bear the name of George, a cheerful omen. England had not been lucky with her Georges; and this elderly king with his 'Goddammes', his good humour, his rolling sailor's gait and his charming, plain little wife, who so obligingly mothered his numerous bastards ranging from girls of her own age to nursery toddlers, might well be the best of a bad lot.

Thus the verdict in the clubs of St James's, while bets among the blades ran high. 'Five thousand to one there'll be another regency before the year is out. The fellow's as crazy as his father.'

General opinion feared he was.

From the moment he left Bushey on his drive to St James's for the proclamation, wearing a suit of appropriate navy blue with a black crape band round his arm, sole deference to the departed, his craziness was only too apparent.

Unrecognised along the way by the villagers of Twickenham, Putney and Hammersmith, he was hailed at Hyde Park turnpike by the toll-gate keeper, who likewise had no knowledge of this genial old gentleman's identity. Broadly smiling, the King handed him a crown piece with the jocular injunction, 'You'd best keep it. That's the last silver coin you're like to see stamped with George's head!'

It would seem his sudden glory was mounting to his own.

Yet his coronation, and by his command, was not to be remarkable for glory. He would have 'no fuss, no botheration', so, in effect rumour gave it, as from that arch-gossip, Mr Creevey. 'My brother George's crowning cost the country half a million. This is no time,' he told his ministers, 'to burden the nation with a lot of unnecessary expense.'

'Not so crazy after all.' Thus Mary Anne to her husband, who brought her this latest royal dictum from the Lobby of the House. 'And if those Whigs jibe at him for wanting to recoup old George's waste of money —'

'It is not the Whigs who jibe at him,' Wyndham glumly interposed, 'it is the Tories.'

'Well, you can't blame them for that,' she hastily capitulated. 'They'll not be so eager to back him now they look to be thrown out. Wellington has bungled badly. It was a good thing for us he resigned. Just because he's the greatest general of all time it don't go to say he's a great politician. I think it's daft to make a statesman of a soldier. Let's only hope the King won't be overruled by Grey. Even old nosey Wellington would be better than him. If Rosina is to be believed, Grey will stop at nothing to bring in reform. Mark you, it's bound to be, but not as the Whigs 'ud have it. Was ever anything so silly as this ten-pound household franchise which is part — so Rosina tells me, having it from Edward — of their Whiggish policy when, or *if*, they should come in, which for all our sakes, God send they don't.'

Wyndham cast a glance at her where she sat in a window seat fronting the park, her head bent on her needlework, an open bandbox at her side spilling silks and ribbons, artificial flowers. A smile warmed his face as he watched her, noting the glossy mouse-brown hair smoothly parted to spring in wide clusters of curls. Pretty creature! Such a child, as — despite the speeding years — he still thought of her. She had that quality of agelessness which stayed with her all her life long. The slender outlines of her figure were unchanged; her skin, petal fair and unlined; her eyes clear and, as a child's, long-lashed as when he first had seen her fifteen years ago. Yet he would never cease to wonder at and perhaps to disapprove her astonishing grasp of affairs far beyond her province or, one would have thought, her comprehension. And with the shadow of a frown behind his smile Wyndham asked, 'What are you at so busily?'

'A bonnet for the "Half-Crownation", as Edward Bulwer says they call it, whoever "they" may be. If the King can be stingy at his crowning, so can I!' Taking a large untrimmed poke from the bandbox, she placed it on her head and told him with a laughing nod, 'This won't cost me more than half a crown with all these bits and pieces I've kept by me from my overstock.' She rummaged among the bits and pieces. 'I've an ostrich feather somewhere that 'ud be just the thing. I'd like to see the procession, though I doubt me I'll have more'n a glimpse of it from a stand in Piccadilly. You wouldn't see anything but crowds from here. I suppose you as a Member will be given a seat in the abbey, but wives, of course, don't count.' And throwing aside the bonnet she went to him, saying, 'I heard something else from Rosina. Something that you ought to know. With a dissolution pending you'll have to stand again. Yes,' as she saw the doubtful negative forming on his lips, 'you must! Not for that rotten little borough of Aldeburgh — why do they call them "rotten" boroughs? — which has never been and never will be any good to you. It's finished. Not worth the salt of the sea that's swamping it. But there's another, better seat for you in store. I'll tell you —'

And she told.

'Yesterday, while Rosina and I were chattering over the teacups of the great event, her second baby — and about time, too! — Edward came in and he said that Maidstone — Wyn, do listen, this is important. Edward said that Maidstone — Wyn, do you hear? Don't look so bored. *Maidstone*, which up till now has been held by two Whigs in succession, is spoiling for a change. Edward hinted that the change might be himself. Huh! Much hope for him, or any maw-worm of a Radical.'

'Maw-worm?' queried Wyndham, eyebrows up.

'It's what Gran'fer Evans used to call the farm lads when he laid about them with his stick, as I,' she chuckled, 'would lay about the Whigs had I the voice to speak, and as you *must* have the voice to speak. You can't let Edward or a Whig walk in while you sit here twiddlin' your thumbs. I give you Maidstone, Wyn, for what it's worth, which at least may well be worth — consideration.'

Consideration, duly given, was to bring about its ultimate advantage, not only for her husband, but, far-distantly, for Mary Anne.

ELEVEN

At the window of her boudoir, a telescope glued to her eye, she took note of a newcomer in the afternoon procession passing into or out of the park. Like some recurrent figure translated to her fancy as an oft-repeated symbol in a mazy arabesque, was this singular young gentleman who, unfailingly, appeared attendant on one or other of three ladies, none of whom was known to Mary Anne. But while clearer inspection through the telescope discovered these three to be undoubted beauties, it was their escort on whom the eye of Mary Anne was fixed.

'Nina, just you take a look through here.' She handed the telescope to Nina Rook, sewing in the window seat; that same Nina, once her mother's maid-of-all-work and who, since Mary Anne's removal to London, had been her personal attendant. 'Quick! When the fourth carriage passes out — they're held up for a few minutes — I want you to tell me what you see, or if *I'm* seeing things. Sure to goodness I could swear he's wearing rings outside his gloves, his hair in curls down to his shoulders and — poppy-red pantaloons!'

Obediently Nina set aside her needlework and, taking the telescope, held it to her eye. 'I can't see naught, ma'am,' she said, screwing her face into a series of contortions.

'Silly! You have to twist it round to suit your sight. I've focused it for mine but yours'll be different. Here, let me —' Mary Anne deftly adjusted the lens. 'Now then, is that better?'

'Yes, ma'am, 'tis a bit better, but 'tis still kind o' blurry, like.'

'Then go on twisting till you get it right. Be quick, they're moving on. Now here comes the fourth carriage. Can you see him?'

'Oh, yes, ma'am, I do! Was there ever such a funny-lookin' — Rings they be, ma'am, and worn outside his gloves. An' his hair, too,' giggled Nina, 'all in ringlets black an' shinin' like a lady's, and them red pantaloons. Would 'e be one o' they play-actors, ma'am?'

'Here, give it to me.' Mary Anne snatched at the telescope, but before she could readjust the lens the carriage had passed on down Park Lane. 'If he's not a play-actor,' she said, 'he ought to be; or, likely he's a foreigner. No Englishman would make such a guy of himself.'

The lavender dusk of early spring shrouded the grassy spaces of Hyde Park, enveloping in wraith-like mist the budding tree branches, lifting skeleton arms to a dove-coloured sky. Slowly the park emptied; and, as she turned from the window to the cheerful fire-glow that lighted the darkening room, a multitudinous sound, as of a muffled roar, halted her.

She stood stock still; and Nina, the colour fled from her round pippin face, whispered, 'Sure, ma'am, it be they rioters agin.'

'Yes.' Mary Anne went back to her stance at the window, peering out. 'And some of the carriages will run into them and be held up. They've chosen the right time for it, the devils.'

'They'll be hackin' down the railings yonder, ma'am, as they done las' week, an' murder too,' said Nina, with ghoulish enjoyment. 'So be they kicked a Peeler in his private parts and cracked open the 'ead of another, as talk gives it in the servants'. All that they took him off to 'ospital where 'e died. Beasts of 'ell they be, an' God forgive me though I say it.'

'The House will be rising now.' Mary Anne tapped a fretful heel. 'I'll have no peace till your master is safe home. If those devils could set upon the Queen, as they did the other night when she was driving to St James's from the opera, they'd not scruple to attack a Tory Member.'

'Lord save us! 'Ere they come!' Nina made as if to duck beneath a table and was caught back.

'Go down and stay down. And tell the men to bolt the doors and bar the windows. Hurry.'

She hurried.

Mary Anne drew the curtains close across the panes, leaving a chink through which, with the aid of her telescope, she swept the amorphous vista of the park. All was still; no movement, nor sight of the marauders, yet that ominous sound of them persisted, coming nearer, ever nearer; until their war-cry from a thousand throats rose up to smite the air, penetrating the closed fastness of her windows... 'The Bill, the Bill, and nothing but the Bill!'

'They'll be at the turnpike now,' she muttered. 'Wellington's house is their target. Those iron shutters he put up won't help him — Lord God! What's that?' A louder uproar and a splintering crash broke the quiet of the room.

'Madam!' Her butler, a man of natural calm, stood in the doorway. 'The mob are riotin' at the gates of H'apsley 'Ouse and smashin' the windows of all H'anti-reformers along 'ere in Park Lane. May I suggest it is not safe for madam to stand behind glass?'

She wheeled round. 'Send word at once to your master at the House that he must wait until the rioters disperse. But don't send a man in livery lest he be set upon.'

'Very good, madam.'

He had performed his duty as head of the staff, and in his master's absence. If madam chose to ignore his advice the responsibility was hers, not his. But as he bowed and withdrew she called to him, 'No. I won't have him go, neither. The mob is fighting mad. They'd do him a mischief, livery or no. Listen.' Another shattering of glass, and yells of 'Down with the Duke! Up with the Bill!' rang out in mutineering savagery.

'What on earth,' cried Mary Anne, 'can those Peelers be about to let them run riot like this? Is there no law and order in the — And now what's that?'

'That' was a clatter of hooves and wheels below to send her flying to the window. Pulling the curtains apart she saw the carriage drawn up to the kerb and, in a stream of light from the open doorway, Wyndham carefully descending. 'God be thanked,' she breathed, 'he's home.' And within seconds was down the stairs and in the hall to meet him. 'Here's a nice to-do! I wonder they let you through… I've been so anxious.'

'I told Thomas to take a roundabout route to avoid them. These outbreaks are very disagreeable.' Handing his hat to a lackey while another relieved him of his coat, 'The fuse is lit,' he said, 'to set the Bill aflame. Lord John Russell sprang a march on us today, and Grey is closeted now with the King. Another general election looks to be in the offing.'

'And so does your seat for Maidstone.' She breathed a long sigh of relief. 'You must be tired out after all this. You had best go to bed. I'll have a meal brought to you there.'

A dish of broiled chicken laced with a bottle of wine and a rum souffle to follow were served to him. She sat on the bed while he ate.

'Do you not have any?' he asked her.

'I'll have something later. I'm not hungry.' Nor would she let him tell her of the session in the House. 'I can hear all from you tomorrow. Rest now and forget it. We'll beat those Whigs and that little viper, Lord John. I've faith in this new King. He's dead set against reform, and more than ever since that attack on the poor little Queen — if only Grey don't get at him, soft-soaping. Eat up your souffle, it'll spoil else. He's a good chef, that one, even though he is a Frenchie. I wonder why the French are always so much better than us in cookery.'

'And what of you, my dear? Won't you try it?'

'I don't like the taste of rum. I ordered it special for you. I'll have a glass of wine.' And as she sipped she thought: *Bless him, he takes all this too much to heart;* and her own heart twisted to see the thinning hair turned grey at his temples, and a pale tinge about his lips.

'Wyn,' she told him, casually, for she knew him nervous of his health, 'I wish you'd see Sir Henry. I think you need a tonic. All this bother with the Bill is so fatiguing.'

'I have no need to see a doctor. And it's not the Bill — it's this sitting all day on a hard bench —' He rubbed his back in the lumbar region where it ached.

But he did not tell her that only the day before he had consulted Sir Henry Halford who had warned him, 'If you want to make old bones you will go easy. Your heart is not so good as it should be. I detect a murmur — no, no, nothing serious, but take care of it. None of us is a steam engine, you know.'

Propped by pillows, a stone hot-water bottle placed by Mary Anne against his back, he recalled Sir Henry Halford's words. *Steam engine...* More change in this swiftly changing world. And idly watching her while she made herself ready for bed, her long hair falling loose about her shoulders, 'These railways,' he murmured. 'You will live to see the iron horse replace the horse of flesh, but I ... may not.'

'See what?' At her dressing table, combing out her curls, she paused to find him in her looking-glass still with that paleness about his mouth, and gazing into space. Staying her comb in mid-air she said again, and fearfully, 'What is it you may not, God forbid, live to see?'

'I was thinking — here, take this thing away. It's burning me.'

She removed the bottle and told him, 'I'll give your back a rub.'

'No, not now. You can tomorrow if it isn't better. Egad! I'd sooner a whole day and night in the saddle than six hours on a bench — I was thinking of these new railroads they're building. No good can come of such a monstrous innovation.'

'Tempting providence, I call it.' Mary Anne laid down the comb, let fall her wrapper and stood there in her long-sleeved lace frilled nightdress. 'What next, for goodness' sake, will they invent?'

'The tempo of the world,' Wyndham said, 'is set to speed.'

'Well, if that's so, I wish all you anti-reformers would speed yourselves to outrace the Whigs and their precious Bill. All this palaver and then what's to do?' She picked up her dressing gown and laid it on a chair. 'Another election, with the Tories thrown out unless they put up a fight. But they *won't* fight. They're too gentleman-like. What we want is one who'll stand up and slash at them with his tongue to give 'em back as good, or as bad, as they give. I only hope,' she added with a side glance at him — *So peaked! He ought to take a tonic* — 'that you'll not find the strain of the next campaign too much for you.'

He gave her his indulgent smile. 'It won't be too much for me. It may be too much for you, since it is never Wyndham Lewis but his wife who wins his seat.'

She dimpled at him. 'Go along! I only do what any wife who's worth her salt 'ud do.'

'But not any wife who may be worth her salt knows *how* to do... That's a very pretty nightdress you are wearing.'

'Do you like it? I made it myself. As for knowing how to do, like you was saying, that's because most wives don't bother to know *what* to do, outside of their own homes; but of course, if they have children their place is *in* the home, and not gallivantin' up and down the country cryin' "Vote for him!" I'm the exception since I haven't any children, nor ... which reminds me.' She crossed to her dressing table to snuff the candles on it; then turned down a lamp, and came over to the bedside. 'I had a letter from John today. He has a month's furlough and wants to spend a few days of it with us.'

'With the price,' Wyndham grimly suggested, 'of a horse and a woman thrown in.'

'What a thing to say!' cried Mary Anne indignantly. 'As if he would.'

'As if he wouldn't,' muttered Wyndham.

She groped her way into bed and with her cheek on the pillow said, 'I've been thinking we might rope him in to do some canvassing at Maidstone.'

'Rope?' queried Wyndham of the darkness.

'*Bring* him in then, to the hustings. His voice 'ud carry like a foghorn being used to shout orders on parade... Oh, no, Wyn, you're too tired... Must you?'

'Yes.' His lips crushed down upon her shrinking mouth. 'I must.'

TWELVE

During the spring and summer of 1831 the current topic of talk in St James's was not the pending coronation but the political crisis. The general election, that returned the first Whig Ministry for three and twenty years, had resulted in a general combustion. From Land's End to John o' Groats the United Kingdom thundered with the repercussional effects of the fight between the Tories and the Whigs, while the future of Britain hung in the balance to make of democracy the triumphant emergence of enduring liberties, or the most colossal blunder in the history of politics.

That the Tory banner, unfurled by Lewis at Maidstone, lost him the day by forty-eight votes in a total of fourteen thousand, was not for want of effort on the part of Mary Anne.

As in the past she turned her glib verbosity to her husband's cause; and more than that, her bank balance, the pin money with which he so lavishly supplied her on condition that she didn't give it all to John who was, as usual, badgering her for a loan.

'No fear!' Wyndham was assured. 'I'm done with helping John. We know money opens doors, but I've opened Johnny's door once too often. I now want every penny you — and I — can spare to *bolt* the doors of those damned Whigs who —'

'Damned?' Wyndham's eyes bulged slightly. 'My dear child!'

'Damned they are and damned they will be — to perdition before I've finished with them.'

'Or unless,' Wyndham gloomily inhaled snuff, 'they finish me.'

'Not,' said Mary Anne, 'if I can help it.'

They stayed at an inn in Maidstone for election week, when, taking John with her on the eve of the poll, she was moved to slide a twenty-pound note into his pocket — 'For drinks to the voters in the taverns, and don't you dare put it on a horse,' she warned him and came back, although uncertainly defeated, in fighting fettle to the last.

'The scurvy hounds! I doubt if we'll get in at the telling.' So she ragefully reported to Wyndham. 'They're playing reform for all they're worth. What do you think they threw down as their trump card?'

'Well,' Wyndham twinkled, 'and what?'

Dramatically flinging up an arm, '"We'll draw the sword of reform,"' she recited, '"to knock out the eyes of all nomination borough men. You've been robbed of your rights —"' This, from him on the platform in the market place, and as squint-eyed hank o' gallows meat as ever I did see. I was standing by while you was addressing your lot from outside the town hall.'

At which Wyndham, red-flushed, thumped a fist on a small table at his elbow and upset his coffee cup. 'I will not have you stand alone among those hooligans!'

'I was not alone. I had John with me. And now look here what you've done.' Mopping up the spilt coffee with her handkerchief, 'They'll make us pay for that,' she said, '*and* through the nose! They're red-hot Whigs in this inn. And you don't have to fuss. I can look after myself. Besides, I'm too small to be noticed in a crowd. As for John, standing head and shoulders higher than me and almost all of those reforming — or should I say, performing — beasts, he'd have been a match for any one of 'em. And he was, too, the way he let out a yell to take the Whig's words from his mouth and fling them back, as I'd already primed him. "Dolts! Idiots!" roared John. "Don't you be hoodwinked by false promises and hopes. Do you want to plunge your country into civil war? For it'll come, sure as fate, if you follow-me-leader to lead you into lawlessness and the overthrow, may God forbid, of Monarchy. I," shouted John at 'em, "have fought to win your wars, and we've never been defeated yet in a fair fight." I wish you could have heard him. I'd set him going and he couldn't stop. A tendency,' she said with laughter in her eyes, 'which is common to the Evanses. We're all talkers, once we get going. And believe me, John got going with a voice on him to drown the Whig's, who stood on the platform with his mouth moving, but no words coming from it that could be heard above John's shouting and the booing and the yelling.

'If,' pronounced Wyndham sententiously, 'I had known you would lay yourself open to —'

'Be quiet. I didn't lay myself open to anything. I — or rather John and me together — laid the Whig open, if you like! Hung, drawn and quartered he was, the whey-faced louse.'

Wyndham shuddered.

'I tell you,' disregardful of the shudder she went careering on, 'he hadn't a bite left in him before we'd done. And when, at his last gasp, he pops up squealing, "Every man under *us* will govern himself with the right to vote," "What good will that do him?" says John. "A vote won't fill his empty belly nor give him the price of a loaf of bread." (That was me again.) "If the Whigs come in they'll be making laws to break the laws and to break you!" But for all we done — I mean did — I'm afraid we haven't got 'em,' she disconsolately added. 'You should have seen their ugly faces swarmin' round us. They booed John and me, the whole pack o' them.'

Again Wyndham thumped his fist. 'I do *not* approve of you taking part in this electioneering. Suppose you had been recognised as the wife of the Tory candidate, rubbing shoulders with that rabble?'

'Well, and suppose? It's the rabble vote we want, isn't it? We'll need all sorts to bring you in — that is, if we *do* bring you in.'

'John,' pronounced Wyndham with frigid persistence, 'had no right to take you there.'

'He didn't. I took him. I've done it before and I'll do it again. What do you fancy for your supper? You can have gammon and spinach or loin of lamb with onion sauce, or both.'

Wyndham gave up. 'Whatever you please, my dear.'

Despite Wyndham's defeat as candidate for Maidstone he had earned the respect of his fellow Tories in the House. While they were all agreed that his star was unlikely to shine in a galaxy, its steady if faint glimmer gave promise of unalterable permanence, as witness the poor majority gained by the Whig at Maidstone. There were some, doubtless prompted by Lady Cork, last survivor of the *Ancien Régime*, who suggested Wyndham Lewis owed his previous constituency to his wife, 'that voluble, pushing young person!' ('And not so young, neither,' was the verdict of those Tory wives whose husbands had also lost their seats in the recent triumph of the Whigs.)

Yet if her own sex shrugged disdainful shoulders at the Bulwers' Mary Anne, the men — as their women were chagrined to discover — seemed to be absurdly magnetised. So soon did she appear at a dinner, soirée, ball, outlandishly dressed, her hair in those ridiculous exaggerated curls, she was surrounded. Even D'Orsay, a charmer not easily charmed, would forsake his Blessington to dance attendance on *'la petite*

Louise', so did he gracefully effeminise her married name. As for Edward Bulwer, he encouraged her to tell — out of Wyndham's earshot — risqué, near to ribald little tales with a wide-eyed naivety to convulse her audience… Well, but what could you expect of one born in the gutter, or next door to it?

'The little Lewis', according to Rosina, had come under the protection of the estimable Wyndham, who had apprenticed her to millinery. This semi-factual hypothesis offered some varied convergence. Lewis had first seen and followed her, walking barefoot to and from a needle factory in Bristol, where she had been employed as a 'hand', this based on talk possibly originated from the Pantgwynlais contingent. And how she had managed to snaffle him, unless by a false bait, who. could tell? Certainly not those ladies who sat unpartnered at a rout and in far less demand for the waltz than *la petite Louise*, chattering away to D'Orsay in her appalling French and in an accent even worse than was her English. As for her brother, this Major Evans, so-called — suddenly produced for the coronation and with not the least resemblance between them — but that fatuous husband of hers would swallow anything.

Having passed unscathed through similar fires in those early days at Clifton, Mary Anne went undisturbed by Rosina's kindly warning.

'As your friend, I tell you, love, that scandalous reports concerning your personal life in the past are bruited everywhere. You could bring, or at least you should threaten, an action for slander to put an end to this evil talk.'

'Better be talked about evilly,' smiled Mary Anne, 'than never to be talked about at all. Pray, my dear,' she offered her a box of bonbons, 'try one of these marshmallows made by my chef. They are delicious. No? Do you fear to grow fat?'

'I am giving you some sound advice which you can take or leave, but in your own interests,' rejoined Rosina sharply, pricked by that reference to 'fat', 'I suggest you do not trespass on *too* many private preserves.'

Mary Anne, still smiling, popped into her mouth a marshmallow. 'Whose preserves? Yours?'

'The Blessington and D'Orsay,' continued Rosina disdaining this enquiry, 'are coming to my soirée tomorrow and you will do well to discourage his attentions lest she turn hers more markedly to Edward, as tit for tat to her pimp!' She broke into laughter, unmirthful. 'He sits at her feet and reads *Eugene Aram* to her by the hour while he lays her eulogies as balm to the wounds inflicted by the savage attacks of the critics, most of whom are Tory scouts who will never forgive or forget his easy triumph at St Ives. Cornwall is fiercely for reform — My darling!' This endearment was addressed, not to Mary Anne, but to the toy spaniel she nursed on her knee. She was always surrounded by dogs that she professed to love better than humans. 'But in spite of the critics and their determined efforts to kill *Eugene* — only because Edward is an outstanding success and they, the critics, are for the most part disgruntled would-be authors who can't find a publisher for their muck — in *spite* of their beastliness, Edward holds the heart of the reading public. But that is not enough for him. Oh, no. He must have adulation, and the Blessington lays it on thick. So, my dear, the more you flirt with D'Orsay, who doesn't care two pins for you or any woman, not even his wife — in name only, poor child, being still a virgin as everyone knows — so will the Blessington try to win her mincing fribble back to her by using Edward as a foil. I tell you —' Rosina twisted the necklace at her throat in such a gust of fury that the string broke, scattering pearls in all directions.

'Lucky this is a carpeted and not a polished floor,' calmly remarked Mary Anne, down on hands and knees to gather fallen pearls, 'they'd have rolled all over the place, else.' She gathered a handful and scrambled to her feet. 'I think I've found them all. The rest are still on the string.'

Rosina shrugged an indifferent shoulder. 'It is of no consequence. They are only imitation. My real pearls are with *mon oncle*, and I have not the cash to redeem them.' Taking the pearls she dropped them in her reticule. 'I've had to dismiss my marvel of a chef, which reminds me...' Thoughtfully starry-eyed, Rosina touched a finger to her lips, 'I wonder if I dare ... no,' determinedly she shook her head, 'I daren't. It is too much of a presumption —'

'If,' prompted Mary Anne, 'you wish to borrow Pierre for your rout tomorrow night, you have already dared — a week ago. I told you then that I would ask him, and I have. And he won't.'

'How vile of him!' screamed Rosina.

'But,' Mary Anne coolly continued, 'I have ordered him to make you some cold dishes for your buffet — oyster patties, mousse of salmon, jellied chickens trimmed with truffles and something he calls *l'aspic de blanc de volay* — but don't ask me what it means. I'll have them sent round to you tomorrow morning in a hamper.'

'You precious dear!' Placing the dog on a cushion Rosina bounced up from the settee to embrace her. 'You are the most angelic of all creatures! Only you must, you positively *must* allow me to pay you for these delicacies. Yes?'

'Yes,' unexpectedly assented Mary Anne. 'But not in coin.'

The last round in the battle for reform had reached its height, yet never had the season of parties, balls and dinners been more feverishly gay. At the houses of Lady Blessington and Mrs Edward Bulwer, those two rival hostesses of Mayfair, the lower Tories and the higher Whigs met and intermingled, their swords, for the meantime, amicably sheathed.

And to the most brilliant of these assemblies at the Bulwers' house in Hertford Street on an April evening in 1832, Mr and Mrs Wyndham Lewis were impressively announced by one of half a dozen hired flunkeys in red plush.

Light from a myriad candles struck rainbow sparks from crystal chandeliers on jewelled throats and heads, casting metallic gleams on scarves of gold and silver gauze, to die away amid the folds of multi-coloured satin; bathing a shoulder in shadow or defining the feature of a face, none lovelier there than Rosina's.

Exquisite in amber, her sleek dark hair drawn from her forehead in a Grecian knot at the back of her head, she stood with Edward to receive her guests. The cacophony of women's voices, high and shrill as starlings, rose above the deep subdued murmur of their attendant men. More subdued, too, were the pastel greys and blues and buffs of their swallow-tailed suits harmoniously blended with that fragmentary mosaic.

Her hand tucked in the crook of Wyndham's arm, Mary Anne surveyed the room, or as much as she could see of it for the increasing crowd.

'Ah, the little Lewis! I've been lookin' for you everywhere. What a jamboree.' With a perfunctory nod for Wyndham, Lady Cork was at her elbow, a startlingly youthful figure in a full-skirted ankle-length gown *à la Taglione*. This octogenarian countess had, in her heyday, been a beauty and a toast; and now, although her world of a past century had vanished, she stayed, as might some ancient monument, mellowed but unmarred by the relentless touch of ages. Her teeth had fallen out, her mouth had fallen in and she wore a flaxen wig and jewels worthy of an empress. Forthright, diminutive, with a ready wit, a readier tongue and a deep gruff voice, surprisingly inapposite, issuing from so small a body, she had pounced on Mary Anne to say, 'I hoped ye'd be here. I like you and your lavender eyes.' Her own, set in a network of wrinkles, whimsically explored the droll little figure with its wide bunched curls and self-made conspicuous candy-pink gown. 'You have that something about you,' quacked the dowager, 'which in my day would have made men want to wring your neck or tumble you.' She put up a quizzing glass. 'Here's Melbourne, all eyes for Caroline Norton. He has a *tendresse* for a Caroline. His first was a handful if you like! But she died in his arms with Byron's name on her lips. 'Mad, bad, and dangerous —' So he was, and so was she. This Caroline's a granddaughter of Dick Sheridan. Pity 'tis a man must die to live. He hadn't a rag to his back nor a groat in his purse when they laid him in the abbey to rank with the immortals. There's irony for you, and trouble on the brew now for Norton. He's not one to be cuckolded. Ha! that's a word long out o' your reckoning, hey? Yet when I was a girl the lads still used to sing it, "Cuckolds all awry". It was a century old even then.'

Up went the quizzing glass again. 'D'you see that bolt-eyed, pudden-faced fellow sidling round Melbourne and the Norton? That's Creevey — the devil of a Whig — ears wide to grub up all he can and what he can't he'll guess at. Here, let's sit. My legs aren't so spry as yours that I can stand on 'em for hours. The Blessin'ton is getting up from that settee. We had best go take it.' And as if starting for a marathon, the lady made off on the arm of Wyndham with Mary Anne hard put to keep the pace.

'She's a good-lookin' piece, is the Blessin' as they call her,' squawked the dowager at the top of her voice. 'Seduced at fifteen and married to a madman before she hooked Blessin'ton, and he scarce dead and buried when she digs her claws into her stepdaughter's pimpish husband. No good'll come of *that*. She's gettin' stout. D'Orsay don't like 'em stout. Here, is it true,' the lady made a cut with her fan at the starched frill of Wyndham's shirt front, '*you* ought to know, or I'll lay your wife knows better — Bute says she won your seat for you at Cardiff — that Grey is on his knees to the King begging him create peers from the Whigs, and so pass the Bill through the Lords? Sharp practice, hey? But our Billy is not to be caught. There's more sense in one of his gouty big toes than in the whole bulk of his brothers.'

'The creation of peers has, I believe, been suggested by Lord Grey,' was Wyndham's cautious answer, 'but His Majesty, I understand, is obdurate.'

'Long may he remain so!' And with such vehemence did the lady wag her head that a cluster of curls pinned to the wig fell off, and in their falling were retrieved by Mary Anne.

'The deuce take my woman!' cried her ladyship. 'Obleege me by stickin' 'em on again, my dear.' Then, as, stifling her giggles, Mary Anne 'obleeged', 'I'd have had the creature in the stocks for this, some twenty years ago, but not now, oh, no, not now. Our dependents are our equals or as near as dammit now, thanks to these tub-thumpin' Radicals and what-not, preaching brotherhood of man a-top of barrels at street corners. String 'em up, I say, on the nearest gallows tree. They're traitors to the monarchy. And what a monarchy, God save the mark! A lot o' crossbred guzzlin' Germans. We've never had a true blue English monarch since the days of Brandy Nan, as they used to call her — but that was even before *my* time. Drat my teeth!'

The dowager covered her mouth and, through her fingers, superfluously mumbled, 'They're new. They don't fit. I'll have to take 'em out.'

And with shocking nonchalance she took them out, lifted her overskirt and slid them in the pocket of her petticoat; then, side-glassing the company, she delightedly exclaimed, 'Hah, there he is! My latest beau, back from the Grand Tour and making a bee-line for the Norton. How she does pick 'em out — or pick 'em up? Have you read his new book? Full o' dukes. Much he knows of dukes — knows more of duchesses, from all accounts. But clever, no denyin'. I must catch him quick before he's grabbed.' And with astonishing agility the dowager darted away.

'I wish I might grow old as young as that,' said Mary Anne.

'H'm.' Wyndham took snuff and remarked, 'How soon can we leave? This looks as if it will go on all night.'

'Mr Lewis, sir, a word with you.

One whom she recognised as Sir Charles Wetherall, a short, squat, florid gentleman, Recorder for Bristol, buttonholed Wyndham to launch forth on a diatribe against the recent reform riots in that city. Supported by a cavalcade of magistrates and Tory squires, he had made an imprudent public entry, with disastrous result to which a purple bruise over one swollen eyelid and a plaster on his forehead bore token. 'Sir!' In Wyndham's down-bent ear he exhaled his fury. 'If I tell you that the constables were overpowered by the mob, the railings of the Mansion House torn up and used as weapons, along with brickbats, stones, hurled at us, as I, Goddamme' — the splenetic knight touched his plaster tenderly — 'have cause enough to know with six stitches, sir, sewn into me. 'Pon honour, Mr Lewis —'

Mary Anne's attention wandered. The company, now somewhat less congested, had formed into groups. Lady Blessington, surrounded by her worshippers and that nasty Mr Creevey, his gossiping tongue hanging out, waiting for an opportunity to make himself seen and heard; that rumbustious O'Connell, too, the Irish Radical, bawling his anarchistic views — -just hark at him! I wonder at Edward bringing him here. Rosina'll have at him for this, you bet!

'*Madame! Enchanté!*'

Perfumed, becurled, bewhiskered, arbiter of elegance in lilac, with primrose pantaloons and a waistcoat of silver brocade, D'Orsay bowed before her, lifting to his reddened lips her mittened hand. A hasty downward glance revealed a trace of scarlet on her knuckles. A dimple hovered at the corner of her mouth.

'*Ay bien, M'sew le Comte, common sa vah?*'

'The better, madame, for this so charming sight of you.'

'Go along!' She unfurled a highly coloured silken fan where rather wooden shepherds and shepherdesses sported in *a fête champêtre.*

'*Ah, mais! Ça c'est exquise!*' with gushful insincerity cried D'Orsay. 'After Watteau, is it not?'

'A very long time after What-oh, I should think,' said Mary Anne; for in truth it was one of those trifles salvaged from her overstock-in-trade and which, although quite valueless, she still cherished from sentiment.

D'Orsay ran an experienced eye over this so comical *petite bourgeoise* in just the wrong shade of pink, the heart-shaped bodice seductively pointed below the slender waist, two upstanding sprays of flowers perched among the bows of silver ribbon in her not-too-well-coiffed hair. But her skin! '*Délicieuse,*' exclaimed D'Orsay, '*comme le pétale d'une rose.*' From his fingertips he wafted her a kiss; and, his eyes probing lower to the valley of her breasts where a provocative ruche of lace suggested more than was meant to conceal, 'You make hungry —' he murmured ardently — 'how is it your Shakespeare says? — you make hungry where most you satisfy. *Mais!* He shrugged his immaculate shoulders, 'The mere sight of you can never satisfy. It can only make more hungry.'

'*M'sew le Comte,*' her gaze sliding past the fulsome D'Orsay, 'who,' she demanded, 'is that article draped against the mantelshelf in the canary-coloured waistcoat and green velvet trews, engaged with Lady Cork? I see him everywhere.'

'He?' Following her glance D'Orsay protruded a petulant lip. He was unused to indifferent response to his advances. 'Yes, you *will* see him everywhere. He is our latest *arriviste*, and much *en faveur* with the ladies. They adore him.'

'*Ayvidemong,*' she said, cuttingly, 'but if he is not too much *"en faveur"* with these adoring ladies, I wish you to present him — to me.'

'He will be honoured.' Beneath the careful rouge on his cheekbones, the vexed D'Orsay pinkened. '*Attendez un petit moment, chère madame.*' He turned to thread his way among the groups of guests to him whose macassared ringlets almost swept his shoulders, whose rings of semi-precious stones were worn outside his white kid gloves, and whose bevy of adorers, resenting interruption, ceased at D'Orsay's approach, to adore.

What a sight! He's like something from a circus, reflected Mary Anne, watching D'Orsay stoop to whisper in his ear. He turned his head and then his eyes, full and dark, on hers to hold them; and at that look, warm and glowing, a queer emotion seized her; the briefest pause in time as if the past, the present, and the future met and for one fleeting second fused.

She stood, her breath quickening between her parted lips as he crossed the room, panther-swift, in the wake of D'Orsay.

'Madame,' D'Orsay fluttered his fingers and eyelids from one to the other, 'allow me to present...'

Bowing, eyes lowered, eyes up, hand on heart, 'I am charmed,' said young Mr Disraeli.

THIRTEEN

From Benjamin Disraeli to his sister Sarah, April 28th, 1832:

The soirée last night at Bulwer's was really brilliant ... Many ladies of distinction there. I was introduced 'by particular desire' to Mrs Wyndham Lewis; a pretty little woman, a flirt and a rattle, indeed gifted with a volubility I should think unequalled and of which I can convey no idea...

Faced for the first time with him whom she had so often viewed from afar, her 'volubility' may have been increased by nervousness or determination to impress the unimpressionable.

'I hear you have just returned from the Grand Tour. What a *won*derful experience, and *how* I envy you,' said she in accents tonnishly italicised.

At which, with no expression save boredom in his face, he offered her an arm. 'If madam would care to take refreshment?'

To the buffet in the dining room, now virtually deserted, he conducted her, placed her on a settee, summoned a footman. She demanded oyster patties and champagne; and while she sipped, munched, and ceaselessly 'rattled', he stood and silently surveyed her.

'Pray, Mr Disraeli, be seated.'

'Thank you, ma'am, I prefer to stand.'

'You must tell me of your travels. Where did your in — your in*tin*eray take you? Did you go to Greece and Turkey? I would give my heart to go to Turkey and visit the harems. Did you visit the — no, of course, the only gentlemen allowed in there are the Sultan and those fat what-you-may-call-'ems, as in the Arabian Nights. I have read all about them in a French translation of the original Persian, or would it be Arabic? Very improper. I expect you will be writing a book of your adventures. Do have an oyster patty. I can highly recommend them. My chef's — um — Rosina's oyster patties are delicious.'

'I do not care for oysters.'

A lengthy pause. She tried again, brightly.

'I read *all* your *marvellous* books,' said she who had not read either of them; but she had read one scathing review of *The Young Duke*, the single exception to the paeons of praise from other literary critics, and which suggested to *Parasites, sycophants, toad-eaters and tuft-hunters, this book as full of comfort to their calling.* Reversing the charge against it to extol, she lavishly quoted from Rosina's hosanna to the works of Edward. 'Such eloquence, such brilliant sardonic — er — humour, such courage of attack! You should stand for Parliament. My husband stands for Parliament, but the Whig beat him last time. Dare one ask where *your* sympathies lie? Your writing so cleverly disguises them that one cannot tell which party you favour, Whig or Tory?'

That, she judged, was safely non-committal, and his rejoinder disconcertingly oblique. 'I am undeserving of your grace.'

'Come, sir,' she tapped a toe, 'I ask — are you a Whig or a Tory?'

He appeared to ruminate. 'Am I a Whig or a Tory? I forget. As a Tory I admire antiquity.' His low-lidded glance wandered to the door, where Lady Cork on Bulwer's arm was animatedly telling him, 'What do you think? My old parrot, which is at least my age and that I always thought to be a he, has laid an egg!' Disraeli's eyes returned to Mary Anne's. 'Or should one say, an admirable ruin?'

She smothered a giggle. 'Sir, for shame!'

And, as if there had been no digression, 'Yes,' he continued, 'I think I am a Tory, but then the Whigs give such good dinners.'

'I,' she said, 'can give you a better dinner at my house, if I may have the pleasure of your company, than you would have in that of any Whig.'

The only response to this was another bow, another pause, and: 'I wonder.' Laconically he smoothed back a ringlet that had strayed from the parting on his temple to fall across his cheek. 'The best dinners I have eaten were not served in Whig or Tory mansions, nor in a Sultan's palace, but in a chop-house hard by Seven Dials, a locality as far removed from Mayfair as hell from heaven is. Yet the Tories are so moral, and morality,' the merest gleam of a smile dawned behind that sardonic mask of his, 'has always been my *forte*, but the Whigs dress so much better than the Tories.'

'In which case,' slyly she looked him over from his jet black perfumed hair to the sparkling buckles on his shoes, 'you must be a Whig, for your dress would appear to be as much your fortay as your morals, of which I can know nothing, since in your books,' she hazarded a guess, to scratch him on the raw, 'you seem never to write of yourself.'

And watching a dusky flush mount to his eyebrows she demurely added, 'I am confident that modesty is the surest road to success. Pray, sir,' her remarkably even white teeth became visible, 'do not think me presumptuous, if I say that I appreciate your reluctance to write of yourself, to speak of yourself, or indeed, unless urged, to speak at all. For my part,' her lashes flickered, 'I confess I prefer a silent melancholy man.'

'I have no doubt,' said he, drily, 'of that.'

On the short drive home with Wyndham, 'I hope,' said Mary Anne, 'you were not too bored with that tiresome Sir Charles. I cannot say that I was greatly entertained by Mr Disraeli whose manners, if not his wits, are wanting.'

'At least Mr Disraeli's attention to you for almost the whole evening,' Wyndham said frostily, 'was by no means wanting.'

'Attention — I like that!' she retorted. 'He would barely condescend to *look* at me, let alone talk to me. A conceited young jackanapes, that's what he is.'

The carriage drew up at the kerb. A footman handed her out, while Wyndham stayed to give an order to the coachman. 'And what a name,' she resumed when Wyndham joined her in the hall. 'Is his name as much a pose as all the rest of him?'

'His name,' replied Wyndham, 'speaks for him and his race. He is a Jew.'

'Oh!' She half turned to say across her shoulder as she mounted the stairs, 'That, then, accounts for all. I never thought … good gracious me! A Jew.'

It came as a shock. The only Jew with whom, hitherto, she had been very briefly acquainted was a certain purveyor of second-hand goods in a slum quarter of Bristol. She remembered him as a bearded individual with a nose like a scimitar, a dewdrop on the end of it and a touching tale of a crippled wife and six young children. To him she had sold, at the time of her marriage, the entire contents of her salon for a guinea the lot; a counterfeit guinea as it proved to be, and his tale as false as his coin. For, as she subsequently heard from Mr Yate, this Jewish gentleman was not only a bachelor and, presumably, childless, but the wealthy owner of some profitable holdings in the lowest slum quarters of Bristol. She took it hardly and vowed henceforth to be wary of Jews. And now Mr Disraeli…

'But,' said Rosina when, over the teacups, the question arose, 'he isn't a Jew. He's a Christian. He and his brothers and sister were baptised when they were children. There was some fuss to do with the synagogue, whose elders made their father a warden without his consent, and then when old Isaac — the father — wrote an abusive letter of refusal they fined him forty pounds for it, or so Edward told me. He knows more of Disraeli than I do, for I detest the creature, and wouldn't have him in my house but for Edward's insistence. He adores him, as so do all these fools of women who sicken me the way they crawl at his feet. Caroline Norton raves over his "beauty". Beauty! I've seen,' declared Rosina, 'a better-looking toad.'

Mary Anne sucked in her underlip. 'Foreign-looking, maybe. I would have thought him Italian, but never a Jew.'

'My dear, the man's a mountebank, a charlatan. A flash in the pan, here today and gone tomorrow...'

Tomorrow and tomorrow, a succession of tomorrows, and still he was not gone. He stayed, and continue to flash.

No function was complete unless graced by his presence; the desk in his chambers at Duke Street, St James's, was strewn with invitations from feminine devotees; his rooms blossomed with their floral tributes, and when Lady Cork proclaimed him 'the best ton in town' his social success was assured.

Mothers of not-so-young unmarried daughters, discarding racial prejudice, cast speculative eyes at Disraeli whose latest novels *Contarini Fleming*, published in 1832, and *Alroy* in '33, must have brought him in, they guessed, a pretty penny; besides that his father was said to have inherited a fortune. But if 'Dizzy', as the ladies fondly called him, toyed with the idea of marriage, *As for love,* he wrote to sister Sarah, *all my friends who have married for love either beat their wives or live apart from them...*

Had he in mind the cat and dog existence of the Bulwers? *I may commit many follies in life, but I never intend to marry for love.*

Nor did he intend to marry at all. Life's unfettered exploration was far too exciting an adventure to renounce for domesticity. He was no longer silent or melancholy now. He lived in a whirl of febrile enjoyment that brought from his father an ironical rebuke: *I wish your organisation allowed you to write calmer letters.*

Calm! How could he be calm with fame at his elbow and leading politicians glancing covertly in his direction? *Nature has given me an awful ambition and fiery passions,* he confided to the diary his father urged him to keep, that he might 'sober down' before he went to bed.

If his 'fiery passions' led him to an amorous intrigue with a young person of the name of Henrietta, his 'awful ambition' was to lead him further still.

The turning point came in that fateful spring of '32 when at a stag dinner party, he found himself seated at table beside Sir Robert Peel. Here was a man born, not of noble blood but, as himself, of the wealthy middle classes, whose father had bought him a seat in Parliament and who, at the age of three and twenty, had become secretary of state. One, who, if the Tories should win the next election, would be prime minister.

Peel most gracious, he reported to the doting Sarah, *a very great man indeed … Yet I observed that he attacked his turbot with his knife.* A solecism that placed him a rung lower on the social ladder than even his admiring young acolyte. And recalling the great Peel's graciousness, why, he demanded, should not he, Disraeli, enter Parliament? He reviewed his situation, weighing carefully his assets against his liabilities. In his case there could be no question of a bought seat, since, despite the generous allowance made him by his father, he was up to his ears in debt and had been forced to borrow from certain of his brethren in Crutched Friars. He had no background nor status other than that of society's darling, and his notoriety as a fashionable novelist. He was an outsider, a foreigner, a Jew: Christianised no doubt, but still a Jew. These his liabilities. His assets? Only one; unswerving belief in himself.

He haunted the gallery of the House of Commons; he listened to the speeches of statesmen whose names rang round the world of politics, but whose blue blood from which those names had sprung paled to insignificance beside the royal purple blood of Judah. They, who when his ancestors were kings, were woad-painted barbarians. *Angels, not Angles.* Yes, one might admire their blond hair, their fine features, broad shoulders, deportment. *But between ourselves,* he told Sarah, *I could floor them all with my devil of a tongue.* He was confident he could *carry everything before me in that House.*

He had yet to find a seat in it.

'What do you think?' Whispers flew behind the fans at every rout. 'Dizzy is standing for High Wycombe as a Radical.'

A Radical!

'I'll never speak to him again,' cried Mary Anne when she heard this latest news from Lady Cork.

'You will be lucky if *he* speaks to *you* again,' was the dowager's reply to that. 'He is more than ever cocksurely in demand since his sensational appearance on the porch of the Red Lion at High Wycombe. Never has that village seen the like of him.'

He was the talk not only of 'that village' but of London Town from Mile End to Mayfair. Mary Anne, ears tingling, heard how 'Dizzy' in his pre-election speech had burst upon the gaping yokels in a fantasia of frills, knee-breeches, black velvet coat lined with pink satin, a gold-headed cane, and the curls.

The stupefied natives of Wycombe who stood up-staring at this astounding apparition were further astonished to hear, not the puerile mincing speech they had expected, but a powerful torrent of eloquence delivered in a voice that carried far along the High Street. His reception was terrific.

I made them all mad, he bragged to Sarah. *A great many absolutely cried. I have never made so many friends or converted so many enemies. All the women are on my side and wear my colours, pink and white.*

One woman did not; one, of all those who flocked around him, sympathetically indignant over his defeat, neither wore his colours nor was she on his side when, to his twittering audience, he announced, 'I'll make an end of the factious slang of Whig and Tory. Two names with one meaning.'

'Yes, indeed! How right! How true —'

'How false!' broke in the voice of Mary Anne, received with shocked flutters and a loud cackle from her hostess, Lady Cork.

'Look out! She'll rally you on every point to put you down.'

'Or put me up.' And although he spoke to Lady Cork it was at Mary Anne he looked, with a danger spark in his eyes that met hers across the agitated turbans. 'I am flattered. Nothing is more encouraging or of greater use to a young man about to make his bow to life —' accompanied by an exaggeratedly profound obeisance — 'than a woman's kindly criticism.'

'Fiddle!' muttered Mary Anne.

'Madam,' his eyes still holding hers, 'you said —?'

'I can never repeat what I say, for what's on my lung leaps out on my tongue and is at once forgotten.' She turned, chin high, and to Lady Cork she sketched a curtsy. 'A thousand thanks for a most agreeable evening, but I beg your ladyship will excuse me for leaving so early. My husband attends a party meeting at Apsley House by special request of the duke,' she threw this out to the company in general, 'and I would not have him home before me.'

'Must you go, m'dear? You've not been here five minutes. Well, well, that's as it should be and very seldom is. A wife should wait, arms open, for her husband, and not go gallivantin' round with another woman's husband. Aha! That's a cap to fit a-plenty heads. Goodbye then, if you must. Bring that man of yours to dine with me on Monday, and we'll drink damnation to the Whigs.'

'I will,' said Mary Anne, 'full measure, and a double draught to drown a — Radical!'

She flounced away, darting a look at him, who took this with a razing of his chin between a thumb and finger to hide his twisted smile.

Up the wide marble stairs to fetch her cloak, and down again into the pillared hall went Mary Anne. A lounging footman sprang to attention; another flung open the door, calling her name to the line of waiting carriages. She was conducted to hers ... and was followed.

'Madam, may I be permitted to attend you to your house since your husband is not here?'

The lamplight fell full on his face, gilding the ebony halo of his curls; shone in his eyes to gild them, too, that mocked hers, dipped in shadow.

'I thank you, sir, but as you see,' she gestured her immobile footman standing at the ready, 'I am well attended.'

'Your servant, ma'am.' He bowed, he backed; she beckoned.

'Not to appear ungracious, if you will ... you may.'

She stepped in; he stepped after her.

The door was slammed. The footman sprang to the box; the carriage moved on.

'As for you,' she threw a look at him seated beside her, his arms folded across his laced shirt front, 'you should be ashamed of yourself, hoodwinkin' those sillies who grab at the words you hand out to them like the children down by my home in Devon used to grab at the pies handed out by a travelling pieman. If that's the way you hope to enter Parliament, then I tell you straight, you won't.'

'I will, and — I choose my words to fit my company.'

'Touchay! But I am not of your company, so that don't apply to me.'

'The loss, alas, is mine.'

In the cheek half turned from him he discerned a straying dimple. 'Have you heard,' he drew nearer to ask, 'that an ass loves to hear himself bray? And that every ass thinks himself worthy to stand with the King's horses?'

'An ass didn't stand with the King's horses at Wycombe, no — nor in the Horgean stables of Whig mules.'

'The Whigs have failed me.'

'How failed you, if you was standing Radical?'

'Even an ass may borrow the prerogative of woman and change his mind.'

'Qui sexcuse sackuse, to account for your two faces.'

'My —?'

'Two faces. You wear a mask to suit your audience and speak what they would have you say and not what's in your heart to say.'

And while narrowly he watched the charming uptilt of her nose, 'Do you know,' he sank his voice, 'what is in my heart to say?'

She slanted him another look, contemplative and half suspicious of this suggestively intimate tone.

'Only you and your God can know that,' she told him primly. 'But this I do know,' and she nodded, 'or at least I think I know, that you will get in at all costs by the back door if you can't get in at the front — and let your party go hang. You are two-faced.'

'Ah, but *vera redit facies, dissimulata petit.*'

'Say that in English. I don't understand Greek nor Latin, and I can't ever remember which came first, the Greeks or the Romans.'

He slipped her a smile and said it in English. 'The true face returns, that which is assumed passes away.'

'Yes.' She swung her head round. He saw the glint of her teeth in the dark. 'You may be clever. I believe you to be clever, and you should go far, but not if you go jumping through hoops like a circus clown, this way, that way, to stand with the Radicals, then with the Whigs, and then — what next?'

'The Whigs,' and now he was not smiling any more, 'have cast me off. They shall repent it.' The carriage halted. 'This drive,' said he, 'has been all too short. Will you not tell your man to take us up to — Hampstead? There is much that I would say to you. The night is young, the moon is high —'

'Moonshine!' she scoffed. 'Which is all I have to say to *you*. I swore I'd never speak to you again when I was told how you had made your bow to life — at High Wycombe.' A twinkling hint of mockery was in her eyes; and his, meeting hers, seemed to find it difficult to disengage. Then, with a little laugh and peering through the window: 'There's a light in the dining room,' she said, 'which means my husband is home and will be in a taking to find me not there.'

'Allow me.' Disraeli sprang up, and forestalling the footman, he handed her out.

On the pavement she paused to say, 'And now, having broken my word to myself and exchanged words with you — a deal too many — won't you come in and take pot luck with us? There's veal-and-ham pie and cold chicken. You're welcome.'

'Madam does me too much honour.'

'Fudge!' She gathered her skirts to mount the steps and, as the door was opened, 'Where,' she asked, 'will you be standing next?'

'On my head,' said he; and bowing low, 'I thank you very kindly, ma'am, but I will not come in.'

The triumph of the Whigs was short-lived. The King's hostility to reform and his determination to reinstate a Tory Cabinet were decisive factors in the retirement of Grey. The return of the Tories returned also Wyndham Lewis to head the poll at Maidstone.

Once again Mary Anne had been unsparing in her efforts of support; once again she toured the town, calling on houses of likely or unlikely voters, fondling their children, hob-nobbing with their wives, while all through the last weeks of the electoral campaign speculation ran high as to which colours, Whig or Tory, would be flaunted in the House. That irrepressible gossip, Mr Creevey, writing round to his ladies, dubiously ventured: *You know I am not by nature a Radical, yet I am rapidly becoming one, or anything else that may be most opposed to the horrid Tories.* But Mr Creevey and his fellow Whigs did not speculate for long. In November '34 the 'horrid Tories', under Peel, came in, the first Reform Parliament went out, and the adventurous Mr Disraeli, wrecked on the rocks of Radicalism to founder in a backwash of defeated Whiggery, seized upon a Tory lifeline. There he clung.

'Yet I do not feel in any way a beaten man,' he told his supporters at Wycombe after another unsuccessful attempt. 'Perhaps it is because I am used to it.'

Gone were the mannerisms, gone the flowing ringlets, the rings, the knee-breeches, lace ruffles and all. No mountebank was he who resignedly accepted this further defeat, but a decorous, earnest young man in a sombre suit of raven blue.

'I have fought my battle and have lost by a majority of fourteen … I am now a cypher; yet, if the devotion of my energies to your cause can ever avail you, I beg you to call upon me.'

They roared for him, surrounded him, they marvelled at his modesty, unaware it was as much an affectation as his previous flamboyance; unaware too, that the day before he had penned those very words to the Duke of Wellington. But … a cypher? They doubted it. So did Mary Anne when a sad-faced young gentleman in Quakerish grey, with evidence of a recent haircut, called at Grosvenor Gate to enquire after Mr Wyndham Lewis, who, he had heard, was laid low with a chill.

Such visits, on some pretext or other, were not infrequent; for, if at their first meeting she had been piqued by his indifference, his interest in the 'pretty little rattle' had increased. Her malapropisms, her humour, artless or artfully naive, both amused and intrigued him. She was *enfant terrible* with a surprisingly shrewd perspicacity, to edge her platitudes with subtle innuendo. The evanescent pleasure-seeking women of his circle had long ceased to fascinate, as did their flippancies and surface adoration. Something of his father's quiet cynicism was noted by his sister in the letters from the lion cub, now grown into a lion. 'Sa', as he called her, may have traced between the lines a touch of malice when, after dining at the Bulwers', he wrote of his hostess, *she was a blaze of jewels and looked like Juno, only instead of a peacock she had a dog in her lap…* From which it would appear that the jewels had been redeemed for the occasion from *mon oncle.*

But if Mary Anne enjoyed a muted triumph in the knowledge that the 'best ton in Town' preferred her company to that of the Junoesque Rosina, she offered no encouragement to his advances. His elaborate speeches, his homage, the grapes and flowers brought from the hothouses at Bradenham and gracefully presented, were not so gracefully received.

On the occasion of his visit during Wyndham's convalescence, 'Are these,' she enquired, laying aside a basket of peaches, 'a *bonne booshe* to sweeten the taste of an offensive remark you made of me at the Bulwers' the other night when Rosina partnered us for dinner?'

He expressed profoundest shock. 'An offensive remark *I* made of *you*, to — Good God!' Horrified incredulity was in his voice. 'I am at a loss to understand to what you can possibly allude.'

She bent over her knitting. She was always knitting or sewing or something, when he called. Her lips moved to a murmur: 'One plain, two purl, knit two together —' and with an upward look from under those lashes she said, sulky-mouthed, 'If you didn't want to take me down to dinner you needn't holler it out for everyone to hear.'

'Madam, I greatly fear,' said he with a face of stone, 'that you must be hallucinated.'

'And you don't have to make it worse by being rude. I am not hallucinated, or, if you prefer it, daft.' The ball of wool dropped from her lap; and as she dived to retrieve it, so did he; their heads collided. Rosy-cheeked, her eyes brimming with laughter. 'I'll be obliged,' she told him, 'if you'll hold out your hands so I may wind it on them. It'll be easier for me if you kneel down.'

He knelt down. 'I am, as always, at your feet.' And when, obediently, he held out his hands, she, winding rapidly, said, 'I'm making shawls for my brats.'

'For your —?'

'Brats. At Maidstone. Since Wyndham has come into his own again he must nurse his interests, and I his constituents' babies. I've never seen such a flux of babies, newborn or about to be, as there is in Maidstone. Lift up your hands and don't stick out your thumbs. Hold them closer. That's the way. Yes, I was saying, as you may or may not choose to remember, how you told Mrs Bulwer in my hearing when she asked you to take me down to dinner, "Anyone rather than that insufferable woman".'

His eyebrows shot up to histrionic altitudes. 'Child! You are utterly mistaken. I would never … I swear…'

'You don't have to swear, nor to shout. I'm not deaf. And don't call me child when you know I'm almost old enough to be your mother. Quite old enough if I'd been born a Hindu. They marry at ten in India… Your hands, *if* you please. How d'you think I can wind with you throwin' yourself about like that? I know what I heard. "That insufferable woman," you said, and then, "Oh, well, if Allah wills it," or some such heathenish remark, and so you *had* to take me in to dinner, whether you wanted to or not. Rosina'll never have done quizzing me. Everyone's entitled to his likes and dislikes, and yours is most evidently — me!'

She gave a little sniff, and as the lashes lifted he saw that her eyes were suspiciously bright.

'You did say it, you know you did. There's some may think you a droll and a wag to poke fun at a person who's not what they call *comme il foe*, and who don't follow the fashion in dress nor in talk like the baa-in' of sheep. Let 'em sneer. Much I care. I'll lay there's not one of those beauties of yours who'd have faced a crowd of hecklers and booing Whigs at Maidstone to help her man into his seat as did I, though I say it as shouldn't to blow my own trumpet. You can get up now.' She relieved his outstretched hands of wool. 'I can wind it better on a chair-back.'

He remained static, head down.

'I am mortified, shaken, I am wounded,' he laid a hand on his heart, 'to the core. That you, whom I respect, revere above all women, can believe me guilty of uttering so vulgar, so gauche a *bêtise* — and in public — bereaves me of all words —'

'It don't sound like it.' And relentingly, he looked so shame-faced, and so young! 'Stay and have a cup o' tea with Wyndham. He's down in the dumps and will be glad of your company to cheer him... And here *is* tea. Get up, do. Whatever will the servants think?'

He got up. The door opened to admit the butler preceding a footman with a tea tray and cake stand.

'Take it upstairs to your master's room. Mr Disraeli and I will have tea with him there.' And as the men withdrew, 'He is better of his chill,' she said, 'so you won't catch it.' Her level brows contracted. 'But I'm a little worried. I've had Sir Henry Halford here in consultation because my husband complains of a pain in his chest. The doctor calls it indigestion, but Sir Henry, he says he has a — what is it? — cardiac murmur. Nothing serious, only he'll have to go easy and not overdo it. He's at it hammer and tongs in his constituency, and then there's those long sessions in the House. I've a mind to suggest he takes in a fellow member to help him.'

Disraeli stood stock still.

'Can Maidstone carry a second Conservative seat?'

'That's as may be.' She gave him a slow sidelong look.

'And will be if we — if they — find the right man.'

FOURTEEN

The new year brought disturbing news from Mrs Yate. For some time past her letters had been anxiously concerned with the health of Mr Yate. Having long since retired from his Mastership of Ceremonies, he had been impelled, on medical advice, as so his wife reported, to lead a life of leisure. He was still leisurely leading it when Mary Anne received a frantic appeal from her mother to come to her at once. Mr Yate had been *Taken with a Seizure and was Sinking*. But by the time that she arrived at Clifton Mr Yate had sunk.

Since John was with his regiment in Iceland, and Wyndham had been unable to accompany her owing to his parliamentary duties, Mary Anne had all to do superintending the funeral arrangements and consoling the grief-stricken widow; and when the last rites were thankfully over she persuaded Mrs Yate to return with her to London.

'It won't be for long,' she told Wyndham, who did not greatly welcome the prospect of an indefinite visit from his mother-in-law, never at her happiest cheerful and now transformed into a woe-bedecked Niobe. 'I couldn't leave her there alone in her trouble. She must bide here for a while, and then I'll ask Miss Graham if she would care to take her as a paying guest. She might be glad of her company.'

Miss Graham might well have been glad of Mrs Yate's company, notwithstanding she now stood in no need of pecuniary assistance. Soon after Mary Anne's marriage Miss Graham's circumstances had been mysteriously *Elevated by a God-sent gift*, so, in a much italicised letter peppered with exclamation points, she had imparted to her 'Dearest Mrs Lewis'. It seems Miss Graham had received from a firm of solicitors in Cardiff:

...The most wonderful Surprize! An annuity, my dear, of Five and Twenty pounds!! Per Annum! Quite a little Fortune for poor little Me! But the Donor of this Benificence insists he shall remain Anonymous! I am sure it is a He and am positively Certain Who — I must not Mention Names, Head over Ears (if you know what I mean) in my more youthful days, and altho' I have not heard of his Demise my Heart tells me that he has Passed On and in his passing he remembered Her whom he so ardently Desired!! (This word, faintly erased, was replaced by *Adored*).

If Mary Anne had her suspicions as to the identity of this anonymous donor, she kept her own counsel and Miss Graham her illusions. But when Mrs Yate was approached with her daughter's suggestion, 'Never in this world,' she declared, 'will I share a home with that flippertygib of mutton dressed as lamb. Sooner than live with her I will follow my dear departed to his grave. Of course, if you wish to be rid of me I will take myself and my sorrows away. I can tell when I'm not wanted.'

'Now, now, that's unkind in you, Ma. You know that Wyndham and I are only too glad,' Mary Anne said without gladness, 'to have you here, but I thought you would prefer to live in Clifton where you have so many friends.'

'What better friend than her daughter should a mother have?' wept Mrs Yate. 'Her own flesh and blood who turns me out neck and crop as if I were a leper.'

Manufacturing patience, Mary Anne replied, 'No one is turning you out neck and crop, leper or nothing, but neither

Wyndham nor I would be happy to think you were living at Clifton alone.'

'I shall always be alone,' sobbed Mrs Yate, 'until I am called to meet my maker and your dear papa in glory.'

'You'll be meeting two of my dear papas in glory,' was the inexcusable reminder, 'but in the meantime we must think what's best for you to do while you're waiting to be called.'

'To mock me in my misery! Have you no reverence, no heart, you wicked girl — for girl you are to me although you're forty—'

'Forty-one,' said Mary Anne.

'— but I am not yet so beggared that I can't afford to pay my board and keep even though my son-in-law may be rich as Creases, and in this p-palace of a house with all these servants I had hoped you could have found a room, or even an attic, for your widowed mother in the eve-eve-evening of her life…'

'So you see I couldn't help myself but tell her she could stay,' was Mary Anne's report of this to Wyndham, who, on condition that Mrs Yate be given her private apartments, 'And not,' he stipulated, 'that she share our table or our rooms,' agreed to accept the inevitable.

'You must know your own business best,' was Rosina's summary of the situation, 'but believe me, you are taking a risk. Mothers and mothers-in-law are the devil to raise hell between husband and wife, as Edward's bitch of a mother has raised hell between us — to break our lives.'

This was not the first of many hints dropped by Rosina that the sorry drama of her marriage was soon to be played out; nevertheless, it came as a shock to Mary Anne, who had seen and deplored the increasingly bitter hostilities between these two, whose frequent savage quarrels had bled them of their love.

Rosina's account of these brawls presented her as an angel of virtue and him as a monster of vice whose 'physical cruelty and brutal assaults' she displayed in minor bruises on her body.

But while Mary Anne expressed consolatory disgust at Edward's maltreatment of his wife in private and his taunts and abuse of her in public, she inclined to the belief that Rosina may have been the first aggressor, to attack and to receive chastisement due in self-defence. Edward may also have been tried beyond endurance. Rosina's constant complaint, that he neglected her for his work, called forth the not unreasonable retort that he must be chained to his desk in order to pay debts incurred by her reckless extravagance. Moreover, the money she wheedled out of him she spent on herself and not on their children, in whom neither parent showed the smallest interest; indeed, both seemed to lack all sense of parental duty or affection.

A last attempt to call a truce and save their marriage was proposed by Edward in the spring of '35, when, with *Pompeii* in view, he decided to visit Naples and suggested Rosina should go with him. She delightedly agreed, but was not so delighted to find that, unknown to her, he had arranged for his latest attraction and her complaisant husband to meet them in Paris *en route*. Edward's infatuation for this somewhat raffish lady who, according to Rosina, he would 'fondle and paw' in full view of his wife and 'that trollop's husband, if husband he is' — went far to wreck all possibility of a reconciliation.

Things were at a pretty pass when the Bulwers, more than ever now at enmity, were back in Hertford Street. Not only was Mary Anne treated to the tale of the Paris debacle and 'that trollop's' part in it, but she found herself involved in the ensuing crisis when, all hope of reunion abandoned, the two resolved to separate. Edward took himself to Albany where, 'undisturbed,' he said, 'by constant rows, he could commune with his Muse in peace.'

And to Albany one evening Rosina pursued him, 'to find,' so to sundry of her circle she reported, 'his Muse in white muslin, seated on his knee.'

It was all over Town the next day. A few weeks later, on plea of incompatibility, A deed of separation, by special request of Rosina, was signed and witnessed in the presence and at the house of Mary Anne.

So much immersed was she in the Bulwers' marital disarrangements that matters of more personal concern were left for a while in abeyance. Yet she found time to keep a watchful eye on the political barometer that had risen again to favour the Whigs with Melbourne in office, Peel out of it, and Disraeli once more in the news.

Determined to identify himself with either one or other of the two great parties, and 'those old hacks,' as he called Melbourne and his Cabinet, 'having cast him off,' he decided to enter the tiltyard at Taunton, armed *cap à pie* for the Tories. Astonishing apocalypse! And his speech on the hustings even more sensational than had been his previous oratory at Wycombe, as was also his appearance. Discarding the subdued mode of dress he had latterly adopted, he reverted to his former parrot-gay accoutrements and came attired in one of the new tight-waisted frock coats of bottle green, a vest of divers colours adorned with a glitter of gold chains, and gaudy patterned pantaloons. But, as before, the moment he began to speak his audience ceased to wonder at the sight of him and stood electrified at the sound of him. Relentlessly he hurled at them his powerful denunciation of the Whigs that provoked his hecklers to a frenzy and his supporters to *such a show of hands,* he wrote to Sarah, *as no Blue candidate ever did before … The potwallopers at Taunton are as eloquent as those of Athens.*

But despite his own Athenian eloquence and the loyal demonstration of his party, he found himself again defeated, and with calamitous result when, at a dinner held in his honour by the local Tories, he gave them a rehash of his oration with some vitriolic enlargement levelled at the Irish Radical, O'Connell. It was unfortunate that this gentleman, of whom Disraeli had once been an ardent disciple, should have seen a bowdlerised summary of the Taunton speech reported in a Dublin newspaper.

O'Connell's reply to 'this piece of gratuitous impertinence', expressed in a volley of vituperation, was gleefully seized upon and publicised by the national press.

'For goodness' sake,' gasped Mary Anne at breakfast, from behind the *Morning Herald* and the tea urn, 'here's a pretty how-d'ye-do. Whatever next will he be up to?'

Over *The Times*, Wyndham asked testily, 'Who will be up to what?'

'Him. Disraeli. Isn't it in your paper? He seems to have got himself into hot water with that bog-trottin' son of a — h'm.' And dodging the tea urn and Wyndham's frosted stare, 'I see you've left your chop,' she said with a pretty show of housewifely concern. 'I'm afraid they're too fresh-killed. I shall have to complain to the butcher. Won't you try the devilled kidneys?'

'Yes… They…' he answered absently while he scanned the open page. 'I can find no mention here of Disraeli and — whom did you say?'

'O'Connell. He writes the most dreadful letter about Dizzy… The devilled kidneys, Charles. No, not for me, your master.

Listen, Wyn, I'll read it. Huh! The beast. Would you believe? He, this tub-thumping potwalloper —'

'Pot —?'

'— walloper. It's what Dizzy called the Taunton Blues. Don't you remember? When he dined with us the other night he told how he had "squabashed" them — his word, not mine. I never knew such a one for turning defeat into a victory.'

Wyndham lifted a nostril. 'He certainly has the knack of cutting his losses to meet his weather-cock convictions.'

'And the courage of them too, whichever way they blow. Just imagine him slashing out right and left at that fire-eating Radical for *an incendiary and traitor*, as O'Connell quotes him here. A case of the pot — or the walloper — and the kettle, no mistake.'

'Ha — hum!' Clearing his throat of some morning catarrh, Wyndham again searched the pages of *The Times*. 'Ah, yes, I have it now... *An egregious liar both in action and in words... utter abhorrence... entertain for such a reptile... perfidy, depravity.* Hum, strong, very... Let's see what more the choleric O'Connell has to say of... Ha! Yes, his name. That's always a sure target. *His name shows that he is of Jewish origin. I do not use it as a term of reproach —*'

'Very kind of him,' burst forth Mary Anne, 'the dirty hound!'

'*There are many most respectable Jews, but there are, as in every other people, some of the lowest and most disgusting grade of moral turpitude, and of those I look upon Mr Disraeli as the worst. He has just the qualities of the impenitent thief on the Cross.* Pah!' Wyndham laid aside the paper to attack the cooling kidneys. 'These are the vindictive vapourings one has come to expect from the Irish rabble.'

'Blasphemy, more like,' she flashed. 'That skunk of an O'Connell! I wonder at *The Times* daring to print it. What do you think Dizzy will do about this?'

'If he has any sense he will ignore it as the usual inaccuracy of the press.'

But Dizzy did not ignore it, and in order that there should be no inaccuracy of the press in his retort, he sent a copy of his letter to every newspaper throughout the kingdom.

Although you have long placed yourself outside the pale of civilization, still I am one who will not be insulted even by a Yahoo without chastising it ... We shall meet at Philippi; and rest assured that I will seize the opportunity of inflicting upon you a castigation which will make you remember and repent the insults you have heaped upon
  Benjamin Disraeli.

The fat was in the fire, but the fire did not burn; for O'Connell, who had already killed one man at pistol-point, had taken a solemn vow that, no matter what the provocation, he would never fight again.

Then Disraeli, with one eye on publicity and his blood at boiling pitch, challenged O'Connell's son, Morgan, to make the *amende honorable* on his father's behalf, and asked D'Orsay to stand as his second. D'Orsay, however, was unwilling to oblige. He excused himself on the grounds that, as a foreigner, he could not interfere in a political duel. Another friend was found to manage the affair and to leave his card upon O'Connell junior.

Disraeli spent the intervening hours of that day impatiently awaiting the result. When evening came and no reply from the O'Connells, father or son, was forthcoming, he dressed himself in his most dandiacal fashion of embroidered waistcoat, knee breeches, lace frills and all the rest of it, and betook him to the opera.

In the stalls, resplendent, he sat, sunned in the welcoming smiles of the ladies. Immediately above him, in a box on the first tier, he sighted Mr and Mrs Wyndham Lewis. In a gown of lavender blue with those bunched curls either side her face — and what a complexion! Tinted like the foxglove — she looked most delectable, he thought. She smiled down at him and drew her husband's attention to 'Mr Disraeli'; he saw her mouth his name, and, rising, bowed to both of them and sat again, and wondered: *Well, why not? She has him in her pocket…* Then the curtain rose, but he heard nothing of Grisi or the opera. During the *entr'acte*, the hand-wavings, fan-flutterings and beckonings from stalls and boxes invited him to make his choice. He made it.

'Why, you must have read our minds!' cried Mary Anne when he presented himself in the doorway of her box. 'I was just telling Wyndham to go down and ask you if you would care to sit with us here. Won't you join us?'

'Your servant, ma'am, and — with all my heart.' Watched by numerous envious eyes he bent over her hand where his lips seemed to linger; and to Wyndham, who had risen, he bowed again. 'Sir, have I your permission?'

'By all means. Delighted.' But Wyndham's tone conveyed little delight as he produced a gold snuff-box, tapped, opened, and wordlessly offered it.

Disraeli took a cautious pinch, applied it to his nose and promptly sneezed. 'An admirable — ah-a'tchew! — and potent blend. I thank you, sir, but I fear I am not addicted to the a-ah-cult.'

The orchestra was tuning up. In the auditorium the feathered turbans swayed and rippled as if stirred by a breeze; Mary Anne unfurled a fan; and when Disraeli, comforting his streaming eyes and nostrils with a perfumed handkerchief, sank into the seat beside her, she, under cover of the chorus and the fan, gave to his ear a whispered commentary on his case.

'It might have served you better had you left that rat O'Connell to stew in his poisonous juice. You've asked for trouble, and you'll get it. I'm told he's a demon shot... Bravo! Encore! Not that I don't think you'd be a match for him, *or* his son, only they say he's killed one man, and the son, he winged another — Lord Alvanley, I think it was — for calling him a bloated Tory. Lord! how that man does bellow. Why do singers run to fat? Even Grisi, though I'll grant she's lovely in the face, must measure at least forty in the bust. I hope you'll think twice before you'll call him out. You should never have got yourself mixed up with that low trash. I'm surprised, I really am, that you should sink to their level.'

Disraeli took this reproof with a folding of his lips and arms, and the remark, 'I always find something ridiculous in a chorus yelling itself hoarse with all its mouths wide open as if it would swallow the house.'

Mary Anne hunched a shoulder. 'One might as well talk to the back of a hackney for all the good it'll do. Very well then, go and *be* killed, and don't say I didn't warn you. Mercy me! My ears'll split. Is this the last of it? Thank God for that.'

Wyndham, leaning over the red velvet ledge of the box, was vigorously clapping, the audience shouting, the curtain falling, and rising again to the curtsies of Grisi and a storm of applause to hit the roof. The shower of bouquets flung at the feet of the diva was returned with hand-kissings, eyes up to the boxes and down to the stalls, a curtsy right to the tenor, left to the bass, a hand graciously extended to the bowing *chef d'orchestre*, to the first and second fiddles and all the lesser fry who, half risen from their stools in sheepish response, sat down again to fidget with their scores. Disraeli, wresting a carnation from his buttonhole, dramatically flung it at the Grisi as she sank to her eleventh curtsy; but his tribute, falling short, hit the conductor on the nose.

'A fine shot!' laughed Mary Anne. 'It'll be a poor look out for you if your bullet goes so wide of its mark!'

'What's this of bullets?' Wyndham asked as he wrapped her in her cloak.

'Nothing of bullets … we *hope*. Mr Disraeli, won't you come home with us to supper?'

Mr Disraeli went home with them to supper, and was regaled with cold chicken and champagne.

Later, when Mary Anne, having left him and her husband to their port, had retired to bed, Wyndham — at his dressing-room door and half in and half out of his nightshirt — woke her, announcing: 'Talk — talk! I thought he would never have gone.'

'Who?' Shaken from her first sleep she hazily enquired, 'What's the time?'

'Past three.' Wyndham pulled on his tasselled nightcap. 'That young man suggests I take him in with me for Maidstone at the next election.'

Mary Anne, now wide awake, sat up. 'No! Him?' Her tone expressed the liveliest amaze. 'He actually dared to ask you *that*?'

'He didn't ask,' said Wyndham stiffly. 'He hinted; a broad enough hint, I admit.'

'The sauce of it! I hope you put him in his place.' And as Wyndham turned down the lamp on a small centre table and carefully climbed into bed, she slid her tongue in her cheek to tell him, 'It would, of course, be fatal.'

'Injudicious, perhaps,' he leaned out to snuff the candle on the bedside commode, 'but not — or why — fatal?'

A shroud of semi-darkness, and a moment's silence fell upon the room, then, 'But surely,' she protested, 'you would never think of sharing your seat with anyone, least of all *him*. He is so wildly rash and outspoken. Look how he flies a red flag in the face of O'Connell, the Radical bull. He'd never stay the course as a Tory.'

'You sang a very different tune, and to his praises,' Wyndham reminded her, 'only a week or two ago.'

'That was before he called out O'Connell. He must be crazy mad to get himself mixed up in a scandal with that scum. Mind you...' Rolling over on her back she gazed at the ceiling where, by the glimmer of a candle on her side of the bed, was revealed a circle of fat cupids from which suspended a crystal chandelier. In the hanging lustres a furtive gleam of light shone like a winking eye. 'Mind you,' she murmured, 'the Tories might do worse than have someone who'd knock the stuffin' out of them.'

'My dear girl!'

'There you go. You're all the same, you Tories. You jib at plain speaking. Stuffy, that's what they are — not you, love —' she put out a hand to feel for and stroke the bristle of hair beneath his nightcap — '*them*. But as for taking in Disraeli, that's going to extremes. He'd be another Guy Fawkes to set the House a-fire.'

'Part of the House,' said Wyndham sleepily, 'was set on fire in November '34 so that we must be herded together in the Court of Requests, until...' His voice trailed off. Then suddenly, as if hit between the eyes, he jerked up his head. 'By Jove, and isn't that just what we want? With all due respect to your judgement, my dear, you are inclined to see no farther than —' and now his hand went seeking to alight upon her nose — 'than *this*. You allow your indignation at that young man's foolhardy, but none the less courageous, challenge to O'Connell to obscure your perspective. In politics we must take the long view and not be carried away by — a-a-ah —' A prodigious yawn swallowed his words; his chin dropped. He stretched himself sideways under the bedclothes while his feet went groping for the warmth of hers. 'I'll have,' he yawned again, 'to think it over.'

'You're cold as frogs,' said Mary Anne. 'That girl's forgot the warming-pan.' She snuggled down into the pillows, and to herself she grinned. 'I should think it over twice, if I was you.'

Meanwhile the subject of this intimate discussion went on his homeward way in deepest thought. Maidstone… Yes, with her behind him to galvanise that pompous ass, her husband, into action he might yet, as she once had impudently told him, 'get in at the back door if he couldn't get in at the front.' But how, weighed down by a millstone of debts round his neck and a pack of blood-sucking creditor curs at his heels? Well, let them yap. He could chuck them a bone — or a book — and stave them off. That for tomorrow. But for today?

By the railings of Hyde Park he stood a while watching the ghostly mists of dawn uprisen from the night's chilled earth. In the shadowed nebulae of distance tree branches traced a formless frieze against the sky, pricked with slow-fading stars. The city slept, but in the lifting dark those verdant acres pulsed with life, untamed, unseen; the tiny rustle of some wild creature in the grass; the savage cry of the swift-winged killer, the piercing shriek of its captured prey; sound symbols of nature, primitive, carnal, and as ruthless in those green aisles of a London park as in uncharted jungle depths… A hush, fear-fallen, hung heavy for a moment, then, as if a clutching hand had loosed its hold on each small feathered throat, the air was filled with the sweet faint chirp of waking birds; and from somewhere in some lodge-keeper's yard the first cock crowed.

A couple of hackneys loaded with drunks rattled rowdily by, splashing mud from puddles undried after recent rains. At the corner of Park Lane a high-hatted Peeler cast a suspicious look and his lantern's gleam at the dandified young gentleman aimlessly sauntering, stopping to stare, eyes up at the weakening stars and down to his spattered silk-stockinged legs, muttering, cursing, and on again stalked by the Peeler who, unsure if his man were felon or fop and deciding on the latter, let him go.

Along Piccadilly, still muttering, he went, past the houses of the great whose right it was, by virtue of their breed and birth, to rule 'this earth, this realm, this England'... Yes, from which no drop of English blood coursed through *his* veins. By what right, or in what smallest part of it — if any — would his memory be planted? On some unobtrusive gravestone in a village churchyard? *Here lies Benjamin Disraeli, master of jibes, of flouts and sneers, who believed posterity to be a pack-horse with himself astride the load of baggage as — prime minister!* Hah, even that!

He recalled his meeting with Lord Melbourne at one of Caroline Norton's assemblies just before his first misfired attempt at High Wycombe. The debonair Whig leader, grizzled, handsomely debauched, had asked him in his attractive, lazy drawl, 'Well, young man, and what is it you want to be?' And his unhesitating answer for all the room to hear: 'I want to be prime minister.'

'Ho, you do, do you?' Those keen grey eyes had probed, to flay without words, this insolent young cub, this Jew who dared rush in where Christians...

'Bah! Be damned to them!' He thumped his gold-topped cane on the pavement. 'The ape may yet be on the side of the angels!' He didn't know he spoke aloud until he heard his voice; nor did he see a prowling figure sneak out from a side alley till she came at him with whispers.

The light of a street lamp revealed her in her tattered finery, dismayingly, a child. The frayed silk of her low-cut bodice uncovered one immature breast, its nipple caked with dirt. Her face, under a bedraggled tinselled cap was hunger-pinched, unchildishly hollowed. Pointing her tongue at him between her painted lips, she murmured invitation and laid a coaxing hand upon his sleeve. Revolted, he shook her off and hurried on, heedless of the volley of obscenities hurled after him in shrill gutter-urchin treble; and at the sound of it, stabbed by her pitiful youth, he retraced his steps. Avidly she met him, wriggling her hips in grotesque imitation of the elders of her trade.

'Good God,' he uttered softly, 'how old, in heaven's — or hell's name — are you?'

'Old enough, me darlin', to give you what you want and what you'd die to 'ave. If I tell you —' and in nauseating glib recitative she told, until he cut her short and digging in his pocket, brought out a handful of coins.

'Here,' gingerly he tendered a gold piece, 'take this and go.'

Eyes popping, she grabbed at it, bit on it and came at him again, offering her painted grin. 'Sure I'll go if you'll go with me, darlin. I can pleasure you as you 'ave never known an that you'll beg for more until you'se —'

'I told you, go, be off!' He backed from a stink in her breath of onions, patchouli and, paramount, of gin. 'And don't spend it on drink.'

'Yah! Fuck you!' Gathering a mouthful of spit she discharged it in his face with another choice flavour of words. 'And *you* can go fuck yourself!'

Disgustedly he turned from her and heard at his heels a whimper as she pattered beside him.

'T'ain't my fault. If there was more like you there'd be less of us — like me.'

He watched her scuttle away into the dark and resuming his walk, *What a world,* he reflected, it is, *of shiftless unrealities and mealy-mouthed hypocrisies, fostering corruption. We preach of Christ and in the same breath murder Him who said, 'Suffer little children...' We should weep to see that child soaked in vice, not of her will but of ours, who turn a blind eye and deaf ear to it, and her excruciation. She and all such miserable young creatures, homeless, unwanted, unnamed, should, if I had voice in it, be cared for, schooled and guided. But is this she-whelp of the gutter more degraded than the women of my kind? What is there to choose between the enticements of the boudoir or the brothel? The one sells her young body for the price of a meal, and the other for the price of a cuckold... Barter, so runs the course of life and so run I, in a cesspool of political lies and insincerities. No, by God! I'll either get in or get out on the strength of my beliefs. But what beliefs have I in an England ruled by Downing Street? Once it was ruled by Elizabeth. The Crown has become the figurehead of a vessel with two captains at the helm and at each other's throats, while the ship of State founders in the quicksands of disunity. What we need is...*

Again he halted and, still sky-gazing, crossed over the road into St James's Street, and was almost run down by a cabriolet. Dodging under the horse's neck and impervious to the imprecations of the driver, who pulled up just in time with a jarring scrape of wheels, *What we need, and* must *have,* he thought, *is a co-operative Government. Only by some such union between the Tory and Radical masses can the country be saved from a decayed degeneracy such as the decline of Spain during these three hundred years since we defied the might of her Armada … Strange how England has prospered under her queens. Man's instinctive homage to the matriarch, the eternal quest and craving for a return to the womb. Even the last of the Stuarts, poor brandy-sodden Anne, raised, to inspire, a Marlborough… And soon,* he said to himself, *there'll be another queen of England.*

As he let himself into his lodgings he could hear the early clatter of the kitchen, the clink of china and cutlery, the sound of men's voices, and a girl's raucous song as she scrubbed.

There were no letters for him among those on the hall table, only bills, recognised by the names of the senders boldly printed on the envelopes. Without opening these he tore them in half and went up to his room where he dropped them in the waste-paper basket. Then, fully dressed, he flung himself on the bed, was asleep the next minute… And awakened.

'Sir, beggin' your pardon.' The *valet de chambre*, long inured to discretion, stood over him. 'There are some persons below demanding to see you. Shall I tell them you are not at home?'

'What?' Dazedly blinking, Disraeli sat up. 'Who —?'

'They,' an apologetic cough preceded the information, 'I think, sir, they be Peelers.'

'Pee —? Duns more like. Kick them out.'

But they were in, pounding up the stairs to shake the house, and, undeterred by remonstrance from the valet, 'You,' demanded the bewhiskered burly leader of the three, 'are Benjamin Disraeli?' Without waiting for an affirmative, 'In the name of the law,' he gloatingly announced, 'you are taken into custody and will accompany me to the police office of Mary-le-Bone.'

Death and damnation.

Shamed to the uttermost deeps of despair he, who in secret hope had climbed Olympus crowned with glory, was hustled down the stairs by two uniformed officials and driven away in a hackney cab.

FIFTEEN

'Well, there's nothing so bad but it mightn't be worse,' was Mary Anne's doubtful consolation when, a few days later, a chastened young gentleman presented himself with red roses, a long face, and longer tale of his recent unhappy experience. 'You can thank your stars you're not in gaol.'

'Which,' was the morose reply, 'should be, in lawful case, my present habitat.'

'Count your blessings,' she said briskly. 'And see you keep the peace, as you're bound over now to do.'

'On a surety of five hundred borrowed pounds, to plunge me further in the mire of my debts.'

She gave him no quarter for that. 'A fine politician you are with one foot, if not both, in the Fleet!'

'The Fleet is filled with better men than I.'

'Yes,' she nodded unkindly agreement, 'and you don't have to search the Fleet to find them.' Then, while silently he swallowed this, 'Is it true,' she bestowed on him a look of limpid wonder, 'that you asked Wyndham to bring you in with him for Maidstone?' And while he stared back at her, dumb as a boot, 'As if,' she continued, inhaling his bouquet — 'these are delicious — as if so hot a Tory as Wyndham would dream of hand-and-gloving it with a turncoat Radical that gets himself arrested for challenging another — and what another, too! That blackguard O'Connell, to make you the talk o' the town.' She got up to pull the bell-rope, and to the footman who appeared in answer, 'Bring,' she ordered, 'a vawse for these, and tea. You will stay to tea, Mr Disraeli?'

Mr Disraeli did not stay to tea. He left in a huff, ears a-tingle with her warning: 'You'd best go on writing books and leave off writing letters, to land you into trouble with the police. Success won't come to you by waging newspaper war against a dirty hound who hasn't got the guts to answer back when he's called out. Yes, guts I said, and you needn't look at me down that long nose of yours. I'm not one to mince my words, and you are not so lady-mouthed that you can't take 'em. I tell you this…' She surveyed her arrangement of the roses in the 'vawse', carefully placing a spray of maidenhair fern among the velvety dark blooms to receive a thorny prick. Hastily withdrawing her hand to suck an ooze of blood from her thumb, 'Speak,' she said, 'as strong as you like in the House, if you find a seat, which after this to-do I doubt you ever will, but to speak so strong in print and give the news-scavengers a feast at your expense is courting failure.'

'Madam,' he bowed and straightened, gazing through her as if she were a window, 'if by courting failure I may be a brilliant failure, better far that I should fail than achieve — mediocre success. I will bid you a very good day.'

And he took himself off.

But also he took her advice. With writs out against him for his debts, and the sheriff's officers planted on his doorstep, he directed his pen, not to the writing of letters but to a political tract entitled *A Vindication of the British Constitution dedicated to a Noble Learned Lord*.

The 'Noble Learned Lord' was Tory Chancellor Lyndhurst who, more amused than scandalised by 'Dizzy's newspaper war' against O'Connell, invited him to dinner with the Lords of the Exchequer. *Rather dull* was his account of it to sister 'Sa', *but we had a swan, very white and tender, stuffed with truffles and the best company there…*

The 'stuffing', not only of truffles but of 'the best company there', included a sober-faced, elderly young man who, although some six years Disraeli's junior, was already under-secretary of state. And if the swan so 'white and tender' turned to gall in Dizzy's mouth at the reminder of this fellow's triumphant emergence from Eton and Oxford (with a double first), and his subsequent success as Tory Member for Newark, young Mr Disraeli's greeting to the younger Mr Gladstone lacked nothing of laudatory warmth. And if Mr Gladstone gazed serenely over the head of this 'Hebraic outsider' in his Joseph's coat of many political colours, he accepted the 'outsider's' panegyrics with a self-depreciatory shrug and a murmured, 'Sir, I trust I may be worthy of your esteemed regard,' uttered in his carefully well-modulated Oxford voice.

But that first meeting between these two, though neither could foresee the linking of their names on Parliament's roll of honour, drove Disraeli to his desk, more than ever determined to win his coveted seat in the House, and without Eton, Oxford, or a double first to back him … and without petticoat patronage either.

And deliberately he held himself aloof from Mary Anne.

Once again the London season with its gilded dissipations of dinners, balls and routs was at its height. Once again, in the leafy squares of Mayfair and Belgravia, lighted windows gave access to flower-decked balconies under gaily striped awnings. And, as always in the summer months, the refrain of the waltz drew a ragged herd of idlers come from their lairs to listen, wonder-struck, staring up to gain a glimpse of glittering figures that moved in slow gyration to the lilting measure of the violins. And once again, on those green and golden afternoons, an endless procession of carriages drove through Grosvenor Gate to the park.

To Mrs Yate the enjoyment of drives in her daughter's barouche could never be staled by custom. Whether accompanied, or preferably not, by Mary Anne, Mrs Yate felt herself to be the equal of any lady in the land. True, she was untitled, but her carriage — or rather Mary Anne's carriage, which was one and the same as her own — carried a crest on its panels. Her daughter visited and entertained Nobility. Mrs Yate had talked with countesses, or at least with one countess, at tea, on those rare occasions when Mary Anne invited her to meet her lady friends. Not that all of them were ladies by any means considering the scandals attached to their names, but not so far, thank heaven, to the name of Mary Anne.

'I am reading,' Mrs Yate informed her daughter on one of these excursions to the park, 'or rather *trying* to read — it's so dreadfully wordy and long-winded — a novel by that daring Mr Who-is-it who writes those shocking letters to the newspapers and got himself locked up for fighting a duel.'

'If by that daring Mr Who-is-it,' said Mary Anne, 'you mean Mr Disraeli, he didn't fight a duel. His man refused to answer when he called him out.'

'Well, whether he did or didn't fight a duel, he got himself locked up. The newspapers were full of it. I am glad to know he no longer visits at our house. I have only met him once and that by accident when he came in unexpected, so you had to introduce your mother whether you liked it or not, it being one of the stipulations laid down when I took residence with you as the Guest of Charity, that I keep strictly to my own apartments. Not that I mind,' declared Mrs Yate with every indication of minding very much, 'for I wouldn't want to take up company with Jews and jailbirds, no matter they write books and stand for Parliament — Just look at those sleeves, like bolsters. Such a hideous fashion. I am thinking of having my last year's maroon remodelled by a little woman I know of in — dear me, we are stopping again. I have never seen the park so crowded.'

Indeed, the press of carriages, coaches, tandems, four-in-hands and horsemen, striving to curb their fretted mounts to walking pace, caused a continuous block. Lined up by the Achilles statue the stream of equipages with their occupants in gowns of variegated colours, gave the impression of a brightly patterned carpet outspread for a giant's stride.

Under the drowsy sun-dazzled trees the motley parade of Fashion, leaning on the arms of their escorts, promenaded to an incessant interchange of chit-chat, greetings, and women's laughter like a carillon of bells; and in unconscious mimicry of gentlemanly bows, the attempted downward ease of an arched neck, foam-bespattered from the torture of the bearing rein.

A couple of riders edged their way in single file to the barrier between Mary Anne's barouche and a coroneted coach. The very old lady inside it, whom Mrs Yate, from over her shoulder and under her parasol, noted was dressed far too young and painted far too high, hailed the first of the two horsemen with a crook of her gloved finger and a smile to the fullest display of a mouthful of porcelain teeth.

'Count, you odious creature! Why were you not at my soirée last night? Aha! I'll lay you had other and more tasty fish to fry.'

The gentleman thus addressed turned his head, and encountering the eyes of Mary Anne, bowed from the saddle effusively to her and then to his interlocutress. 'Miladi, I am desolate! *Hélas*, I was summoned to the sick-bed of *ma tante*.'

'That,' snickered 'miladi', 'I can well believe, but I have never heard her called your *tante* before. However, you missed nothing but a party of frumps arriving in shoals — none under seventy, and Wellin'ton. He'd go anywhere for a free meal.'

'Isn't that,' Mrs Yate nudged Mary Anne, 'the Countess of Cork behind us?'

'Yes.'

'And who,' another nudge, 'is that foreign-looking gentleman she's talking to? What whiskers! So palpably dyed, and I declare he's rouged. As for Lady Cork, countess or nothing, it don't speak well of her manners to shout across at him like that. And isn't the other one leaning over the barrier that Mr Disraeli? Yes, it is. He'll fall off his horse if he don't take care — kissing hands with — goodness me! — if it isn't Mrs Bulwer. I wonder she dare show herself in high society after that disgraceful rupture with her husband. She surely isn't walking in the park alone? Oh, no, she has a lady with her, or one who might pass for a lady. I've heard she has taken to drink since the breaking of her marriage. Talk gets about, you know, even if I'm not allowed to meet your friends except on sufferance.'

'I wish he'd move on,' said Mary Anne, dodging her coachman's broad back to look ahead, 'or we'll be stuck here all day.' And to the coachman she called, 'Can't you take us out of this crush?'

'I will try, ma'am.' But while manoeuvring to do so, the companion of the 'foreign-looking' gentleman brought his horse alongside.

'Mrs Wyndham Lewis — as I live! Or do my eyes deceive my heart, which for so long has sought a sight of you?'

'I think,' said Mary Anne, her face closing as a sea anemone closes to a touch, 'that you have met my mother.'

'Indeed, ma'am,' he bowed again, 'for my pleasure.'

'I am reading a book of yours, Mr Disraeli,' said Mrs Yate graciously. 'I find it most enjoyable.'

'Madam, to afford my readers enjoyment is my purpose, but not always the reward of my poor efforts. I greatly value your esteem.'

'Well, I'm sure that's very...' Taken with the flushes, Mrs Yate was lost, for once, of words.

'Dizzy!' From behind the Lewis carriage he, in his turn, was croakingly hailed. 'Come here, abomination, and explain, if you can, your absence from our giddy whirl. I have not seen or heard of you in ages. Have you gone into retreat, or are you in love?'

'In love, madam?' He swept his hat from his head. 'How could I possibly avoid the tender passion when faced with such ineffable charm and condescension as yours?'

'Pish! Don't pass the trumpery patter of your novels on to me.'

'As for retreat,' he continued, 'I am bound to admit that of late I have striven to lead a life of meditation.'

'On your sins?' quacked her ladyship. 'Come to me tonight and confess 'em. I can't ask you to dine. My cook is out and my kitchen-maid in trouble, so she's out too, but maybe Mrs Lewis who, if I mistake me not, is trying to hide herself under her poke, and the prettiest of pokes it is, will offer you — Hey, Mary Anne, will you dine Dizzy this evening and send him round afterwards to play backgammon — or the deuce with me?'

'So now,' Disraeli edged his horse nearer, to tell Mary Anne, 'you will have to be my hostess, will you, nil you.'

'I do not,' she said coldly, 'keep open house at a moment's notice. Count D'Orsay, kindly oblige me by moving your horse that we may drive on.'

'*Pardon, madame!*' Pulling his mare back on her haunches D'Orsay unavailingly endeavoured to oblige, but clamped between the barrier and vehicles in that solid block, advance was impossible. '*Nom de nom!*' he muttered. 'Here we are and here we rest. For myself I ask no sweeter rest. May I also, madame, be invited to dine with you this evening? We none of us see Dizzy these days since he has been elected a member of the Carlton Club. He spends his time testing the *fauteuil* intelligence of that august body, or should one say bodies?'

Mrs Yate stiffened.

'*Mais, à propos le corps, ou le coeur,*' resumed D'Orsay, '*tais-toi, ma belle* —' reining in his peevish mount — 'Dizzy, have you heard — but *sans doute* you have — how Lyndhurst is courting a lady young enough to be his granddaughter? Second marriages are *de rigueur*, and always a compliment to the first. For me, one marriage is enough.' He pouted his reddened lips and, shrugging, said, 'Marry once is an experiment, marry twice — is an excess. *Ecoute-moi, mon ami*, a word for your ear alone.' But the word for the ear of his '*ami*' alone, went considerably farther than its mark: 'Remain out of love if you can, but do not remain out of marriage. If you meet with a rich widow — then take her.'

'D'you hear that, Dizzy?' simpered Lady Cork. 'Here's your chance. I am rich and have been a widow these — God bless my soul! — I forget how many years. I've lived through three reigns but I'll not live through a fourth. Wellin'ton tells me the King is on his last legs, but he still stands on 'em.'

'The King,' Disraeli bared his head, 'will die like an old lion.'

'Yes,' the dowager nodded, 'a sea lion. I knew him when he was a midshipman.' Her faded eyes locked beyond the arabesque of parasols and bonnets on the promenade to the green distance. '"Snotty", his messmates called him, for the trick he had of wiping his nose on his finger. A pretty, chubby flaxen-haired boy he was then, with a head like a pineapple. Ah, well! *Tout passe, tout casse…*'

'*Mais tout lasse*, never,' D'Orsay added softly, 'for you.'

'For me, no.' She brought her eyes back to his with a sudden flare of light in them. 'I am not yet weary of living. When I am, I'll go out like a snuffed candle… Ah, we're free of this jam at last.'

And as the carriages moved on, 'Well, really,' exploded Mrs Yate, who having held herself in was bursting to let herself out. 'She may be a countess, but I consider it the worst of taste to be so forward with the gentlemen, and at her age, too. She can't be right… I'd no idea the King was so poorly, although I had heard he's been ailing for some time, and just imagine! That slip of a girl will be… Why, what are all those people staring at, and to whom do the gentlemen raise their hats?'

'To that slip of a girl,' said Mary Anne, 'come out for her afternoon drive.'

And scarcely to be seen, dwarfed almost to extinction by the overpowering presence of her mama, the Duchess of Kent, beaming acknowledgement right and left from the royal barouche drawn by four Windsor greys. Her diminutive daughter, obedient to the word of command, waved a tiny mittened hand to the curtsies and bows. She wore a chip bonnet wreathed with daisies shading her prominent pale blue eyes; her mouth was slightly open, showing small projecting teeth.

'Well, I never,' whispered Mrs Yate, 'what a plain little niminy miss it is. You'd never look at her twice in a crowd.'

And that same afternoon when returned from her drive, this 'plain little niminy miss' wrote to Leopold, King of the Belgians:

You know, of course, dear Uncle, how very ill the King is, it may all be over at any moment ... Consequently, since Wednesday all my lessons are stopped as the news may arrive very suddenly.

It did: at six o'clock in the morning with the sound of carriage wheels in the courtyard of Kensington Palace, where a young girl asleep in her narrow white bed stirred in her dreams, and woke.

SIXTEEN

From Benjamin Disraeli to his sister Sarah, Friday June 30th, 1837:

The clouds have at length dispelled, and my prospects are bright as the day. At six o'clock this evening I start for Maidstone with Wyndham Lewis.

But how bright his prospects on the accession to the throne of an eighteen-year-old queen, his wildest ambitious boyhood's dreams could not envisage. Sufficient for the day that dispelled those clouds of doubt, mistrust and disreputability which for so long had obscured the light of monarchy.

She, who, on that summer's morning, held her first council at a country palace in a garden where in almost novitiate seclusion she had lived her little guarded life, was as entirely unknown to him as to almost all her subjects. Even many of the personages, peers and bishops, ministers of state, assembled there to homage that childish fair-haired figure in its mourning black, were seeing her for the first time; and seeing, marvelled at her youthful dignity, her amazing self-possession. They marvelled more when, in a clear, unfaltering voice she read her speech to them. Then she rose, and with a glance at that circle of masculine faces and forms, while those slightly prominent blue eyes lingered for a moment on the grizzled head of Lord Melbourne, she went from that room as she had come to it, alone. And not a man who watched her go, so small, so very young, and yet so regally composed, but did not see in her a symbol, a regeneration. It was as if a dead orchard, blighted by long winter frosts, had miraculously blossomed overnight.

Overnight, too, for Disraeli, the miraculous had happened, or, as more sanely he reviewed it, cause and effect had conjoined to bring about a metamorphosis. He, who for so long had scanned a lost horizon, now saw the dawn of hope deferred, at last to be fulfilled.

With the dissolution of Parliament and the general election that followed the sovereign's death, came the offer to Disraeli to stand with Wyndham Lewis as co-candidate for Maidstone.

If he had anticipated any such contingency arising from his friendship with the sitting member or the sitting member's wife, his deliberate avoidance of the latter, and a resultant coolness on her part when, unavoidably, they met must, he thought, have 'squabashed' his one chance of getting in and further barred the way to keep him out. Nor, on the evening of that afternoon encounter in the park when, despite her tacit refusal to invite him for dinner, he presented himself in full fig at her door, did the omens augur better for his coveted constituency. Although Wyndham accorded him politest welcome, hers was most markedly chill. At table, still unthawed, she sat, bereft of her 'unequalled volubility'. No deaf-mute could have been less responsive to Disraeli's effusive hyperbole until, 'My love,' her husband anxiously enquired, 'are you not well?'

'I am perfectly well.' And there could be but little doubt of that, as their guest's low-lidded glance appraised. She wore a gown of her favourite lavender blue, reflected in the deeper mist blue of her eyes. Her always flawless skin, 'tinted like the foxglove', held in either cheek a flush that owed nothing to the hare's foot. Amusedly he watched her relishing her food with an appetite that belied her slender figure and did ample justice to her chef's eight courses. *And, damme,* he wondered, *do they feast in such Lucullan splendour every night,* à deux*?* Or is this spread produced in honour of me? Not very likely, since his presence appeared to be decidedly *de trop.* And so, from cordial address to ptarmigan in aspic he turned to address himself to her.

'I sought you in vain at the opera last night. You were not in your usual box.'

'No,' said Mary Anne.

The butler filled his champagne glass, and, lifting it, Disraeli offered her a silent toast and perseveringly continued, 'I have never heard Mario in finer fettle.'

'Oh?'

'We have only attended the opera once this season,' put in Wyndham. 'We seldom have the time — or rather I have not the time, nor am I disposed, at the end of a session in the House, to sit through a caterwaul of noise. I would sooner listen to my wife,' he gave her his thin smile, 'whose singing does not offend my eardrums.'

'You sing?' Again Disraeli turned a rapt glance in her direction. 'Your accomplishments are legion, matched only by your modesty that withholds from us — your friends — your many gifts, each one a fresh surprise. May I not beg the inestimable favour of a song from you later, as the crowning delight of —'

'Here,' with a jerk of her chin Mary Anne drew his attention to the footman at his elbow, 'he's waiting to serve you potatoes.'

'Potatoes!' exclaimed Dizzy in tones of astonishment, as Raleigh might have uttered in the moment of discovery. 'And crisped, I see.'

'No,' said Mary Anne, 'fried — in curaçao.'

'*Merveilleux,*' he murmured. 'My congratulations on your choice of epicurean delights.'

With an audible sniff, distinctly disdainful, she passed him the cruet. 'I thank you, ma'am, but such perfection of flavour needs no superfluous spice. Do you know the story of the French marquis whose guest at table helped himself to pepper? Whereupon his host observed, "I see, monsieur, I must dismiss my chef."'

'Good, very good,' Wyndham unenthusiastically applauded. 'Your health, sir.'

'And yours, sir. And yours, madam,' received in silence. 'An excellent vintage, Mr Lewis.'

Thus, from ptarmigan to *gâteaux glacés* did their guest, with small support from his host and none from his hostess, sustain a lively spume of small talk, light as the froth of spun sugar on the dish of brandied cherries offered as finale to dessert.

Mary Anne rose from the table. 'I'll leave you two together with your port.' The gentlemen were on their feet, the butler at the door; she passed through it and said across her shoulder to Disraeli, 'As I'll not be seeing you later I'll bid you goodnight. Being stuck in the park in that blazing sun has given me the headache.'

'There, I knew it!' exclaimed Wyndham, and made as if to follow her. 'I'll send your woman to you with a cachet.'

'I am exceedingly distressed,' began Disraeli, 'not only on account of your indisposition, but that I am to be deprived of—'

'My husband,' she broke in curtly, 'has something to say to you —' she darted Wyndham a meaningful look — 'so it's best I was out of the way.'

And out she went.

The 'something', when the servants had retired, that her husband had to say to him and said, with a certain unease, was in respect of a recent visit from the sheriff's officers by whom Disraeli had been intercepted on the road to his father's house at Bradenham from London, 'Such an — hum — unfortunate occurrence,' hemmed Wyndham, 'might prove prejudicial to your nomination as my co-candidate, which project has already been — ah — broached by me, Pray, sir,' he passed the decanter, 'refill.'

So that's it, is it? The little devil! blurted Dizzy's mind. *She must have had that brought to her — by whom? Rosina? Lady Cork? These damned women and their wagging tongues work more mischief in a drawing room than a wolf pack of O'Connells in the House. Yes,* she *has put him up to this. And why?*

'I thank you, sir,' he replenished his glass. 'I am shamefacedly bound to admit —' looking not in the least shamefaced — 'that the blows have been rapid and violent, with demands pouring in from all quarters for the past twelve months. But with the royalties due from my latest novel I hope to clear myself.'

'I am relieved to hear it,' Wyndham doubtfully replied. 'Having given serious consideration to your possible candidature, I feared that my colleagues at Maidstone would not have offered much encouragement to my intent, in view of — ah — your financial — hum — embarrassments.'

'That, my dear sir,' with careful precision Disraeli peeled a walnut, 'is quite understandable, and I appreciate a cautionary hesitation on your part and that of your working associates. However, you may rest assured that if in any way I can assist your electoral campaign, I beg you to call upon me.'

Releasing a breath with the air of a rider to hounds who has cleared a formidable fence, 'I am confident,' said Wyndham, 'that you will prove yourself an admirable ally. I have unbounded faith in your oratorical ability.'

'Which,' returned Disraeli, rising, 'will ever be at your disposal.' He glanced at the clock. 'And now, sir, I fear I must take my leave. I am pledged to play backgammon with Lady Cork this evening. Pray convey my best regards to Mrs Wyndham. I trust she will soon be well of her malaise.'

But he did not play backgammon with Lady Cork that evening; instead, he paid a visit to an obliging gentleman of his acquaintance in Crutched Friars, who — although, as explained at some hand-spreading length, he was not accustomed to doing business out of hours — he would be happy to accommodate Mr Disraeli if Mr Disraeli would accommodate him with regard to the settlement of 'that other little matter.'

Since Mr Disraeli could not accommodate him with regard to 'that other little matter', more than the security offered and reluctantly accepted of a diamond ring, a gold watch and three pearl studs, he returned to his lodging minus these accessories and with a bulging shirt front, in a state of dejection that was almost suicidal.

Under these gloomy auspices it was the more surprising that, within the next ten days, a deputation from Maidstone should have been despatched post-haste to ferret out Mr Disraeli.

They ran him to earth at the Carlton Club with the announcement of his nomination as prospective candidate with Wyndham Lewis, for that stronghold of the Tories; more surprising still the change in Mary Anne's demeanour when he came to the house in Grosvenor Gate all set for his journey to Kent. Breathless, curls bobbing, hands outstretched to be taken in his, she ran down the stairs to greet him where he waited in the hall.

'I am glad — so very glad,' she panted. 'I had hoped — but some of those old Tories are so stick-in-the-mud and so bigoted — can't see further than their noses — and never coming near us and after your row with O'Connell and other things besides —'

'What other things besides?'

His hands, still holding hers, tightened on her fingers as he seized upon this one coherent tag.

'Just,' she told him vaguely, 'things. I was afraid I overdid it the way I cried you down to make Wyndham cry you up.'

'Well, I'm —' Unpredictable, the vagaries of woman. 'Never shall I plumb the depths of your delicious inconsistencies. From your passable impersonation of an iceberg when last we met, you now present me with —' he released her hands to make a helpless gesture — 'with this heartwarming incandescence. I am more than grateful, overwhelmed by —'

'Cut the puffery!'

She hunched her shoulder with that impudent touch of the gamine which had always irresistibly intrigued him. 'And which,' he subjoined softly, 'brings you to me as you must have been when aged exactly twelve.'

'I hope to goodness,' she retorted, 'that you won't go treating the electors to any of your high-flown stuff. Speak plain and to the point so they can understand you. Don't talk above their heads, and don't play-act... Your cravat's all crooked. Come here, I'll straighten it.' Her fingers, cool and soft, brushed his chin as she made the adjustment. 'And don't go to the hustings dressed up to the nines. They've not come to see a peep show.' Standing back to survey him, her head on one side, 'It's a load off my mind,' she said. 'I thought you'd done for yourself this time for good and all, or at least with the Tories at Maidstone.

They're such a stuffy lot there, but Wyndham always wanted you.'

And watching her wide uplifted look and those parted lips, so invitingly, so childishly red, he lost himself, for a second, in a whisper: 'Was it only Wyndham who wanted me?' And which, if heard, was disconcertingly dismissed with another last instruction.

'Be sure to ask him for the brandy balls.'

'Brandy —?'

'— balls. For the children. I always fill them up with sweets when I go canvassing, but they like brandy balls the best. I've packed pounds of them in Wyndham's bags, enough for him and you. And don't forget — God help you! — to kiss the little dears. Oh, yes — and the flea powder. You'll need it.'

He took with him a last glimpse of her standing on the doorstep to speed him and her husband on their way, with the light of the westering sun on her face and the warmth of it in her eyes.

SEVENTEEN

From Mrs Wyndham Lewis to her brother, Major Evans, July 29th, 1837:

> *Mark what I say, mark what I prophesy! Mr Disraeli will in a very few years be one of the greatest men of his day. His great talents, backed by his friends Lord Lyndhurst and Lord Chandos, with Wyndham's power to keep him in Parliament, will insure his success. They call him my Parliamentary Protégé…*

Her 'Parliamentary Protégé's' success insured at Maidstone was followed by a letter to his 'Dear Mrs Wyndham', giving her a glowing account of his electoral reception and his *delight on entering the County of Bucks, to find the walls of every town plastered over with pink placards (my colour at Wycombe) and our united names Lewis and Disraeli.* He concluded with an invitation to his father's house at Bradenham: *We all wish very much that Mr Wyndham and yourself would pay us a visit among our beechen groves. We have nothing to offer you but simple pleasures, a sylvan scene and an affectionate hearth…*

'Do you think these "simple pleasures" he offers will include fishing?' asked Wyndham, having read and frowned over the letter handed him by Mary Anne.

'How should I know?'

'Do you want to go to — where is it — Bradenham? And where *is* Bradenham?'

'In Buckinghamshire. And I don't particularly *want* to go, but I don't see how we can refuse your co-member.'

'H'm. The Blues were shouting "Shylock!" and "Old Clo'es!" at him from the hustings. I wonder was I wise to bring him in? After all, he *is* a Jew.'

'So,' said Mary Anne, 'was Jesus.' And she went away to write her letter of acceptance, leaving Wyndham visibly appalled.

She was charmed with the family of her 'Parliamentary Protégé' when she paid her first visit to the 'beechen groves' of Bradenham. She was enchanted with the house, its 'sylvan scene', its flower gardens, terraced lawns, a finer house than Pantgwynlais… *Most of the rooms are 30 and 40 feet long, plenty of servants, horses, dogs, and a library full of the rarest books…* This again to brother John. Of her 'protégé's' father, *How,* she asks, *shall I describe him? The most lovable, perfect old gentleman I ever met with, and his manners are so high bred and natural. Miss Disraeli is handsome and talented and two brothers…*

Which is all she has to say of them. And of *our political pet, the eldest, commonly called Dizzy, you know Wyndham brought him in for Maidstone with himself.*

Indeed, the whole household, other than the 'perfect old gentleman', appeared to revolve in an orbit of perpetual adoration around this brilliant luminary. The handsome Miss Disraeli, however, whose talents were subservient to, if not entirely eclipsed by, the dazzle of Dizzy, did pause in her worshipful circuit to declare Mrs Wyndham to be 'the quaintest little creature, so delightfully original, remarkably intelligent and such very lovely eyes'. While the two brothers, Jem and Ralph — short for Jacobus and Raphael — were agreed as to the eyes and the originality, the intelligence was likely less remarkable to them than to their sister. The laudations of her lode-star poured into Sarah's ear may have increased her favourable impression of this 'quaintest little creature's' perspicacity.

And Mary Anne was in her element; for, despite that she had gained, or more correctly forced an entry to and been accepted by society, she was still a trifle conscious of her anomalous position in that exclusive circle which held for her no right of way. But in the homely atmosphere of Bradenham, and between herself and these people, who, though British born, were of an alien race, she felt a certain kinship. True, their mode of life conformed exactly to the pattern required by the land of their adoption; yet that hint of the exotic, more exaggerated in the eldest son, was to some degree perceptible in all of them with exception of their mother. Small, grey, with the pathetic eyes of a marmoset, Maria D'Israeli went enveloped, as it were, in an aura of apology for her ineffectual existence not only as the wife of him whom she believed to be the wisest, most erudite of men, but the mother of the god-like Benjamin. In fact, the whole household appeared to be a temple of idolatory in which even the servants were admitted as tyros, in particular one: Giovanni Battista Falcieri, called 'Tita'.

Formerly valet to Byron, he was discovered by Dizzy at Malta when on his Grand Tour, brought back by him to England, and deposited at Bradenham. There for the next thirty years he stayed as major-domo, personal attendant, bodyguard or what you will, to the master of the house.

It was a day or two after her arrival that Mary Anne first came upon this interesting personage while walking with Dizzy in the grounds. He had shown her the rose garden, the hothouses, the grape vines, the peaches; but when he would have gathered some she stayed him. 'No, don't! They're not near ripe for picking. Ours come sooner than this, being milder in Wales than here, and they're not ready yet.'

'So you know everything of horticulture,' said he, 'as of all else.'

'It's Wyndham, not me, who knows about botany — which I suppose is what you mean by horticulture — or at least he knows the Latin names of flowers, which I don't. But I do know something of gardening, landscape gardening, that's to say. You should have seen Pantgwynlais when I first came to live there — all the beds laid out so stiff and tidy. I like a garden to look natural.' And shading her eyes with her hand she said, 'That yew hedge wants a bit o' trimming. It 'ud grow twice as —' She broke off with a startled, 'Lord alive! What's this?'

'This,' said Dizzy solemnly, 'is Tita.' Risen from behind a clump of berberis and towering above them.

Mary Anne stood petrified. He was gigantic: six foot four, and proportionately wide. His head was adorned with a scarlet fez, his face with fierce black mustachios and a thicket of beard that hung down to his uncovered chest. Baggy red breeches were tucked into a pair of gilt-spurred riding boots, and he wore around his middle an embroidered leather belt in which were stuck two daggers.

Mary Anne hurriedly backed away.

'Don't be alarmed,' was Dizzy's dubious assurance. 'Although he fought like a tiger for the cause of the Greeks in the Albanian war and has, to my knowledge, stabbed three men to their deaths, and should opportunity arise would not hesitate to stab a dozen more, he is love and loyalty personified and mild as a lamb.'

'He looks it,' she muttered, retreating farther as Tita, with one hand on a dagger-hilt, advanced.

'Me,' he told her with a grin to split his face, '*Italiano. Signora* spik-a *Italiano*, yes?'

She moistened her lips and said, 'No.'

'*Signora* stay long?' interrogated Tita. 'This very nice-a place, no?'

'Yes.' And for a moment conversation languished while she cautiously prepared for flight. Then Tita, drawing one of his two daggers, flourished it ferociously, demanding, 'You like I cut a *fiori*?'

'What,' she asked faintly, 'does he want?'

'He wants to know if you would like him to cut you some flowers.'

'Oh … I … tell him thank you very much. What is "thank you" in Italian?'

'*Grazie.*'

'*Gratzee* very much,' said Mary Anne.

'*Prego,*' murmured Tita with that grin and a bow; and baring his head he clasped dagger and fez to his heart. '*A riverderla, Excellenza.*'

'What's that about an excellent river?' she asked as they moved away. 'Is there fishing in these parts? If so, Wyndham will be pleased. He likes a bit of fishing.'

'Oh, God,' breathed out Dizzy on a whispered laugh, 'you are — you really are —'

'Well?' Suspiciously she eyed him. 'I am really what?'

'Adorable.'

'That is not what you began to say.'

'I forget what I began to say. I remember only —' he stopped to pluck a sprig of lavender and laid it to his lips — 'what I must never dare to say.' And watching a flush, not of the sun, warm her lifted face, he added lightly, 'Unless when I stand upon a husting.'

'Yes,' she flared in a flurry of vexation, 'when you stand —
to climb the greasy poll!'

'The greasy pole,' he echoed to give the word a twist, 'and I'll
hoist my flag a-top of it, you'll see!'

If those few days at Bradenham were for Mary Anne too short,
for Wyndham they were all too long. There was no fishing, and
although the best horses in the stables were at his disposal for
hacking, the cubbing season being still some weeks ahead, the
daily rides through 'beechen groves' and 'sylvan scenes' soon
palled. In the evenings after dinner, which at Bradenham was
fashionably late, there would be a game of whist for those who
cared to play, which Wyndham did not and Mrs Wyndham did,
partnered by Dizzy against the two brothers; or Miss Disraeli
would give further proof of her talent at the piano in a
selection of the latest modern music by 'this new composer,
Chopin'; or she would sing Heine in German and de Musset in
French, adapted by herself to her own composition; very
talented indeed. And once, but once only, Mary Anne was
persuaded to sing and gave them, 'She'll be comin' round the
mountain when she comes, Singin' I-I-ip-pi-ip-pi-I' to convulse
Dizzy and the two brothers, to scandalise Wyndham and bring
her a scolding in bed.

'Where on earth did you learn that really rather vulgar —?
Miss Disraeli and her mother, I could see, were quite shocked.'

'It isn't vulgar, it's Welsh, as you ought to know. I thought
you'd be pleased. And it's your fault for telling them I sing. As
for "Mrs", she's in a state of continuous shock, and "Miss" is a
Blue, so nothing would shock her. Highly intellectual. A bit too
high for me. She ought to be married, that's her trouble. But
she'll never marry now. She told me she had been engaged to
Dizzy's best friend and that he died of smallpox when they

were abroad together. I must say I'll be sorry to leave. I've enjoyed myself here, if you haven't. I hope they will ask us again. I like them all, especially the old gentleman.' (Who the day before she left invited her to his sanctum, an unusual concession, to show her his valuable collection of etchings.)

While Isaac D'Israeli had insisted on having his children baptised, he himself followed no faith either of Christian or Jew, yet he refused to delete the apostrophe from his name, choosing to preserve the implication of his racial origin. At the same time he could not see why, as he was wont to say, his children, born of and into a progressive western civilisation, should conform to the rites and rituals practised by a nomadic tribe of Arabs who lived in a state of semi-barbarism some several thousand years ago.

There was little physical resemblance between Isaac and his sons and daughter, all of whom were unmistakably Semitic. Not so their father. Corpulent, paunchy, fair skinned and pippin-faced, he might — were it not for his Voltairean philosophy and the patriarchal black velvet cap he habitually wore clamped down on his wiry white hair — have been any old English country squire; and although he had lived through one of the most eventful periods in history, he held himself aloof from and avoided politics. He refused, he said, to understand them.

Seated on his right hand at table, Mary Anne would study that smiling, rosy-cheeked face and those full dark eyes, myopically peering from behind thick-lensed spectacles. It was something in the expression of those eyes, despite the spectacles, and in the intonation of his voice that stirred in her some dormant memory. Often she would ask herself where she had seen him before. But it was not till she inspected his etchings that she knew.

He had laid out on the table his portfolio of treasures: Dürer, Hollar, the two Drevets, a Van de Bruggen; and while she, who knew nothing of their quality, could appreciate their charm, one less remarkable than any of these arrested her attention.

'This!' She turned excitedly to Isaac. 'I know this place. Isn't it Brampford Speke in Devon?'

He leaned over her shoulder to look, peering through his spectacles. 'Yes, I think ... the date. Can you read the date? Your eyes are younger than mine.'

'It says 1804, and that,' Mary Anne told him on a breathless rush of words, 'is my old home in Devon where I used to live, and this horse here —' an eager finger hovered, a hair's breadth from the dark ivory and umber of crumbling walls, a thatched roof, a stable door — 'he's the spit of our old Rory. I'd know him anywhere. I used to ride him on May Day perched up on his bare back, and I'd plait his mane and tail fine with coloured ribbons, paper flowers... Yes! That's Sowdons — Granfer Evans's farm at Brampford Speke. However did you come by it, Mr D'Israeli?'

'How? Now, let me see...' He peered closer. 'I bought it ... yes, I bought it at a curio shop in Exeter where I was ordered for my health, a slight weakness of the chest, to spend the winter months in Devonshire... Dear me, yes, many years ago, before my marriage. But although it has a certain rustic naivety, this print is not a masterpiece. It should not have been placed among the ... I must have slipped it in unwittingly. So you come from Devon, do you? A beautiful county.'

'Yes. And now I know —' she started up from her seat excitedly to tell him — 'I know where I've seen you before. You came to our farm when I was milking the cows in the old stables which Granfer — my grandfather — converted to cowsheds, and you walked into the yard — you must have taken the footpath through our barley field and you asked if you could have a drink o' milk, and I took you to the dairy and you gave me a crown piece. Now, isn't this an extraordinary coincidence!'

'The whole of life,' said Isaac, 'is coincidence, or accident. The accident of birth, of death. Nothing is ordained. We come, we go, and so we pass away. I am no fatalist. But if you are interested in Devonshire, this of Exmoor,' he tenderly unfolded the wrappings of another, 'is a little gem of the English School, unsigned, by a master unknown, yet the influence of the younger Faber, born in Holland though dominantly English, is indubitable. Do you observe his sense of isolation, these wind-drifted clouds in a limitless sky? The delicate articulation of his pointwork? Exquisite.'

'Yes,' said Mary Anne. 'But you *did* come to our farm, and you spoke to me. You told me my eyes was like love-in-a-mist.'

'Ah, if you are interested in flower-pieces I can show you a mezzotint of... Now, where is it? In another portfolio, I think... And here is the loveliest of all. A Hollar. Do you know Hollar? People sometimes say to me, "What can you see in Hollar?" "Almost everything," I tell them.'

'Who,' asked Mary Anne, 'did the one of my old home?'

'Your old home? Indeed? Most interesting. Now, this —' reverentially Isaac uncovered and placed before her — 'is one of the earliest and greatest masters of the point, Albrecht Dürer.'

'Yes, I'm sure. But,' she pleaded, 'don't you think it strange and ... and rather wonderful that I should be looking at pictures now, with you, and when we first met I was milking cows in a stable?'

'A stable,' mused Isaac, 'was once the scene of something still more strange and wonderful.' He went over to a triptych on the wall depicting the Nativity. 'This is a Lorenzo Monaco, or more likely of the School of Lorenzo.'

'Then you do believe in —' blundered Mary Anne; and glanced uncomfortably aside from his gentle questioning smile.

'I believe in ... what?'

'Fate,' she finished lamely.

'If by Fate you would mean the secret things that belong to me and to my gods, then,' he closed the portfolio, 'I do believe.' And, still vaguely smiling, he went with her to the door saying with a courtly bow, 'It has been my great pleasure to show you my etchings.'

'And mine,' she said, 'to have a look at them.'

But he might, she thought, *have given me that one of Sowdons, seeing that he doesn't set much store by it. And Sowdons it is, I wouldn't mind betting — old Rory, the stables and all.* It had been on the tip of her tongue to ask him for it, only that she'd have had to show it round to the family, and then he ... they, had they cared to reckon up — would have guessed her age to have been ten, eleven, maybe twelve years old before he — before any one of them — was born.

EIGHTEEN

In November of that year the young Queen opened her first Parliament with Melbourne, her 'dear Lord M' to lead her and the Whigs, brought in again at the general election. And in that same month Rosina came to London on one of her bi-annual visits from Dublin where, since her breach with Bulwer, she had taken a house for herself and her children. Uninvited she descended upon Mary Anne with a quantity of luggage, two lap dogs, and 'not a rag to her back, for you couldn't be seen dead in a ditch in anything the Dublin shops could offer,' and not a single hotel in this 'beast of a London' would take her precious darlings. She hated to intrude, but if Mary Anne would 'be an angel' and let her stay till she had bought some clothes…

So we find the pair of them in Mary Anne's boudoir on a raw and foggy afternoon; Rosina, lounging on a sofa with her 'precious darlings' spread about her, and Mary Anne industriously sewing something long and white.

'What,' Rosina asked her idly, 'are you making?'

'I'm not making, I'm mending Wyndham's nightshirt. He is so broad in the chest he bursts his seams.'

'Don't!' gasped Rosina. 'You'll kill me. Can he not afford to buy a new nightshirt, or is this the only one he has?'

Mary Anne, in silence, went on stitching. Her sleek down-bent head with its bunches of side curls showed not a thread of grey.

'I can't imagine,' said Rosina, 'how you manage to keep your complexion and figure. You look years younger than your age. And here am I at thirty-four, a hag. Don't fidget, heart of mine.' She lifted one of the dogs in her arms to smother it with kisses. 'They are so sweet together, these two — husband and wife. He adores her, don't you, my precious? What an example he sets to man — the higher animal, as he is pleased to call himself — who combines cunning with evil and greed and lust and every foul and filthy beastliness. Can you wonder I love dogs more than any human? More even than my own children? Dogs give you their hearts and souls — for they certainly have souls, haven't you, my blesseds? Little loving dog souls. *My* hell, when I die, will be dogless.'

Mary Anne glanced at the clock, put aside the nightshirt and got up to pull the bell; and to 'Plush and Powder' at the door, 'Tell Chef,' she said, 'not to roast the pheasants till the master comes home.'

'Very good, madam.'

'"'Till the maister comes 'ome," mimicked Rosina, exaggerating the least suggestion of a burr. 'Such housewifely devotion deserves its reward, priced above rubies, as the bracelet you are wearing testifies. Is this Wyndham's latest offering to the shrine of wedded bliss, or to his conscience?' A smile dragged the corners of her mouth. 'When Edward bought me jewellery I always knew he was involved in some violently torrid *affaire*. But no one would suspect the exemplary Wyndham of indulging in ex-marital orgies unless with a whore, who since the days of the Greek *hetaerae* has always been accepted by a lawful wife as her husband's gentlemanly privilege.'

Mary Anne, in patience and in pity, let her talk. All the bitterness of Rosina's broken love had turned to relentless hate, not only for Edward but for life itself, to regurgitate in a squalid recital of her woes, halted by the entrance of 'Plush and Powder' to tend lamps and draw the curtains. And when these rites were over, 'What,' asked Rosina in her smiling voice, 'of your much-vaunted "Parliamentary Protégé"?'

Mary Anne re-threaded her needle. 'What of him?'

'That is what I'm asking you. Has he made his maiden speech yet?'

'Not that I know of. I'd have heard from Wyndham if he had. But I'll tell you this —' swiftly her needle flew, darning an infinitesimal hole in the white fabric — 'that when he does speak, his name will be made. That's sure.'

'As sure,' smiled Rosina, 'as he is sure of you?' And watching the red fly to her cheeks, drawn from that lightly poised cut, 'His name,' she said in her languid, one-toned voice, 'is made already. In Dublin. As a literary scarecrow, a miserable poltroon, a thing of straw and rubbish, a craven dullard — there's no end to it. The Irish Radicals will never forgive nor forget how he has turned his coat, or his trouser seat, to backside himself on any party's bench and never mind by what low means he gets there. Edward always used to say that Dizzy is as crooked as an eel… Excuse me a moment.' Her restless eyes wandered; she moistened her lips. 'Nature calls. Watch my babies for me.'

But Mary Anne watched her as she moved to the door, her head a little drooping as if overweighted by the heavy hair wound round in snake-like coils. Her gown of vivid scarlet, tightly moulded to her figure, enhanced its provocative curves. She had stoutened, a trifle coarsened, but was still lovely. She went, leaving the door ajar, and was gone for half an hour. A log fell in the grate; the fire sank lower, and the room was full of the acrid smell of burning ash. One of the dogs began, experimentally, to sniff at the leg of a chair.

Mary Anne pulled the bell again. 'More logs. And sweep the hearth. And you can take him —' she pointed to the dog — 'he wants to go out. Better take them both.'

But as the footman lifted them singly by their scruffs, Rosina rushed in to fling at him, ragefully, 'Don't you dare! Put them down. You are not to touch them with your great beefy hands.'

He put them down, and, with scowling apology, went.

'I won't have your swinish servants touch my dogs, d'you hear?' Rosina came threateningly close, standing over Mary Anne. 'Why do you sit at your sewing of a shirt — or's it a shroud — like a seamstress? That's lit'ration, which Edward always used to say is the insignia o' Grub Street.' Her words went sliding on a giggle. 'But I forgot — in course! You *were* a seamstress till you hooked your sanct'monious fox-huntin' gentleman… That shirt of his. I'll wager he don't take it off at night to uncover's nakedness — *or* yours. I know's sort. Think's sinful to 'njoy what he can have for nothing.' Her laugh rang out, discordant, harsh, with a whiff of cloves and brandy.

'You've been drinking again,' said Mary Anne.

'Don' know what you mean by "again".' She lowered herself on to an ottoman. 'I've had my med'cine as prescribe' by my doctor as an'dyne — pain-killer — for the headache.'

'Headache?' Mary Anne looked at her steadily.

'Or God's eternally dam' heart-ache,' Rosina stared wonderingly down at her hands, turning their long tapered fingers this way and that as if she had discovered them for the first time.

The footman returned with a basket of logs. Banefully she stared at him while he mended the fire and swept the hearth. Her eyes beneath their swollen lids were slits of blue, the whites of them faintly bloodshot, and when the man had gone,

'At what time,' she asked, 'do you dine in this fine house of yours? My stomach squeaks with hunger. Does the faithful wife wait up till all hours f'r husband? I'm sure he 'preciates your willing slavery, but I don't see why I should starve.'

'I will have a tray sent up to you if you would care to go to bed.'

'Bed? Who with? I've no bedfellow. My bed is empty, cold — corpse-cold — a cast-off wife, despised 'cause she's never clamped horns on her husband — so much by other men is she desired. Me, also faithfu' wife. Fel — Felicity should be my name, as I've named this one.' Lifting the bitch to her knee, she placed a kiss on its satin smooth head. 'And this,' she took up the dog who nuzzled adoringly into her neck, 'is Fidelius. Mated and loving as once I … we…' Tears brimmed and crawled down her cheeks.

Mary Anne laid aside her work and went to her. 'Come, Rosina, let me take you to your room. Come, my dear, with me.' Soothing, supporting her who still held an armful of dogs, Mary Anne led her away.

It was past midnight when Wyndham returned from the House, which had been sitting in debate.

'Peel,' he said, 'made one of the finest speeches I have ever heard. He'll break the bulk of the Government Party.' He dropped into a chair, passing a hand across his forehead. There was a bluish look about his shaven lips and a hollowness under the high cheekbones.

'You're tired,' said Mary Anne in quick concern. 'I'll have your supper served to you here. It is all ready. I'll ring.' But as she made for the bell he stayed her.

'No, don't. I had supper with Dizzy and the rest, at the Carlton. Oysters, Guinness, broiled bones — but I could do with a half-pint of champagne.'

The champagne was brought. He drank it, no heel-taps; and, thankfully, Mary Anne saw his eyes brighten and his normal red-veined flush replace that mottled pallor.

'Did Dizzy speak today?' she asked.

'No.'

'When d'you think he...?'

'Very soon now. If you care to take a chance, next week or the week after.'

She took her chance, and her seat, in the ladies' gallery on December 6, having had it from Wyndham that it was almost certain the Speaker would 'give Dizzy his eye' on that day. So, with Rosina, whose visit seemed to be unending, she found herself behind a latticed grille facing the Speaker's chair and segregated by a wooden fence from unconcealed, more privileged, male spectators. Since only twenty-four tickets were available for Members' wives or women friends, and as Wyndham in his long parliamentary career had risen to speak only once and would likely never speak again, Mary Anne had not pressed for admission to the gallery until Dizzy's first appearance in the House.

There were scarcely more than a dozen other women seated there behind the latticed screen. Lady Peel, a high-nosed beauty in a lilac quilted bonnet, acknowledged, with a gracious bow, the presence of Mrs Wyndham Lewis, markedly ignoring that of Mrs Bulwer and of a stout red-faced lady in purple on the other side of Mary Anne with two empty seats between. A smell of aniseed emanating from the empurpled lady — she had an unpleasantly bronchial cough — was prevalent above the scent of lavender and musk; of cloth, of velvet, stale perspiration, mothballs, camphor, and from Rosina, cloves.

'We might as well,' she whispered, 'be in purdah, shut off here as if we were untouchables.' She was peering through the lattice to seek out Bulwer on the Radical benches.

Over by the entrance the Irish contingent was assembled in full force, headed by O'Connell.

'We have him to thank,' and from behind the screen Mary Anne regrettably poked her tongue at 'him', 'who, along with his wolf pack, hounded out the Tories. We'd have had the majority, else. They split the vote.'

'There he is!' Rosina had eyes for none but Bulwer. Light shone on his fawn-coloured hair, his calm aloof face, his slight, still boyish figure — 'Like a lily on a dung-heap, set about with blowflies. God knows why he should have chosen to plant himself with them.'

Mary Anne was searching, too, to find, not him she sought, but Wyndham, seated on the Opposition benches behind little Lord John Russell, the smallest Member of the House, in an old-fashioned cut-away coat and wide-brimmed hat. Beside him, tall as he was short, Sir Robert Peel, the Tory chief. But where was —?

Rosina jogged her arm. 'There's Palmerston, the old rip! He should be sitting with the Irish, as he is an Irish peer and can't sit in the Lords. He'd have his hand under your petticoats as soon as wink the eye.'

A roving eye it was, too, looking up at Mary Anne as she looked down at him, ruddy-cheeked, dyed whiskers, heavy-jowled; a fine figure of a man was the lady-killing Foreign Secretary. And she, who had met him on several occasions, had good reason not to doubt Rosina's word.

'He'll be prime minister one of these days,' said Rosina.

But Mary Anne, still hunting, had now found.

He was seated behind Peel, with the table on which stood the ministerial red box dividing the Cabinet benches from the Opposition. Yes, there he was... Not too foppish, but over-dressed enough in that white embroidered waistcoat and gold chains — like the Mayor and Corporation. And that much-too-black cravat. Very pale. 'What a buzz,' she murmured. 'Someone's up and speaking, but you can't hear what he says, with all this chattering.' Her teeth were chattering too, but not with cold.

The Speaker in his robes and wig looked to be asleep. His eyes were closed. And to think you had to wait for that old man to...

The lady in purple, with a creak of corsets, leaned forward, and so did Rosina. 'It's the Irishman up.'

'O'Connell,' breathed Mary Anne, clutching her Paisley shawl about her shoulders. And now she did feel cold, was shivering. Don't they ever heat this place? No fires — more than in Dizzy's eyes, like burning coals, as he turned his head to watch and hear O'Connell.

That rich voice, with its succulent brogue, rolled round the House in broad echoes, conveying not one word to Mary Anne. She said, 'You'd think those Irish would at least keep quiet while this one does the talking.' Yes, and what a one! *We'll meet at Philippi...* Well, they were meeting now.

Rosina nipped her arm. 'There goes your "protégé" sidling up to Stanley. Did you meet Lord Stanley at my parties? He often used to come. I could have had him if I'd wanted... Supercilious devil!'

The velvet brim of Mary Anne's bonnet brushed the latticed grille as she pressed for a closer view of O'Connell.

'What a voice the man has, like a bull's.' Rising loud above the gabble of the benchers.

'…will I, who have sacrificed a fine professional income in defence of my country's rights be vilified, traduced by a renegade —' ('That's a dig at your Dizzy,' whispered Rosina.)

'No, I will not!' At which the lady in purple said, 'Hear, hear!', coughed something into her handkerchief and beamed round at Mary Anne, who returned her a basilisk stare. Mrs O'Connell, for sure!

Then amid the vociferous applause of the Irish band and a cough and 'Huzza!' from the lady in purple, O'Connell sat down, and Disraeli stood up.

Mary Anne lowered her eyes. Her hands were so tightly clenched that even through her gloves she could feel the bite of her nails in her palms. She had a singing in her ears and a misting of her sight that seemed suddenly, wishfully blinded. Then, as she lifted her head, vision and hearing were clarified, and the throb of her heart ceased its hurry.

He began quietly by asking the usual indulgence of the House allowed to those who speak for the first time. But his mincing tone brought hoots of laughter from the Irish and the Radicals. He took it good-humouredly enough to laugh with them, at himself. 'I am not insensible of the difficulties of my position —' more laughter, cries of 'Question!' and some booing — 'and I shall be glad to receive indulgence even from the honourable Members opposite. If, however, the honourable gentlemen do not wish me to…'

Shouts of 'No, we don't!' cat-calls, drumming of feet and more laughter crushed the words in his mouth.

From behind the lattice, Mary Anne saw how his face looked to be drained of blood, his lips as if grafted upon steel. She glanced aside at Rosina; she too was laughing silently. The lady in purple was laughing to splutter out a cough-drop from her mouth on to her lap. She picked it up and put it back again. The gallery was full of sibilants — *Diz-his-Diz-hiss* — and from Rosina a whisper: 'The fool! He asked for this — to follow on after O'Connell.'

He had, however, succeeded in gaining some partial attention, and despite the accompanying chorus of boos, moos and donkey-brayings from the Irish, he turned his batteries upon them with a broadside directed at 'the stains of borough-mongering that since the Reform Bill has assumed a deeper, darker hue...' But the cheers of his supporting Tories were lost in a retaliating cannonade of howls.

'If the honourable Members think fair to interrupt me —'

Roars again of laughter, whistling, and cries of, 'Go on, we're not stopping you!'

Oh, God, prayed Mary Anne from her watch of torment, *make him stop! Why won't he stop?* He wouldn't stop... His lips, parchment white, were drawn back against his teeth in a grin like a skull's, while with hand upraised and jewelled index finger pointing, he flung corrosive irony at 'the noble Lord Tityrus of the Treasury Bench —' Lord John, who appeared to have shrunk, that nothing of him but his enormous hat and little feet in buckled shoes placed primly on the boards in the first position, could be seen — 'and that other noble Lord, secure on his pedestal of power —' *Who?* Mary Anne frenziedly wondered, staring about. *Not Melbourne. He's not here. He's in the Lords* — 'wielding in one hand the keys of St Peter and in the other —'

The conclusion of that was gone in a hailstorm of laughter and guffaws, crashing down in demoniacal waves until, 'Now, Mr Speaker, we see the philosophical prejudice of man...' gave him heartening cheers from his supporters, and here and there an isolated echo from the Opposition.

'Cheers?' Up went his hand again. 'Yes, gentlemen, I would gladly have a cheer, even though it comes from my opponents, but I am not surprised at this reception. I have begun several things several times —' jeering cries of 'Hear, hear'! — 'and very many have predicted I should fail when I often have succeeded…'

It was no use. They roared at him, those Irish. They yelled at him, 'Sit down!' and baited him with hoggish squeals and grunts and taunts of 'Jew! Jew! Take a bit of pork, put it on a fork, and give it to the Jew, Jew, Jew!'

Very still he stood; all of him was still, his lips carved to that smile of a death's head, and the sombre black of his cravat and those glittering gold chains were like the trappings of some mummified lost figure of the East. A sob tore at the throat of Mary Anne. She covered her mouth, stifling the sound of it that none but she could hear for that murderous mockery of laughter.

Then, all at once, from his rigid immobility his fisted hands were raised high above his head, while in a voice, awful in its strength, striking to petrify the glutted House to silence, he cried out, 'Aye, sirs, I sit down now, but the time will come when you will hear me!'

She drove Rosina home, left her there, and drove back to the House. 'Watch for your master,' she told the footman. 'I will wait.'

She waited a long time, her mind a wilful blank. She dared not think, dared not re-live those soul-searing moments when she had seen her hopes, and his, mauled, trampled on, destroyed. Was this to be the end of all her careful scheming? And why… why should she have set her heart on giving him his chance to raise him up and then to bring him down? Her 'Parliamentary Protégé'... In any case, what right had she, a nobody from nowhere, to stick her nose in politics and make of him a laughing-stock? Never, she solemnly vowed, would she hear him speak in the House again until... But what hope of highest honours for him now? He had dropped to the depths. He had failed her, and himself... Brr, this cold! She ought to have worn her sealskin. If Wyn didn't come soon she'd go home.

The sodden dusk closed down upon the wintry afternoon. The paving stones of Palace Yard oozed a dark greasy slime, reflecting a bilious flicker from carriage lamps just lighted by the footmen. The arched entrance to the Commons yawned, dark and wide as the mouth of a giant, to spew forth a vomit of hurrying men, coming, going, halting, merging in groups of twos and threes. She could hear the murmur of their voices and their laughter... No, dear God, not that! Were they laughing still?

She tapped on the window. The footman opened the door of the carriage. 'Go in,' she said, 'and ask if your master has left.'

But even as she spoke she saw Wyndham come out, not alone. Two others were with him. That one, muffled to the chin, was it...? No. Too tall. It was Bulwer. And the other, short, stout, laughing. Would they never cease to laugh? Who was he?

She saw the footman touch his hat; saw Wyndham turn and gesture those two to the carriage. Head-shakings, hand-shakings, bows, and away they walked. Thank goodness.

The footman swung open the door and Wyndham got in. 'My love! You should not have waited for me in this wretched cold.'

'I had to. I couldn't ... I wanted...' Her voice dwindled.

The door was closed. The footman climbed on to the box and the carriage rattled over the cobbles and out of the yard.

'What,' she made her lips firm to ask, 'what are they all saying?'

'I didn't hear much.' Wyndham raised himself from the seat to tuck the fur rug under him. 'Are you quite comfortable, my dear? I haven't taken the rug from you, I hope?'

'What *did* you hear?'

'From the general opinion I gathered that he acquitted himself very well.'

'Very…' She gave a little gasp. 'Very *well?*'

'Under the circumstances, certainly. Both Peel and Stanley thought so. I heard Peel tell Stanley in the Lobby that though some of our crowd were disappointed and talked despondently of failure, Peel gave it them at the top of his voice, "Anything but failure. Just the reverse."'

'But,' she felt something snap inside her, 'those jeers, those horrible animal noises —'

'All to the good, my dear. As I was saying —' He interrupted himself to peer out, cleaning with his gloved finger a space in the breath-misted window. 'An uncommonly nasty night, and a thickening of fog.' He took up a speaking tube, the latest innovation, and called through it, 'You'll have to go slow. Hold them back. We don't want an accident.' And to Mary Anne, 'Shiel told me — that was Shiel who came out with me and Bulwer — that his coachman knocked down an old person in Fleet Street driving home in the fog last night. Ran over her and broke her leg. He had to pay up to keep her quiet.'

'Who —' Mary Anne swallowed — 'who is Shiel? And was that all he had to tell you, about running over an old person?'

'That and other things. Ecod! It's pretty thick here. Can't see the kerb. That fellow had better get down and give us a lead.'

And with the tube to his mouth again, 'Here, Parker, let James down to walk ahead with one of the lamps... What? Oh, well, if you can see where you are going. I won't have broken knees in my stables. It's very slippery.' He hung up the tube. 'Obstinate devil. I told him not to bring out the new young horse this weather — the one I bought to match with the bay mare. She's steady enough, but I am not so sure of the youngster. You were saying...?'

She was not saying, she was praying: *Send me patience!* And then, 'What of Shiel,' she asked. 'Who is he?'

'Shiel? One of the older Irish Members, less extreme than O'Connell, but his staunch supporter. And this I did hear, and saw him break in on a gang of young Radicals all greatly enjoying Dizzy's downfall, as they called it, with Bulwer loud as any in their midst —'

'Yes!' flashed Mary Anne, 'and you come out with him and that staunch supporter of O'Connell's, all toadying together!'

'One of the first lessons,' said Wyndham, taking snuff. 'Nothing better than this for dispelling fog from the nose. Women used to take snuff in my mother's time — not all, but some, and I fancy Lady Cork does still.' He returned the gold box to his pocket. 'I was about to say that one of the first lessons I learned when I first entered Parliament, is that no matter how bitter the enmities within the House, once out of it all parties call a truce, until the next election.'

'Yes, but what,' Mary Anne asked with infinite calm, 'had Shiel to say of this day's disgraceful doings?'

'Hah, yes! Both Shiel, and Bulwer, too, congratulated me on Dizzy's 'sensational' — they called it — 'debut', although Bulwer could not forbear a cut at his rig and the gold chains, which I also thought a pity. I believed he had outgrown his dandyism. Shiel, however, was quite enthusiastic. 'You call it a failure,' he says, rounding on the Radicals and Bulwer, 'I call it a crashing success! My debut,' he told them, '*was* a dead-dull-as-ditchwater failure. I was listened to in silence. Not a cheer, not a laugh, not a question. Not a word.' You know,' admitted Wyndham, 'it was much the same with me. Respectful silence and no more. This buzz that brought the House about his ears today will at least give him a second hearing. They will all be waiting now to have at him again. As Shiel put it, though I have my doubts of that, 'if ever the spirit of oratory was in a man it is in him'.'

'Well…' Mary Anne let out a long held breath. 'You do surprise me,' she said.

As Dizzy two weeks later surprised the House. Nothing could have been more correct than his deportment, more modest his suit of unadorned grey, nor less sensational his speech on the Copyright Bill. Primed by Shiel, who invited him to dinner and gave him some fatherly advice with an eye to a possible recapture for the Radicals, he offered not a loophole for jeers. 'Call their bluff,' Shiel had told him. 'Don't argue and don't reason with um, at all. Drone on. Be precise, and be dull if ye can. Quote dates and figures to give 'um the yaws, so they'll be wantin' a taste o' your blarney.'

This advice to the letter he followed, and was received, he reported to Sarah, 'with glorification… Hear, hear from John Russell and Co. Hear, hear from the leader of the Rads…' And sat down amid cheers from all parties and an uproarious ovation from his own.

'Which,' recounted Wyndham, bringing news of it to Mary Anne, 'is the more remarkable in that, to my mind and a good many others, he gave them the most boring speech I ever heard. Half the House was in a doze, and the rest so busy making notes of what they would have to say if, or when, they caught the Speaker's eye, that they made no attempt to listen. As for the Speaker, I distinctly heard him snore.'

Mary Anne began to laugh. She mustn't laugh. There had been laughter enough to break her. But she had to laugh, she couldn't stop. The pent-up flood of anxiety and misery was rising in a threatened outburst of hysteria... 'I can't ... I can't get over it!' She was helpless, shaken by a paroxysm of the giggles. 'That old Speaker in his wig and...' She held her side, 'Oh, Lord, I've got a stitch. And *that's* your politicians! They're like a lot o' monkeys in a zoo. One minute they'll be gibbering and fighting and gnashing their teeth at each other, and the next they'll be pl-playing with their tails or eating a ba-banana or fast asleep and snor ... Oh, dear!'

Wyndham, who did not greatly relish this zoological comparison, said stiffly, 'At all events, he has redeemed his bad beginning. And now he is well up in the saddle we can only hope that he will keep his seat.'

Mary Anne wiped her eyes. 'So long as those grinnin' apes don't go at him again to pull him down.'

But the new year found him still in the saddle and more than ever in demand at social functions. His letters to Sarah were peppered with names from the peerage, headed by dukes and ending with WLs. For if the Wyndham Lewises were nothing much to brag about at Bradenham, they figured largely in the pattern of that coronation year. And what a year! Never had spring danced so joyously in the royal parks where every afternoon the girl Queen rode out, attended by a cavalcade of courtiers, with her *excellent kind dear Lord Melbourne* beside her. Or in the evening after dinner she would call for music and a dance, *the quadrille, of course. I only dance quadrilles.* Never the valse, not even at her first ball, *a lovely Ball so gay and nice.* And she *felt so happy and so merry.* She had *never heard anything so beautiful as Strauss's band.* She enjoyed everything. Her riding, her dancing, her food. She had a youngster's healthy appetite for food. *Little Vic,* wrote that indefatigable scribe Mr Creevey, still scribbling round to all his friends, *eats quite as heartily as she laughs. I think we may say she gobbles.* And she was always laughing, *opening her mouth,* chuckled Mr Creevey, *as wide as it will go, showing not very pretty gums.*

But whether she were laughing or gobbling or dancing or riding or listening to her *excellent dear Lord M* reading despatches *in that fine soft voice of his,* and telling her tales of his boyhood (and *how handsome he must have looked with his hair worn long as boys did then!*) she was happy, *so very happy,* she ecstatically wrote to Uncle Leopold.

Then to the play to see Mr Kean act Hamlet *so beautifully, though not at all good-looking in the face.* And how gratifying and *moving* it was, to be sure, to hear them play 'God Save the Queen', and to see everybody standing, craning necks to stare at her, seated in the royal box. *Oh, but not rudely staring, it was only because they were so interested...* Not that anything much of her little plump figure in its schoolgirlish little white gown could be seen, more than her little fair head and her little smiling face, above the velvet-draped ledge of the box banked high with flowers.

'And who, dear Lord M, was that foreign-looking person with the very black hair in the opposite box? And the pretty lady with him in those wide sleeves and the large, rather sour-faced gentleman?'

Lord M knew all the answers. 'Mr Disraeli? Such a peculiar name. A new Member? How interesting. Is he a Whig? No? Oh.' But the sovereign must never show preference, although we might perhaps be allowed to tell dear Lord M, in strictest confidence, that we hoped the Whigs would stay, so he might be *always* our prime minister… And the lady? Very animated, is she not? And those *very* wide bunches of curls. So droll! As if they were put on to match the sleeves!'

The gums were shown at fullest view through a peal of laughter, swiftly quenched as the curtain rose on the last act.

'So very sad,' sighed 'little Vic' when it was over, 'and Mr Kean's conception of the part so difficult to follow, one might almost say incomprehensible, but his actions and attitudes are *very* good'… And so home to bed in her very *own* room, not to be shared any more with dear Mama. It had really torn her heart to see Mama's tears when the bed had been taken away, but after all we *were* the Queen of England and *must* be allowed to sleep alone, except for darling Dash in his basket, or until… But one need not have to think of *that*. Not for years and years.

NINETEEN

And for Mary Anne as for the little Queen, the days sped gladly by in those first joyous months of Victoria's reign. At the play, at dinners, concerts, routs, that ubiquitous trio, Dizzy and the two 'WLs' caused amused remark among the ladies of the Whigs. Inevitable, naturally, since Lewis put him in and little Lewis put him up… What, she? But of course! Everybody knows she holds the purse strings, and you may be sure she has a pretty penny put by for her 'Protégé' to square his debts and make her worth his pains!

On forked tongues expectant whispers floated. Would it be a repetition of the Norton-Melbourne case? And if so, in *this* case, the jury might not be so gracious to a turncoat Tory Member as to the leader of the Whigs. As for that mole-blind husband of hers — and such an imperishable bore! — one could but hope his sight would be restored, if not his senses. Oh, but did you see her at the Salisburys' last evening? She positively *pushed* her way in after the dinner given by the Lyndhursts. And her gown! Too frightful. Like something from a pantomime. Yes. And her behaviour! The nods and winks and play-acting and ogling of the duke, one might well believe that in her *far-away* youth she had abandoned millinery for the boards. She must have given poor Dizzy no peace till he presented her to Wellington who, although in his dotage, still had an eye for anything not of the highest *monde*! And there they were, the three of them, the duke and Dizzy and the little Lewis cracking jokes and drinking punch together in a corner. And did you *see*…? And did you *hear*…?

'And did you know,' delightedly cried Mary Anne at breakfast the next morning, reading from *The Times*, 'that we are named among those present at the Salisburys'? It's a very long list. Is it in your paper? Have a look among the Ls. It's alphabetic —'

A knife, dropped from her husband's hand, clattered on the crockery.

'What?' Fear loudened her voice as she looked across at him, so deathly pale. 'What is it?'

'I…' He leaned back in his chair, and struggled to say, '…feel … faint.'

She flew to his side. His eyelids sank; his head lolled forwards, and, while frenziedly she strove to loosen his cravat, a dreadful sound gushed from those greying lips that moved as if to speak again, fell open, moved no more.

PART THREE: FLOWERING THORN

TWENTY

On an April afternoon of capricious sun and showers, Miss Graham, a trifle more shrunken, but girlish and golden as ever, was holding her bi-weekly audience. To be sure, there were few of her former cronies left, since she had outlived almost all of them, yet these later perennials who had now replaced a seeded crop had come to accept Miss Graham as presiding goddess of the Pump Room.

Gathering her circle about her she served, between sips of the waters and in a voice suitably hushed, the latest titbit garnered not only from the news-sheets but from that which she could vouch for on her own authority.

'My dears, when I saw the announcement in the *Bristol Courier* I wrote to her at once but received no answer.'

'...answer,' came the sighing echo, as of a Greek chorus. 'Fancy that!'

'Yes, and I wrote twice before I received a printed card, very black-edged, thanking me for 'kind sympathy and condolence'. And then, my dears, I wrote to her again, and this time the letter *was* answered, not by her, by Mrs Yate. You remember Mrs Yate?'

The chorus, generally, remembered Mrs Yate.

'And Mr Yate? *Such* a charming man — Master of the Ceremonies — but he had to retire on account of his ill health.'

Only one very old lady remembered Mr Yate, and gave her opinion as to the cause of his ill health, which Miss Graham indignantly refuted. 'Dear me, no! You are most wrongfully mistaken. I never saw him once the worse for… Always perfectly correct, and so well spoken.'

'Saw him myself,' obstinately stated the old lady, 'in a stupor.'

'Yes, poor man, to his misfortune. *Quite* paralytic at the end. But let us speak no slander,' chirped Miss Graham, 'no, nor listen to it, especially of the dead.'

'…the dead,' sighed the chorus.

Stifling a giggle as 'not quite' for the occasion, 'Poor soul, her memory,' murmured Miss Graham, 'she being — you know — so *old*. I was in my cradle when she first came to live here.'

At which the chorus rather tactlessly agreed that indeed she must be very, very old.

A pause ensued for sipping. Miss Graham pulled a little face and gave a little scream. 'Oh! I have never known the waters quite so salt… And so Mrs Yate, she wrote me she was dealing with her daughter's correspondence, because poor Mrs Lewis is now in Pants —'

'Pants?' was the scandalised concerted query.

'— or whatever — hee, hee! — the outlandish name in Welsh is for Greenmeadow. And she also told me,' another pause, more pregnant, 'how he … *went*. Suddenly. At breakfast. Sitting in his chair.'

'…chair,' breathed the chorus.

'Yes, imagine the shock! She was with him at the time. And so, considering that I have known her since we were girls together, what could I do but take the coach for Wales there and then, and offer my condolence and my sympathy in person?'

'…person,' buzzed the chorus approvingly.

'I found her, poor dear,' Miss Graham piped her eye, 'in a great to-do of packing. She is leaving Pants — Greenmeadow. Her husband only leased it from an elder brother, and the other Mrs Lewises were with her, bustling about — at least one of them was — and *so* domineering she quite overpowered poor little me. From what I gathered she is being turned out.'

'…out?' came the eager repetition.

'And she could only offer me a bed for one night as all the guest rooms were at sixes and sevens so I had to go back next morning, for I could *possibly* have made the journey in one day, though I told her I would willingly have stayed a month to see her through her trouble.'

'…trouble,' cooed the chorus.

'She must,' was the hopeful suggestion from one isolated voice, 'be beside herself with grief.'

'One would have thought so, but not a sign of tears. Perfectly composed. Black quite becomes her, and of course she will be enormously rich. Coal, or pig —'

'*Pig?*'

'Pig-iron. Foundries or something. And coal. Oh, yes, that is how he made his fortune. Much richer than his brothers. She will have at least four thousand pounds a year.'

'… a *year?*'

'Yes, my dears, and I would be thankful for as much in pence. Good gracious me, is that the time? The new vicar is coming to tea, and I have nothing ready. He has a passion for my — ratafees. So sad he is a widower, but I do not think that he — hee, hee! — will be a widower for long. I must fly.'

'At her age, too,' twittered the chorus as Miss Graham winged away. 'She is seventy-five if a minute, and only think of little Mrs Lewis coming in for all that money and she once a milliner — or worse.'

Much worse, as everybody knew, and providential dispensation most unfair.

Most unfair also, to the minds of the sisters-in-law Lewis, was the dispensation of providence, or of Poor Dear Wyndham's will, bequeathing to his widow a life interest in the whole of his estate and not a penny to his next of kin, until her death! A will, were it made in his right senses and of his own volition…

'Oh, but surely, Mrs Henry,' ventured Mrs William, 'you do not think —?'

Mrs Henry did not dare, she said, to think, but putting two and two together she could draw her own conclusions — and two and two, when all is said, make four. Thousand. A year. For life.

'Could one,' suggested Mrs William, 'dispute … I mean, if not in his right senses?'

'My dear Mrs William,' authoritatively stated Mrs Henry, 'to bring evidence to bear on such a case would be impossible.'

'But to go so very suddenly, and she alone with him when he … at breakfast. And not in his bed like a Christian. Such an unnatural time and place to die.'

'My husband,' said Mrs Henry darkly, 'is of the same opinion. We can only hope he made his peace with God before he went. We had — I tell you this in confidence — we *had* considered a post mortem under the unhappy circumstances of his death. Only that Sir Henry Halford, the late King's physician, declared our poor Wyndham died of heart failure.'

Both ladies deeply sighed.

'However,' piously continued Mrs Henry, 'it is not for you, Mrs William, nor for me, to question and dispute the will of the Almighty, even though we might dispute the lawful will of man. And here we are.'

Here they were indeed, driving up to Pantgwynlais in Mrs Henry's carriage to visit Mrs Wyndham, and give gratuitous

advice in the painful duties of packing up and moving out —
'As soon, we hope,' Mrs Henry said aside to Mrs William while
they waited at the door to be admitted, 'as may be.'

Into the drawing room, bereft of half its furniture, the
remainder draped in dust sheets, swept Mrs Henry, followed at
her heels by Mrs William, and received by Mrs Wyndham with
chilly interchange of pecks.

'My dear Mrs Wyndham, and how are you feeling?'

'Thanking you,' said Mrs Wyndham, 'right as rain.' Mrs
Henry remarked — but did not look — that she was glad to
hear it. Her eyes, like boiled gooseberries, travelled from Mrs
Wyndham's head down to her toes and up to her face,
colourless save for her mouth, which Mrs Henry believed to be
painted — so *much* too red. And was she not also too
youthfully dressed for her years, in that very juvenile black with
those white bands at neck and wrist? Correct for a widow, no
doubt, but not enough crape and no weeds to her cap. Then,
as Mrs Henry's eyes wandered to the empty wall above the
mantelpiece, her black-upholstered body stiffened.

'That,' she pointed. 'That portrait of our poor dear departed.
Where is it?'

'On its way home,' said Mary Anne.

'Home? Where? Whose home?'

'My home, at Grosvenor Gate. Here —' she whisked a dust
sheet from an ottoman — 'you don't have to stand. You can
sit on this until the removal men cart it away. There's two
pantechnicons out at the back. They are packing up the kitchen
things first, and then they'll be coming round for these.'

'But the portrait,' persisted Mrs Henry, 'of my brother?'

'— in-law,' said Mary Anne.

Mrs Henry flushed a dark puce red. 'In *law* indeed, which
brings me to my point. In *law*,' she stressed the word, 'this

house and all within it belongs to us — that is to say, to Mrs William's and my husband, as poor Wyndham's next of kin. Which you, in *law*, are not. I am bound to remind you, Mrs Wyndham, that you have no right to that portrait of your husband, which is a family heirloom.'

'Oh, no,' Mary Anne rejoined coolly, 'it isn't. That portrait is mine. When Wyndham had my likeness painted ten years ago I asked him to have his done too, and he did, and he gave it to me for my birthday. So now if you'll excuse me —' she made for the door — 'I must go and see what those men out there are up to.'

'Should we not also,' suggested Mrs William, as the door closed with something of a slam, 'go and see? I am sadly in need of new saucepans, and she told me only last Christmas that she had bought a dozen of the latest thing in copper. I should like to have those saucepans.'

'As so, my dear, you shall.'

'As so, my dear, you shan't!'

To say that Mary Anne burst open the door would be an understatement. If a cyclone had blown in upon these two elderly crape-adorned ladies it could not have caused more disturbance. Her voluminous petticoats upset a three-legged table and the vase of daffodils upon it, splashing water over Mrs Henry's aggressively black breast.

'Well, really, Mrs Wyndham!' she expostulated. 'Really —'

'Yes, really, really, really! I'm sick of it,' blazed Mary Anne. 'Day in, day out, these three weeks that I've been here settling Wyndham's affairs, you two have been nagging at me, digging at me, mewing at me, making *cat's* meat of me now that I am on my own and no man to stand by me. But, ladies, let me remind you that I, as executrix of my husband's will, can allow nothing to leave this house without I say so. See?'

'Indeed,' Mrs Henry uttered awfully, 'I am bound to resent, as I am sure does Mrs William —'

'Yes,' from Mrs William came the piping tremolo, 'indeed —'

'— this unwarranted attack. I would hesitate,' Mrs Henry continued, 'to accuse you of eavesdropping, but —'

'You'd better!' ominously interrupted Mary Anne.

'Mrs William,' said Mrs Henry in a penetrating undertone, 'we must make allowances. The poor woman is out of her mind. The shock — you understand? We had best be gone.'

They went.

From her bedroom window Mary Anne watched the shattered ladies drive away. *And let's only hope,* she said to herself, *you don't come back!*

Long she stood gazing out at the familiar well-loved gardens. She had made much of her gardens, planting a row of poplars along the drive, grown from saplings, and now so tall in less than twenty years... And that monkey tree on the front lawn flinging out its prickly arms in all queer sorts of shapes and sizes. She would miss her monkey tree. She had heard tell in the old days down in Devon that monkey trees brought ill luck to a house. It had brought no ill luck to hers ... till now. But better for his sake that he had gone so peacefully, unknowing. Cruel for her, though not for him. When her time should come, please God, it would be just that way: soft and quiet, sudden, with no pain.

Her eyes followed the sloping green of meadowland to the valley of the river. A marvellous sweet day it was, the air full of birdsong, the orchard full of blossom, and everywhere a burgeoning of hawthorn in the hedges. Never had been such a spring as this sad, lonely spring, her last here at Greenmeadow; never surely such a wealth of primroses starring the woodland way that led across a stile through the field down to the Taff.

And, as she watched the dappled light and shadow on the water, shining silver blue in the fierce downpour of sun to catch each gossamer drift of cloud reflection, her eyes filled... So often had she watched at this same window and at this same time of spring for him whom she would never see again, come walking homewards from the towpath, his rod across his shoulder, his basket at his side... And from that haunting memory, from the sight of that gay callous empty green, she turned; and in the window seat she sat, to take from the pocket of her petticoat a letter, creased, crumpled with much reading. Yet once more, though she knew it by heart, she must read it again.

It is natural, after such severe trials as you have recently experienced, and such petty vexations as you are now forced to encounter that you should give way to feelings of loneliness and sorrow ... But you must not brood over the past ... You are too young to feel that life has not a fresh spring of felicity in store for you...

Too young! Her lips trembled on a sigh. If only she *were* too young.

I fear that you are at present in a miserable circle of narrow-minded people incapable of any generous emotion and any genial sympathy; but this is an infliction that will not last, and I recommend you by all means to command your temper and watch over your interests.

Yes, well, she *was* watching over her interests, but had not 'by all means' command of her temper.

A smile came upon her lips as she recalled how she had ousted not only Mrs Henry and her echo Mrs William, but the brothers Lewis when they had given her to understand that this, her country home throughout her married life, was to be her home no longer: that she would not be permitted to renew the lease which had run out last quarter, and since Henry owned the freehold of Pantgwynlais she would be requested to remove herself and her belongings at her earliest convenience. Moreover, that legal advice should rightly be sought to disprove her husband's will as 'unorthodox', so the brothers called it, in allowing her not only a life tenancy of the London property but an income out of all proportion to her needs. Very well, *let* them disprove it! They couldn't. She had, as Dizzy would have said, 'squabashed' them. She, too, had sought legal advice and had been assured by Wyndham's lawyer that the will was indisputable, 'A valid, right and proper will for her protection, since, in the event of her remarrying and, had the capital been left to her absolutely, she might have then become the prey of any fortune-hunting adventurer.'

In the event of her remarrying. As if she ever would! Her life with Wyndham, bless him, had been easy and happy, but — what of Rosina? She married for love, a passionate, romantic love, and where did it lead her? To lifelong separation and drink. Marriage at its best, or worst, must always be a gamble.

Then, as she folded and replaced the letter, Nina, with an armful of fresh-laundered linen, came bustling into the room. Nina, now nearing her forties, was spherical, round as a ball, her face still rosy as the rosiest of cider apples; nor, in her long association with Mayfair's 'Plush and Powder', had she lost her loyal heart or her Somersetshire accent.

'I'll be packin', ma'am, of these,' she said, 'as you won't be wearin' of 'em now, 'avin' plenty to go on with.' And while she busied herself at cupboards and drawers, her mistress returned to the window to look … and look again.

'Nina, come here.'

'Yes, ma'am?'

'Do you see what I see?'

'Where, ma'am? I don't see nowt.'

Nor could Mary Anne, for the serried rows of poplars that now obscured that first glimpse of a figure advancing at funereal pace.

Lifting the window sash she leaned out head and shoulders to see him emerge from the drive's elbow, a blob of black amid the green, in tight-waisted frock coat, high hat swathed in crape, black gloves, and an ebony black-tasselled cane. He paused in his walk, removed a glove, and, stooping to the primroses in the grass verge, plucked and arranged himself a buttonhole, and passed on to the front of the house out of sight.

'Ooh, yes'm, I did see 'un, then.' Nina, who had not outgrown her adenoids, was breathing heavily down Mary Anne's neck. 'An' I did 'ear talk o' gem'man what come by coach this mornin' to the Cow and Snuffers, but I never thought to ask 'un 'oo t'ud be.'

A pink flush warmed the face of Mary Anne. 'Give me a clean tucker and band for my cap. Then go down,' she said calmly, 'and tell Mr Disraeli to wait.'

In the ghostly-sheeted drawing room he waited, and he waited. Why so long? Did she resent his coming? And why, he may have asked himself, *had* he come bumping down to Wales in the racket of a stagecoach to arrive bone-shaken in the early morning, at an inn called — of all improbable names — the Cow and Snuffers?

Subduing a grin, he took from his breast pocket a handkerchief bordered in black an inch wide, bent to flick the dust of his walk from his boots, and, straightening up, shot his cuffs to display a narrower edging of black. A circular and ancient wall-mirror returned him a view of himself, diminished, lopsided, an ink blot in the whiteness of the room. But ... were primroses not a trifle gay for the occasion? He removed the buttonhole, slipped the flowers in his pocket and, satisfied that he now presented a sufficiently doleful appearance, he began to rehearse the speech he had prepared to account for his intrusion.

Your wistful little letter has brought me here post-haste in the capacity of guide, philosopher and — no, let us not revert to clichés — *in the capacity of a faithful friend in so far as my advice and sympathy can sustain and comfort you in your severe affliction. The courage with which you have met your most tragic bereavement fills me with unbounded admiration. Rest assured that I and my family, who, from my* — no — *who from their first acquaintance have loved you...*

The door opened: he turned, his recitative ready; but at sight of her standing there, her eyes so large, her face so small and young under the widow's cap, her lips parting to a voiceless cry of welcome, he had not one word to say... Yet when he took her hands stretched blindly out to him, and held them close against his heart, in that revealing moment, though neither of them knew it, all was said.

TWENTY-ONE

The visit to the improbably named Cow and Snuffers of a gentleman with a name equally improbable, gave rise to liveliest conjecture in the parlour of the inn. Tankards rose and sank and rose again, were emptied and refilled, while word went round of her up at the House and of him in his black clothes with his black hair and pale in the face as might be from foreign parts, or as was said of him a lawyer. Heads nodded. A lawyer, indeed.

'And if a lawyer is it,' said Huw Morgan from over the mountain, having worked man and boy this forty years at Pantgwynlais, 'who will go walk in the moonshine with whispers and to kiss inside the palm and close the hand on it, eye-gazing, then will I be a lawyer, mind!'

Which occasioned much laughter and more talk to go about until it reached the ears of the ladies Lewis, who received this latest scandal to damnify 'that creature' past redemption. And it would seem that Mary Anne more than once lost *command of her temper* to give blazing account of *that odious place and those odious persons* whom Disraeli in answer hoped *will be speedily banished from our memories…* He longs for her return and prays she will *come to Town cheerful and happy.*

She came to Town at the end of May, and if not yet cheerful or happy, London most certainly was, in anticipatory excitement of the young Queen's coronation.

At four in the morning of the great day, the guns and the bands and the tramping of feet in the park woke 'little Vic', who *got up at seven*, she confided to her journal, *feeling very strong and well…*

The clatter and noise of it all woke Mary Anne also, to look from her window at the swarms of people hurrying along Park Lane on the way to Constitution Hill. Then, as she watched those milling crowds below, her attention was suddenly focused on one, cloaked, knee-breeched, cocked-hatted, who pushed his way through the thronged pavement to the steps of the house, ran up them, and… Good heavens, in court dress, too! After having told her that nothing would induce him to sit in the abbey for seven or eight hours decked out like a flunkey. And here, at her bedroom door, one of her own flunkeys, similarly 'decked', was announcing, 'Mr Disraeli, ma'am, h'asks h'urgently to see you if you could h'oblige him.'

'Tell him I will be down in two minutes.'

But the two minutes lengthened to ten, while she frantically searched her wardrobe. She had given Nina leave to go with others of the staff who wanted to see the procession. And now where on earth had Nina put that new black satin dressing gown? All these were coloured. Well, then, white would have to do. But her hair — in curlers! She tore them off; no time to put it up. She combed it out and let it fall in long shining ripples to her waist. *What a sight! Can't be helped.* He'd be too full of himself to mind her, or her hair in rat's tails.

'Here's a nice time to call,' was her greeting from the doorway of the library. 'And goodness me! Aren't you grand? I thought you said you wouldn't go.'

'Nor did I think I would, since my purse does not run to a costume of this kind. However, last night I decided to hire one, but it didn't arrive until half past two this morning. I feel very much of a jackdaw togged out as a peacock. How do I look?' He strutted up and down for her approval. 'Does it fit?'

'Like a glove. But Dizzy,' her eyes were full of laughter, 'you are very flushed. Is it fever or … you aren't *rouged*, are you?'

'A little of both, my dear. I have been in a frenzy waiting for this rig from last evening until dawn, but having made up my mind to see her crowned I would have gone to the abbey in my nightshirt rather than not go at all. As for this —' he touched a pinkened cheek — 'how could I appear in gala dress and on such an occasion with my peculiar face of a cadaver?'

'I don't know what is a cadaver, but I do know,' she eyed him critically, 'that I like you pale best. I wish I was going with you there.'

'And I wish I was staying with you here.' He came close to her, saying, 'I have never yet seen you with your hair *au naturel*.' Taking a strand of it he delicately sniffed and murmured, 'Violets … and all kinds of flower scents make up the scent of you. If I had my way you should always wear your hair long and loose, like this.' He gave the silken ends a teasing jerk.

'Here, don't —' But as she pulled away from him her hair, entangled in his fingers, held her fast. 'That hurts!' She tugged; he tugged. 'What,' she panted, scarlet, 'do you think you are about?'

'God knows,' came the staggering answer, 'what I think I am about. I only know what I want to be about. And if you look at me like that, I'll —'

A terrific bang of guns rocked the sky and shook the windows, and sent Mary Anne, still chained to him, right into his arms, to find her lips surrendered, and possessed.

'This,' he tore his mouth from hers to say, 'is what I should *not* be about, and what I've longed and longed to…'

'Are you … have you,' disengaging, she managed to articulate, 'gone mad?'

'Yes,' he panted, in a heat, 'if to think of you all day and dream of you all night, as no sane man should dream and keep his reason, then, God help me, I *am* mad. Idiotically, gloriously—'

Another, louder explosion rent the air followed by the cheering of a multitude.

'The signal!' He dashed to the door. 'I should be in my seat. I shall never get there to *be* in my seat. I must go. Don't want to go. Will have to go. But I'll be back. By four o'clock. In good time for you to drive me down to Richmond. I was riding yesterday at Richmond. The park —' Still talking he talked himself out of the room with her after him.

'Your hat! You've forgotten your hat.'

'— the park,' he said, receiving the hat, 'is at its loveliest now. We will feed the fallow deer and have supper at an inn, and take a row-boat in the moonlight, and then —'

'You've put your hat on back to front,' said Mary Anne.

Richmond in the moonlight, supper for two at a table in a garden with the scent of stock and heliotrope bordering a path that led down to the landing stage... Day fallen, to spread a bridge of dusk between evening and the risen moon above the chalk-white river: the glide of the boat in the grape-bloom dark, when night brooded in the treetops and colour faded out of things, and there was silence broken only by the plash of oars, the cry of owls, and somewhere, suddenly, the liquid golden throbbing of a nightingale's song... Richmond in the sunlight to make a glory of copper-green bracken: the drive down in the phaeton to meet a groom at the gates with two horses, and the ride together along hilly grass tracks, black streamers floating from her tall hat to her challenge, 'Come, I'll race you!' lying forwards on her horse's neck, full tilt under hanging branches, past herds of grazing deer scampered by his warning shout, ''Ware rabbits!' The stumble of her horse with his foot in a burrow to throw her off, and Dizzy, white-faced beside her on his knees in the tussocky turf.

'How *can* you be so reckless. Are you hurt?'

And her laughing answer as she scrambled up, brushing dead leaves, mould and grass stains from her habit, 'Hurt? To fall cushion soft! Would you have me ride a rocking horse?'

'You might have done yourself a mischief.'

'Done this lad a mischief, more like.' Expertly she felt her horse's hocks, soothed him, tightened his girths and, disdaining help, remounted.

'I didn't know,' Dizzy said in wonder, as they turned towards the gates, 'that you, besides all else, are an accomplished horsewoman.'

'Accomplished my — fiddle! Wyndham, bless him, always used to say I rode like a cowboy, and that's not surprising since my first mount was a steer and I learned to break in shire horses, and ride 'em too, bare-backed, before ever —' let him have it — 'you were born!'

So those joy-filled summer weeks fled by. *The happiest summer of my life!* wrote the little crowned Queen to her Uncle Leopold; and, for Mary Anne, a second blooming.

But despite Dizzy's singular behaviour on Coronation Day, rides in Richmond Park and moonlight excursions on the Thames, he did not again forget himself in more than semi-comic adoration. At his insistence that it would have been her husband's wish she should not lead a life of solitary confinement, but to go about and decorously entertain, she did.

In July, a few chosen friends were invited to watch the Review in Hyde Park: D'Orsay, Lady Cork, the Lyndhursts,

Rosina, who, again on a visit to London, invited herself; and Dizzy, who invited Lord Rolle. This gouty and very old peer had caused quite a stir in the abbey at the crowning when he tripped over his robes as he knelt to do homage, fell down the steps, and, according to Dizzy, was 'stuck there unable to rise till the Queen charmed all present by stepping down from the throne to help him up.'

And at Grosvenor Gate Lord Rolle, rather shakily upheld by two lackeys, like heraldic symbols supporting, with Mary Anne and Dizzy on either side, watched the Review from the drawing-room balcony while the other guests watched from behind window curtains below. For 'it would never do,' declared Mrs Yate, 'that people should see you entertaining, and poor Wyndham scarce buried four months. I don't know, I'm sure, how you have the face to go horse-riding in Richmond and gadding about in your weeds with that Mr Disraeli. And now to be giving a party!'

'It won't,' said Mary Anne, 'be a party.'

But it was, with a popping of corks to the popping of guns and a cold collation later in the dining room. Then, when all the guests had gone and the park lay bathed in the last of the sun, he, who had left with the others, returned.

'Have you forgotten something?' Her eyes were wide upon him where he stood in gala dress, having rushed home to change and back again. 'I thought you were going to the Londonderry banquet?'

'I was. I am. I have this to say.' And jerkily he said it. 'Before I leave. For Maidstone.'

'Maidstone?'

'Tomorrow. My constituency. I must tell. I cannot wait to tell. Hear me now, and having heard let me know if I may … hope.'

'Hope?' Her heart jumped, but she answered him coolly enough. 'Hope for what? Your seat is certain. The by-election—'

'Damn the by-election! Why do you wilfully misunderstand? Is it so impossible? I see it is. Forgive me.' And as suddenly as he had come, he went.

Well!

What to make of this? Or of the two letters that followed his departure, hurriedly penned at each stage of the journey.

ROCHESTER.
July 26th.
Pressed as I am for time and about to make a speech of which I have not an idea ready, I send you this scrawl from a wretched pot-house to tell you that you have not been the whole day one moment absent from my thoughts.

MAIDSTONE.
July 27th.
I arrived here just half an hour before the meeting, and under the inspiration of a glass of brandy and water I contrived to collect some nonsense, but what I shall say at the dinner today I can't devise… Let me avail myself of this moment which I seize in a room full of bustle and chatter to tell you how much I love you…

If by this written avowal it would seem that he had lost his heart, she kept her head. His letters went unanswered. Back in London he called with fruit, flowers and messages from Bradenham, to be told at the door that madam was not at home. An intentional rebuff?

Abysmal misery.

He rushed down to Bradenham to confide in Sarah and contrive an invitation. Would she accept it? Would she not, or would she? He loved her. He adored her, he wanted her, or did he? If he could only know his mind — and hers!

And then, God be praised, she came to Bradenham, but in no happier case was he to have her there, made much of by 'Sa', the two brothers, his mother, his father, but never by him, whom she allowed no single opportunity to see or speak with her alone. Her avoidance was deliberate, her coolness unmistakable. She couldn't bear him near her. Why?

She drove him crazy.

Not until the day before she left did he track her down and corner her — with Sarah — in the rose walk, a cul-de-sac from which she could not escape him unless she climbed the wall. Not that he doubted if put to it she would. If she could mount a horse in her habit and unaided, she would not hesitate to climb an eight-foot wall in petticoats.

A comprehensive sign sent Sarah off with mumblings of the vicar's wife to tea, and gave him an eleventh-hour chance to speak.

He spoke, to less purpose than passion, until his words ran down in an affronted silence when he saw the rose she held raised to her lips, to hide — Good God! — her laughter. Yes! She laughed at *him*, who frenziedly appealing, had told her, 'I adore you. I cannot live without you. I owe everything to you. You have made me what I am. Without you beside me my career is finished. Ambition, my future — what are these compared to this consuming urge? You will be the ruin of me if I am to lose you...' Would she not give him hope, for this suspense was agony and death?

And now that rose, no redder than her lips, so red were they as if at the slightest finger touch they would spurt blood —

and her small body, so strangely enticingly virginal, shaken with inward — what? Emotion? Tears? Oh, no, with the giggles. Like a schoolgirl.

'I amuse you.' His voice struck at her, hoarse as a crow's. 'You find me tremendously funny, as did the House when I was up on my feet to throw pearls before swine. I am accustomed, by this time, to being received as a comic turn. This performance of mine offered gratis would cost you a florin in a sideshow at Cremorne.'

'Listen…' Would he *listen*?

He would not. 'You must have known and seen, and split your sides to know and see your conquest, while you play me as a puppet on a string.'

'Don't talk so wildly. I am not yet adjusted to my… Can you not understand? It isn't circumspect that you should…' She faltered. 'And barely six months since Wyndham… pray be reasonable.'

'Reasonable? I have been reasonable and contained too long. I can be contained no longer. I love you and I want you and by heaven I will have you —'

'Dizzy!' she bade him sharply, 'control yourself.' She began to be alarmed. Whether feigned or not, he was in a taking, with beads of sweat about his forehead where a vein stood out like gristle; his face, not pale now, was fiercely flushed. He would have a stroke if he went on like this. There was something menacing and desperate in the way he seized and crushed her hand. She felt the fever in his blood and her own leaped to meet it, but resolutely she repulsed him, wrenching her fingers from that too fervent grip, hardening her heart against the bewitching trick of his smile, swift as a sun-flash in a stormy sky, and as swiftly fading when she found voice to tell him, 'You may believe you love me, but I … do not.'

'You do not. I see. You hate me. I am odious. Repulsive. Is that what you would say?'

'No, it is *not* what I would say. Don't be idiotic.'

'Idiotic? Hell's torment!' His groan and the clutch at his hair recalled the actions and attitudes of Mr Kean in *Hamlet*. 'Is the hunger of my love, my desire, to be discarded, spurned, mocked as — idiotic? How can I convince you?'

'Not by all this play-acting.' The rose was at her mouth again. 'I'll lay you've said the same a hundred times and to a hundred women.'

'No. *Ten* hundred times, and to *ten* hundred women. Go on. I am enjoying this. You rip aside my weaknesses, expose me to myself as — idiotic. A sentimental lecher with the morals of a chimpanzee. I compliment you on your penetrating powers of discernment. Let me go!'

'No one's stopping you,' said Mary Anne.

For half a minute he stood in controlled exasperation, taking in the charming oval of her face, the clusters of side curls under the widow's cap that lent to her mourning black a note of raffishly incongruous sophistication.

'God knows,' was at last dragged out of him, 'what there is in you that brings me to this pass. Yet, if I may believe myself, though you do not believe, I think my life is bound indissolubly with yours. I may be deluded. I hope I am deluded. If so, in time, I *may* be restored to sanity, and find you no more than a flowering thorn to be plucked out of my heart. In the meantime, I swear —' he neared her, the breath of his words on her lips — 'before God I swear it,' he repeated with forced quiet, 'that I will make you want me as much as ever I have wanted you.'

Her eyes were closing, her head lifting, her body swaying as if to sway into his arms.

'Will you,' he whispered, 'love me … ever?'

'I can't. I daren't. I must not let myself.' He saw a tear steal from under her eyelid. She drew away from him; he heard a sigh. 'If only you were fifty.'

'Fifty!' He stood staring at her blankly. Incalculable creature. Then, light dawning, it was now his turn to laugh, unamused and loud. 'Aha! I understand. Your taste is for a vintage well matured and mellowed, bottled in the peerage. Our friend the duke — or Melbourne. Both are your ardent admirers. Or even the decrepit and venerable Rolle can offer you what I cannot. I have no coronet to lay at your feet, but that may yet come when I *am* fifty. Ah, well,' he shrugged, and he was smiling, 'so now we have it. I am too young for you.'

'No.' She pressed a tooth down on her underlip. 'I am too old … for you.'

That broke him and he took her. She let herself be taken. In one unguarded moment he had shattered her defences. She could no more resist.

'You have me utterly,' he murmured, his hot eager mouth on hers. 'I am yours, and I am … devastated.'

As, in that timeless second, so was she, to know herself handfasted, sealed, confessed.

Confessed but not committed. Although by this tempestuous approach he had stormed her citadel, she still retained to reassemble, a retaliative store of ammunition.

Not one wink did she sleep on the night of that encounter in the garden, while with pitiless self-searching she reviewed her case and his.

Why should he, with his brilliant future marked for fame, he, who could take his choice of women better placed and graced than she in birth and breeding, beauty, youth, choose to fling himself at her whose youth was gone? There lay the bitterest sting of her doubt. Her age. The same difference in years as had been between herself and Wyndham, only now *she* was the elder. She must not in fairness to him encourage this infatuation, for that was all it could be: an infatuation. She dared not take the risk ... of what? Of marriage? But he had not once mentioned marriage. What then did he want of her?

And as she re-lived his words, his touch, she fused and flamed with exquisite revival of sense upsurged, surprised and, for the first time, awakened. Yes, through all these years of married life she had been starved of love, if this were love, this sweet drenching madness... She stood before her looking-glass, lighted the candles either side of it, and with merciless precision surveyed her mirrored face. Not a line, not a blemish, no sagging of the contours, no thickening of flesh? Her waist still measured eighteen inches. Her hands... She had heard that a woman's age can always be guessed by the hands. What of hers? She spread them out; small, soft, white. Her arms? But what use to go over her points as if she were a brood mare? Time cannot be cheated and, some day, time would find her out, to find her old ... too old for him.

She crushed her hands to her hot cheeks, and going to the window opened the casement. A wonderfully calm autumnal night of stars with a small golden disc of a moon hanging high above a yew tree; not a breeze to stir the clinging warmth, heavy with the smell of wood-smoke and the scent of a cigar that came to her with the sound of footsteps on the terrace. She heard voices, low in murmurs, as they strolled, he and his father. The end of a sentence drifted up... 'your own mind best, my son.'

And his answer: '...know my mind, have weighed the pros and cons. When or if I marry it must be for...'

She drew away from the window, closing the curtains, shutting out the night, fearing to hear more lest she should hear too much. 'And if,' she muttered savagely, 'you know your mind then so do I, to weigh less pros than cons for me — with *you*, young man!'

She went to bed at last, rose unrefreshed and rang for Nina. 'See to the packing. We leave here at nine o'clock sharp.'

She left with fond farewells to all the family, but not to him, who may also have been sleepless, as he did not appear at breakfast. She scribbled him a note of apology for having gone without bidding him goodbye, and drove up to London pursued by a letter expressing 'stupefaction' at her hasty departure from which he had not yet recovered. He had *scarcely left his room, scarcely spoken to anyone. The charm is broken, the magic is fled. What future joy, prosperity, what fortune, even fame, can compensate for this anguish?* Which went unanswered to bring him, still in 'anguish', tearing after her to London.

'May I,' he demanded, 'be allowed five minutes' audience? I have that to say which cannot be written.'

'Very well.' She glanced at the clock. 'Five minutes only. I am dining with the Lyndhursts this evening and must rest before I go, so you'd better be quick and begin.'

'I don't know how to begin.' He stood before her, his chin in his stock, his thick eyebrows meeting in a dark frown, as he watched where she sat at her knitting. That everlasting knitting!

'My patience,' he said, with dangerous calm, 'is exhausted. I do not hope that you can understand — any more than a kitten understands the love pangs of a tiger — the sufferings of doubt, despair, that you have caused me. And you sit and you — knit.'

'Why shouldn't I knit? You ought to be pleased that I make shawls and comforts for the old folk at Maidstone, the wives of your constituents. I always did for Wyndham to hand round to them at Christmas, and now I am doing it for you. And this,' a smile strayed, 'is all the thanks I get for it.'

A pause. He moved away, travelling uneasily about the room, fingering knick-knacks, peering at a silhouette of Wyndham on the wall.

'Your five minutes is up,' she said.

He turned, glaring down at her who was busily unravelling a knot in the wool.

'You,' he said chokingly, 'are driving me mad. Mary Anne!' He flung himself beside her on the couch, gripped her by the shoulders and turned her face to his. 'I can't — I cannot, I *will* not,' he gave the shoulders a shake, 'go on like this. I love you. I want to *be* with you, to live with you, never to be away from you. I give you all of myself if you will take me.'

She stole a glance, not smiling now. He felt the tremble of her body, but her face was closed as if a shutter had slid down to hide her from him; her lips parted to speak, but not a word, scarcely a breath came from them.

'Will you,' he whispered, 'give me what I ask? If I dare hope that there is love between us, will you … marry me?'

She did not stir; a faint scent of violets filled an empty void. His hands slackened on her shoulders, fell; he bowed his head. And through the stillness and the silence she raised her eyes slowly, defensively, to tell him, 'No, Dizzy. No, my dear.'

'No?' He stared at her, white-lipped. 'You mean that?'

'I mean,' she covered her eyes from his searching, 'I don't know what I mean,' she said in a small lost voice, the colour draining from her face; and in that moment she had for him an infinite tender beauty. 'I must,' her lips quivered on the words, 'I must have time. I want to be sure, not only of you, but of … myself. Give me a year.' She had now recovered from her momentary weakness; her voice strengthened and steadied. 'I want to learn more about you. I must have a year to study you and your character.'

'Study me and my —' Anger forced the words from him in raucous amaze. 'God alive! You have known me — how long? Six years.'

'Yes.' She nodded. 'I have known you six years as Wyndham's friend and colleague. But what do I know of you as a … as you would have me know you? I am…' For a second she faltered and went on resolutely, 'I am older, much older than you. It would not be right to tie you down just because you think you are in love.'

'I don't think. I know.' He caught her in his arms. 'What is age in eternity when a thousand years are but as yesterday? You and your race are young, and I and my race are old with all the wisdom and the sorrows of my people in my blood. That I find myself enmeshed in love against my will is no new thing. It has grown in me. I have fought against it, believe me I have fought. Do you suppose I *want* to be enslaved by you?'

His mouth found and rested lightly upon hers in a touch that was the very ghost of passion; and for a long time there was no sound in the room more than the guttering of one of the candles in a branched gilt stand on a table at the couch-head. Then, even in that moment when their joined breathing quickened to a gentle frenzy of desire, she slipped away from him, stretched an arm to extinguish the burnt wick, could not reach so far and stood, methodically to snuff the smoking wax, and light and wave an aromatic pastille to disperse the smell of it.

He watched her in a dumb fury of frustration. What to make of her? Was she the most experienced or the most artless of coquettes, to tantalise with promises unspoken and withdrawn in the coolest of dismissals, still waving the pastille, to wave him to the door?

'Go now. Your five minutes is fifteen. If what is to be may be, it cannot be yet. Not for a year at least… So now you know.'

A year! A lifetime. But with that half promise he must be content and strive to *bear up* against his *sorrowful lot*. So on his return to Bradenham he wrote to her. He could not reconcile love and separation. *My ideas of love are the perpetual enjoyment of the society of the sweet being to whom I am devoted, the sharing of every thought, every charm, every care. Perhaps I sigh for a state that can never be mine.*

It looked uncommonly like it, since these almost daily effusions went, for the most part, unanswered; yet there is some evidence of a reply, possibly relegated to the fire sooner than retain it as perpetual reminder of *your words that recall to me most fully, vividly and painfully the wretchedness of my situation … I will not allow any feelings of false pride to prevent me from expressing my deep mortification at your strange and prolonged silence … What must be the inevitable end of this estrangement?*

A vile low disorder looked to be the end of it. *I am lying on a sofa so utterly wretched that I cannot convey to you a faint idea of my prostration … I am sure you never wish to show your power over me because I have never wished to conceal it, but indeed this last week is something too terrible to think of…*

Alarmed at his state, his 'sweet being' appears to have relented enough to offer him the hope of a reunion and to bring forth this paean of joy:

I am mad with love. My passion is frenzy. The prospect of our immediate meeting overwhelms and entrances me. I pass my nights and days in scenes of strange and fascinating rapture. Lose not a moment in coming … I cannot wait.

She made him wait until after the New Year, *the happiest of New Years, and indeed I hope and believe it will be,* he wrote, *the happiest of our lives!* By which it would seem she had relented even so far as to consider a betrothal. *But not yet,* again she insisted that the year must run its course before there could be any question of an open engagement between them. On that point was she adamant. *Nobody — but nobody, must know of it. You promise?*

He promised; and for a week or two at least none did know of it more than all the family at Bradenham; and D'Orsay, his friend and confidant, he *must* know of it, pledged to secrecy, of course; and Chandos, who already knew of it, and dear old Lady Cork, who would be only too delighted to know of it. And so from ear to ear and mouth to mouth the news went flying to alight on the lips of Rosina, now Lady Bulwer-Lytton, since Melbourne had bestowed a baronetcy on Edward, from whom, however, she still lived apart.

In London after Christmas, and, as always, self-invited to Grosvenor Gate, she made the very best, or worst, of her opportunity to tax Mary Anne while out shopping in Bond Street, with: 'This amazing information brought to me, my dear, by — you will never guess — my milliner!'

'Your —?'

'Milliner, my love. Such persons, as *you* should know, hear all the talk first-hand, and yesterday, while fitting my head with an advance model for the spring on which I would ask you to cast your professional eye —'

'With all the pleasure in the world, my love.'

'How sweet-natured you are, to be sure. There is the shop, just opposite. Madame Pompadour. All the Queen's ladies swear by her, but not our little Vic. Her pokes are too *fright*fully Lehzen. Tell your coachman to pull up, my love.'

The coachman pulled up and the ladies got out.

Madame Pompadour of Bond Street, who bore in countenance, bust and deportment, a distinct resemblance to Madame 'Thing' of Exeter, pridefully produced her creation of green satin straw trimmed with matching bows of gauze, blue lilies, pink roses and one ostrich tip.

'This,' said Mary Anne with a deft touch to a rose, 'would look a sight better under than over the brim, and I'd dispense with the ostrich tip too, if it was mine. The least trimming the better if one is not, let us say, seventeen.'

'As *you* say, my love,' purred Rosina.

'And as I say,' the Pompadour stated, with a glare and in Frenchified cockney, 'this poke is the most fashionable style for this season. Only yesterday the Lady Lynd'urst she says to me, "Pom-pom," she says, "your bonnets are always in advance of the mode and of the most *chic*."'

'Yes, Pom-pom, we know your taste to be perfection,' Rosina offered her most ravishing smile, 'but you see, Mrs Lewis is herself exceptionally gifted with a flair for millinery. She makes all her own bonnets and caps, even, alas,' sighed Rosina, 'her weeds. But you will not, will you, my love, be in weeds much longer?'

'As *you* say, my love,' echoed Mary Anne with a smile as ravishing as Rosina's own.

'And as Lady Lynd'urst says,' went on the Pompadour, her glare, her bust, and her cockney French a trifle more pronounced, 'and as I may say as to be the first of 'umbler persons in the *monde*, to congratulate Mrs Wyndham Lewis on what I take to be 'er engagement, in the hope I may 'ave the pleasure to make 'er *bonnet de noce*.'

'I have not the least idea,' achieved Mary Anne in tones of crushing astonishment, 'what on earth you are talking about.'

'A thousand pardons, madame,' the Pompadour gave a near Frenchified shrug and a spread of her hands, 'if I intrude on a *petit secret*, no? It was only that my Lady Lynd'urst, whose *bonnet de noce* I made for her when she marry with that very old Lord, and she so much younger than 'im —'

'Better be much younger than much older,' broke in Rosina, removing the bonnet with an upward glance at Mary Anne. 'Don't change the rose, Pom-pom. Mrs Lewis is thinking of the mode in days gone by, long, long ago. Is that not so, my love? And if I pay cash down, dear creature, will you give me discount?'

'*Chère madame!* With the greatest pleasure would I give you discount if my last *petit billet* 'ave been paid, which it is not. I am always 'appy to accommodate my ladies, but...' Another spread of the hands.

'How much,' asked Mary Anne, opening her reticule, 'do you want for it?'

'Not what *I* want, madame. What I o*ffer*, at a price to give away, for three guineas.'

'Yes, we know all about that. Here are three sovereigns.' Mary Anne dropped them into the Pompadour's outstretched palm. 'You can let madam off the shillings.'

'Mary Anne, my love!' gasped Rosina, 'how too utterly ... but I cannot allow ... I am not yet so pauperised as to...'

'Not another word, my love,' with ineffable sweetness uttered Mary Anne. 'It is my pleasure.'

And out to the carriage she swept, followed by a startled Rosina.

'What is the meaning of this sudden embarrassing spurt of generosity?' she queried as the footman closed them in.

'Shall we say hush money?' smiled Mary Anne.

'I can't imagine —'

'Can you not? I know my Rosina. And I know how she has fattened on the cream from the Londonderry saucers lapped up since she came to town to spill it into Georgie Lyndhurst's ear, and so to the Pompadour *née* Black — of Whitechapel. Who better than I,' was the ingenuous reminder, 'should know how talk flies from a rose on a bonnet to the jewels on the crown of the Queen?'

'As so you should — from past experience.' Rosina's smile, now a trifle starched, answered hers.

'And as you should not,' retorted Mary Anne, 'so keep your tattle under that adder's tongue of yours and hold it there.'

'As I would were I not your friend, your only friend, your truest friend. I tell you this most honestly and from my heart sincerely.' And nothing could have been more honest and sincere than the tearful look in Rosina's lovely eyes. 'I would not invite your confidence if I did not think it my duty to tell you how your name has been coupled — to your detriment — with Dizzy's ever since poor Wyndham died. A liaison, well —' Rosina laid her hand on Mary Anne's and squeezed it knowingly — 'that, at *your* time of life, one could understand. Much may be excused in the newly widowed of uncertain age, who finds little comfort in an empty bed. But to contemplate — I fear to say it — marriage with —'

'Why do you fear to say it?' Mary Anne's voice was as cold as the hand she withdrew from Rosina's.

'Because, my love, I cannot believe you would be so foolish as to let yourself be gulled by the artful flattery of a fortune-hunting adventurer. Do you not realise how fatal such a marriage would be?'

'There is no question of marriage between Disraeli and myself.'

'Oh, yes, there is. D'Orsay —'

'D'Orsay?'

'D'Orsay, my dear, had it all round the town in half an hour, and came bursting in on me and Georgie Lyndhurst only yesterday, hot with it, saying, 'The incredible has happened. Dizzy is *fiancé* with *la petite Louise*'. You know he always calls you that?'

'And you believed him?'

'I believe the evidence of my own eyes and ears. Did I not see him here with you in July at the Review in the park? People were nodding and winking at each other even then, greatly diverted at Dizzy's somewhat too obvious intention to grab at an income for life and the chance to be free of his debts. Everyone knows he hasn't a penny to bless himself with and will *have* to marry money — to say nothing of a mansion in Grosvenor Gate. My dear, you can't — you really cannot make yourself a laughing-stock by marrying a man almost young enough to be your son. By the way, does he know your age?'

'He knows I am older than he.'

'Does he know how much older?'

Mary Anne released her bitten underlip with an ooze of blood upon it. 'He has never asked my age, but if weighed in the balance of —'

'— of your bank balance?' asked the smiling Rosina.

'Even that,' was the equally smiling response. 'But in spite of my age and my bank balance, and if he is not quite so madly in love as he professes to be, he seems to think I would make him a suitable wife.'

'As so would anyone,' scoffed Rosina, 'make him a suitable wife along with four thousand a year. Frankly, Mary Anne, I did credit you with more sense than to throw yourself away on a trumpery charlatan. Compare what you can give him in exchange for what he can give you. His novels? Second-rate. His parliamentary career? He may, by sheer impudence, live down that disastrous false start of his, but he will never romp home a winner on the parliamentary racecourse. However, I am glad you realise that his primary motive is not love. How could it be? After all, the difference in your ages apart, it isn't as if —' Rosina settled herself complacently against the padded cushions of the carriage — 'as if you were a beauty.'

'Unfortunately no. And here we are at home.'

'And there,' said Rosina 'is Dizzy at your door, which he hopes to make his own.'

He was admitted; the door remained open. The footman came down from the box.

'Tell Charles,' Mary Anne bade him, 'to show Mr Disraeli to my boudoir.'

'Very good, madam.'

The ladies followed him up the steps. 'Will you excuse me, Rosina, if I ask you not to join us?'

'Of course, my dear. And do, pray, be firm. You will, won't you, be very *very* firm? For your own sake, for his sake —'

'And for God's sake,' inelegantly cut in Mary Anne, 'shut you your jaw! You've said enough.'

But not enough to satisfy Rosina, who could have said a great deal more. Her bedroom was on the same floor as that of her hostess's boudoir, and the temptation, strengthened by a dose from a flask, 'medicinally prescribed', prompted her to loiter in the corridor during the interview between Mary Anne and the importunate Mr Disraeli.

Glancing about to assure herself that she went unwatched by prowling maids or inquisitive footmen, Rosina knelt at the keyhole, pressed her shell-like ear against it, and heard a voice low and, yes, thankfully firm; but the words were at first indistinguishable, a gentle stream in a monotone with that slight Devonian burr, and then loud like a whip to lash: 'If I was fooled by your high-falutin' talk and your letters to take them for truth, I've come to my senses at last.'

Good, good! Rosina shook hands with herself and pressed her ear closer.

'You do me the gravest, most cruel injustice.' That from him, bitingly calm. Ah, if one could see! Rosina could not; yet her mind's eye pictured the two of them, he with his pale face turned a bilious lemon as if about to be sick, as he looked in the Commons on the day of his great fiasco, and she eye-blinking up at him to show off her lashes... 'I trusted you, believed in you as his friend. I was grateful for your sympathy and for your ... affection. I thought...' Rosina missed the rest of that; and, hearing a rustle behind her, was at once frantically searching for a dropped bracelet torn from her wrist, as Nina, carrying a vase of red roses, came up the stairs.

''Ave your ladyship lost somethin'?'

'Yes, Nina. I am looking for my — ah, here it is. The clasp is loose. I must take it to be mended before I wear it again. What exquisite roses.'

'Yes'm. Count D'Orsay 'as just left 'em for madam.'

D'Orsay too! Rosina took herself off to her room to be soothed with another medicinal dose, while the scene in the boudoir played itself out.

'That you should accuse me of the lowest possible motives in my declaration is the more bitter than your refusal of my love.' He stood before her, every fibre taut; and as always when deeply stirred, white-lipped.

'Your *love*?' With slow deliberation she took up a fan to screen her face from the warmth of the fire or from his watchful gaze which flinched from hers at that scornfully soft echo. 'Beyond everything,' she said, 'beyond all my fears and doubts of you and your sincerity, you have proved yourself for what you are.'

'What am I?' His shoulders wriggled slightly, as if at that question he restrained a laugh.

'Careful, Disraeli.' The colour faded from her cheeks; she lowered the fan. 'Let us be done with play-acting. Drop your mask — that two-faced mask of yours which has served you and your purpose well with me, and will serve you — with me — no longer. You've bragged once too often and too loud of this, your latest conquest.' Her chin lifted, and her eyes, full, unwavering, met his. 'You have bandied my name and our secret, or what I trusted was our secret, in every drawing room and every club and maybe in every bawdy-house in town, so prinked you are and proud you are to make of me your — fool!'

She could feel his look upon her in a brooding cynical detachment, while from some far-off vacancy she heard him say, 'You strike deep. You have done that which my enemies have failed to do. You have broken my spirit, have poisoned my faith in myself.'

'Words, words! You was ever one for words. But you can overstep the mark of fine dramatics.' And, although with dimpling playfulness, she nodded, her fingers crushed the frail ivory sticks of the fan she held, with a sound as of elfin bones cracked. 'I'll believe you when I see your spirit broken, which not I nor any woman, no, nor any man, will ever see. That much I'll grant you. Oh, yes, you're strong and I am weak, with the foolish weakness of a woman who was "ever in such humour" — how does Shakespeare give it? — "wooed"? Yes, but "never in such humour to be won"'. She gazed ruefully down at the splintered fan. 'Well, there it is. And since we don't have to split hairs in this last talk between us, I ask you now that you may answer honestly — would you have come a-courting in such indecent haste had I four hundred and not four thousand a year? And that's putting my price at its lowest. Probate gives me close on five thousand a year, but I've no doubt you priced me higher.'

'As a matter of fact I did. I estimated your worth at *ten* thousand a year.'

Her lashes flickered. She looked at him with a half-appraising, half-speculative air, her head a little on one side; and rising from her seat she glided to a bell-rope, laid a hand upon it and said in a small, almost a child's voice, 'I had come to love you, Dizzy — yes, I loved you, and I found you — not the rock on which I thought to build my future life, but the thing you are — of straw. Go now. I wish never to see or speak to you again. The farce is ended.' And to the footman at the door, 'A hackney cab for Mr Disraeli — or do you prefer to walk?'

He walked, blindly following his footsteps where they led along Park Lane into Piccadilly, and past the market gardens of Old Brompton. Taking a hedgerowed lane to the left, he came to Chelsea and stood on the embankment watching the brown-sailed skiffs and heavy barges trailing their shadows in the pewter-coloured water. The tide was low and the last wintry rays of the sun shone in sharp-pointed iridescence on the mud-beach where the voices of half-naked urchins mingled with the plaintive mew of gulls flying inland from the sea. A foetid stench of sewer refuse came to his nostrils; his gorge rose. He mastered nausea and his stunned thoughts, crowding so close upon him that he seemed plunged in a confused bedlam state of semiconsciousness.

Then, as he watched that gruesome mockery of childhood, sense returned to ask himself, *What massacre of innocents is this — and what a stink! The sanitary conditions of our noble, save the mark, metropolis and its environment are our disgrace. Wonder it is we have not more cholera and typhus. This must be looked into, and these starveling waifs protected. How to right this monstrous wrong? But how? God knows I have rammed it home enough — or not enough? — to both front benches who oppose me. The Poor Law Amendment Act must be again amended, even though they throw me out for it.* Yes, even that, as Peel had broadly hinted, if he wished to climb to the top he had better keep his Poor Law opinions to himself. 'We don't want to see you a Tory-Radical, my boy.' *Do you not? Well, in God's good time we'll see what we will see!*

He gazed across the serene expanse of river, soothed by the wistful charm of the hazed distance wreathed in lavender scarves of mist about the farther shore, where the graceful mansions of Anne's day shouldered a mushroom growth of warehouses, stark against the fading sky; progressive present nudging elbows with the past. Then, as shocked awareness filtered through from the lifting curtain of his self-determined anodyne: *This, then,* he said to himself with that same ironical detachment in which he had heard her condemnation, *this is the end.* She had told him so plainly enough... He felt an inward bruising as if he had been spiritually flogged, but never beaten. No. His will, his pride might be corroded, but not by her destroyed.

Resentment was flooded in a wave of indignation. She to reject, and with such cool implacable resistance, the offer of himself, of *him*, Disraeli! The inconceivable, outrageous insolence of it, that she should dare…

'A a'penny, mister, for Gawd's sake? Ain't 'ad bite to eat since yesterday.'

A couple of those sewer rats were edging up to him; their little old pinched faces looked to be smeared with a mildewy slime, apish, sub-human, a hideous excrescence on the soul of man. He dug out of his pocket a handful of silver, flung it at their bare filth-blackened feet, and hurried away.

Well! He still had his mission, he still could strike a blow for life's derelicts and for the younger generation. Young England! A new movement. He would head a crusade to search for, and find, Utopia.

The afternoon had dwindled into evening, the sky was dark and overhung with snow-clouds; not a star, no moon, and a creeping fog to chill him to the marrow. He ached with tiredness and cold when he came to the rooms in Park Street, near Grosvenor Gate, where he had recently moved from St James's.

He looked over his letters: more bills. Nothing from her, as he may have half expected. But why should he expect? She had done with him, told him to go, and he had gone.

He ordered a sandwich and a hot toddy, and sat warming his hands on the steaming tankard. His teeth chattered against the drinking-cup, a delicately wrought silver piece of the time of the second Charles, purloined from among his father's treasures.

Long he sat there, brooding, while alternately he shivered and was hot, burned and was cold, and thought himself sick enough to die; until, with a muttered 'God-damme! I'll give it her now,' he shook off his rigors, went to his desk, drew up his chair and wrote:

I would have endeavoured to have spoken to you of that which it was necessary you should know, and I wished to have spoken with the calmness which was natural to one humiliated and distressed. I succeeded so far as to be desired to quit your house for ever.

I avow when I first made my advances to you I was influenced by no romantic feeling. My father had long wished me to marry and I was not blind to worldly advantages ... but I had already proved that my heart was not to be purchased...

Now for your fortune: I write the sheer truth. That fortune proved to be much less than I or the world imagined. It was in fact, as far as I was concerned, a fortune that could not benefit me in the slightest degree; it was merely a fortune not greater than your station required...

I have entered into these ungracious details because you reproached me with my interested views. I would not condescend to be the minion of a Princess; not all the gold of Ophir would ever lead me to the altar... My nature demands that my life should be perpetual love.

I told you once that my heart was inextricably engaged to you, and from that moment I devoted to you all the passion of my being ... I will not upbraid you, I will only blame myself. I seek not to conceal my state. It is not sorrow, it is not wretchedness, it is anguish.

Farewell. I will not affect to wish you happiness for it is not in your nature to obtain it. For a few years you may flutter in some frivolous circle, but the time will come when you will recall to your memory the passionate heart that you have forfeited and the genius you have betrayed.

He did not know himself ridiculous, he only knew himself in love; and perhaps now, while smarting from this deep cut to his pride, for the first time did he know it.

He sealed and sent the letter by hand, betook him to the Carlton, and was cornered by Chandos, who had just succeeded to his father's dukedom of Buckingham. Tucking his hand under Dizzy's arm he led him off to the coffee room saying, 'Dine with me, Dis. I want you to come to Melbourne's place tomorrow. I am collecting a deputation — off the record — to bombard him with his beating about the Corn Law bush. He will have to come to a decision, for if I mistake me not, he is at heart a thoroughgoing Tory — and a farmer. You look pretty glum. What's up?'

'Nothing's up. All's down.'

'Aha? Has the bewitching little widow thrown you over?'

'I have thrown myself over. Let us see what is on the menu.' And he addressed himself to the choice of: 'Dried salmon, woodcock pie, and … yes, I think a point steak grilled and well underdone. I like them red and juicy — and a bottle of Beaune. You will drink with me if I dine with you?'

'With the greatest of pleasure.'

And when the dried salmon, the steak and the woodcock pie were set before them, 'Now, my dear Dis,' said Buckingham, savouring the glass beneath his nose, 'a good vintage, this — let me tell you, since I am in a position to speak as an outsider in the Lords and with no axe to grind in the Commons, that you are not in highest favour with your party, who accuse you of siding against them with the Rads. We know a crisis is pending, prompted by those sons of Reform — or Belial — the Chartists. We know also that wrongs must be righted, but not imaginary vote-catching wrongs which never can be righted by pulling the strings of political power, that every man may find his own level.'

'My level is found. As a scion of a race that has suffered persecution for eighteen hundred years, I support the persecuted.'

'H'm, h'm.' Buckingham served his teeth with an ivory toothpick and, pocketing it, told him, 'If I may offer a comradely criticism, one of your greatest faults is a tendency to turn each facet of an argument to your personal account. This rankling grievance against your origin is shared by none of us. Believe me, we all appreciate and recognise that you would not be the man of parts you are, were it not for this same racial origin which you deplore.'

'I do *not* deplore it!' flashed Disraeli. 'But because of it I am perhaps more acutely aware of human responsibilities to all creeds and to all people than, shall we say, yourself and others born of a later race than mine.' He tilted the remainder of the bottle into Buckingham's glass. 'I intend to support the petition of the Chartists when it comes, even though I am put down for it. I never fight small game. I go straight to the leading stag of the herd, and if neither the Whig nor Tory hounds choose to run with me, well,' he gave an airy shrug, 'I'll run alone.'

'Yes.' The blunt corners of Buckingham's womanish mouth were wryly uplifted. 'You are always the crusader *par excellence*. So go to it, my boy, and all luck to you.' And he added lightly, 'What is this I hear of your engagement to the little Lewis?'

'I don't know what you have heard, but I can say that if it is of an engagement between myself and Mrs Wyndham Lewis,' he deliberately stressed the name in full, 'you have been misinformed. Waiter! Another bottle of the same... Ah, D'Orsay, well met! Will you join us? Waiter, make it two bottles.'

D'Orsay, who had strolled up to their table with every intention of joining them, sat and accepted his share of the two bottles. So ended the evening in mutual conviviality, endowed with another bottle of Beaune, followed by Cognac and Tokay. And in happier state than when he had left them, Disraeli walked, rather unsteadily, home.

A note awaited him on his hall table. He tore it open and read:

For God's sake come to me. I am ill and almost distracted. I will answer all you wish. I never desired you to leave the house nor implied or thought a word about money ... I have not been a widow a year. I often feel the impropriety of my present position ... I am devoted to you.

'And so,' said D'Orsay when he met a radiant Dizzy at the Carlton the next morning, 'it is not *blague*. It is true, then? You do not intrigue, you risk no false step, you take your rich widow and — marry her!'

TWENTY-TWO

Marriage was in the air. That same year another young gentleman on holiday in Rome met and fell in love with pretty Miss Catherine Glynne, whose mama beamed upon and encouraged the attentions of William Ewart Gladstone, MP. No question here of an impecunious suitor over burdened with debts.

Born with a spoon not of silver, but gold, in his mouth, Mr Gladstone's perfectly correct, if none the less fervent, approach to the charming Miss Glynne was the antithesis of Mr Disraeli's passionate advances to his lady. Indeed, love was the least topic of discussion on the lips of Mr Gladstone, who confided to the blushful Catherine that his wish had been to take holy orders, but that his father had opposed his vocation and ordained him for a political career.

'Yet the Church and the State,' Mr Gladstone said, 'walk hand in hand.' As so did he and Miss Catherine when, with Mama discreetly at a distance, they explored the palaces of buried Caesars and the scattered marble tokens of a lost empire where roses twined among the carven curls of little vestal virgins; and there, in that treasured place of pagan memory, did Mr Gladstone — but always most correctly — declare himself.

And as the summer drew to its close so did the little Queen declare herself to her 'Dearest Cousin Albert'.

Rhapsodically and endlessly her diary extols him: *his beautiful blue eyes, his exquisite nose, and such a pretty mouth with delicate mustachios and slight, very slight whiskers, a beautiful figure, broad in the shoulders... And what a pleasure it is to look at Albert when he gallops and valses, he does it so beautifully.* But of course the Queen must not gallop or valse, even with her Albert. She could, however, sit with Lord M and adore. And Uncle Leopold was told: *I am the happiest, happiest Being that ever existed. I do not think it possible for anyone in the world to be* happier *or as happy as I am.*

Equally happy were the affianced Miss Glynne and the widowed Mrs Lewis who, discarding her weeds, blossomed forth in white muslins adorned with lilac ribbons; or gossamer grey confections flounced to the eighteen-inch waist.

The announcement of her betrothal caused much feminine laughter concerning Dizzy's preference for the 'elderly', as witness the Blessington and the Londonderry, to say nothing of Great-grandmama Cork, which disturbed Mary Anne not at all. As for Dizzy, he walked on air. He was in love, *madly, idiotically,* and, as so he proclaimed to his adored, he loved her *more truly, more tenderly each day. All my hopes of happiness are centred in your sweet affections* — further to vex those who, if younger and more beautiful, were not so well, in worldly goods, endowed. 'For certainly,' went talk of it, 'nothing but her money could have caught him. Only look at her, and hear her when she lets herself go!'

And all through that radiant summer she did let herself go, in subdued entertainment at Grosvenor Gate to Dizzy's friends, for she had few of her own. Or she would accept invitations from the Lyndhursts and Buckingham to the play, or to quiet evening parties; and on one occasion to a picnic in celebration of her engagement arranged for her by Bulwer-Lytton who, since his baronetcy, had taken his mother's name.

They were to meet at his cottage on the Thames below Richmond, but they arrived late to find that their host and his other guests, wearied of waiting, had gone on ahead by steamboat. Edward had left word, should they come, for them to follow and join them at the appointed place. Two more tardy guests were there already, mooning about the cottage garden, undecided what to do. One, a small stout, puffy little man, Dizzy recognised as Prince Louis Napoleon, a refugee from France; the other his equerry, the Comte de Persigny. Having often met the Prince at the Blessington-D'Orsay *ménage*, Disraeli presented himself and Mary Anne, suggesting they should hire a boat and row in the wake of the steamer. There happened to be a boat lingering at the landing stage; this the Prince hailed, and refusing the offer of the boatman to row, saying he preferred to row himself, the four of them embarked.

Mary Anne sat with Dizzy in the bows, de Persigny in the stern to steer, and the Prince, with apologies to Madame, divested himself of his coat, took the oars and pushed off into mid-stream.

For a while all went well. The Prince, perspiring freely, for the day was warm, plied his oars with a will. The attention of de Persigny, however, was centred more on Mary Anne than on his rudder-lines, causing him to steer a precarious course in the backwash of a passing pleasure steamer. The boat rocked; Mary Anne screamed, 'For goodness' sake look what you're doing!' And Dizzy, flinging a protective arm about her waist, strenuously urged the flustered count to 'Keep her out, man. Keep her out!'

The Prince, with the sweat rolling down his face on to waxed ends of his moustache, making a Lilliputian mop of the black tuft beneath his lower lip, valiantly strove to keep her out, while his discomfited henchman, pulling first one and then the other rudder-line, swung her round, bows foremost, hard towards the bank.

'Steady on!' cried Dizzy, 'What the deuce —' as, with a jerk that sent Mary Anne sprawling face downwards to her knees and brought Dizzy to his feet at perilous risk of a capsize, the boat swung round again, her stern in a tangle of rushes.

'You'll catch a crab!' shrieked Mary Anne. 'Put up your oars, Prince. Here, give that to me.' Regardless of the Prince's protests and Dizzy's attempt to drag her back, she snatched a scull from His Highness and shoved it with all her force against the bank. The boat cast off into mid-stream again. 'Now, you, Count, pull!' she told him. 'Don't sit there staring like a stuffed image. *Pull!* Here, you, Diz,' to him who assured of no imminent danger was in splutters of laughter, 'you'd best change places with the count, who don't seem to know his right hand from his left… No, better not, or we'll all be in the river. As for Your Highness —' still manfully sculling — 'don't go diggin' your oars in so deep. You shouldn't have taken the sculls if you don't know how to use them. Just look at my dress, all covered in mud.'

His mortified Highness, whose face had assumed the appearance of a beetroot just off the boil, went on rowing, the count went on pulling, Dizzy went on laughing, and Mary Anne, spreading out her splashed skirts to dry in the sun, went on giving orders, until they landed on the island at Hampton to find the picnic in full swing.

The ladies of the party could not have been more sympathetic at the ruin of Mary Anne's gown, the Prince more contrite, and the count more adhesive to her whose side he never left for the remainder of the day.

One may be sure there was some snickering from certain ladies, not so favoured by His Highness and his gentlemen regarding 'the Lewis's ridiculous rig-out, and the way she quizzes and ogles the Prince…' Who greatly appeared to enjoy it.

So the day ended merrily enough without further mishap, and with Mary Anne in highest royal favour. Then back to the cottage in the row-boat, but this time Dizzy sculled his love alone.

Extracts from account book and diary of Mrs Wyndham Lewis:
O de Cologne
Gloves 2/6
Greenwich 2 dinners including pint of champagne, steamer, cab home, 19/-
Swan & Edgar 4 lambs wool stockings
In Purse: £308.10.
Married: 28.8.1839
Dear Dizzy became my husband.

PART FOUR: THE PRIMROSE PATH

TWENTY-THREE

The first week of the honeymoon was spent at Tunbridge Wells where, incessantly, it poured with rain to keep them in their rooms day in, night out; an incarceration which *we find very agreeable,* the elated bridegroom wrote to sister 'Sa', who had no doubt of it. From the Pantiles to Baden-Baden, declared by the bride to be *scarcely more lively than Tunbridge Wells,* they went on to Munich and finished up in Paris. Mary Anne rioted in shopping expeditions, visits to the Embassy, dinner parties, plays, and *looked particularly well in her new costumes,* reported Dizzy. And so again to London in November, and life for Mary Anne began again.

It was a life unshadowed. Whatever doubt of his love she may have harboured in the past was now dissolved. Her wedding night was her fulfilment, so long awaited and at last fulfilled. 'And yet,' he marvelled in the gentle aftermath of consummation, 'you are still *demi-vierge.* This, then —' even at this moment must he analyse and delve into the reason for his joy of her — 'is the secret of your hold on me and your attraction for all men.'

During the round of entertainments that followed the Queen's marriage, she accompanied him everywhere. The nine days' wonder of the captivated Dizzy and his capture had died down. Hostesses vied with one another to secure not him alone, but her, for their dinners. 'One never knows what she will come out with next. She is always so amusing.'

Her remarks were repeated behind fans amid little shrieks of laughter. Talking of sculptures: 'Oh, but you should see my

Dizzy in his bath…' Of a picture, and this at breakfast during a house party at Lady Somebody-or-other's, when she complained to her hostess of a certain 'indecent oil painting' in their bedroom: 'Dizzy says it is Venus and Adonis, and I've been kept awake half the night, trying to turn his attention from *her* — to me! But it's nothing so good as the Venus he has in our bedroom at home.'

'That,' her gallant host replied to cover his lady's confusion, 'I can well believe.'

She may have mischievously set herself to shock, and, encouraged by Dizzy, succeeded. He delighted in her gamine disregard for society's conventions, while intimate association with her every mood was a voluptuous experience of which he never tired. His pleasure in her body was increased by exploration of her mind. Yet, if analytically he studied her, she, who had demanded a year in which to study him, whimsically continued her observance after marriage with a respective summary of their peculiarities:

HE
Very calm
Never irritable
Bad humoured
Very patient
Very studious
Often says what he does not think
No vanity
Conceited
No self-love
He is seldom amused
He is a genius

SHE
Very effervescent
Very irritable
Good humoured
No patience
Very idle
Never says what she does not think
Much vanity
No conceit
Much self-love
Everything amuses her
She is a dunce

One can fancy how she wrote that, tongue in cheek; for if posterity accepts him as a genius she is equally and certainly no dunce. That Disraeli sought and followed her advice on his literary work is shown in the dedication of *Sybil*:

To one whose sweet voice has often encouraged and whose taste and judgement have ever guided these pages; the most severe of critics but a perfect wife!

Nor was it only in the writing of a novel that he called upon her judgement. At the general election of 1841 that brought Peel in with his Conservatives, the new name for the old Tories, Disraeli, who had previously withdrawn himself from Maidstone, stood instead for Shrewsbury, with Mary Anne at his side in the forefront of the fight.

'We had a sharp contest but were never for a moment doubtful,' was Dizzy's report of it to Bradenham. 'They *did* against me, wrote against me, said against me all they could find or invent, but I licked them.'

One may believe Mary Anne had her share in the licking, since, at the close of the poll when Disraeli was chaired, which he found to be 'gorgeous but fatiguing', he presented his wife to an enthusiastically receptive crowd as 'she who has won the seat for us, not I!' Then, after quaffing *a triumphal cup*, so he gives it to Sarah, *at forty different spots in Salop*, they retired to bed overcome with victory and quaffing, and danced a Highland Fling together in their nightgowns, a not uncommon demonstration of jubilance on the part of this curious pair.

'And now,' panted Mary Anne, dropping down on the hearthrug with a deep contented sigh, 'you'll be in the Cabinet for sure.'

'I wonder.' He leaned against the mantelshelf, the laughter gone out of his eyes.

'Well of course,' she said quickly, 'you are bound to be called to the Ministry. Peel can't overlook you after this.'

'I think he will.'

'I think he won't! And if he does, you will have to ram yourself down his throat. You are not going to stand by and let smaller men get in before you. Let him know how you've won your four fights with all the odds against. It was wonderful the way you had those farmers eating the Corn Laws out of your hand. You smashed the Whig — beg his pardon — the Liberal, on that score alone. Huh! A fine name to give themselves, I'll say. So liberal they'd snatch the cheese-mites from a cheese to bring grist to their mill. I told 'em as much, not in so many words but as near as makes no matter. Did you hear me shouting out to them at the back of the crowd? But it's not *what* you say as how you say it that tells.'

'Yes, and you said it,' he pulled her up into his arms, 'that every man of them was wanting to do to you,' he kissed her long and skilfully, 'just this.'

And later, drowsily snuggled in his arms, 'What you'll have to do,' she murmured, half asleep, 'is write to Peel. If he don't recognise you now you must put your pride in your pocket and *make* him!'

But day followed day, and those two at Grosvenor Gate were still anxiously awaiting word from Downing Street. None came.

At the end of the week, unable to endure the suspense of uncertainty, Disraeli wrote a letter to his Chief, asking for a Ministry appointment: a bold step. Without bombast or persiflage he presented his case:

...on which I cannot be silent. I have had to struggle against a storm of political hate and malice from the moment I enrolled myself under your banner, and have been sustained under these trials by the conviction that the day would come when the foremost man in the country would publicly testify that he had some respect for my ability.

He ends with a fervent appeal to Sir Robert's *magnanimity and justice* to save him from *the intolerable humiliation of being passed at this moment unrecognized.*

He left the copy of the letter on his desk, where it was found and read by Mary Anne. Lying wakeful beside him while he slept, she thought about that letter. Yes, he had pocketed his pride, but what if Peel should remain stubborn in spite of it? She knew her Dizzy. She knew how he would brood, lose heart, to lose himself, his faith, his future... No! Anything but that.

What if *she* wrote a letter to Peel? She had met him on several occasions, had talked to him, had found him a pig-headed rock of a man with one weakness, shrewdly observed: he must stand well in the eyes of the world. He must, at all costs, be popular to combat the Queen's dislike of 'that odd cold man', as it was reported she had called him. *Punch, or the London Charivari*, an amusing new outspoken weekly journal, had pilloried him in an imaginary dialogue with the Queen. How they had laughed at it, she and Dizzy. Yes, and how the world would laugh at her sly digs at Peel and his pomposity, and *Punch*'s ridicule. A hint, a word dropped here and there, all the big Opposition men had been given a taste of her tongue, but Peel, by damn, would have a mouthful — of spit!

She felt Dizzy stir beside her. She lit a candle and gazed down at him. So young he looked, the merest boy, his mouth softened in sleep; the lashes lying in two dark crescents on his cheeks. A wave of tenderness engulfed her.

'My love,' she whispered, 'my own dear, my little one. They shan't hurt you. They shall *not*. You are great and they are small. We'll show them… That beast of a Peel. The Queen knows him, yes, *she* knows him for what he is. And so do I.'

She got out of bed, took the candle with her and, tip-toe for fear of waking him, went into her communicating boudoir. At her bureau she sat, dipped her quill and wrote.

GROSVENOR GATE.
Saturday night.

Her pen paused; her eyes sought the clock on the mantelshelf. Yes, it was still Saturday night; it wanted two minutes to twelve.

Confidential.
Dear Sir Robert Peel,

I beg you not to be angry with me for my intrusion, but I am overburdened with anxiety. My husband's career is for ever crushed if you do not appreciate him.

Mr Disraeli's exertions are not unknown to you, but there is much he has done that you cannot be aware of, though they have had no other aim but to do you honour, no wish for recompense but your apro — two ps or one? Two and chance it — *approbation. He has stood four most expensive elections since 1834, and gained seats from Whigs in two, and I pledge myself as far as one seat that it shall always be at your command... Do not destroy all his hopes, and make him feel his life has been a mistake.*

She paused again, nibbled the end of her quill and went on: *May I venture to name my own humble but enthusiastic exertions in times gone by for the Party, or rather for your own splendid self?* She chuckled at that 'splendid', and her pen spluttered as if it chuckled with her, and made a blot. She sopped it up with blotting paper and continued: *They will tell you at Maidstone that more than £40,000 was spent through my efforts alone.* And as an afterthought she added: *Be pleased not to answer this, as I do not wish any human being to know I have written to you this humble petition.*

Did one other human being know of it? While it is generally accepted that it was written without her husband's knowledge, the wording and style suggest that it might have been edited by Disraeli before it was sent.

Both his and her letters arrived the same day; hers, as requested, went unanswered; his received a firm and graciously dignified refusal. Grace and dignity, however, could not sweeten the bitter pill of rejection, nor give for it adequate reason; but the pill once swallowed acted as a stimulant.

The smug consolatory comments of his more successful colleagues were acknowledged with the airy rejoinder, 'You rate me too high, my friends. I have far to go before I join you, or some of you, on the front bench.'

He had recently taken to wearing an eyeglass, explained by a minor defect of his sight. Monocled, dapper, with no frills and no curls, he surveyed the House; and sat, arms folded, his hat tilted over his forehead and a narrowed glance for Gladstone who didn't have to eat of humble pie to gain what he had lost; and had been heartily God-blessed by the Chief on his acceptance of high honours: the vice-presidency of the Board of Trade, Master of the Mint, and a privy councillor, to boot. So much for Eton and Oxford, to say nothing of merchandised wealth; a man after Peel's own heart. But let none perceive the jaundiced eye behind the monocle, beaming on young Gladstone who, earnestly devout, always offered up a prayer before he spoke. And gravely, precisely, with perfect slow enunciation was he speaking, while Disraeli, a trifle too pointedly, dozed.

So home to Mary Anne, with all the windows winking cheerful welcome in the light of a hundred candles — 'Lights, plenty of lights!' was her slogan – and a sumptuous supper awaiting him of turtle soup and salmon, roast chicken and champagne.

'Don't fret yourself, love. You'll have Peel on his knees to you before a twelvemonth's gone. You'll see.'

She began counting the cherry stones on her dessert plate. 'This year, next year…'

But this year, next year, were to be darkened by two deaths; first that of her brother John, and a few months later, of her mother. Mrs Yate's illness, obscurely diagnosed as a 'decline', was lightened by a hopeful period of convalescence spent at Bradenham, where Mary Anne accompanied her, and stayed with her there some few weeks.

From Dizzy, left alone for the first time since their marriage, she received daily letters telling her how *wretchedly lonely* he was and giving her news of debates in the House; of a *Thunderbolt Budget* that had introduced, to horrified Members, a *Property or Income Tax* (of sevenpence in the pound) *but Peel can do anything at the moment.*

Only for the moment, in so far as he, who had not forgiven or forgotten that repulse to his appeal, now played for time. He played for near upon three hours in *not only one of the best speeches I ever made,* was his modest report of it to Mary Anne, *but the best ever made in the House.* Yet more than all the approval of his colleagues did he need hers, *for without that stimulus I don't think I could go on... The more we are separated, the more I cling to you.*

As with his predecessor, so had he learned to lean on her; but while Wyndham had been unready to admit his dependence, Disraeli gave all credit to her and *to your sweet heart in disappointment and sorrow and your quick accurate sense to guide me to prosperity and triumph.* Nor did he conceal his devotion; he paraded it for all the world to see.

Like some brightly plumaged small exotic bird she flashed upon London society, his prideful exhibit. Men adored her, women loathed her, but knew better than to criticise or air their views in Dizzy's hearing, with whom it was a case of 'Love me, love my Mary Anne' — in whose 'marble hall he had hung his hat', as the ladies were amusedly agreed.

Yet if any of this reached the ears of Mary Anne, it could not mar her happiness. The nuptial sky stayed blissfully blue until the cloudburst.

It came with the advent of a stranger announced as 'A —' a moment's hesitation decided on, 'a young man', as distinct from 'a young gentleman', 'to speak h'urgent with the master, or failin' 'im he said yourself, ma'am. Shall I show him in?'

He was shown in, smiling, overdressed, and over-polished from his sleek black hair to his shining black boots. Everything shone, a trifle grubbily. His nose, a hooked proboscis, shone; his teeth shone when, with an ingratiating bow, he exposed them to say, 'Mrs Disraeli, I believe?'

'Yes, and who are you?'

'Who I am, madam, is of no consequence. This,' he offered her a something large and sealed, 'will explain my presence, for which I 'umbly ask your pardon. Your servant, ma'am, and always ready to oblige.' With another bow, still smiling, he went.

She tore open the envelope, read the first lines, boldly inscribed in block capitals; she read them twice, disbelieving, and then, damnably convinced, she read no more.

When Dizzy came home that evening he was met not by her of the 'sweet heart', but by a changeling: a shrill-voiced virago, who attacked him with cruel accusation of 'Lies! You won me with your lies and oiled words of love. Huh! Love! As much love in you for me as in a jellyfish. I should have had more sense. I, who have paid out thousands to stave off these sharks. And no sooner do I put you right than you do me wrong. Yes! You took good care to be out when he walked in, a mealy-mouthed son of a dun to come at me with —' And in her husband's face she threw that which in his absence had been served on her. 'And it's not the first of its kind I've seen by a long chalk. My ma had her fill of them with Mr Yate. And you're another, but I'm done with you and your debts. You can pay them yourself or go kick your heels in the Fleet — you with your gab of a chancellorship. That's what you're after — a fine Chancellor of the Exchequer you'll make if you waste the nation's money as you've wasted mine. A low-down trick. I trusted you... You're no better than a thief, running up bills unbeknown to me who has to foot them.'

And again she called him 'thief' with an inexcusable reminder of O'Connell's jibe at him, and watched his lips whiten in a look of unutterable scorn, contempt and — oh, no! Oh, God! — dislike. Then he turned, and without a word he left her.

She stood, her little body shaken, not with sobs, with shock and fear for the consequence of her flare-up of temper, unmeaning and unmeant. What had she said, done — or what would *he* do?

He was packing his bags.

She tore up to his room, found the door locked, and hammered on it. 'Let me in!'

No answer, but she could hear him moving about, opening and shutting drawers and cupboards with a deal of noise and banging.

'Dizzy, let me in. I didn't mean ... my wicked tongue. Forgive...'

Silence; a heavy breathing silence. Then: 'You have said that which is unforgivable.'

'Open the door or I'll —' She clapped her hand to her mouth, stifling a scream, and with her lips to the keyhole, controlling a sob, she asked, 'What are you doing?'

'I am leaving you.'

'No. *No!* Let me *in!*'

She heard him cross the room, more opening of drawers, more banging of cupboards.

'You can't ... I won't. You mustn't...'

For what seemed to be hours she waited there, but he would have to come out by the door unless he climbed out of the window. The banging and slamming went on and on. Was he taking everything he had? His clothes, belongings, everything?

Her knees were weak as water. She sank down on them. More hours of torment, but they were only minutes, passed. At length the key was turned, the door opened. He stood there cloaked and hatted. He carried a portmanteau. She sprang at him, arms clinging.

'Dizzy! My love, my darling. Forgive. It was only... It was such a shock. I didn't expect ... didn't know what I was saying. Give that to me.' She tried to wrest the bag from his hand.

He stood firm and coldly unrelenting. 'Let me pass.' It was awful.

'Where,' she asked him in a cracking whisper, 'are you going?'

'To my club.'

Then she flared again. 'Very well — go! And good riddance.'

To his club he went, and in the smoking room he sat, sunk in despair and neat brandy; and there he was found by Buckingham. To him, a ready sympathiser, he told of a 'terrible domestic crisis. All is over. She has thrown me out... No. I've thrown myself out. Finished!'

Buckingham, greatly tickled but tactfully solemn, advised him to go back to her and not delay his going. 'For you can't,' was his meaningful advice, 'afford to lose her.'

'If I were to lose her,' Dizzy said, with brandied earnestness, 'my life, my career, my whole future, would be ruined. Not financially,' he made haste to add. 'You have no idea what that creature means to me. She has wound herself into my life, and were I parted from her I think I would go on bleeding internally. Eternally.'

'As the Jews would go on bleeding you?' suggested Buckingham, beckoning a waiter. 'In which case — a strong black coffee for Mr Disraeli — you'd best go tell her so.'

Sobered, chastened, braced with strong black coffee, he hurried back to tell her so.

In his nightshirt he crept softly to her room. The firelight revealed her where she lay, curled up like a child in their great four-post bed, her hair a tousled cloak about her shoulders, her long lashes still wet upon her cheeks. He leaned over her. A scent of violets, that always seemed to be her own, was wafted up to him. He caught his breath. She was sleeping sweetly, gently, untroubled; her ripe lips apart and from them came a murmur which sounded like — but couldn't be! — 'Beer. For Chef … One pound … seven…'

Chef? Beer? She could not, he thought, while in anguish he listened to her quiet breathing, have suffered as had he. She did sometimes talk in her sleep, but never surely, of the… Damn and damn and damn her! *Beer. Chef. Hell.* So much for her love, and she to doubt his!

Then, as he stood there in his agony, there came to him the smallest sound, a caught-in sob. His hand hovered, touched a wet cheek. The next moment he had her in his arms, her quivering mouth beneath his own. They had found each other after aeons of misery. Nothing so terrible had ever happened to them; nothing so wonderful as the joy of their reunion.

TWENTY-FOUR

This horrific incident drew them closer together and made their temporary parting, enforced by Mrs Yate's illness, the more unbearable; for, in that same week, Mary Anne, on doctor's orders, took her mother to recuperate at Bradenham. She stayed with her there until the end of the month when the doctor pronounced her well enough to undertake the journey home.

They set out in a post-chaise, hired for speedier travel. Although early spring, the day was cold with a biting wind. Mrs Yate, wrapped in furs, her hands in a muff and her feet on a warming-pan, kept up a running complaint of the shivers, the jolting, the shocking bad roads, and 'a filthy smell of tobacco' to make her feel sick. 'You never know who has been here before you. That's the worst of these hired conveyances.' And as they came to the village of Uxbridge, 'What's amiss here? All these ugly looking men standing about?' In watchfully sinister groups outside the Chequers Inn; and, as the chaise rattled over the cobbles, a burly, thick-set man sprang forwards waving a banner, approximately white, bearing the words boldly printed in black letters: THE PEOPLE'S CHARTER.

The chaise swayed to the startled uprear of the horses, expertly steadied and halted by the post-boy, while from all directions, as at a given signal, a murmurous crowd spread fan-wise across the road to bar the way; a swarming locust crowd with brutish gibbering faces; lean men, stout men, ragged men and all sorts; women too, sluttish and half naked. One, with a wizened baby at her breast, thrust her face at the window of the chaise where Mary Anne was peering out, and shuddered back from the sight of those red-rimmed eyes and foam-flecked lips shrieking a foul word at her. 'Fuck you! Yes, you in your finery, what would keep me and mine in bread for a year. We starve while you go gorge yourselves!'

'Merciful God!' moaned Mrs Yate, her hand to her heart. 'This'll kill me — my palpitations…'

Mary Anne let down the window.

'Don't show yourself!' screamed her mother. 'Sit back.'

There was a second's pause, then, in one convulsive movement, the mob surged forwards while the post-boy's whip lashed frenziedly to right and left, and the chaise rocked as if the ground were smitten in an earthquake.

'Let me get out.' In her terror, Mrs Yate was wrenching at the handle of the door.

'Stay still,' cried Mary Anne. 'I'll deal with them.'

'No, no! Keep down.' But she was up, her head out of the window.

'Good people!' Her voice, shrill and urgent, subdued the clamour to a moment's surprised silence. 'Why do you waylay us? What is it you want?'

'Justice.' He, who seemed to be the spokesman, pushed himself to the forefront of the crowd, flourishing his banner. 'Manhood's suffrage. The right to live as men and not as beasts.'

'Seek justice and you'll find it in the proper quarter,' shouted Mary Anne, 'but not on the Queen's highway. I tell you —'

'The Queen!' A groaning roar rolled up to drown her words. 'Aye, the Queen. What justice will *she* give us? We who go starved while she eats off gold plate?' This from the leader, a rubicund pot-bellied fellow who looked anything but starved, in the blood-stained blue apron of a butcher, his shirt open at the throat displaying the hairs of his chest almost up to his chin. 'What do the Queen care if a loaf of bread costs one and six and our chil'ern go grubbin' in pig troughs for their breakfasts while she dances all night in her palace?'

'Yes!' shrieked the woman who had first accosted Mary Anne. 'What's it to her, if our breasts run dry of milk, that our babes are dead for want o' suck? She who suckles a fine Prince o' Wales! Let her give my babe *her* milk — o' human kindness. She ain't got none!'

'Give us our rights!' And, as if from one mouth, a babel of voices rose up in a threatening chant. 'The People's Rights! The Charter! We want the Charter!' And regardless of the terrified plunging of the horses, the mob closed in upon the chaise; but the post-boy, still manfully laying about with his whip, managed to hold the pair from bolting.

'For pity's sake,' Mrs Yate tugged Mary Anne's pelisse, 'sit *down* or we'll be murdered. Oh, why didn't we travel by the train?'

'Don't keep pulling at me,' hissed Mary Anne. 'I'll quiet them if only *you'll* be quiet.' And raising her hand with something in it, 'Here's to stop your noise and fill your empty bellies!' And among the hurtling crowd she flung her purse.

'Lord, Lord,' moaned Mrs Yate, 'the girl's run mad!'

Not she, but they had run mad, when the netted purse, with a glint of gold in its mesh, soared and fell among that scrambling mass of bodies, who, like wolves upon a prey, were tearing at the silken threads, struggling, fighting among themselves to snatch the loot, hitting out at each other with savage oaths and blows and howls in a hideous massed epilepsy.

'On, on!' cried Mary Anne. And the postilion, urging his frightened horses, drove them at the gallop to scatter the tumbled heap of men and screaming women.

'You see,' head and shoulders still out of the window, Mary Anne looked back at that dust-clouded swarm, 'there can never be share and share alike for them, if that's what they want of their Charter. Each man for himself — snatch and grab.'

'I've come over!' gasped her mother; and promptly fell into a faint.

Alas for Mrs Yate, that alarming experience proved too much for her and her palpitations. She was got home and put to bed and died within the week.

Although not unexpected, her mother's death shattered Mary Anne; both she and Dizzy were in need of a change, and, armed with introductions from D'Orsay to his sister, the Duchesse de Gramont, they made the most of it on holiday in Paris. *But I have left my great gun*, Dizzy wrote to Sarah, *till the last.*

His 'great gun' was none other than Louis Philippe, King of the French; and Disraeli the only stranger there to be received, as the King and Queen were in mourning for the death of their son, the Duc d'Orléans.

In consequence, and much to the disappointment of Mary Anne who had hoped to be presented, no courts were held that season. Louis Philippe, however, much intrigued by this so un-English Englishman gave him private audience on several occasions in his *cabinet privé*, to discuss international affairs. He discussed them in English with an American accent acquired during his three years' refuge in the United States. And he may have given away more than he intended to tell while they supped *tête-à-tête* at St Cloud.

The *specialité de la maison*, and a favourite dish of the King, was cold ham, carved in wafer thin slices: a performance, he explained to his admiring guest, he had learned from a waiter 'in a ninepenny — how you call? — chop-house in London when I was an exile down on my 'ard luck'.

Poor Louis Philippe. Little did he know of still harder luck in store to send him flying for his life, when a few years later the barricades went up in the howling streets of Paris.

But Mary Anne knew Paris only in holiday humour with a grand finale at the opera while she watched from a box, in a black domino, *a masquerade of five hundred witches dancing, five thousand devils whirling and, fancy me!* — was Dizzy's report of it — *walking about in such dissolute devilry*, with an enticing little scarlet imp on his arm whom his wife did not fancy at all. And so back to London exhausted and pale from a rough Channel crossing and devilry.

'It's been fun, but I can't say I'm sorry to be home,' Mary Anne said.

Home! Her home, not his. The thought, a long-hidden grievance, darkly coiled in some corner of his mind, had now risen to strike. He must have a home of his own, bought, if not paid for, by him. A stately home, a country house. All the heroes of Disraeli's novels had town and country houses, so why not he?

He had his eye on a manor in the neighbourhood of Bradenham which had lately come into the market — at a price. And what a price! How to raise it? Not from Mary Anne. On that he was determined. The purchase must be his alone. Nor could he hand his hat round in Old Jewry after that last appalling affair, settled by her with the threat that if he did it again she would leave him. Not that he believed she would, but you could never know with Mary Anne. He dared not risk it.

Come what may, the purchase must be his, not hers. He would have to tap another source: his father.

Old Isaac, whose sight for some years had been failing, was now totally blind; and, knowing he had not long to live, readily agreed to make over a fourth share of the paternal inheritance which could not be less than ten thousand. Yet the manor and its lands would cost more than treble that amount. But financial obstacles had never dismayed Dizzy. He had a host of wealthy influential friends, of whom the most likely were the Bentinck brothers, sons of the Duke of Portland.

To Lord Titchfield, Lords Henry and George — particularly George who, besides that he was a Member of Parliament, owned one of the finest racing stables in England — he applied and was generously supported by all three, who saw in Disraeli a future leader of their party. That he was still heavily in debt when he asked for this fabulous loan did not at all deter him. In for a penny in for a pound — or thirty-five thousand pounds, no matter. An English country gentleman he wished to be and, thanks to the brothers Bentinck, an English country gentleman he was.

The title deeds were signed and sealed and Dizzy rushed home to tell Mary Anne, 'It is done — and you are the Lady of Hughenden!'

TWENTY-FIVE

It was the day of the housewarming. The ground floor had been cleared of all furniture. Flowers, banked in long coffin-like boxes, were ranged round the walls; three hundred gilt chairs, trestle tables for refreshments, and four extra footmen had been hired. On the terrace the musicians were putting up their stands. The piano had been carried out and would be carried in if it rained. 'But it mustn't rain,' said Mary Anne, apprehensively eyeing a curtain of cloud that had shut out the face of the sun. The guests had been invited for three o'clock. It was now half past two and she still in curl-papers and dressing gown was arranging flowers on the buffet table in the dining room.

'Ma'am,' urged Nina, plodding after her, 'do 'ee come. I'll never 'ave you ready.'

'Just coming. Don't fuss. My word, Dizzy,' to him who stood in the doorway, 'aren't you a swell!' In black swallowtails, buff pantaloons and a white embroidered waistcoat. 'I can never compete with this… All right, Nina, I'll be with you in two minutes.'

Dizzy followed her upstairs and sat on the red damask-curtained bed to watch Nina comb out her hair, winding it in corkscrews round her finger to fall in layers of ringlets on her neck; the latest fashion. And now the brand-new dress of lilac taffetas, flounced and full skirted over six petticoats stiffened with buckram, forerunner of the crinoline.

'I look like a balloon,' said Mary Anne.

'You look,' Dizzy told her, 'delicious.' And to Nina, 'Pin back those curls on her forehead — that's better.'

Mary Anne turned sharp about. 'I can hear a carriage. Darling, do go down. One of us must be there to receive.'

He was at the window looking out. 'It's only Sarah and the boys.'

'Oh, I meant to remind her and forgot. Ask if she has remembered to bring the custard glasses. I have only ten dozen, not nearly enough. If she hasn't brought them send one of the men to fetch them in the gig. Quick, Nina, my pearls. And Dizzy, for heaven's sake, go *down*. There's some more coming…' A continuous snail stream of carriages, four-in-hands, phaetons, barouches, and, from Hatfield, the Salisbury coach.

She caught up a scent spray, puffed perfume on her hair, gathered her petticoats and ran to take her place at Dizzy's side.

'How d'you do…? And how d'you do? So glad you could come… And how d'you do? May I present the Duke of Buck — Oh, how d'you do? (My dear, do you like it? I bought the stuff in Paris ages ago and have only just had it made up.) Dear Louise! Are you better of your cold? Do you know Lord… Mrs de Rothschild, Lord Lyndhurst… *How* do you do?' Her face was stiff with smiles but she managed to hiss a word to Dizzy: 'Don't leave it all to me. Can't you do *some* introducing?… Ah, Prince Metternich, how good of you to come.'

Everyone had come. Lord John Russell, Prime Minister, had come; Sir Robert Peel had come, but not his lady. She had refused to come. She would not, she said, set foot inside the house of the man who had execrated her husband… To destroy, with magnificent invective, his once revered chief.

This, his Mosaic eye for an eye, tooth for a tooth revenge on the great Tory leader who had spurned him to find himself denounced, his party split by the malicious wizardry of an oriental conjurer who juggled with the Corn Laws to bring down the House — and Peel. Yet here he was urbanely smiling, towering above the dwarfish Lord John, his usurper in the '46 election that had given the Liberals the lead. Together they moved towards the buffet... And Mr Gladstone had come, with bowing apologies for his wife who exceedingly regretted that she could not come. 'Our youngest is taken with the mumps.'

'Dear me, I am so very sorry. I trust that you and Mrs Gladstone have had the mumps, for if not I believe it is no slight ailment for grown — Ah, Lord Palmerston, so you *have* managed to come. Delighted!'

She felt like a clockwork doll, jerking out mechanical greetings, her eyes everywhere, ears strained for floating scraps of talk...

'Poor old Louis Philippe. No wonder his nerves have given way. His wife dead and six grandchildren at Claremont...'

'The Queen and Albert *very* sympathetic...'

'Yes, so I believe, under the rose...'

'Oh, but my dear, you simply *must* read *Dombey*, quite his best. I cried for a week over the death of little...'

'Oh, do you really think...'

'But of course, my dear, he must be a Rad, the way he... Ah, Mr Disraeli, Lady Lyndhurst and I are discussing Mr Dickens. He is a Radical, is he not? The way he always makes sinners of us and saints of the lower — *What* did you say?'

'I said, madam, that there are but two nations, the rich and the poor.'

'Yes, isn't she surprising? Never looks a day older, but *he* does. He's going grey.'

Mary Anne wheeled round, her gaze searching the back of Dizzy's head. He, with Palmerston, had joined Peel and Lord John at the buffet. So it *was* noticeable. She pulled them out whenever she saw them while cutting his hair — she had always insisted on cutting his hair, the barber made such a mess of it, either too long or too short. *But they say if you pull out one you pull out a dozen...*

'Mrs Disraeli?' She turned. A commanding hand was laid on her arm by an overpowering person in mauve with a dominant chin and a complaint. 'I much regret to have arrived so late, but I came by train and had to take a fly from the station as there was no carriage to meet me.'

'My dear Mrs —' what on earth was the woman's name? — 'I am so *very* sorry, but there were three carriages meeting the trains. I do not see how you could have missed — Ah, Mr Smythe, how nice to see you. Do you know Mrs — um —'

'Perronet-Thompson,' was decisively supplied. (Oh, heavens, yes, wife of an erstwhile opponent of Dizzy's.) 'Mr Smythe is one of my husband's "Young Englanders", Mrs Perronet-Thompson. Now I am sure you are in need of refreshments after your tiresome journey. Mr Smythe, would you be so kind as to take Mrs Perronet-Thompson to... Ah, Lady Jersey, delighted... *And* Lord Stanley. Allow me to present... But of course, you know each other. Lord Stanley, pray take Lady Jersey to the buffet.'

Phew!

There was a pause in the announcing; almost all the guests had now arrived. She gave a hasty glance about her. Yes, and all seemed to have arranged themselves in groups of Conservatives and Liberals. Dizzy had made her invite equal numbers of both. There must be two hundred here at least. She hoped the refreshments would last out... These new stays pinched dreadfully. Nina had laced them too tight and she was dying of thirst.

She edged her way to the buffet, grabbed a glass of lemonade from a tray borne by a passing footman and heard 'Our host has made...' What was this? Lord Palmerston shouting down at Lord John in the bellowing tones of the deaf. '...has made a sandwich of himself between two pieces of very stale bread for squeamish throats to swallow. Hah, hah!' Hah, hah, yes, very funny! And you'll look very funny too when you swallow him whole to stick in *your* throat, you old turkey-cock, inwardly commented Mary Anne; and waited for Lord John's answer in his spinsterish thin voice as he tiptoed up to his Foreign Secretary's inclining ear.

'Our host, as self-appointed Leader of the Opposition...'

'Mary Anne,' Sarah at her elbow, looking worried, 'do you not think we ought to take some of them out on to the terrace? It is so very hot in here.'

'Bother! You have just cut in on something most important, but it's just as well you did, or I might have thrown this,' she raised her glass of lemonade, 'in the face of our little First Lord.'

'Hush, darling, he will hear you.'

'I hope he will, if anyone can hear anything in this din. Yes, for mercy's sake, get them outside... Prime Minister.'

Lord John perked up his clever little face. 'Madam?'

'Pardon me if I intrude on affairs of State, but would you and Lord Palmerston care to see the grounds?'

'With the greatest of pleasure if you will honour —'

The little man's attempted gallantry was swept aside by Palmerston who had seized on the tag of this to say, 'Sure I will!' with a touch of the Irish brogue he affected when stalking the ladies. 'An' is it meself ye'd be asking to walk with you? Faith, I'd walk to the moon to take a turn in *your* pleasure ground, my dear.'

He crooked an arm, and Mary Anne, dimpling up at him, took it and thought, *I'll wager you would, you old rip.* And leaving Sarah to follow with Lord John and other of the guests, she led the way to the terrace.

The rain cloud had vanished; the sun blazed from a brassy blue sky on the hatless heads of the perspiring pianist and fiddlers, valiantly thumping out and scraping at a waltz.

'You can have an interval now,' Mary Anne told them. 'Go indoors and cool yourselves with ices. Lord Palmerston, come and see my peacock. Oh, where is he? The music must have scared him away. Dizzy says we can't have a terrace without peacocks, but we have only one at present. Let's go and find him. He may be roosting in a tree.'

The gardens were her pride. It had taken months to put her house in order, but the gardens would be the work of years.

'I have only just begun to plan the grounds,' she told those who had trooped after her along the beechwood walk. 'I intend to plant a German forest here.'

'Yes,' Dizzy came up while she was talking, 'and believe it or not, she has been digging this path herself, with no help but two old men.'

'And I want all our friends,' she gave Lord Palmerston's arm a little squeeze, 'to plant a tree or shrub at Hughenden.'

'I'll do it now!' he roared. 'This very minute.'

'No, you won't. The soil isn't yet ready for planting. Besides,' she glanced up from under her lashes at the dyed whiskers, the twinkling eyes, the full-lipped leering smile, 'we must know who *are* our friends before they come digging in my — in *our* preserves. A friend today,' she added softly, 'may be an enemy tomorrow.'

Palmerston lowered an ear. 'You said?'

'I said, there is the peacock — in that yew tree.' Mary Anne gave a little grin across her shoulder at Dizzy a step or two behind her. 'Do you see him? Come and look.'

Disraeli turned to the tall grave-faced man at his side. 'My wife finds as much joy in the growing of trees as do you in the … felling of them, Gladstone.'

The last carriage had gone; the last sound of hooves and wheels were lost in silence. The sun, a ball of fire, dipped below the wooded hills. From the terrace Mary Anne and Dizzy watched a cloth of gold spread across the deepening sky, patterned in a frieze of homeward flying rooks; then, as the dusk of evening stole in upon the day, a shrill and mournful cry pierced through that drowsy quiet.

'The voice of the peacock,' said Dizzy, 'is heard in the land.'

And she: 'Poor thing, he always calls at sundown. I expect he's lonely having to roost at night all by himself.'

Dizzy slipped an arm round her shoulders. 'We must find him,' he whispered, 'a wife.'

TWENTY-SIX

It was their shared sorrow that Isaac did not live to see them there at Hughenden. He and his wife had died within nine months of each other and before the purchase was completed. But although the death of Isaac D'Israeli did not benefit his eldest son who had anticipated his inheritance, his father bequeathed to 'my beloved daughter-in-law, Mary Anne' his treasured collection of prints. He also bequeathed Tita to the family, but when Bradenham was disbanded and Sarah and the brothers severally dispersed, none knew what to do with him until Dizzy had a brainwave. By some pulling of strings he managed to place Tita as messenger of sorts to the Board of Control, but he was always helpfully at hand for functions at Grosvenor Gate.

Months melted into years, and still Mary Anne was planning, digging, laying her 'magical touch' on Hughenden, as Dizzy said, to make of it a 'pleasance'. This green slice of land with its lavish gifts of wood and field and meadow was an increasing joy to both. And there, in that tree-embossed seclusion, Disraeli's trials, tribulations, the long struggle to retain his slippery hold on the 'greasy pole' were all forgotten. That not one shilling of the purchase loan raised by the Bentinck brothers had been repaid didn't disturb the leader of their party. His future was security enough, and Parliament was watching him. Everyone was watching him. John Russell, warily, was watching him who had flung the stone of David at Goliath Peel to bring him low and cut the House in half.

But Peel could not watch him. Peel was dead, thrown from his horse while out riding after a late night's session. He died four days later, 'at peace with all mankind', thus Gladstone, who had stayed at his bedside to the end, gave it to a shocked group of Peelites in the Carlton. And Stanley was watching him with a cold and calculating eye: Stanley who had threatened Peel at the height of his ascendancy, 'If you take in the Jew I go out.'

The parliamentary squalls that had risen to high gale force, sweeping Lord John off his feet, swept Stanley to Grosvenor Gate, hot haste from the Presence of Her, no longer 'little Vic', but Victoria Regina.

'We are launched!'

The chilly eye had thawed; that delicately chiselled face was radiant with smiles. 'The Queen has asked me to form a government.' A pause: the smile faded; the jocular tone became pontifically grave. 'A protectionist government.'

'Yes?'

The merest flicker of an eyelid gave no indication of what this displaced Israelite was thinking behind that mask of impassivity.

'Her Majesty wished to know whom I intend, or have in mind, to lead the Commons in the event, the imminent event, I fear, of my father's demise and my elevation to —' Confound the fellow! He had pulled a cat on to his knee. A black cat. And Stanley had a horror of cats — 'to the Lords,' he finished, bleakly.

The dark eyelids were lowered, the long sensitive fingers rhythmically stroking the creature's back, arched to its sensuous purring.

'The loss of Lord Derby,' said that lazy voice, 'will be immeasurable, not only to you but to us all in that it will deprive the Commons of our rightful leader... Puss, puss. Good little pusskin.'

Repressing a shudder, Stanley cleared his throat. 'And I have named among others, for Her Majesty's approval, yourself.'

'No, no, pussy, mustn't dig claws... And what did Her Majesty say to that?'

'She said, "I do not approve of Mr Disraeli. I don't like his conduct to poor Sir Robert Peel."'

'Poor Sir Robert Peel.' Was there the faintest hint of mockery in that murmured echo? 'The Queen's former animosity turned to love, at the last, for her "estimable, worthy good Sir Robert."'

A small muscle moved in Stanley's jaw as he watched that ringleted down-bent head, surely even blacker than it used to be? They said his wife cut his hair. Did she dye it too?

'I then persuaded the Queen,' Stanley carefully continued, 'failing further consideration, to accept you — on my guarantee.'

'I am overwhelmed by Her Majesty's most gracious condescension, and by yours, my ... friend. You may rest assured that I am always and entirely at your command. Now pussy, that's naughty. Mustn't spit.'

The cat jumped down and Lord Stanley got up. 'I have yet to interview Gladstone. I will let you know the result.'

The result of that interview with Gladstone, while Stanley dilly-dallied, first with this one then with another, was the complete disintegration of the proposed new government, and of Disraeli's hopes. Once again the proffered cup of office had been dashed from his lips as he stooped to drink.

He took the morning train to Hughenden and Mary Anne for consolation. He found her in the garden in short skirt and gaiters, sweeping up the frost-stiffened leaves from the paths.

The February day was sharp and clear with a keen wind blowing.

'Since when,' he demanded, 'have you turned crossing sweeper?'

'Someone has to do it, and the men are all at work in the Pinetum.' Her name for the forest, a fairy's size as yet.

Walking back arm-in-arm to the house, he gave her an account of the crisis and its finale. 'As usual, when the Queen is in a fix, she sends for Wellington. He advises her to stick to the old crowd. "They're in the mud," he tells Stanley, "so there let them stay while you look about."'

'Yes,' Mary Anne nodded. 'He's a wily old bird, is Wellington. He knows his oats.'

'So back come J Russell and Co, very shaky on the pins, and that is how they stand today.'

'And tomorrow,' she said cheerfully, 'they will topple over. Come indoors, love, you look blue with cold. I didn't expect you till this evening and there's only Irish stew for luncheon, but that'll warm you up. And don't, my darling, take it too much to heart. The Whigs are finished. They'll be sunk in the mud — to their necks. You'll see.'

But in the spring of that year the plight of 'J Russell and Co' was of little concern to the Queen and certainly less to her people. For several months, and every day in the week, Londoners flocked to Hyde Park to watch an army of workmen with pick-axes, shovels, and wagons and cranes, hammering, sawing and cutting down trees, hoisting up scaffolding, building a palace — of glass! This, Prince Albert's great inspiration, was to be the wonder of the world: a monumental effort to promote and encourage international industry and commerce.

The shy, unpopular transplanted German princeling was now the nation's hero, and the Queen beside herself with pride, joy and adoration of her Albert; with gratitude unbounded to Mr Paxton who had designed and accomplished this crystal colossus — under dearest Albert's supervision, of course — Mr Paxton, who had started life as a gardener's boy! Mr Paxton deserved and would be given recognition. *Rise, Sir Joseph…* Oh, the glory and the wonder and the beauty of it! And the park trees, towering inside up to the very dome, and all those little sparrows… What to do with the poor little sparrows, dear duke? Not a sparrow that falls to the ground, but it is only their droppings that fall to the … and will spoil the displays and ladies' bonnets. Would the duke advise us what to do?

'Yes, ma'am,' Wellington advised, 'get a sparrowhawk.'

And then the dawn of the great day. 'The greatest in our history, the most beautiful and imposing, *touching* spectacle,' so Uncle Leopold had account of it. 'Albert's dearest name is immortalised in his great, his *own* conception.' If only Uncle Leopold had been there.

Yet if Uncle Leopold was not there, some forty thousand others were, on that unforgettable first of May in 1851.

Mary Anne and Rosina were there, but not Dizzy; he had more to do, he said, than to sit and be suffocated hours on end in a hothouse. So Mary Anne and Rosina went without him.

The years had not been gentle with Rosina; no trace of the beauty that once had ravished Edward lingered in those time-blurred features, the sagging lips, the pendulous paint-bedaubed cheeks. Unbalanced hatred of her husband had carved deep bitter lines from nose to mouth. At forty-eight she was a wreck of a woman, untidy in her dress, careless of her person; and for all she might have been, for all that she was not, Mary Anne bore with her, pitied her, made her welcome at Grosvenor Gate.

She had come from Dublin especially to see the opening of the Great Exhibition. Her gown of sapphire-blue satin was bursting at the seams, soiled under the armpits and stained down the front of the bodice. Her hair, bundled into a chenille net at the back, was streaked with dye; and on her bonnet of blue straw were perched three bedraggled white feathers. They had arrived early to avoid the crowds, but a long queue of people, some several feet deep, was already waiting at the entrance, and it took a good half hour to reach their seats in the gallery, booked well in advance by Mary Anne.

Under that gigantic dome of glass the air was stifling, and pungent with a variety of smells: of spices from the Orient, the dry bitter smell of palms; the aching scent of lilies, and of women's sickly perfume; a smell of sweat and beer and oranges, where the hoi-polloi below, who had waited all night to get in, were guzzling from paper bags and drinking out of bottles.

The multi-lingual clack of tongues ranging from Japanese to cockney was accompanied by an incessant whir of engines, for the Machine, symbol of modernity, was to be the great attraction of the day: man's triumphant emergence from the limitations of a darker age into a dazzling new enlightenment. But, 'What with this noise and the heat and the stink,' said Rosina, 'I know I shall faint. My head is splitting. I will have to take a cachet, only I can't swallow it without a drink of water. I must go and find a ladies' room.'

'I saw one as we came in at the end of the gallery,' Mary Anne told her. 'Though if you are going, you'd better be quick. The Queen will be here any minute.'

Rosina's exit in that narrow passage between ballooning skirts and trousered knees caused expostulatory remark from benched spectators. 'That's the style! We can spread ourselves out a bit now,' spoke a deep voice in Mary Anne's ear. The owner of the voice, who had moved up into Rosina's place, was a stout shapeless old lady in black bombazine and a large black poke. She wore lace mittens, a beaming smile and a formidable moustache.

'Hot, isn't it?' She produced a handkerchief and mopped her face. 'Squashed here like flies on flypaper. Is your friend coming back?'

'Yes, I —'

A fanfare of trumpets within, and a booming of guns without, broke in on Mary Anne's reply to announce the Queen's arrival. The throb of machinery was hushed. All heads were turned, all eyes fixed on that dumpy little figure as, with amazing dignity, she moved towards her improvised throne: an Indian chair, covered with a richly brocaded elephant cloth. Her silver threaded gown of rose-pink silk flashed with jewels and the glitter of the Star. A coronet of diamonds circled the smooth, fair head; and as she mounted the carpeted steps to her chair another burst of cheering resounded in echoing wave upon wave through the vast crystal hall.

For a second she was seen to hesitate; those near her saw her eyes fill, her lips tremble as, with the dawn of a smile, she acknowledged that deep-throated welcome.

Immediately behind her, leading the Prince of Wales by the hand, came her consort in full dress uniform. The organ thundered the National Anthem; choristers sang it; then, as the last notes died down, the Prince stepped forward to deliver his speech in so strong a German accent and so low a voice that scarcely one word of it was audible to people in the gallery.

'Teutonic barber's block,' muttered the old lady. 'Waste of the nation's money, I call it. Can't see what good it will do. Here comes your friend.'

Rosina's return and her murmured apologies as she edged her way along that restricted space, momentarily eclipsing all view of the Queen and Albert, were received with indignant exclamations.

'Really, madam!'

'This is too much —'

'You might have waited until —'

More cheers, somewhat less vociferous, greeted the end of the Prince's address, followed by a prayer from the Archbishop of Canterbury, a singing of the Hallelujah Chorus, and the Great Exhibition was declared open.

'Thank goodness for that,' whispered Rosina on a breath of spirituous cachous. 'I suppose we can now go and look at the stalls.'

Bathed in that silvery translucent light the thronged aisles presented a bewildering kaleidoscopic pageant. The magnificent robes of Indian potentates, the gold laced uniforms, the harsh bright colours of women's gowns, formed an intricate pattern against that astonishing display of exhibits drawn from the wealth of all nations.

There were rugs from Persia, carpets from Turkey, tapestries from Gobelins, a gem-like fantasia of amethyst, ruby, lapis-lazuli and emerald, blent with the opalescent pearl of silks from Lyons. There were leopard skins from Africa and sables from the Czar; rare porcelain from China and kimonos from Japan; jewels from India worth a Maharajah's ransom; and from the Queen her priceless own exhibit, reposing on a velvet cushion in a gas-lit gilded cage: the world's most famous diamond, the Koh-i-noor.

There was steel from Sheffield and pottery from Staffordshire, tortoise-shell from Italy and gay rich shawls from Spain; from the Swiss were clocks and watches, one no larger than a pea, mounted in a finger-ring, of perfect craftsmanship yet so infinitesimal it needed a magnifying glass to tell the time. Mary Anne bought a clock from Switzerland to hang upon a wall. It was of painted china wreathed with rosebuds, its weight a pine cone of carved lead. Rosina bought some handkerchiefs, and at the same stall, bearing the name of a famous Belfast firm, Mary Anne saw the old lady who had spoken to her in the gallery buying hand-embroidered linen sheets.

'I wish them sent,' she told the assistant, handing him a card. 'Here is my name and address.'

Rosina wanted to see the machinery, but Mary Anne said, 'You can go by yourself. I must sit. I can't stand on my legs any longer.' On every side the crowd pushed and jostled her, trod on her toes. 'I'll wait for you here if I can find a seat. Only pray don't be long.'

The old lady looked round. 'Oh, it's you.' She nodded, beaming, and her black poke, loosely tied under her flabby chin, slipped to the back of her head. 'They have charged me twice as much for these than they would cost in Regent Street. A great to-do about nothing. And who's going to pay for all this? *We'll* pay. We always do. Free trade? Pah! Good day to you.' And with another nod and a word to the assistant, 'Don't you lose that card, young man,' the old lady waddled away.

Mary Anne was still searching for a seat when Rosina came back. 'I couldn't get anywhere near the machines, and such a horrible noise — my poor head. I shall have to take another cachet.'

'No, you don't.' Mary Anne grabbed her by the arm, casting an eye on Rosina's reticule, which showed a conspicuous bulge. 'You've had quite enough of your cachets. We're going home.'

TWENTY-SEVEN

It was during the August recess that Mary Anne became aware of Dizzy's latest 'feminine interest', as she called an unknown admirer from Torquay. That, however, did not unduly disturb her. Letters from unknown admirers of his books, his speeches and himself were no novelty to her or to him, who, notoriously careless of his personal correspondence, would give her the letters to read. She carefully kept and filed them all.

They were at tea on the terrace at Hughenden when a footman brought the daily post. She sorted hers; one from Rosina, a couple of bills — 'Oh, and another from Torquay. No mistaking her scrawl. Here, take it.'

He took it, broke the seal, glanced over the four single pages of heavily embossed notepaper, laid them aside and went on with his tea.

Mary Anne, feeding cucumber sandwiches to the peacock and his wife, asked idly, 'Well, what has she to say this time?'

'She wishes to make my acquaintance.'

'Does she so?' She looked sharply round. 'I thought that would be the next thing. I told you not to send her *Tancred*. How can you hope to sell your books if you go giving away free copies to every woman who adores you through the post?'

'Not every woman, only one,' Dizzy unconvincingly assured her, 'and that, if you remember, was because she wrote to say her bookseller in Torquay had sold out of all his copies.'

'Then why couldn't she have asked him to order more instead of cadging one from you? A fine way to found a free library! I have a good mind to try it myself on Mr Thackeray.'

'You won't,' murmured Dizzy, 'get very far with him.'

'No, I don't suppose I will. He has to live by his pen and not on his wife.'

And having said that she could have bitten out her tongue; and he, throwing a lump of sugar at the peacock, said, 'He's moulting.'

'I'm a beast!' she burst forth. 'I didn't mean it — you know I didn't mean it. But you shouldn't always be telling me you married me for money.'

'Yes, but I am also always telling you that if I married you again it would be for love.'

'You're safe enough there,' she retorted, 'knowing that you couldn't marry me again unless we were divorced, as we very likely will be if you go scraping acquaintance with every — let me see the letter.'

He passed it; she read it, her face darkening, and a vertical line between her brows. Then: 'This woman,' she declared in a tone of finality, 'is mad. Only a lunatic would ask you — *you*, whom the whole world watches — to meet her at the Crystal Palace as if you were the grocer's boy and she the housemaid, walking out!' She tossed the letter back to him, crumbled a biscuit and flung the pieces at the peacock. She had been weeding and was in her gardening dress, the short skirt, open-throated smock, and the gaiters. Her floppy straw hat lay at her feet.

Dizzy folded the letter, slipped it in his pocket and picked up the hat. 'Put it on, darling. You will have sunstroke if you go bare-headed.'

She snatched the hat, laid it on her knees and said, 'Do you intend to accept this — invitation?'

'I have not made up my mind.' Reflectively he stroked his chin, decorated with a little goatee beard, a recent indulgence to the disgust of Mary Anne. 'It might,' he admitted, 'be amusing.'

Their eyes crossed. His held a twinkle, hers were stormy.

'Very amusing, I'm sure, especially to newspaper men dodging behind statues to jot down the twitterings of what a little bird — one of the sparrows nesting in the trees inside the Crystal Palace — had to tell of Mr Disraeli's rendezvous with a — goodness knows what!'

'In that rig of yours,' he drawled, the twinkle deepening, 'you are deliciously epicene. Half girl, half Ganymedes. Shall we,' he inconsequently added, 'go together?'

'Go together where?'

'To meet the — a — goodness knows what.'

'Oh, your inamorata from Torquay. No, thank you. If, as is evident, the creature is insane, I prefer to keep out of her way. But you go, by all means, if you care to run the risk of a knife in your ribs unless you give her what she wants. A madwoman can be very dangerous when she has an *idée fixe*, and her *idée* is evidently fixed — on you!'

He sighed. 'You shatter me. From her letters, which I thought to be remarkably perceptive and intelligent, I had hoped, despite increasing age and my — disguised — grey hairs, that I had made a conquest.'

She eyed him coldly. 'You aren't — you can't be serious.'

'I may be too serious to be taken seriously.'

'As so,' she snapped, 'it would seem is Mrs — who is it? I can never read her signature.'

'Brydges Willyams, spelled twice with a Y. And Sarah.'

'For gracious sake! You haven't come to Christian names already?'

'Christian names, no. Jewish, yes. The lady claims to be related to my family.'

'You didn't show me *that* letter.'

'Did I not? You have an earwig on your neck.'

'Ooph! Take it off.'

He took it off.

'I don't believe a word of it!' blurted Mary Anne. 'She's an artful one, she is. And nothing so mad as I thought. So that is why you gave her *Tancred*, in the hope to find in her your "Rose of Sharon", as she hopes to find in you her "Asian mystery". A fellow feeling.' She gave him that with an impudent grin. 'I see it all.'

'Not quite all. Do you think you could discourage Mr Micawber —' his name for the peacock because he was always waiting for something to turn up — 'and listen to me for a moment?'

'I am listening. Go on.'

He went on. 'The point is, I believe this lady to be of some social importance in the county of Devon, which as you may or may not know, is a Liberal stronghold. An ardent Tory supporter in a hotbed of Whigs might be worth cultivating.'

'And you intend to cultivate your "Rose of Sharon"? She may need some careful pruning.' She got to her feet, extending a finger at the goatee. 'As so will this. It makes you look part Uncle Sam, part satyr.'

'God's life,' he breathed, 'but you are wonderful.' And reaching for her soil-stained hands he took them to kiss. 'Such dirty little hands. You ought to wear gardening gloves. I love you and I love you and — I love you, Mary Anne.'

'Yes, that's all very fine, but,' a dimple hovered, 'wait until you see — and cross — your Brydges!'

It is, however, doubtful if Disraeli would have been involved in this singular affair were it not for Mary Anne's insistence. Once assured that his interest in his 'inamorata' from Torquay was less romantic than political, she gave him no peace until he agreed to make the assignation.

'But,' he stipulated, 'on one condition — that you come with me. I refuse to face her alone.'

'Don't be an ass. Much support you will get for the party in the West with a wife tacked on to your tail. And why so bashful of a sudden? You, who will go to any lengths to win the ladies — for their husbands' votes. Did you do as I advised, and ask the Member for South Devon if he knows anything of her?'

'I did. And he doesn't. Has never heard of her — nor, I gather, has anybody else.'

'Well, he *will* hear of her — from you. It's a good thing,' she reflected, 'that I am so un-jealous as to allow your fancy's freedom a full rein. But at least if you meet her you will know if she be worth your while or — your wiles.'

And thus it came about that an interview with his mysterious correspondent was arranged to take place at the crystal fountain inside the exhibition. That Mary Anne had urged, indeed had driven him, to this encounter may have a little piqued him, and the more so since she so persistently had emphasized her lack of jealousy. Was she then, he asked himself, indifferent to the consequences that might ensue from such an equivocal approach? Or, hideous suspicion, had she taken a lover and wished to divert his too exigent attentions from herself? No, God! Never that. For if she were not jealous he was.

Imagination harrowingly courted the vision of some seductive youth — she always had been drawn to youth. George Smythe, for instance, the original of 'Coningsby', who wrote her distinctly amorous poems and almost as amorous letters… And Lord John Manners with his silken curls and sloe-dark eyes; or Stanley's beautiful young son, all were heirs to great estates and titles, and her professed adorers who delighted in her naughty innuendoes and openly declared that they would sooner spend an evening, or a night, with 'Mrs Dizzy' than with a bread-and-butter miss of seventeen. Yes, any one of these exquisite youths, his 'Young Englanders', might well be his supplanter; yet although they were younger than he, they were not very young any more. It came as a shock. Time was speeding by, too fast. But life might still offer a swansong adventure.

He had chosen to walk through the park to his tryst. The lady had made the appointment for eleven o'clock in the morning when the exhibition, she wrote, would be less crowded than in the afternoon. Mary Anne, who had made him shave his tufted chin, had also supervised his toilet. Arriving at the entrance he caught a glimpse of himself in a wall of palm-darkened glass: raven blue frock coat, tight-waisted and slimming; check trousers of a lighter blue and white; eminently satisfactory was that dimmed reflection. Tilting his hat to a slightly rakish angle he sauntered in.

Excitement seized him. Again he wished that Mary Anne had not been quite so anxious to encourage this diversion, less now from doubt of her ulterior motive, than that her knowledge of it tended to deprive the situation of its charm.

It was a few minutes after eleven when he gained the centre hall. Not a vast crowd, but an increasing number were already there to view or to stroll, or to buy. He took a hasty glance around. What a vulgar monstrosity of a thing — this crystal palace, with Albertian taste and influence predominant, as everywhere in every home, including his. Mary Anne, following the fashion, filled the rooms with cumbersome mahogany, horsehair sofas, antimacassars of Berlin wool and frightful wax fruit in glass cages... He quickened his steps to the fountain, relieved to find that the lady had not yet arrived. The wide circular seat surrounding the pool was unoccupied save for a stout elderly party eating an apple and nursing a large and rather shabby sealskin bag.

Carefully lifting his coat-tails, he sat facing the entrance, and with his back to and as far from the elderly party as possible. He did not greatly welcome a witness to the meeting.

Screwing in his eyeglass he scrutinised newcomers, to discover in the distance a small hesitant figure in a modest grey mantle and a bonnet thickly veiled. She seemed to be searching for someone, and he wondered if this could be... No. She had wandered off in an opposite direction to look at a display of Brussels lace.

He pulled out his watch. A quarter past eleven; she was late. Her last letter gave an address in Bryanston Square, so she had not far to come. Then again he saw, and seeing, his heart sank. This, undoubtedly was she: a tall determined, horse-faced woman searching round about to make straight for him and the fountain. Suddenly she swerved, she stopped, she called: 'Matilda! Theresa!' And swooped to grab a pair of identical little girl twins. His heart bounced up again, when, with a child attached to each hand, she hurried past the fountain to accompanying squeals of, 'Oh no, Miss Smellypot,' it sounded like, or something, 'we didn't hide on purpose, no we didn't, truly.'

He would give her another five minutes and no more. What a fool, what a thrice besotted fool was he to have landed himself in this fantastic situation! He had been trapped. It was a hoax contrived by some mischievous journalist who thought to make a coup for his rag-tail press. He could visualise the

Opposition laughing itself sick at a Grub Street cartoon of 'A Frog he would a-wooing go to make a Great Exhibition of himself', offering a nosegay labelled 'Protection' to a smirking John Russell in petticoats…

And then, again he saw and this time he knew. Intuition, something more: the knowledge that at last he had found what all his life he had sought; his Ideal. His monocle gave her to him, dark and beautiful beyond his dreams, although more Spanish, he would say, than Jewish. And what eyes! Black-lashed and large as a gazelle's. Unhesitatingly, and with what imperious grace, she advanced to the circular seat, sank down upon it with the faintest little sigh, her silken skirts billowing about her like the petals of a rose — his Rose of Sharon! For a second he sat, drinking in her loveliness, the delicate aquiline nose, the curve of her chin, her cheek, peach-coloured, under a bonnet swathed in creamy gauze. His pulse raced. Foolish, foolish Mary Anne to give him his 'fancy's freedom' and 'full rein', for *this*.

He braced himself; he stood, removed his hat and, bowing, said, 'Madam, I think … I hope you are expecting … me?'

'Sir!'

Indignation blazed from those eyes, her face crimsoned. 'How *dare* you accost… Here is my husband. He will … Charles!' She sprang up and hastened forward saying shrewishly and high, 'Why are you so late? I have been waiting ages.'

'Not ages, my dear, surely. It is barely half past —'

'Long enough for some dreadful man to —' Quietly, profanely, and to the point, he cursed. He must get away before this husband, this red-faced person with a military air, should make a scene. A fine to-do for Disraeli to be called

305

upon to give an explanation of his conduct. He must go. At once. Sneak out by a side entrance before she…

They were coming back. She had her Charles by his arm and was talking — no, shouting — into his face. A proper bitch!

He wheeled about and was frantically searching for an exit, when he heard himself deeply and throatily hailed.

'Mr Disraeli, I believe?'

The elderly party, whom he had clean forgotten, beckoned him, saying, 'I did not see you arrive. You are very late.'

'…?' His tongue went dry and tasted suddenly of lemons.

'It is Mr Disraeli, is it not? No mistaking the cartoons of you in *Punch*.'

Horror heaped on horror held him palsied. No, not this! It couldn't be this — this elephantine nightmare!

'You don't have to stand. Sit down.' She patted the seat, flicking from it the cores of some two or three apples. 'There are no cartoons of me, more's the pity, for they'd never have done laughing.' She chuckled juicily, rummaged in the sealskin bag, and held out to him a card printed in bold copperplate. 'You have seen my letters, now you see me — in the flesh, and plenty of it!' Another and juicier chuckle. Her chins shook. 'Not so bad for near on eighty, eh?'

Clutching the card, he mechanically bowed; his lips moved, a croaking sound came from them, but no words.

'Don't be shy.' Again the seat was patted. 'I shan't eat you.' Her little beady eyes brimmed with good humour until they almost disappeared in the rolls of rosy fat around their sockets. 'Come along then, sit you down.' Still rummaging inside the sealskin bag she pulled from it a sheaf of parchment. 'And now, young man,' said Mrs Brydges Willyams, 'we'll talk business.'

An eagerly expectant wife awaited his return. He had told her he would not be back until the afternoon as he had an appointment at the Carlton with Stanley, who, since the death of his father, had succeeded to the earldom of Derby.

'Well?' She plied him with questions: 'What is she like? Is she young? Is she pretty?'

'More than pretty.' A far-away look came into his eyes. 'She is — how shall I describe the indescribable?'

A lengthy pause; then faintly, 'We know she is a Mrs. Is her husband alive?'

'She is a widow.'

'Oh? A rich widow?'

'I did not,' he said coldly, 'discuss the state of her finances.'

'What *did* you discuss?'

He passed a hand across his forehead. 'How can I know? When one clips Elysium to find the epitome of an ideal — in the flesh,' a spasm crossed his face, 'it is so rare, so precious an experience, that one is lifted to extra-mundane heights. I am not yet down to earth. Forgive me.'

'It seems,' she said miserably, 'that you must be … in love. All the lovers in your books talk this way when they're in love. Are you,' she whispered, 'in love?'

'For your dear sake I fear to say,' his gaze slipped past her, 'that I am. She came, I saw; was conquered. Whoever loved that loved not at first sight?'

'Evidently, since you are so full of quotations. A sure sign. But for your dear sake,' a quiver slurred her voice, 'I will try to accept what I always knew must come some day. I was too happy … I knew it couldn't last.'

He was pricked by a moment's remorse. Too bad to make her suffer; yet it fed his self-esteem to think she did. He had suffered enough on her account today, sending him out on this fool's errand, so let her pay for it. 'I have never disguised from you,' he reminded her gently, 'that my nature demands perpetual love.'

'Yes, you wrote that to me once when you thought you had lost me, before we were married.' She hid her face in her hands and spoke through them tearfully. 'Is *my* perpetual love, then, not enough? God help me! I have brought this on myself. It was I who sent you to her. You said —' she dropped her hands and seemed to be grappling with the fear of asking that — 'you *did* say she is beautiful? And young?'

'Eternally young. A glorious creature. The living re-creation of my Rose of Sharon.'

'Has she a moustache?'

'A…?'

'I only wondered. These Jewesses — and Spanish women, too — they are, as a rule, so very dark they often grow hairs on the face and sometimes on the chest, according to my dressmaker.'

'I cannot particularise,' he said stiffly, 'as to that of her manifold attractions … yet.'

'A hope, deferred perhaps?'

She hid her face again: a sobbing breath came from her and a spluttering sound, followed by a peal of laughter. 'Oh, my Dizzy! You sublime idiot. You are — you really are the worst possible liar. You will have to do better than this if you want to lead the House. Oh dear!' She held her side. 'It hurts to laugh.'

But he was unamused. 'What the devil —?'

'Wait. I have something to show you, and don't you come after me. Stay there.'

She ran out of the room, and was back within five minutes in a modest grey mantle and a bonnet thickly veiled.

'Here I am, and as I was. You didn't see me — or did you? But if you did, you wouldn't have recognised me. You can't see a thing, even with your eyeglass, at a distance of more than ten yards.'

'You don't mean to say,' was the rather strained enquiry, 'that you were there, after repeatedly refusing to go with me?'

'I refused to go *with* you, but I never said I wouldn't go at all. You don't suppose I would have sent you off alone to meet some stray female cat whom neither you nor anybody else has ever heard of? You might have laid yourself open to anything — blackmail, slander, seduction, or,' she looked at him slyly, 'you might even have fallen in love.'

His mouth twitched. 'I have,' he said, 'fallen in love.'

'What! With my old lady?'

'Yours?'

'Yes, mine. She was in the next seat to Rosina at the opening of the exhibition, and we exchanged a few words. I remembered her at once. Who could forget her? She weighs half a ton, and that Sairey Gamp poke — and the moustache. I arrived before you did and she was there already, eating apples and staring about but she didn't look at me although I walked right past her. Of course it never entered my mind that she was your "inamorata". But what I can't conceive is why she should ask you to meet her at the Crystal Palace and not at her hotel, or wherever she is staying.'

'I will tell you why. The fact of the matter is —'

And the fact of the matter was that Mrs Brydges Willyams, on a visit to a married niece, did not wish the niece to know of her intention to ask Disraeli if he would act as executor to her will, on the understanding that if he did agree to act in such capacity he would also be her residuary legatee.

'Good Lord!' Mary Anne drew in a long breath. 'Does that mean she's going to leave you all her money? Then she *must* be mad.'

'On the contrary,' was the frigid reply, 'I thought her remarkably sane. As a childless widow with no near relatives other than a niece, who is already well provided for, and because of her connection with my family — her father was a Mendez da Costa, and she, like myself, was baptised — she has chosen to regard me as her possible heir. Strange as it may seem to you,' he added, growing chillier, 'this very intelligent and perceptive old lady has unbounded faith in me and in my future. She is confident, and I trust not unduly optimistic in her conviction, that I am destined for a — why do you laugh?'

'I can't help it,' giggled Mary Anne, 'when you put on that voice. You sound like Gladstone speechifying.'

'And when, may I ask, have you heard Gladstone speechifying?'

'In a dozen drawing rooms. He can't even speak about the weather without giving you chapter and verse for it. But as for your — and my — old lady, of course she has unbounded faith in you. Haven't we all? What age is she?'

'Near upon eighty.'

'Hmm. And she may live to be a hundred. So what have you decided? Will you act as her executor?'

Dizzy pulled a long lip. 'I shall have to take legal advice before I give her my decision. She is willing to wait, and by the way, she invites us to visit her at Torquay this autumn.'

'Us? Me too?'

'You too. She is returning to Devon tomorrow and is sending bulbs for your garden, and lobsters —'

'Lobsters! For my garden?'

'Lobsters for me. She asked if I liked them. I told her I did, and so she will send us a surfeit. When I left her she slipped a sealed envelope into my hand with this in it —' he took from his pocket a thousand pound note — 'for my election expenses.'

'Well!' Mary Anne drew in another long breath. 'An inheritance, lobsters and bulbs, and then *this* — in one morning. I can't say you've wasted much time.'

TWENTY-EIGHT

Summer fled, chased by October gales. At her window Mary Anne watched the copper-clad leaves whirl in the rollicking dance of the winds to lie in tumbled heaps along the paths, on the lawns, in the lake where floated two grey downy cygnets, named Hero and Leander by Dizzy. The flame of creeper on the walls rusted and fell. Winter followed hard on autumn's heels, but not the promised visit to Torquay. That must be postponed, pending a Government crisis. The House was in a ferment: all of France was in a ferment with revolution in the air and Lord Palmerston 'not turned out', he collared Dizzy in the Lobby to tell him, 'I was kicked out', for his open and unauthorised approval of Louis Napoleon's *coup d'état*.

Affairs are very stirring, Dizzy wrote to Sarah. John Russell and Co were uneasily stirring, and Mary Anne and Dizzy in the greatest stir of all.

On a February morning, leaving her Pinetum, the peacocks and the cygnets, now almost grown to swans, she drove pell-mell to London. The House sat late, and Dizzy, who was due back at Hughenden the next day, saw all the windows alight at Grosvenor Gate and his wife at the door to meet him when he returned at midnight.

'I had to come. I couldn't wait until tomorrow, but not a word until you've supped. There's cold chicken and champagne — yes, darling, you must eat.'

He couldn't eat; he wouldn't eat. 'I have no taste, no appetite. I've talked too much. They *all* talked too much, and said, as usual, nothing, though they made a lot of noise. Johnny and Co very sick, but still in.'

'Oh, God, how long — how long will they stay in?'

'Months and months, or weeks and weeks,' he filled the champagne glass and slowly sipped, 'or —' The sound of a carriage pulling up at the kerb turned him sharp about. He went to the window, drew aside the curtain. 'Or hours,' he finished quietly, 'and hours.'

'Lord Derby, sir,' announced the butler. 'I have shown his lordship to the Blue Room.'

Mary Anne, with her knuckles to her mouth, watched Dizzy drink again, set down his empty glass and pour himself another.

Go, go — can't you go? she screamed within her; and watched him go, pausing at a wall mirror to adjust his cravat, smooth back from his forehead a wandering curl, and take from his breast pocket a lace-edged handkerchief; a scent of amber came to her. She bit her knuckles. *Go!* And silently followed him in her stockinged feet. Outside the Blue Room door, her ear at the keyhole, she listened to that low-voiced conference. She heard enough of it to send her flying to her bedroom with a magnum of champagne.

Dizzy came to bed an hour later to find a slightly inebriated Mary Anne gleefully declaring, 'I've backed — the Derby *Winner!*' And flinging up her arms she went reeling round the room in her chemise to a spur-of-the moment improvisation and the tune of that jolly old jig:

'*Oh dear, what can the matter be,*
Oh dear, what can the matter be,
Oh dear ,what can the matter be,
Johnny is gone — hip-hooray!

He hoped to have stayed then he'd bring a new Bill in
But Derby said No and the House wasn't willin'
For Johnny and Co to be stuck there and still in
The mud — so they sent him away!'

When Dizzy, who had overslept after these night revels, awoke next morning he found an empty bed and a note pinned to his pillow, addressed to:

THE RIGHT HONOURABLE THE CHANCELLOR OF THE EXCHEQUER.
Bless you, my darling, your own happy devoted wife wishes you joy. I hope you will make as good a Ch. of the Exch. as you have been a husband to your
Mary Anne.'

'All these new ministers,' complained the Queen to Wellington, 'are strange to us, unknown to us, with exception of Lord Derby. We do not *like* a change of government, but Lord Derby *is* the Government, and so — My dear Duke, pray be seated.'

'Who, ma'am, who?'

'I said,' pronounced the Queen distinctly, 'pray be *seated*.'

'Thank 'ee, ma'am.'

Wellington creakingly sat. The Queen's pale eyes goggled at that spare bent frame, the flesh so tightly stretched across the bones of his leathery lined face that he looked to be all nose. The poor dear duke, so old, and so very, *very* deaf. Much more deaf than Lord Palmerston, who heard perfectly well in one ear.

The Queen raised her voice. 'We told Lord Derby, with whom we discussed the question of our Household, that we make two firm conditions. The persons who comprise our court shall *not* be on the verge of bankruptcy, and their moral characters must be above reproach. We shall never *never* forget the unfortunate affair of Lady Flora Hastings. That her virtue was proved beyond all doubt could not dispel the unsavoury slander attached to the name of a lady of our court.'

'Trust Lord Derby, ma'am,' heartily hazarded Wellington, 'for that.'

'We said —' what *could* the duke have thought we said? — 'that a rigorous moral tone must be upheld by all newcomers to our court. We dread another scandal.'

'Rest easy, ma'am,' a muted guffaw rumbled up from the duke's skinny depths. 'When I asked Lord Derby if he were much fatigued with rocking the Cabinet's cradle, he said, "No, after a long protracted lying-in I and my litter are doing very well."'

The Queen gave a little cough behind a plump jewelled hand, and a chilly glance at that thin white-headed figure. The duke's remarks were certainly at times a trifle odd.

She tried again. 'We receive elaborate reports of proceedings in the House of Commons from Mr Disraeli, written much in the style of his books. I understand he produces his budget in a day or two. We shall be interested to —'

'Who, ma'am, who?' The duke leaned forwards, a hand behind his ear.

The Queen raised her voice a tone higher. 'The budget. We shall be interested to hear the details of Mr Disraeli's first budget!'

'Hah!' The duke wrinkled his great nose. 'He'll drop a load on 'em if I know Dizzy.'

'Dizzy?'

'Everyone calls him Dizzy, ma'am.'

'Indeed?' The Queen achieved a little joke. 'It is to be hoped the House will not turn *dizzy* when they hear his budget speech.'

'Who — who, ma'am?'

'I said —' No, better not repeat it. 'I was speaking of Mr Disraeli. We were not much impressed in his favour. We thought his manner somewhat — if one may say so in strictest confidence, dear Duke —'

But with Albert in the window teaching Bertie to play chess, and her ladies in the anteroom listening, all ears — so tiresome to have to shout — *no* conversation with the poor dear duke could be held in strictest confidence.

'Check, Papa,' crowed the Prince of Wales.

'Yes, my boy, but you will now see what comes. I move my queen, and say to you check-mate.'

'Oh, no, Papa! That isn't fair. You should have first called check to me like I did to you.'

'*Aber doch!* You teach your father, is it, and say to me not fair? As so you your lessons will not learn, so will you not this game learn. You will not give to concentrate your mind. You are *Dummkopf, mein Sohn.*'

'But, Papa, I —'

'Bertie!'

'Yes, Mama?' The heir apparent sent a haunted look in Majesty's direction.

'Stand, Bertie,' his father bade him. 'You shall not sit when you the Queen address.'

Bertie stood, and was commanded: 'Apologise at once to your dear papa for your most disrespectful remark, and — leave the room.'

The heir licked his lips and swallowed twice. 'I apologise, Papa.'

A glacial stare from those icy blue eyes.

'And to your *Mutter*, Bertie. What to the Queen say you for your bad manners?'

'I did not mean to be bad-mannered, ma'am. I am sorry, Mama, I —'

'The Queen has bid you go.' The Consort pointed to the door. 'So go you. Now.'

'Yes, sir.' Head down, the heir slunk off and was halted.

'Wait! Have you again your manners forget? Do you not the duke *Auf Wiedersehen* bid?'

A mumbled '*Auf Wiedersehen*, Duke' preceded a gleam in the eyes of the heir as they alighted on the medals dangling to the old man's shaky bow.

Lingering in the corridor, a small boy came shyly to the duke as he left the Presence.

'Duke, sir … May I … please will you…?'

'Hey? Who — who?'

The duke bent his silvery head. He must bend very low to catch that hushed voice, saying close into his large and rather dirty ear full of greyish white hairs, 'Will you tell me sometime about … these?' A stumpy finger reverently touched the gold medals. 'I would like to hear about the battle straight from you, Duke, if I may.' But one might never hear it straight from him unless one heard it soon. 'If next time you come I could —'

'Sir!' A hand was clamped on his shoulder. A sneaking, spying equerry had caught him. 'Your Royal Highness must not detain the duke. Your Grace's pardon. The Prince must not keep his tutor waiting. The Prince's recreation hour is long past. Come, sir, if you please.'

Recreation, was interjected inwardly, *my foot!*

A nod, a bow, and — was it a wink? — from the duke; a last longing look at the medals, and the laggard heir ('so very idle,' his mama complained, '*always* behind with his lessons'), was, inexorably, walked away.

TWENTY-NINE

At the time of Disraeli's maiden speech, Mary Anne vowed she would never hear him speak in the House again until he spoke as prime minister; and she had kept that vow. Nor when he presented his first and then his second budget, which he said would make or mar the Government, did she alter her decision.

That Disraeli's overnight promotion had received a storm of critical abuse from all parties, neither dismayed nor surprised him. He had been prepared for it. It was generally accepted that the Leader of the Opposition should lead the House of Commons with a prime minister in the House of Lords. But … to give the Exchequer to one who knew nothing of finance, a spinner of words but never a spinner of money, unless to send it spinning down the drain, was an unparalleled error of judgement, said the scoffers, for Derby to rue.

The Liberal press, quick to seize on old Wellington's parrot-cry when the list of Cabinet names was read out to him, few of which he knew and none that he could hear, promptly dubbed the Derby Cabinet the 'Who-Who' Ministry.

Disraeli, however, was not to be put down, though he may have been put out by newspaper cackle and the grins of 'J Russell & Co'. When he tried on his black-and-gold Chancellor's robes before kissing hands with the Queen, 'You will find it,' they warned him, 'very heavy.'

'Oh, no,' he retorted, 'I find it uncommonly light.'

On the last day of the budget debate, Mary Anne drove with him to the House. He had just recovered from a bout of influenza and was far from well. Night after night, throughout that week, he had sat in apathetic silence, arms folded, legs outstretched, his hat tilted over his eyes, apparently unmoved by and impervious to his denouncers for his alleged abandonment of Protection.

Like terriers in a rat hunt they fell on to savage his malt tax, his beer tax, his tea tax, his house tax. And now his turn had come.

Mary Anne anxiously watched him, so pale and so thin! He had lost weight in his illness, yet always, when his body weakened, his spirit strengthened to soar.

Before they left she gave him a stiff drink of egg-nog and a kiss in the hall behind the back of 'Plush and Powder', to the whispered words, 'Pour boiling oil on those beasts tonight and scald 'em!'

Down the steps to the carriage where a new young footman held open the door, Dizzy followed her. Nina was at an upper window looking out to see them go.

'Dear soul, she is as proud of you as I am.' Mary Anne waved to her; the footman slammed the door. She snatched her hand away — but not in time. Her fingers were crushed to the bone.

A strangled cry escaped her. Dizzy turned his head. 'What is it?'

'I … I thought I saw the cat run under the wheels but … it ran back again.'

He mustn't know. He was going into battle. Nothing must deflect him from the fight.

She felt a dampness oozing through her glove. Good! If it bled it wouldn't hurt so much. Once when a window sash had squashed her finger it had bled and didn't hurt … so very much. But this was different. This, after the first frozen shock of it, was a slow grinding agony. The muscles of her arm went taut; her face sagged, bathed in clammy dew. She *must not* faint. She must talk.

'Yes, I wish I could hear you tonight, but I must keep my promise to myself...' And this torture, too. 'You would prefer me not to be there, wouldn't ... you?'

'Yes and no. On the whole, no.'

She pressed her face to the window; her hot breath was like steam on the glass, yet she was cold, death-cold on the rack of this fiendish screw of pain.

'How the days draw in. It is almost dusk, and not yet four o'clock. It will soon be Christmas. We will have a great celebration for Christmas — the Lyndhursts, the Buckinghams and Mrs Brydges Will ... yams.' *Hold it, hold it. You mustn't be sick.* 'Does my talk ... does it fidget you to hear me talk?'

'I love to hear you talk.'

Then, for God's sake, talk.

'I meant to tell you ... Louise de Rothschild told me that John Russell reads *Coningsby* to his wife in bed every night, and when she asked him which parts he ... he liked the best he said the politics, Tadpole and Taper. But Lady John ... she likes the love scenes best ... cries over them. Just fancy Johnnie reading ... you! I didn't credit him with such good taste.'

Her ears buzzed. Some hellish little demon was beating at her fingers with a tiny red-hot hammer; slowly at first. One. Two. Three. Then, in quick succession, onetwothree ... *bang!*

Something splintered. The bones of her hand ... or her head?

Again he turned his. 'What did you say?'

'Did I ... say?' They were passing the palace. 'I was wondering if the Standard ... but of course the Queen will not leave Windsor until after ... the debate.'

Soon be there now.

'If only your father could have lived to see you Chancellor of the...' How much longer could one keep this up? Surreptitiously with her uninjured left hand she pinched her cheeks to bring some colour to them. He mustn't see her looking like a ghost. And of course it *would* have to be the right hand. If the carriage drew up at the left and he took her hand, then he wouldn't know, but if he saw and touched *this* mangled mess ... Yes, by damn, it was! Round to the right to pull up on the right. She hid her hand in the folds of her gown.

Disraeli stepped carefully over her feet. The young footman — clumsy oaf! — was there to help him out.

'I may be late. I doubt that we'll be through with it under five or six hours, but if I can send word to tell you how it goes, I will.'

'Yes, darling, do.' She held out her left hand to him, he took and kissed it. She fixed a smile, nodding brightly. 'God be with you.'

He lifted his hat. The sharp wind crisped his curls; his eyes clung to hers, then, returning her smile, he squared his shoulders and walked quickly into the House.

Never had a budget been so violently derided, scorned, attacked. Never had a Chancellor faced such bitter enmity while under the scourge of his assailants he sat, cold, unmoved, and changeless as the Sphinx... Then came the deluge, inside and outside the House.

Although it was mid-winter a terrific thunderstorm crashed over Westminster to blast the sky, to strike with lightning flash upon flash through the tall windows, above and around that quivering figure sprung from his torpor to his feet to hurl at his denouncers his scorching defiance.

'I have been told to withdraw my budget. Sir,' a finger like a rapier-point shot out at Gladstone who faced him, onyx-eyed, dark-crested, lips set in a hard firm line that he looked to have no mouth. 'A greater man than I or the Honourable Member opposite,' that fiery voice rose up to drown the thunder, 'Pitt — the younger Pitt — withdrew his budget as more recent others have done, but *I* will not submit to degradation!'

Those who saw and heard him believed some diabolic agent had inspired that astonishing, unceasing flow of rhetoric, that tempestuous challenge flung down in the teeth of the storm.

With her eyes on the clock Mary Anne paced her room, her blue-black fingers hidden in a shawl. She had found a bottle of laudanum in her medicine chest, very old and stale, but it served to take the edge off the worst of the pain. She wouldn't let Nina send for the doctor nor apply a poultice. 'Your master mustn't know. I forbid you to tell him. He has quite enough on his mind without this. He should be home any minute now.'

But minutes passed to hours, and still he did not come. Hail pelted a devil's tattoo at the windows. The distant roar of thunder was like the boom of guns.

At nine-thirty a message was brought from the Parliamentary Secretary to the Treasury.

'You will be anxious to know how matters go. The Chancellor has made a wonderful effort. He has been speaking for nearly four hours with unrelaxed energy and spirit…'

Not until one o'clock in the morning, when his energy and spirit were exhausted, did he sit amid the frenzied applause of his party and the heavy silence of the Opposition, roused to frantic cheers when Gladstone rose in disdainful calm superiority to speak.

And now, for the first time were these two great champions met in the tiltyard for the tourney that was to last their lives long.

The storm had passed with the night, when, at four o'clock on that black December morning, Gladstone's cold dry moralising condemnation ceased on the words: 'I must tell the Right Honourable gentleman that whatever he has learned, and he has learned much, he has not yet learned the limits of discretion...'

Up in the gallery Derby, waiting the fate of his Ministry, dropped his head on his arms with a groan: 'Dull! Dull!' Yes, after that brilliant oratory it was dull, yet it had won the day. The Derby Government was beaten by a paltry nineteen votes, and the Disraeli budget destroyed.

'We aren't the Who-Who's any more,' sobbed Mary Anne, 'we are the In-and-Outs.'

There were no celebrations at Hughenden that Christmas. The new year limped in sadly, and not until the August of that year did the Disraelis pay the promised visit to Mrs Brydges Willyams. Nor did Dizzy's ultimate refusal to act as executor to the old lady's will affect that strange triumvirate of friendship. Year in, year out, came gifts of lobsters, bulbs and roses from Torquay, with an almost weekly interchange from Hughenden of letters, trout or partridges; and if Dizzy had no time to write, Mary Anne wrote for him. *Your constant kind and affectionate thoughts add much to the happiness of our lives...* A happiness that may have been increased by hopefully great expectations.

But personal interests were soon to be eclipsed in events that shook the nation. The unprecedented winter storm that had crashed its thunder on Parliament's House was thought by some to be a warning of greater storm to come.

In the spring of '54 an expeditionary force of the Grenadier Guards with bands playing, crowds cheering, marched through the streets of London on their way to the docks.

We are, and indeed the whole country is, wrote the Queen to Uncle Leopold, *entirely engrossed with one idea, one anxious thought — the Crimea.*

Death and disease and disaster; victory drowned in the blood baths of Alma, Sebastopol, Inkerman. Calamitous news was brought to Mary Anne by Dizzy, raging at 'this weakling government that goes to war without an army. It is murder — *murder* to send out forces in their heroic hundreds to wreck themselves against a hundred thousand masses of barbarians. By God! Were I a younger man I'd charter a ship to take me there and see for myself just how little and too late have been the efforts of our smug, inefficient war-lords to amend these appalling conditions. No supplies — or when they do come, they come too late. No ammunition, and a thousand boots all for one foot.'

'Yes, and if you go I'll go with you. We *must* go!' cried Mary Anne excitedly. 'We could borrow a yacht from someone or ask Mrs Brydges Willyams to find us a trawler. And I will offer myself to that Miss Nightingale. I'm a good nurse. I'm strong — and strong-stomached. Miss Nightingale needs someone like me who won't faint at awful sights and smells.'

But Dizzy, who had not thought to be taken at his word, now greatly regretted it since she must always be at him to follow it up, until she too went down with influenza and a touch of pleurisy in the current epidemic. 'That settles it,' he told her when she was convalescent and much debilitated.

'You'll have to give up all idea of nursing. You're not strong enough now. At one time the doctor gave me little hope of your recovery.'

A blatant lie, but anything to stop her dragging him with her to go sailing off in a tramp steamer, fishing boat, or collier, and be sunk in the Black Sea by the Russian Fleet, or hacked to pieces by Cossacks if they landed. He preferred to fight his battles under cover in the House. So Mary Anne must content herself with knitting comforters and Balaclava helmets, and making bandages from linen sheets.

The war dragged on. The Queen conferred medals. 'From the highest Prince of the Blood to the lowest private, *all* must receive the same distinction. The Queen's heart bleeds for them as if for our nearest and dearest.' Oh, the sorrow, the pity, and the pride of those splendid heroes, charging to their deaths! Mr Tennyson must be asked to write a poem on that immortal Six Hundred ... Which gave the Queen to think that giving medals to *all* the brave soldiers who fought in the war was not enough. One special medal 'For Valour' must be given to the very *bravest* of the brave, to be called the Victoria Cross.

The peace treaty was signed. The survivors came back to a grateful country's uproarious welcome. Some came back to stately homes and some came back to hovels. But if the halt and the maimed and the blind of these were soon forgotten, they all had their medals, and a few had the Queen's cross 'For Valour' proudly displayed when they stood armless, sightless, or on wooden legs in gutters with trays of matches slung from their scarred necks. Not for them the celebrations, the banquets and the balls that followed the signing of the Peace. Letters from Grosvenor Gate to Torquay told of *London gone mad with fêtes and festivities every night, and an invitation to the Palace where we had the honour of dining.*

Did Mary Anne, seated in state as guest of the Queen, with the French Ambassador on her right and a naval lord on her left, recall her letters to John written in those far-off days when she had woven fantasies of herself as hostess to the 'high nobility and our noble hero, the great duke' whose old bones, buried with unparalleled pomp, lay mouldering in Westminster Abbey? Did she remember, as she curtsied to her sovereign, a 'plain little slip of a girl' in a daisy-wreathed bonnet driving through the park with her mama?

And now, at the head of her table in the great banqueting hall under its richly carved and gilded ceiling, the walls hung with crimson brocade and life-sized portraits of kings, queens and emperors quick and dead, she sat, the descendant of many, the equal in majesty of all. She was still plain, still little, her plump and homely figure lost of its youth in frequent child-bearing, yet in that brilliant galaxy of uniforms and diamond-besparkled gowns she shone among them in her splendour like a star.

To Disraeli, watching those light alert eyes dart from one ministerial face to another, from Palmerston, chief of her government, to Gladstone, who now carried the weight of the Chancellor's robes — and always back again, adoringly, to Albert — it seemed as if not blood but quicksilver ran in her veins. What force, or mulish obstinacy, or what remote Elizabethan heritage of spiritual might lay behind that calm wide brow, that backward chin, those forward teeth and the shrill laugh to show 'not very pretty gums'?

Dish after dish, course after course were served on gold plate by an army of lackeys in red plush. The incessant hum of foreign accents, lilting, guttural, metallic, to the subdued accompaniment of the quiet English drawl, was interrupted by the Queen's clear, precise voice cutting in to cause all tongues to cease.

'Oh, but I never catch cold now that I take my daily shower bath.' And the gums were exposed to their fullest.

Under cover of Palmerston's genial, 'Haw, ma'am! Your Majesty puts me to shame. I must steel myself to cut the ice in the Serpentine o' mornings,' Mary Anne heard a murmur from the French Ambassador, the Comte de Persigny.

'If, madame, I do not have the chance to speak with your husband tonight, will you tell him from me there is a friend, a very great friend of his and yours, madame, since many years ago, who would be delighted if you and Mr Disraeli will visit him in Paris. Will you give him this word from me, madame? My friend is most anxious to see again Mr Disraeli — and you.'

She looked up at the dark narrow face of the Frenchman and then across at Dizzy. A telepathic message passed between them, a nod, a lowered eyelid.

'We did —' she stayed a spoonful of *Bombe Victoria* halfway to her lips — 'we did intend to visit Paris in the autumn, but so much depends…'

At her pause de Persigny cocked an enquiring eye at Palmerston and added softly, *'Oui, madame?'*

'All depends,' repeated Mary Anne, 'upon the … weather.'

The weather proved fair for the visit to Paris, with a warm welcome awaiting them from their mysterious 'friend'.

'Banqueting with kings and queens,' said Mary Anne, 'becomes a habit.'

'A habit,' remarked Dizzy, measuring a dose of physic from a phial, 'that does not turn your head although it turns my stomach.' Grimacing, he gingerly swallowed the dose, retched, and surveyed his furred tongue in a hand mirror. 'Eleven nights running have we dined out, and you look as fresh as a primrose, and I — like an over-ripe cheese.'

'Yes, you do,' she told him briskly. 'You had better lie down and rest while I go out to do my shopping. You must be at your best for our last night here.'

He groaned. 'For one whole accursed week have I talked riddles with Nap. I have parried and thrust, our foils well-buttoned, and have shuffled and dealt marked cards with Nap. And tonight again will I dine and wine and eat of frogs — with Nap.'

'Ugh!' Mary Anne pulled a face. 'They weren't really, were they, frogs? I thought they were chicken breasts, and ate them! I won't go. You can tell Eugenie I am sick or dead or dying. I refuse to dine with them again, and eat frogs.'

'My dear love, for our love's sake you will go with me to the Tuileries tonight and sit at the Emperor's table, and, if the Imperial menu decrees it, you will eat of the Emperor's frogs. An acquired taste admittedly, and nothing much to mine. You will wear your new strawberry-and-cream satin gown, and you will look upon the Emperor with your most limpid look from eyes that are like bluest water seen through rain. You will flutter these —' he touched her lashes — 'that do not shorten but grow longer with the years.'

'So do my teeth, but they are at least my own.'

'And you will say,' continued Dizzy, 'as you sip the wine of France, '*Voilà, mon Empereur*! I drink this gracious cordial to you and to our cordial intent'.'

'I shall do nothing of the sort.' Mary Anne tied her bonnet strings under her chin. 'He is not my Emperor, and if France had any sense or pride he would not be hers.' She took a fur-trimmed mantle from the bed. 'Help me into this.' He helped her into that. 'I am off now to buy stays for Sarah, some perfume for myself called *"Baizay d'Amour"*, and for you —'

'For me a buttonhole. A pink — a very pink — malmaison to match your gown, and a bottle of chypre-scented oil for my hair.'

Divesting himself of his coat and trousers, and wrapped in a purple dressing gown patterned with white peacocks, he stood at the window gazing down upon the coloured movement of the street. The rooms of their hotel were on the fourth floor, with a glimpse across slate rooftops to an horizon blurred by the far hills of Chaillot. Under the pale Parisian sky, shot with a winter gleam of sun, that city of palaces, towers and spires, of glittering shops and boulevards, as lovely in their plane-treed nakedness as when the leaves were full, lay like some spilled treasure casket, reflecting in the rippled waters of the Seine a thousand varying images.

A light breeze swept along the pavements, flirting with lifted petticoats as their owners stepped from carriages, teasing the feathers in their bonnets; then scampering off to pull at the manes of cab-horses ranked in waiting file, each with its head in a nosebag while their sturdy drivers slapped arms across their chests against the cold, and kept one eye alert for custom and one on the wine shop at the corner to gauge if time could be snatched for a swill. And always the river, like a silver thread in golden hair, glided through the gilt-hazed city, underneath its bridges, past its quays, and so through poplar-bordered fields into the open country: on and ever on to the narrow strip of sea that severed France from England.

'Paris,' mused Dizzy, 'is a beautiful woman, and London is an ugly man. But she, possessed of every tantalising feline femininity, turns tigress at the first scent of blood; while he, stolid, bull-necked, slow to rise, is a Minotaur when risen.'

Mary Anne, jotting down items on her shopping list, asked, 'Is there anything else you want?'

'Yes.' He came to her taking her face in his hands. 'I want you. You and Paris together,' he whispered, 'have bewitched me.' He kissed her mouth, kissed deeper, long and urgently, saying, out of breath, 'Go now. I must keep my wits and senses for tonight. And that you,' he added as he eased himself away from her, 'can do this to me after — how long? — almost twenty years of married life, is something men might wonder at who have no Mary Anne.'

The dinner at the Tuileries that evening was agreeably informal. Not more than a dozen guests, including equerries and ladies-in-waiting, were seated at the circular table in one of the smaller dining rooms, with the Disraelis in place of honour on the right hand of the Emperor and Empress.

Startlingly gowned in rose velvet and emerald faille looped over a wide wire frame, the first conception of the crinoline, she resembled the shape of an isosceles triangle. In the opinion of Parisiennes, the beauty and charm of Eugenie waxed and waned according to favour bestowed or withdrawn. Mary Anne, although confessedly 'unjealous', had her doubts of the beauty but not of the charm. Those slanting eyes, suggestive of the Chinese rather than the Spaniard, lent to that vivid pointed face an irresistible attraction. Her skin held the greenish pallor generally associated with red hair, and hers was as red as a vixen; vixenish, too, the sharp nose, the needle-sharp white teeth, the quick narrow glances of those hazel-green eyes.

Yet Mary Anne, if critical, would be the first to acknowledge the achievement of a woman who, while better born than she as the daughter of a Spanish Don, had come to queen it above the royal blood of France, strong in competition for the capture of the third Napoleon… And no great catch more than his stolen throne, was he, decided Mary Anne, whose first acquaintance with this tubby little nephew of the Yellow Dwarf from Corsica turned giant to bestride the whole of Europe, once upon a time, did not begin in the Tuileries. Nor had Louis Napoleon, shifty-eyed, fat and potbellied, improved with the passing of years. His heavy-jowled face carried long black mustachios and the now popularised Imperial tuft under his loose lower lip. He spoke fluent English but he spoke it very little. Mary Anne had all to do to keep him going.

Apprehensively she scanned the gold-framed menu, relieved to find no mention of *grenouilles*, unless presented by another name. A dish, suspiciously sauced and fragrantly savoured, was offered. Cautiously she helped herself, tasted, and fell to with relish until Napoleon found voice to say, 'You like, then, madame, *les escargots?*'

Snails! Oh God, oh no! But with Dizzy's eye, behind the monocle upon her, she managed, with a flutter of her lashes, to articulate, *'J'adore lays escargoes, mon Empereur.'*

'Ah, so you speak French, madame.'

'Comme see, comme sah. Mon accent say terreeble.'

'Your accent, madame, is like yourself, delicious.'

Come, we're getting on, or getting off! Relinquishing the remnants of snails on her silver-gilt plate — *not gold, as with us,* she was swift to observe, and which happily had been whisked away — 'May I remind your Majesty,' she ventured, 'of a little outing on the Thames some years ago when you all but drowned me?'

'I, madame? Of what horror am I accused?'

It was on the tip of her tongue to accuse him of countless horrors: of the flight of Louis Philippe, harried by the hounds of France to Normandy and across the Channel in a British steamboat, to find shelter in the arms of England's Queen. But again Dizzy's monocle, fixedly shining, warned away her words. He had the devil's own trick of stealing her thoughts, to send them ricocheting back to her as his. Her eyes, with that in them of the adoration of the Magi, were raised to the Emperor's goggling stare, and a silence fell around the table. Through the hush of it she spoke.

'I will for ever cherish the memory of that unforgotten day when your Majesty ran us on a mud bank — to catch crabs!'

'*Mon dieu*! Is not that just like him?' The emeralds circling Eugenie's white throat flashed to her contemptuous shrug. 'He is no fish man, that one, to catch crabs. He will always try to do more than he can, and knows never when to stop till he drown in his own — how you say? — vomit, or until he will drown someone else in it.'

'*Mon Imperatrice,*' caramel-suave was the voice of Disraeli breaking in on an ominous hush, while the little fat man clenched a little fat fist, his eyes almost out of their sockets. 'I am lost in admiration of your Majesty's exquisite emeralds. In my journeys to the East and in the palaces of Sultans where all the wonders of Aladdin's cave have been revealed to me, never have I seen such loveliness as — this.' But his ardent look was not for emeralds.

A buzz of relief went the round of the table. Mary Anne lifted her brimming goblet.

'Sire, I drink to that first happy meeting with your Majesty in your country's gracious cordial, and to… (Heavens! what came next?) 'and to our present and our future gracious… intent.' Not quite right, but near enough. A glance across at Dizzy was returned with an almost imperceptible nod, followed by the preening Napoleon's prompt reply and a joining of his crystal cup to hers, '*A l'entente cordiale!*'

'A somewhat premature announcement,' murmured a voice at her side. Guiltily she turned to address herself to her neglected right hand neighbour, the Vicomte de Lesseps. Lean and lithe as a greyhound was he, his face gipsy-brown as if bronzed by a sun not of England.

'Have you been basking on Mediterranean shores, Vicomte,' she asked him brightly, 'while we at home grope our way through our pea-soup fogs that Mr Dickens calls "the London Particular"?'

'Ah, your Dickens! Yes, I read and laugh and cry with him in the shadow of the Sphinx.'

She saw his eyes travel to Dizzy, and it seemed as if a message passed of eyebrows twitched, of a one-sided fleeting smile; but this time not to her.

'My husband,' she said, 'is known in our House of Commons as the Sphinx.'

'So rightly named.' The Vicomte's careful English bore scarcely a trace of accent. 'Since Mr Disraeli, like that unfathomable mystery conceived in an age of supermen, holds and keeps the secrets of the world.'

Now what is he *after?* wondered Mary Anne, who had learned to mistrust all courtly speech, and particularly at the court of France.

'So you have been to Egypt? My husband visited Egypt in his youth, and wrote wonderful descriptions of the Pyramids and the deserts. I suppose you too have seen the Pyramids and, of course, the deserts?' Not that she cared, she told herself, whether he had or he hadn't.

'Yes, I have been in the deserts of Egypt, madame, and uncomfortably on the back of a camel, only to find that one was there before me to forestall my inspiration.'

'Oh?' She began to be interested in this quiet, dark-faced man whose conversation was not the usual complimentary small talk of the French. 'If one may ask — who was there before you?'

His eyes veered for a second to their host, engaged in monosyllabic response to the lively chatter of the Duchesse de Gramont on his left. *Fancy giving* me *precedence*, thought Mary Anne, *above a duchess. There's something in the wind tonight, and Dizzy knows it.*

'The first Napoleon, uncle of our Emperor,' said that careful voice in her ear, 'was there before me. And the first — as you say — in the field, or in this case, in the desert.'

'You intrigue me, Vicomte. I must know — or may I not — what is this inspiration?'

He smiled.

'Excavation, shall we call it?'

'I see! You are a — what is it — an archie —?'

'An archaeologist, madame? No. Not in the true sense of the word. I am just a digger in the sand.'

'Do you dig for hidden treasure?'

'Yes, madame, I dig for a treasure which I hope will —'

But just at this moment the Empress gave the ladies their signal to rise, and that was the end of that.

Curtsies to the Emperor, a falling back of other women guests, deferentially to let her pass before them and behind Eugenie; a low bow from de Lesseps and the gentlemen-in-waiting, and so to the state drawing room.

Like birds of paradise in their bright coloured gowns the ladies clustered round the Empress to play, at her command, a parlour game. Quotations and passages from English poets, again in deference to Mary Anne, were dictated by each lady in turn with a missing word to be supplied. Only one of those

335

selected was guessed by Mrs Disraeli: *'To be or not to be, that is the...'*

The score, counted by Eugenie — 'Five to me, six to la Duchesse de Gramont, and one,' shamingly, 'to Mrs Disraeli' — was interrupted by the arrival of the gentlemen, with Gounod, who had been invited after dinner, to entertain at the piano. He gave excerpts from his opera, *La Nonne Sanglante* and an aria from another, unfinished, which, he told the Empress, was based on the story of Faust. He played with much banging and thumping and swaying of the hips and up-rolling of the eyes to the rapture of the ladies, *'Quelle coloratura sublime!'* from Eugenie, and the request from Mary Anne, 'Pray, Monsieur Gounod, give us some more of your Bloody Nun.' A remark that engendered a silence of shock from those of the ladies who, to that extent, understood English; a burst of laughter from Eugenie, titters from the gentlemen, and a raised eyebrow from Napoleon drumming sausage fingers on his chair arm, with a bolting look across the room at de Lesseps and Disraeli, deep in talk together.

By feint of permission from the Empress to examine 'that very beautiful portrait of your Majesty,' Mary Anne contrived to edge herself near enough to catch a low-voiced word or two from de Lesseps. 'Egypt ... the Khedive ... prepared to finance ... European subscription ... hope to turn the first spadeful of earth next year ... If you, Monsieur Disraeli, can persuade...' The rest of that was lost.

And then the answer, lightly, 'My dear Vicomte, it is not for me, it is for Gladstone to persuade... He is my country's banker now.'

The guests were departing, the Empress rising, the Emperor strutting on his fat little legs to join de Lesseps and Dizzy, bowing noses to knees. Mary Anne caught his eye as he straightened. Napoleon turned. The strawberry-and-cream satin ballooned to the ground. A podgy hand with a ruby the size of a carbuncle on its third finger was offered to be kissed. It smelled of carbolic. Nap was known to go in dread of infectious disease.

She was kissed on both cheeks by the Empress and told: 'You are so *funny*. You have no *honte*. I like you. Come soon to Paris again.'

On the drive back to their hotel Mary Anne said, 'You seemed very taken with Eugenie at dinner. Do you think her beautiful?'

'No, I do not. For me she is more *femme futile* than *femme fatale*.'

Mary Anne gave an appreciative crow. 'I bet that'll go into one of your books. And what was de Lesseps saying to you? I heard him mention something about Egypt. He told me he has been digging for treasure in the desert. Has he discovered a gold mine in the sand?'

'He has discovered and is, or will be, digging for water in the sand.'

'Is he what they call a water-diviner, then?'

'He may live in posterity as such when he uncovers the waters under the earth to turn them into a river of gold that will bring vessels by a shorter route from India to — No, by God!' He broke off in a sudden heat of vehemence. 'Not that. Never that.' His face, out-thrust under the glare of street lamps in the Place de la Concorde, was etched in profile, cameo-clear against the interior dark of the carriage. 'No.' He stared before him, his upper lip caught back on a dry tooth. Mary Anne, watching him, knew that look: he was on the track of something, some eagle-winged thought that hovered to swoop — and to clutch.

As from a far-off vacancy she heard him say, and hearing, wondered: 'No, not for France — although she bred him — nor for Germany, nor Russia, nor any Arab upstart chief who stakes a miserable million for his share in that waterflow of commerce between the Indies and Port Said. Not for them a link in that chain of fortresses along the road to India. No fear! We have and we shall hold.'

He groped for and took her hand in a grip to grind her rings into her flesh, while still he gazed with that same fierce intensity, as if beyond the padded lining of the carriage he could see some mirific panorama. 'No, not any of these, nor any such as they, but a little fogbound island in a little trough of sea shall hold the British Lion's share in — the Suez Canal!'

Said Mary Anne, splitting a yawn, 'I can't follow all this. What *are* you talking about?'

'Was I talking? Perhaps I was dreaming — of a dream that may never come true.'

THIRTY

Soon after their return to 'that little fogbound island' the majority of islanders were in a state of panic. The end of the world was in sight. Memory, still fresh in superstitious minds of the unprecedented winter storm that had rocked the Houses of Parliament with presage of war in the Crimea, saw now another and more fearful omen with the arrival of the comet. 'This Awful Thing', streaking through space, lashing its tail at the stars, had been seen, and, by one prophetic Dr Cummings, proclaimed as a warning to the peoples of the earth, whose day of doom on this planet was exactly timed — by Dr Cummings — for June 13, 1857.

In Hyde Park, tub-thumping believers bade straggling sinners come to gape or grin, or suck oranges, or to scream with infantile terror as the case might be, to 'Prepare! Be warned. God's Wrath descends upon you. Purge your hearts of sin ere ye be seized by the Powers of Darkness and flung into the Pit. Repent! Repent before catastrophe descends upon the earth.'

But although, at the eleventh hour, the comet was deflected in its devastating course by Almighty intervention, catastrophe did descend upon the earth, in a far quarter of the globe, to strike with horrific force at Britain's greatest of possessions.

With Mary Anne peeping over his shoulder, Disraeli traced, on a map of the world, the long route round the Cape to India. 'The only way at present,' mused Dizzy, 'by which reinforcements can be brought to the aid of our standing army of a few thousands, mowed down while they strive to keep at bay those overwhelming hordes of mutineers. But if de Lesseps, your water-diviner, shall find another way —'

'You mean if he digs that canal you were dreaming about?'

'I mean if we *had* that canal I was dreaming about, this horror might have been averted.'

Hideous stories filtered through the news-sheets, of slaughter unimaginable and unequalled even by those mangled shades that haunted Balaclava. All Britain stood aghast at the massacre of English women and their children in that welter of blood at Cawnpore: mothers lined up and tortured to their deaths, while they cried mercy for their helpless babes still clutched to their mutilated breasts.

The Queen in her castle heard, and read, and wept, distracted.

'What are we to do? Dear Lord Palmerston, what — what *can* we do? There is not a family in England that does not suffer this dreadful anguish of anxiety for their sons and daughters — and oh, the little children in *all* ranks, India being the place where *everyone* sends their sons. When will we see the end of it?'

A change of government was to see the end of it, with Derby and Disraeli in — and out again.

'Be of good cheer, 'tis I, be not afraid,' was Dizzy's consolation to a tearful Mary Anne. 'Our troops are in fine fettle and with ample numbers for the fight. Next time, please God, when we come in we will *stay* in.'

But how long to wait before the next time, with all these waiting years behind him, while the Tantalus fruits of office, dangled temptingly above his head, were borne away at the first taste? How long before they would be his to take and to enjoy? And how many or how few for her the years to come? Yet she still retained the vigour and activity of youth. Women enviously saw her unchanged and unchanging, with those wide bunches of curls, which could not surely now be all her own? Not a grey hair to be seen, unless dyed or wigged. Opinion inclined to the latter, and to the aid of the hare's foot to produce that permanent 'foxglove' complexion as extolled by her fatuous husband. None could believe him sincere in his avowed affection for, and tolerance of her outrageous remarks, her vulgarisms and her want of tact. No social sense whatsoever. Rosina Lytton, who had known her longer than any, could vouch for it that when she married Lewis she was 'just a common little slut' — and had never learned to be anything else.

Resentment turned to gall in the mouths of those whose husbands may have been somewhat less fatuous, affectionate, or tolerant of them than was Disraeli of his Mary Anne. And when after a short illness his adored Sarah was taken from him, 'I have no one left to me in all the world but you,' he said. 'You must be mother, sister, mistress, wife, and everything' — forgetful of that other Sarah at Mount Braddon in Torquay.

Mrs Brydges Willyams was now to take the place of his beloved 'Sa' as recipient of those almost daily letters, recording every smallest detail of his personal and political life. Another sister. 'Less sister than lover,' so Mary Anne quipped him on that curious relationship with an old woman of ninety. And to this second Sarah he wrote of their visit to Windsor: *It is considered very marked on the part of Her Majesty to ask the wife of a Leader of the Opposition, when many Cabinet Ministers have been asked* without *their wives.* And, 'Very gracious, very communicative' was Disraeli's report of it to Derby.

Equally communicative, it would seem, was Mary Anne.

In the state drawing room while waiting for the Consort and the gentlemen to join the Royal Hostess, the Queen, surrounded by a dreary and decorous circle of court ladies, spoke to each in turn with a slightly arid evidence of unoriginality.

'Did you ride in Windsor Great Park this morning, Lady —?'

'Yes, ma'am, I did ride this morning.'

'I trust you were given a nice horse?'

'Oh, yes, ma'am, a very nice horse.'

'Did you and Lord — go to Scotland in August for the Twelfth, Lady —?'

'No, ma'am, not last August. I was —' A pause from the next addressee, a timid little newlywed. 'I was — we were abroad for our honeymoon, ma'am.'

'Indeed? Your honeymoon. How long have you been married?' A glance from the protruding pale eyes at the blushing young matron's crinoline.

'Six months, ma'am.'

An inclination of the august head: another and more searching glance at the carefully concealed waistline approved this information, and was focused on Mary Anne.

'How long have *you* been married, Mrs Disraeli?'

'Let me see now.' And at once the eyes of all the ladies were expectantly fixed on her who — just fancy! — must needs begin counting on her fingers. 'Twenty-two — no, that was my first. I have been twice married, ma'am.'

'Indeed.'

The button mouth was closed as nearly as could be above the small projecting teeth. The Queen did not ask, she looked, a cold and dreadful question, to be answered, to the relief of everyone and the disappointment of a few, 'I was a widow, ma'am, when I married Mr Disraeli.'

'Indeed? Duchess, a fan if you please. The fire is too warm.'

A fan, hastily supplied by the Mistress of the Robes, was unfurled to shield the royal cheek that showed the least suspicion of a flush. And, still addressing Mrs Disraeli, who, the ladies unanimously agreed, was gowned in the worst possible taste with her tiara all crooked on top of those very false curls, the Queen said, 'There is no greater happiness in life than a happy marriage, as I thank my God I have reason to know.'

'Yes, ma'am, and as I, too, have reason to know. Why, even now, every night of our lives, Dizzy — er — Mr Disraeli and I, we sleep together and in each other's arms.'

The horrified circle held its breath, fearfully waiting and watching. Then the fan was lowered; the eyes blinked, stared, fell, while from those lips came the murmur, scarcely spoken, scarcely heard: 'As so do we.'

But within a few months that happy marriage was ended; and in the fearful suddenness of Albert's death a shutter closed down on the windows of Victoria's life. In the darkened solitude of grief she sank, and to her Uncle Leopold cried, 'The world is gone for me! Cut off at forty-two. It is too cruel, too awful!' Such fierce intensity of feeling was something more than grief. Her repeated cry: 'Too *cruel* — like losing one's body and soul, torn forcibly away, when I hoped, with such instinctive certainty, that God would never part us,' was Majesty's outraged indignation against a merciless Jehovah who had dared wreak His Might in misery on — Her!

Uncle Leopold bore the brunt of it in tear-blotted letters from the *utterly broken-hearted and crushed* widow … *Yet whose one firm resolve, one* irrevocable decision *is that* his *plans,* his *views about everything are to be my law.'*

Albert, it seemed, was more alive when dead than when he had been living. In his life, his plans, his views, and his law, had not always been hers.

Disraeli made the very most of the few occasions he had met and talked with Albert to pour out panegyrical obituaries, both written and verbal in praise of the Consort, to be read or retailed to the desolate Queen. She thanked him from her 'pierced and bleeding heart'. Her black-draped courtiers were told, 'Mr Disraeli is the only — *only* person who appreciated Him. Always, *all* my life I will be grateful to Mr Disraeli.'

Two years later the wedding of the Prince of Wales to the beautiful Danish Princess Alexandra brought further proof of royal gratitude with most signal honour conferred on 'Dear Mr' and (in afterthought) 'Mrs Disraeli', in the presentation of two of the four seats reserved for Her Majesty's personal friends at the ceremony in St George's Chapel, Windsor.

Rosina, on a visit to Hughenden, heard from Mary Anne how 'the Duchess of Marlborough went into hysterics at the sight of me sitting there in the Queen's own pew, particularly as the duchess had given a large party at Blenheim for the Prince only the week before. All the ladies were raging, gnashing their false teeth and tearing their false hair at being passed over for me.'

Rosina snickered. 'Yes, Dizzy always knows how, when or where to butter his bread, and good luck to you both.'

She had long ceased to envy Mary Anne, yet she still took a vicarious interest, if no part, in the activities of a society from which she had been banned, or as she defiantly put it, had 'abandoned for an Irish bog'. She had few enemies and fewer friends. That tawdry world of Mayfair's gay insouciance where she and Edward, in the far-off twenties, had been the leading lights, was no more: a vanished city of the past, sunk beneath the ponderous stolidity and stucco of the mid-Victorians. While Bulwer-Lytton was a household word from the throne of the Queen to every boarding-school miss who read his novels, and his name in the mouths of young enthusiastic democrats in Parliament, the name of his wife was unknown; or forgotten.

'Tell me more — tell me of all your doings,' she languidly requested Mary Anne. But if she were told she paid little attention. She preferred the sound of her own voice to that of any other; and she had developed a tic: a disconcerting spasmodic shake of the head, as if she held an intimate and private conversation with herself. She was unkempt, unhooked, unbuttoned, untidy. Her restless eyes, set in discoloured baggy sacs, were for ever wandering as though on the track of something lost: a thought, a whisper, the phantom of her once joyous youth, or the wintered ashes of her burning hate for Edward that had scorched the summer of her life.

Seated on the terrace in the afternoon sun she screwed her eyes at a Florentine vase filled with blue African lilies. 'Those flowers — what are they?' And without waiting for an answer, 'Tell me whose houses or palaces or castles —' she shook her head, smiling with lips turned down — 'that you have been visiting lately.'

Mary Anne, at her tambour frame, sorted silks before replying, 'I don't think we have been anywhere of much interest lately… Oh, yes, we have. At least it was of interest to me. We have been staying with the Northcotes at Pynes.'

'Who are they? And where is Pynes?'

'He is — or was — Parliamentary Secretary to the Treasury, and Pynes is in…' She held her needle poised above an embroidered rose petal. 'How strange,' she murmured, 'life is.'

'Very strange.' Rosina violently nodded and then shook her head. 'A maze. A wilderness — for me.'

'And for me — full circle.' Mary Anne looked up, gazing out. 'Pynes is a great estate in Devon not far from where I used to live, a long, long time ago. The grandmother of *this* Sir Stafford Northcote would never have deigned to invite me to her house even had she known of my existence, although I was born within a few miles of... Yes, and I made Sir Stafford take me for a drive into Exeter, and I showed him the shop where I was 'prenticed as a milliner, but it isn't a milliner's now. It's a grocer's.'

'I wish,' said Rosina, 'I had brought my Felicity with me. I am wretched without her. You talk about grandmothers. Felicity is a grandmother four times, and I have had *six* Felicities and three Fairies. I ought to have brought her but the last time she came over she was seasick all night, poor angel, and now she's *enceinte* again I daren't risk it. I shouldn't have left her, only she isn't due until next month, and I shall be back before then.' She stooped for the reticule on the flagstones at her feet, took from it and uncorked a silver flask.

'Must you?' Mary Anne stretched a hand to Rosina's wrist. 'Can't you wait until they bring the tea?'

'It is too hot for tea.' She lifted, and tilted the flask to her lips. 'This is barley water. I find it very cooling. I have kidney trouble. The doctor makes me drink barley water, and I always have some by me. My mouth gets so dry.' She re-corked and replaced the flask. 'What were you saying about these people — Pynes? I have never heard of them. But I did hear,' she giggled, 'a killing story about you from — I can't remember who — Georgie Lyndhurst or one of them. Georgie it must have been, she has always had her knife in you for marrying Dizzy. Like all the younger women of our day, she was mad about him. I never could think why. He was — and is — so ugly.'

Mary Anne re-threaded her needle. 'What did you hear from Georgie Lyndhurst about me?'

'You?' Rosina picked something out of her nose. 'Oh, yes, you. Your latest *bon mot* is the talk of — well, now, where was it? At the — I always forget names — where you and Dizzy were staying. You came down to breakfast late after everyone else when they were all stuffing away, and — now I got this from Georgie and you know what a liar she is — you said, "My dear Lady —" Oh, I know who it was, because you were speaking of her husband. Hardinge. "My dear Lady Hardinge,' you said, 'you *have* given me an *embarass dee riches*." I died with laughing, the way Georgie took off your French accent. 'I am the luckiest of women to have slept last night between the greatest soldier and the greatest statesman of our time.' There was a ghastly silence, Georgie said, and then *you* said, "Don't misunderstand me. Lord Hardinge was in the next room and Dizzy in my bed." No wonder you are, or were, in demand with the men, such as are left from the bucks of our day who would take on half a dozen in one night and end up with — I can remember when Edward and I —' Her head gave a violent shake. She reached for the bottle.

'Do put it away,' entreated Mary Anne. 'That is your third nip since we've been sitting here. You will have gout in the stomach if you don't take care.'

'Why should I take care? Who cares for me? I wish I were dead.' Rosina squeezed a tear out of her eye. 'I *ought* to be dead. Why was I born a woman? I would sooner be a cow. A nice fat comfortable cow. You keep cows, don't you? When is that tea coming? How old *are* you, Mary Anne? Whatever age — over seventy? — which you must be, because I'm sixty — you don't look it. You don't look very much different from when you first came to London, except for that wig. It *is* a wig, isn't it? Mine is. I'm bald — in patches. Such a common pushing little piece you were. I shall never forget how at one of my parties, when somebody or other mentioned Dean Swift, you asked for his address that you might send him a card for your soirée. I can't think how you manage to keep so young-looking. You must be a freak. Do you and Dizzy still…?' She leered, picking at her nose again.

'Here,' said Mary Anne hastily, 'is tea.'

Rosina really was too tiring. One would have to rest before dinner. All very well to *look* young; one didn't always feel young. In fact, one was beginning to feel just a little — not old — but the least bit worn out at the end of the season, and that nagging little pain down below. Nothing, of course. Just age … creeping on.

THIRTY-ONE

The dwarf trees at Hughenden had become a thick forest of firs. In her pony trap Mary Anne, with Dizzy jogging beside her on his old grey mare, would take him a tour of the estate to show him her latest improvements. Hardly a week went by without some fresh surprise to offer: the vases she had ordered from Florence planted with acanthus lilies and geraniums, a riot of crimson and blue, or a Japanese cherry, a miraculous spray of silvery pink outflung against a cobalt sky which might have been Italian: a rustic arbour, a carpet of hyacinthine-hued anemones, or the search for hidden violets in the moss of the beechen woods. 'Violets,' he told her, 'are inseparably entwined in the scent and thought of you.'

And always on their homeward way they would pause at a flower-decked grave hard by the little church of Hughenden, the resting place of Mrs Brydges Willyams, whose much loved stout old spirit stayed with them in more substantial memory, of all that she had died possessed, amounting to some thirty thousand pounds.

Yet, although this long-awaited windfall had freed Disraeli from his debts and the heavy interest extracted on loans from the bearded brethren of Crutched Friars, his wife was hard put, even with strictest economy, to maintain the position his political prominence demanded, even in those days when it cost little enough to live and nothing at all to die. Electioneering campaigns, subscriptions to party funds, dinners and receptions at Grosvenor Gate, took the better part of her entire income. The villagers said she was mean. She had to be; she must hoard and screw and scrape every shilling she could save for the time when he would come into his own. But how long, how much longer to wait while time's pitiless flight, gathering speed down the declining years passed him by, to leave him waiting still.

Then suddenly, Palmerston, pride of the Liberals, who with one short interval had marched at their head for ten years, was to march with them no more. That grand old chief, as vigorous at eighty as he had been at forty, still stalking the ladies, still dyeing his whiskers, still eating his eight-course dinners every night, was struck down when elected as head of his party again.

'Poor dear Lord Palmerston,' sighed the Queen, who could not forgive or forget how, when commanded to Osborne a few weeks after her agonising loss, he had come to audience gaily arrayed in a brown overcoat, green gloves, grey trousers and a bright blue cravat. Such very ill taste! How different, how markedly different from Mr Disraeli who — in deepest black — had so sincerely mourned her Dear One, and who wrote such a beautiful private and *personal* letter, she confided to her tactfully lachrymose ladies, saying that the Prince was the only person he had ever known to realise the Ideal. The only character in English history, sobbed the Queen, whom Mr Disraeli says can in *any* respect bear comparison to that incomparable nature, Sir Philip Sidney. The same high tone, the same universal accomplishment, the same blended tenderness and vigour... So touching.

The butter was laid on inches thick with more to come, when: 'How strongly had Mr Disraeli pleaded, nay, more, insisted on the erection,' in accordance with Majesty's desire, 'of a monument to that immortal memory.'

Disraeli's address to the House, who had already agreed to a Government grant for the building of the thing and was disposed to grant no more, was a masterpiece of emotional rhetoric, received in stony silence, interspersed with titters and a hoot or two from the back benchers.

'The monument,' he declared, 'should represent the very character of the Prince in its proportion, the beauty of its ornaments, and in its enduring nature to be recognised by a grateful and admiring people.'

If the recognition of the people may not have been quite so grateful and admiring as was Mr Disraeli's intent, its nature is enduring and, despite its hideosity, has endured, less as a memorial to Albert than as the symbol of an age solidly great, an empire irrevocably lost.

But he who was to weld that empire into the power of the Crown still played his waiting game.

The ageing sphinx-like countenance with one jet black curl plastered on its balding forehead, the impassive figure carved as if from granite which for so long had led his Opposition army against the rival force of Gladstone, would not lead in Opposition much longer. Soon, very soon, the lid would close on John, now Earl, Russell, that little Jack-in-Lord-Palmerston's box.

It closed on the stale old cry of 'Reform!' squeaked from the lips of John Russell in the Lords, to be taken up in strenuous debate by Gladstone, his mouthpiece, in the Commons. And when Gladstone cautiously compromised by reducing the ten-pound householder's vote to seven, only the most extreme Whigs of his party were with him. The rest of them, ex-Palmerstonians tailing the jaunty spectre of 'Old Pam', were shocked by, indifferent to, or demanding 'all or nothing' rather than Gladstone's half measure which lost him his seat for Oxford University, to lose him his leadership too.

And now, for the third time, Derby steered the ship of state with Disraeli beside him on the look-out for breakers ahead.

They broke — to flood Hyde Park in a howling mob for the 'all-or-nothings' who had no use for 'bit-by-bit reform'. They tore up the railings, they trampled on the flower beds, threw stones at Tory windows in Park Lane, but not at Mary Anne's.

From Dizzy in the House came anxious word, 'Keep under cover and do not show yourself,' brought by special messenger, none other than Tita. Hers not to question his coming at that precise moment of danger; Tita worked in his own mysterious ways always to be in the front of a fight.

'Me, I go out to them. I kill them, yes?'

'No,' decisively said Mary Anne.

Tita, a servant of the Board of Control, Board of Trade, or whatever Board of the moment in which Disraeli could manage to push him, only to find him pushed out, had changed as little with the years as had Mary Anne. He had, it is true, trimmed his now more grey than black beard, wore a brass-buttoned livery and a high hat instead of a sword-belted shirt and a fez, but he was still known to carry a dagger or two in his pockets.

'Me, I go out to them,' doggedly reiterated Tita. 'I strike at them — so!' He smote his fist at the air. 'I stop their noise. Yes?'

'No, you will not!' cried Mary Anne, who, telescope to eye, was in greater fear of what Tita would do than of what the rioters were doing. 'Look! Here come the soldiers to scuttle them.'

And scuttle them they did, like swarms of beetles disturbed in a cellar by the light.

'Me, I go 'elp the soldiers,' was Tita's frustrated contribution to the dispersal of the riot. And 'A very tame riot indeed,' was

Mary Anne's account of it to Dizzy. 'The Chartist row at Uxbridge, although a flea-bite to this, was much more fun.'

Fun! He gazed at her, deflated. Mr Walpole, the Home Secretary, had burst into tears when told of up-torn railings, ruined flower beds, stones hurled at windows — Walpole's in Park Lane smashed to smithereens — and here was Mary Anne, the unpredictable and unafraid, admitting she had thoroughly enjoyed the 'fun'.

'As so,' she said, 'did they. All within range of my spyglass looked to be out on a spree. It wasn't much worse, and certainly no noisier, than Hampstead Heath on Bank Holiday. You should have seen them skedaddle when the troops came marching up. I laughed.'

'But the Whigs,' murmured Dizzy, 'won't laugh when I … By God, yes!' He turned, hands behind his back, pacing the room with his loping, pantherish stride; and she, watching his face, held her breath. She knew that smouldering light in his eyes as if sparked from some deep upspringing flame. His body stiffened and he spoke — not to her, to that inner voice, his *alter ego*, from whom even she, who shared his every thought, must be divided. And as if in answer to that voice's unheard question: 'You are right,' he said. 'It may be a leap in the dark, but I'll try it. Yes, I'll try it! I'll serve them with the juice of their own stew.'

And within six months, long enough for it to simmer, he served it hot on the table of the Whigs to choke them with the Bill that gave to each householder, no matter what the rental, were it ten or seven pounds, the right to one vote. With his Machiavellian 'leap in the dark' he had done what the Whigs for thirty years had vainly striven to do.

The House sat in awed silence before it burst into a terrific storm of cheering from all sides. Even Gladstone, mortified, glowering, offered the other chilly cheek to accord him 'an insolent triumph'. Excited members fell upon him in the Lobby and dragged him off to the Carlton to sup with them and celebrate, but 'No,' he said. 'My wife waits for me at home. I must go to her.'

He went to her, and was met with a blaze of lights in the windows, a pie, specially ordered from Fortnum and Mason's, and a bottle of champagne. He ate half the pie, drank all the champagne, and just a little drunk with victory wine, 'And with you,' he said, 'who, *in vino veritas* are still as much my mistress as my wife, we will … to bed.'

There was at this time a newcomer to Grosvenor Gate, one Montague Corry, a young man of good looks and good parts. He had first attracted the attention of Disraeli during a visit to the Duke of Cleveland's country house. Having watched from a distance, and formed a favourable opinion of this very earnest young man, who seemed possessed of all the qualities that go to make a perfect private secretary, Disraeli unexpectedly surprised him, on a wet afternoon, performing a vigorous solo dance and singing an almost, but not quite, improper song to a giggling circle of young ladies.

The appearance of the Chancellor of the Exchequer in the midst of this young company who believed him well out of the way, caused some general embarrassment, and to Mr Corry much confusion. But the habitually impassive Chancellor's mask betrayed nothing of censure, amusement or anything else. The stammered apologies of the scarlet Mr Corry were received with a long blank stare as the Chancellor marched to the bookcase, took down a volume, and without another word or second look marched out again.

The giggles of the girls, now verging on hysterics, and the comfortless remark from Lord Dalmeny, the son by a former marriage of the Duchess of Cleveland — 'That's dished your chance with the Chance-o'Law, my boy —' were quenched by a shrill voice at the end of the room. 'He who'll make a pun will pick a pocket. Come over here, Mr Corry, and you too, Dalmeny. I want a word with you both.'

The young ladies exchanged glances and whispers.

'*That* old thing at it again...'

'I didn't know she was there...'

'What a fright in that hideous flame-coloured gown, and that wig all awry...'

'Yes, of course it's a wig, and so old-fashioned, those bunches of curls, like something out of the Ark...'

'But, my dear, she *is* out of the Ark. My grandmama remembers her when she was four ... no, silly, when my grandmama was four. Whatever are they doing now?'

Whatever they were doing now, meaning the two young gentlemen commanded over there, was to sit each on an arm of the 'old thing's' chair, apparently greatly amused by the 'word' given to each ear in turn.

'Just look at her!' uttered the eldest young lady, an acidulous old maid of twenty-two, who had been unsuccessfully 'out' for five seasons. ('But what could you expect with that nose and that carroty hair?') 'How can she dare behave so? With a foot stuck out on the knee of Lord Dalmeny — did you ever! — to fasten her shoe.'

The crinolines swayed to the forward movement of the vestals as they fluttered after the three or four other young gentlemen who, with one accord, had deserted them to gather round Mrs Disraeli. What could she be saying to make them laugh so loud?

'Nothing that is fit for *us*,' said the eldest young lady, 'to hear. All that nodding and winking — so vulgar.'

She may have had more reason than any to resent this monopoly of the young gentlemen, and of Lord Dalmeny in particular, who had partnered her twice at the ball last night and told her she waltzed like a dream. *Very* marked attention from the future Earl of Rosebery, and, though neither the eldest young lady nor Lord Dalmeny himself could foresee, from a future prime minister too.

But how shockingly shattering *this* for the eldest young lady to hear: 'I've found a charmer, Dalmeny, for you. Come to Hughenden next week and you will meet her. A Miss Hannah Rothschild. As rich as she's handsome, which don't often go together.'

More nods and more winks and the tap of her fan to the chin of Mr Corry as he leaned down to her, she looking up to make eyes at him, saying, 'For you, something more to your taste than a wife, be she never so rich or so handsome. And for me — you may sing that song again, and you don't have to leave out the spice!'

'The rain has stopped,' said the eldest young lady. 'Let us go out and play at croquet.'

They went out and played at croquet with a sepulchral striking of mallets against wooden balls for all the world as if they played with skulls.

Later, when Mr and Mrs Disraeli rested before dinner in their room, she on the bed, he in an armchair, 'That young Mr Corry,' she said, 'might be worth watching.'

'He is,' was the answer, 'worth watching. I intend to offer him a private secretaryship.'

'You'd best be quick about it then, or someone else will get in first. He's a good lad, that one. I,' she chuckled, 'have been sounding him.'

'I'll pop the question,' Dizzy said, 'tonight.'

He put up his eyeglass to take a look at her where she lay against the pillows, her hands small and frail as a mouse's hands, limp on the counterpane. Her face, drawn and worn under the rouge, seemed to have shrunk.

'You do too much,' he told her. 'You give too much to me and take too much of me upon yourself. You should rest more.'

'It is you who should rest,' she said, 'not I.'

But soon both were resting; he with sciatica and she with a gastric attack, laid low for several days in separate rooms and for the first time divided while under one roof.

They scribbled notes to each other. His to her she kept.

You have sent me the most amusing and charming letter I ever had. It beats Horace Walpole and Madame Sevigny.

One might wish he had kept hers.

And again: *Grosvenor Gate has become a hospital, but a hospital with you has become a palace. Your own D.*

Then no sooner were they up and about again than Prime Minister Derby was down. His health for some time had given rise to anxiety. His doctors advised his immediate resignation from the onerous strain of his office as Government Chief.

All eyes were now turned on Disraeli, urgently summoned by the Queen to Osborne. A special ship, sent to meet his train at Portsmouth, carried him over the Solent. The next morning Mary Anne received a hasty scrawl: *It is all that I could wish and hope … I was with the Queen an hour yesterday.*

His hour that, at last, had come.

THIRTY-TWO

The House was crowded to capacity, the cheers deafening as Disraeli rose to speak for the first time as Conservative Chief of the Government. In the front seats of the ladies' gallery a small figure in a fur-trimmed velvet mantle sat behind the latticed grille. Few Cabinet ministers' wives, nor those of less important Members, had ventured out on that bitterly raw February day. She sat alone with empty seats on either side of her. She had waited thirty years for this and for the words he spoke, but she heard nothing of them; nor did she see that quiet forceful figure with its thinning hair, its plastered curl, its pendulous lower lip and hollow eyes. One had come there in his place: a youth, strung about with glittering gold chains, standing in rigid immobility, and whose pallor looked to be of death until, with fisted hands raised high above his head, those hyena howls of mockery were drowned in the words: 'The time will come when you *will* hear me.'

Her body weakened. She sat drenched in a wave of happiness too great to bear and live. It was joy, not sorrow, that killed. A darkness came over the picture; she felt herself fading away. The grille was in a curtsy and the House, or her head, in a buzz. Those women ... they were whispering, staring.

Mrs Gladstone rose from her seat and came to her graciously, always so kind. 'Dear Mrs Disraeli, are you not well?'

'Thank you, yes, I am … very well. The heat in here … rather too warm…' With everyone huddled in furs and blue-nosed, and the House like an iceberg.

'Are you sure? You look so poorly.' With angelic magnanimity Mrs Gladstone produced a vinaigrette. 'This will revive you.'

'No, really, how kind, but I am quite…'

He had finished speaking. The session was closed, and she surrounded by mantles and bonnets, such a lot of them. Where had they come from? Many more than she had thought were here, all offering congratulations. 'Thank you, thank you…'

'Yes, a great day in our … and for the party.' But one could not say very much about *that* with Mrs Gladstone heaping coals and smelling salts, and giving her an arm.

'Do let me…'

'Thank you. So kind … I can manage very well.' Surely one wasn't all that old! 'Just a momentary spasm.'

'Too much excitement, perhaps,' forbearingly suggested Mrs Gladstone.

'Mrs Disraeli! I must, I positively must…' Another of them, Lady Russell, sweeping down. 'What a triumph for you.' Just the least reminder with the accent on the 'you' that the triumph for one so far beyond the pale might be thought — malapropos.

'Thank you, thank…' Bow, smile, grin, and bow. 'Yes, quite a crush…' If only they would let her get out of it. 'Thank you so much. Goodbye, goodbye, good…' He was being cheered in the Lobby and in Palace Yard where a multitude waited to watch him come out. But she must go first. She had ordered a hot meal for him. She must see that all was ready.

Her footman was elbowing his way through that bobbing mass of people to meet and take her to the carriage.

'No,' she said, 'find me a hansom. The carriage must wait to bring home the prime minister.'

THIRTY-THREE

'Will you lend your reception rooms to my wife for a night or two?' Disraeli asked his Foreign Secretary, Lord Stanley. 'She can do nothing with Number Ten. She says it is too dingy and decaying.' So on March 26, 1868, Mary Anne held her first levee as the prime minister's wife.

It was a raging night of wind and sleet and hail, but the weather was no deterrent to an immense attendance, both social and political, including the whole Conservative Party, a sprinkling of Liberals, with the Gladstones and the Russells much in evidence, some bishops, and — greatest triumph of all for Lady Russell to see — the Prince and Princess of Wales.

Dizzy in his glory leading about the Princess, as a certain Bishop Wilberforce, also in his glory, noted in his journal, but, contradictorily: *The impenetrable man very low...* Why should he be low when he was so high? And Mrs Disraeli looking very ill and haggard, despite a rather too generous touch of the hare's foot, a great many new curls, a lavish display of new diamonds, and a new orange satin gown with layers and layers of flounces. Like nothing so much as a pagoda, as remarked by Lady Russell. Or, another Liberal suggestion, the Leaning Tower of Pisa! All were agreed her gown and its colour a most unkindly choice with her face under the rouge as yellow as a guinea, and she glued to the Prince, hanging on to his arm. His Royal Highness did not appear to be, it was noticed, best pleased. As for Dizzy — quite beside himself — strutting about with the Princess, bragging and boasting and toasting the royals, and telling everyone, 'Yes! I've climbed to the top of the greasy pole.'

'But he will soon be sliding down again,' Gladstonians hopefully augured. They gave him nine months to the end of the year, when he would find the pole, they had no doubt, a little *too* well greased.

There were primroses from Windsor with a note from Princess Christian *Mama desires me to send the accompanying flowers for Mr Disraeli. She heard him say one day that he was so fond of all spring flowers that she has ventured to send him these...*

And an advance copy of Her Majesty's first publication *Leaves from the Journal of our Life in the Highlands.* So now it was 'We authors, ma'am'.

The small stout figure in its widow's cap had replaced Mrs Brydges Willyams as recipient of letters giving her every scrap of social gossip. 'We are delightfully amused,' she told her ladies. 'Never in our life have we received such letters. Never before have we known *everything.* An ambiguous confession which gave rise to some remark. Never certainly had any of her ministers been permitted and indeed encouraged to take, one might almost say, on bated breath, such highly favoured — liberties.

In September Mr Disraeli was invited to Balmoral; but without Mrs Disraeli, who was, however, given a detailed daily account of that visit, brought on the train by Queen's Messenger. Mary Anne heard of excursions to see the Highland Games at Braemar, and of picnics on the Dee; of dinner with the Queen and a party of eight in the library, *a small square room with good books — very cosy.* And very cosy indeed, were the talks in that room, *with an exquisite view from the windows.* Cosy too, the 'Scotch' shawl in the Balmoral tartan, a compensatory gift from the Queen to atone for the absence of *dear Mrs Disraeli. Her Majesty hopes you will find it warm in the cold weather.*

If the widow at Balmoral were a glorification of that other widow at Torquay, Mr Disraeli was a glorified 'Lord M' … '*Poor* Lord M,' who had never understood the peerless Albert as Mr Disraeli so utterly did. The Queen hoped and prayed that Mr Disraeli would remain in office, for if he did not and there should be another change of government, Mr Gladstone would be her prime minister.

On those few occasions when she had received Mr Gladstone as Chancellor of the Exchequer, 'We were *not* amused to be addressed as if we were a public meeting. So *very* bombastic and punctilious. Perfectly correct, of course, and always full of ceremony, but, oh, how different, how dreadfully different from dear Mr Disraeli's sympathetic, confidential and *human* approach.' Mr Disraeli did not treat her as an institution but, although with all reverence for her sovereign state, he made her feel that his affection, devotion and homage were not only for God's anointed but for herself… Yet, towards the close of the year, and for all her fears and prayers, the dreaded change of Government looked to be a certainty.

Disraeli's Conservatives watched the uproarious welcome accorded to Gladstone in his 'stumpy' tour, so Derby from his sick-bed wrote of it to him who had taken over his leadership. *All this balderdash and braggadocio has done him more harm than good…* Good enough, however, to win him the day. The enfranchised working man, stuffed with Liberal propaganda that they and not the Tories had given him his one-man householder's vote, turned to bite the hand that fed him.

Gladstone, back from his 'stumpy' tour, was felling a tree at Hawarden when the Queen's unwilling message was brought to him. 'The Almighty, Glory be His name,' he proclaimed, eyes to heaven, 'has sustained and spared me for some purpose of His own.'

But not to Victoria's purpose. Nothing more dreadful, since the loss of her Angel, had befallen her than this! The Queen wept. Mary Anne, however, took the defeat of Disraeli's first government with surprising equanimity.

'You have been and will be prime minister again. I am as good as a witch. When you come back you will carry all before you.'

'I have carried too much,' he said, 'behind me. I feel I can carry no more.'

They were at dinner with Montague Corry, now an intimate third at Grosvenor Gate. It was the evening of the day that gave the majority vote of the country to Gladstone.

'But he,' Mary Anne said with oracular cheer, 'won't stay the course. To be thrown out first by Oxford, then by his constituents in Lancashire, and forced to take a mouldy little seat at Greenwich — what a come down for him! And what a come up,' she nodded brightly, 'for you, when... What's this?' The butler was offering a dish of something highly sauced and flavoured.

'*Saumon a l'Italien*, madam.'

'Take it away. I don't fancy this rich stuff. I'll have a boiled egg.'

'My dear,' expostulated Dizzy, 'you have eaten nothing. You left your soup.'

'I can't eat for the sake of eating.'

He gave her an anxious look. She had lost weight; was too thin and too heavily rouged. He never saw her, even in bed, without all that pink on her face.

'You need a tonic,' he said. 'I will send for Sir William.'

'You will not send for Sir William. I am perfectly well. I am just — not hungry. Who could be after an election, and to see those swinish Liberals giving themselves all the credit for your Bill. *That's* what's upset me if you want to know — all their damnable lies, a dirty, sneaking way to push themselves in.'

'Beaune, madam?'

'No. Chablis.'

The butler filled her glass, she drank thirstily and asked for more, 'and some dry toast. And now…' She turned to Dizzy; under the rouge he noted, thankfully, a normal flush, and her eyes were bright and eager. 'Now you will *have* to go to the Lords. You can still lead the Government from the Upper House when the time comes, as it certainly will. I cannot bear to think of you sitting in opposition to that — murderer.'

'My love!' A momentary quiver, which might have been the smile of a ghost, crossed the sphinx-like face.

'He is,' she repeated, 'a murderer. A man who will kill a tree for pleasure is as much a murderer as one who kills for lust. Our pious Mr Gladstone hackin' down trees and walkin' the streets to save sinners and whores — all right, Monty, don't look so shocked — *also* for pleasure — is not fit to cross swords with one who fights clean.' Her glance, skidding from that fixedly impenetrable eye, lingered on the blushing Mr Corry. 'In my young days of the Regency bucks, when we called spades by their names, gentlemen would only fight with gentlemen.'

'Your egg, madam.'

She tapped a spoon on the egg, scooped a mouthful and said, 'I used to be all against you going to the Upper House, but now I think you should. So, Monty, you must back me up and persuade the prime minister into the Lords.'

Mr Corry took his time and a sip of wine before he answered diplomatically: 'I cannot, ma'am, with any confidence recommend the prime minister to take so decisive a step. The Opposition cannot afford to lose our irreplaceable leader.'

'Snipe, sir,' murmured the butler at Disraeli's elbow.

He helped himself to snipe, sampled it and dispassionately said, 'I am of a mind to retire from Parliament.'

'Sir!' Mr Corry blenched. 'Surely not. Parliament would never survive without you.'

'Parliament,' was the inimical reply, 'may not survive *with* me. Parliaments are or should be finished, as the world, or this infinitesimal speck in the universe that man in his arrogance calls the world, ought to be finished. It has gone whirling in space too long and has achieved — what? It has turned apes into men or men into apes. I have never yet discovered which, having discarded the theory of man into angel. But that,' he added, 'does not apply to women, or I should say,' and to Mary Anne he raised his glass with an elaborate bow, 'the perfect wife. Won't you try some of this snipe, my dear?'

'Not with egg. Go on about apes. I like to think that you, if Mr Darwin does not, consider the female of the species may one day grow wings when I shall hope to be rechristened Gabrielle.'

'In my belief,' mused Disraeli, 'Darwin with his missing link has missed his theoretical main point. In the beginning God may have intended the bee or the ant to be lords of creation.'

'But not in His image,' put in Mary Anne. 'I am sure God could never have looked like a bee, or come to that, like an ant.'

At which Mr Corry, hastily drinking, choked into his wine and was bidden by his hostess, 'Hold your breath and count ten.'

'The super-intelligence of these little creatures,' Mr Corry's chief pursued, with callous disregard for his subordinate's convulsions, 'which may have been conceived on a Titanic scale, is vastly superior, on their particular plane, to that of man. This globe of ours was clearly not intended as a permanent habitat for *homo sapiens*, being for the most part —'

'Ow-ow-ouch!' from Mr Corry.

'— for the most part ocean, desert waste, or cannibal-infested jungle with a population — a glass of water for Mr Corry.'

'No — ouch! Sir, thank — I — it — ow-ow-ouch!' achieved the wretched Corry.

'— with a population that since the beginning of time is no more than the spawn of a shoal of herrings.'

'Well,' said Mary Anne, 'if you think that the world and the parliaments that govern it were made for bees and ants and herrings, we had best get out and leave them to get on with it. They couldn't do worse than Gladstone and his lot will do in *this* nasty little part of the world.' She got up from the table with a last word for the empurpled Mr Corry. 'Mind now, persuade him… Poor Monty, it's horrid when something goes down the wrong way.'

The gentlemen were on their feet, while Mr Corry, controlling his whoops, contrived to bow her to the door. In the hall she was met by Nina.

'Sir William 'ave sent a message, ma'am. He will see you tomorrow mornin' at eleven o'clock.'

'Sh! Not so loud. And nothing of this to your master. You understand?'

Relieving herself of Nina's offered arm she slowly mounted the stairs.

Precisely on the stroke of eleven she was shown into the sumptuously furnished waiting room of the eminent physician, Sir William Gull. Only one other patient was there before her, an apoplectic red-faced gentleman, who appeared to be afflicted with the fidgets. He hemmed and he hawed, and he took out his watch; he strode to the window, he pulled down the blind and pulled it up again with so violent a jerk that the tassel came off in his hand.

'Here's a to-do,' he muttered, and returning to the table where Mary Anne sat leafing through a copy of *The Times*, upside down, 'Excuse me, madam, may I ask,' he alarmingly enquired, 'if *you* ever see pink mice?'

'I — not very often,' she found voice to say.

'That,' his head nodded, 'is what I want to know. The fact that you see them at all, shows that I am not the only one who — For what time, if you will pardon the question, is your appointment?'

'For eleven o'clock.'

'Mine is for half past. I came too early. If you would be so kind as to allow me to go first I would be exceedingly obliged.'

'Sir William will see you now, madam.'

'Floored!' ejaculated the fidgety gentleman.

And as she followed the butler through the wide marble hall, her chin high, her lips firm, *At least,* she thought, with a jerk of humour to stifle the drum at her ribs, *I haven't yet come to seeing pink mice...*

Sir William, grey-whiskered, portly and courtly, greeted her with a genial, 'My dear lady! You look younger than ever. What a charming bonnet, and how well it becomes you.' He drew forward a chair. 'Pray be seated.' He seated himself. 'And now — what is the trouble?'

From a dry mouth she told him the trouble.

'Well, Sir William?'

The examination was over. The nurse, who had assisted her to dress, left the room. She faced him across his desk. Light from the tall window fell on her face; the rouge on her cheekbones stood out pitifully harsh against her pallor.

'You can tell me the truth. I am not afraid to hear it.'

He was silent, his eyes lowered, his strong sensitive fingers playing with a silver paper knife. 'Tell me,' she insisted, 'I must know. I *do* know. It is what I thought … isn't it?'

He looked up; his quick bright gaze was on her like a lamp. 'Yes,' he answered gently, 'it is.'

She bowed her head; and he, rising to his feet, stood beside her, a hand on her shoulder. 'But, my dear, we doctors are not infallible.'

'I have every belief that in this case you *are* infallible.' She began to put on her gloves. 'How long —' steadily she returned his look — 'how long do you give me?'

'That is not a question I can answer. You have lived your full allotted span of years, and therefore —'

'Yes,' she broke in quietly. 'And more than my allotted span, but I am not thinking of myself. I am thinking of my husband. He will be so —' her voice dwindled — 'so lost without me.' She had her left glove on now and was carefully smoothing the fingers over her rings. 'You must not tell him, Doctor.' And as she took up the other glove the watchful medical eye was focused on that little thin right hand.

'May I?' He raised her fingers and closely examined them. 'This has been injured. When?'

'Ages ago. It was crushed in a carriage door. My husband knew nothing about it until long afterwards, and he must know nothing of...' She moistened her lips. 'Sir William, you ... you must promise me you will not tell him. He is a great worrier. He has enough to worry him already with the dissolution. He must not have *this*, with everything else, hanging over his head.'

Sir William turned from her to his desk, made a note on the case card and turned to her again. 'The time may come when he will have to know.'

'But not yet ... please. Not until he can't help knowing.' She got up. 'God has been very good to me. He has let me live to see my husband prime minister.'

'And you will live, God willing, to see him prime minister again.'

'Perhaps ... perhaps not.' A smile, fugitive, hurtingly young on that small withered face, strayed to the colourless lips. 'One mustn't be greedy. I have had so much happiness in life. One shouldn't go begging for more. Oh, my glove. I dropped it.'

He retrieved the glove and lifted her hand to his lips. 'You are a very brave woman, and ... you have my promise.'

'Thank you, Doctor. Goodbye.'

She went down to Hughenden the next morning. Dizzy followed by a later train. She wore for dinner that night a new dress of dark crimson velvet and purple, with touches of scarlet. 'You seem so much better, ma'am,' Nina told her, 'since you have seen the doctor.'

'I *am* better, and much … relieved. Sir William finds me just a little below par, but nothing serious. After all, Nina, you and I are no chickens.'

'That be right, ma'am. I'll be sixty-seven come next Martinmas.'

'And I've known you since you were twelve.'

Nina was snow-white, stout and rosy as ever, good for another twenty years by the look of her. What a wife she would have made for a man! But her life was and always had been bound up in Mary Anne's. She would have to do more for Nina than the little something she had left her. There was a cottage at Hughenden. Yes, she would suggest to Dizzy that Nina should be given that cottage when … the time should come.

She heard the carriage in the drive. 'There's your master!'

He was waiting for her in the library, warming his back at the fire, his hands beneath his coat-tails. At sight of her standing there at the door with the glint of diamonds in the dark velvet, he crossed the room to tell her, 'You look, like a dew-spangled fuchsia. What a lovely gown, and what a lovely lady in it.' He took her face between his hands, gazing down at her with a moisture in his eyes. '*My* lady… The Viscountess Beaconsfield.'

'Dizzy!' She caught her breath. 'So you've done it — you go to the Lords. The Queen has given you a peerage?'

'No,' he said, and again he said it, 'no. The Queen gives a peerage to one who deserves it far more than I. One to whom I owe all that I am, and all that I may ever be.' He gathered her closely into his arms. 'The Queen gives a peerage to … you.'

It was ridiculous, unprecedented, unheard of! 'Who but Disraeli would crawl on all fours to the Queen to make *her* a peeress in her own right?'

'Yes, but don't you see the cunning of it? He will have it both ways now. He won't go to the Lords while he still thinks he has a chance as "Mr Disraeli" in the Commons.'

Thus and thus *ad nauseam* from victorious Liberal wives, countered by Tory ladies as 'a graceful gesture. Everyone knows he adores her in spite of her… oddities.'

Tactfully put.

She had come to be, and was generally acknowledged, an eccentric. Those few who could remember the very old Countess of Cork saw her prototype in the very new Viscountess Beaconsfield, who, despite the coronet that within a week of her elevation she had stamped on her notepaper, would never be the Grande Dame of her model.

'And as for the coat of arms!' The Liberal ladies took up the litany. Was there ever to be seen such a coat of arms, as devised by the College of Heralds and flaunted on the panels of her carriage, complete with a grape vine (for Viney), boars' heads, erased on a field (for Evans and the farm, too killing!), supported by an eagle and a lion, holding pendant an escutcheon charged with a castle…

'Why a castle?'

'That for *his* castle … in Spain!'

There was no holding her now that *Punch* had put her into verse:

Long may the gems of that coronet flame
Decking her brow who's more proud of his fame.

Rumour had it she wore her coronet all day, slept in it all night — how too-frightfully uncomfortable! — received in it, and told her guests, 'This, of course, ought to be Dizzy's. I wear it as proxy for him. He could have had a dukedom if he wished.'

More than eccentric. Positively cracked, with the coronet gone *very* much to her head!

Feckless as the straying winds that danced among the springtime daffodils revolved those airy whispers around the carriages and promenaders in Hyde Park, unheard by her whose dauntless spirit defied the onslaught of the enemy within her gates, secretly fought, flung back and kept at bay lest he should know.

She had still so much to give, and so much of him to take upon herself. More and more did he seem to depend on her, when into his heart crept a lurking fear, unfaced, untold: and hidden. Neither guessed that the secret, unshared by the other, was known to them both, while again and again, when all but vanquished, she returned to the attack, marshalling her forces to defend her citadel against the ruthless march of pain.

'I am not ill, dear Diz. Why will you fuss me so? I am only a little run down, but nothing radically wrong…'

Sir William had given her a tonic and told her to entertain, go about, enjoy herself. She would not be treated as an invalid, and of course she would attend the court. The Queen had invited her. She *must* go to court.

She went to court, collapsed and was taken away by him who agonisedly watched over her, hoping against hope when hope was gone, that he might disbelieve.

'But,' he would tell her, 'I am rejoiced to see you getting better every day.'

Although she could no longer walk upstairs unaided, that he must place her feet for her, step by step. 'So stupid, these rheumatics.'

And he, 'Yes, I too have rheumatics.'

'I know, poor darling. Your joints creak like doors that need oiling. I'll rub your back again tonight with that nice balsam…'

So would they keep up the pretence. And when he was detained a day or two in London, for he spent all the time he could possibly spare with her who never left Hughenden now, she scribbled him a note.

My own Dearest,
I feel so grateful for your constant, tender love and kindness. I certainly feel better this evening.
Your own devoted,
BEACONSFIELD.

She showed him how much better she was by inviting guests to Hughenden from Saturday till Monday. She came to dinner, they said, 'gorgeously dressed and wonderfully lively', cracking jokes with them all, full of laughter, painful to hear and more painful to watch that grotesque little object in its wig, its gay trappings, its diamonds, its claw-like wasted hands, ringed to the knuckles. But when she left the men together at the table, he, schooled to betray no emotion, lifted for a moment that calm sardonic mask to reveal himself.

'She suffers so dreadfully,' he told them. 'She doesn't think I know, but I do. Her courage … it tears my heart to see her…'

It tore the hearts of them to see him broken.

Slowly the leaves were falling in those sun-lost autumn days. She was tired, glad to rest, content to lie in her chair by the window looking out on the green lawns of her garden where late asters bloomed with the last of the Michaelmas daisies. She refused to go to bed. 'One spends half one's life in bed and in sleep. When we are old we do not need to sleep … until we must.'

Propped on her pillows she would watch the sky in all its changes: its bright cold morning clearness, a flight of birds across flushed sunsets; the star-woven canopy of night; so many stars, so many worlds... And a slow untroubled moon-cloud on which she seemed to float out of the darkening present into a timeless past where there is no life but memory.

Forms and faces, some long vanished, closed about her, drawing near to take her hand and lead her back along the happy years at Hughenden, through the forest, her forest of pines, and out into the open where a youth with curls on his shoulders and rings on his gloves stood waiting, 'For you. Always and only for you.' Drifting colours, pink and white, for Lewis and Disraeli. *They call him my Parliamentary Protégé...* And a small and narrow house in a small and narrow way and a wedding bell of flowers and Wyndham home from the hunt and her mother's palpitations and Mr Yate in the hiccups and Miss Graham in the giggles and John come from school to tease her, all were here and Granfer Evans too, ''Ands like a boy's 'ands you 'ave,' and she milking the cows in the shadow of the stables. And a stranger in the doorway with the sunlight on his face.

In his book-walled library an old man sat at his fireside watching the flickering logs: the upward leap of the flames, the eager clutch and downward fall into the glowing heart of spent embers. And as he watched he dreamed, to see gathered in the fire a vision of a life long lived: a life that he sometimes prayed would soon be ended. His day, so slow in its dawning, so triumphant in its setting, was done... Was it yesterday, or all his yesterdays when he had brought to Britain the great news from the Congress at Berlin?

Flags were flying, crowds cheering, a frantic joyous multitude to greet him, and he kneeling at the feet of his sovereign whom he had made an empress, to receive from her the Garter. 'My dear, my very dear Lord Beaconsfield, we are so proud, so grateful and so happy...' And he here at Hughenden so utterly alone.

The heavy-lidded eyes left the fire, travelled searchingly about; his nostrils expanded. He sniffed the air like an old dog awakened and alert. That scent... of violets. Yet there were no violets, only primroses, a great bowl of them from Windsor with a card attached and addressed in the Queen's own hand to:

The Prime Minister
The Right Honourable the Earl of Beaconsfield, K.G.

Something warm and wet trickled down the furrowed cheek. He lifted his head; the sparse carefully arranged black curls showed white at their roots, and the tuft on his chin was silver streaked.

He removed his misted monocle, wiped it with his handkerchief and replaced it, gazing up at the portrait above the mantelshelf. The eyes seemed to smile and the pictured face to listen for words below a whisper:

'Peace with Honour... Mary Anne.'

A NOTE TO THE READER

While little is known of the girlhood of Mary Anne Evans, much conjecture concerning her origin was circulated during her two marriages and after her death. The legend that she was a factory girl whom Wyndham Lewis had seen walking barefoot to and from her work, and with whom he fell in love, may have gained some credence from the fact that before he married Mary Anne he had a mistress by whom he had a daughter.

On Lady Beaconsfield's own admission we have it that she kept a milliner's shop, having served her apprenticeship in Exeter. The locality of this milliner's shop has been hitherto obscure. I have, however, reason to identify it as in Culver Street, Clifton, given in the local directory for the year 1815, under the name of Mary Evans, mantua-maker. On a map of Clifton for that same year, Culver Street is indicated as lying parallel with Park Street where Mary Anne was then living with her mother and stepfather, Thomas Yate, her mother's second misalliance. Her first husband, Mary Anne's father, was the son of a tenant farmer in the village of Brampford Speke in Devon. He ran away to sea, became an officer's servant, and ultimately gained a commission in the Royal Navy. Mary Anne lived most of her childhood on this farm, and it is possible that, after her mother's re-marriage, she may, by sheer necessity, have been forced to earn her living as a milliner or mantua-maker. Nor did she attempt to disguise, if she may somewhat have exaggerated, the hardships of her early life.

That Disraeli visited Mary Anne at Pantgwynlais shortly after the death of Wyndham Lewis has been, by some authorities, denied. Yet I have it on the word of a resident in the neighbourhood — the estate is now a developed area — that her grandmother, when a young girl, remembered Disraeli dressed in deepest mourning walking across the fields to Pantgwynlais from the Cow and Snuffers inn where he stayed when he was 'courting' Mrs Lewis.

The Cow and Snuffers, which still exists as a modernised public house, bears proud evidence of this visit in a bust of Disraeli over the door.

If you have enjoyed this novel enough to leave a review on **Amazon** and **Goodreads**, then we would be truly grateful.

Sapere Books

Sapere Books is an exciting new publisher of brilliant fiction and popular history.

To find out more about our latest releases and our monthly bargain books visit our website: **saperebooks.com**

www.ingramcontent.com/pod-product-compliance
Lightning Source LLC
Chambersburg PA
CBHW071246250626
47163CB00002B/347